Sweet Deception

A Veiled Seduction Novel

Heather Snow

A SIGNET ECLIPSE BOOK

SIGNET ECLIPSE
Published by New American Library, a division of
Penguin Group (USA) Inc., 375 Hudson Street,
New York, New York 10014, USA
Penguin Group (Canada), 90 Eglinton Avenue East, Suite 700, Toronto,
Ontario M4P 2Y3, Canada (a division of Pearson Penguin Canada Inc.)
Penguin Books Ltd., 80 Strand, London WC2R 0RL, England
Penguin Ireland, 25 St. Stephen's Green, Dublin 2,
Ireland (a division of Penguin Books Ltd.)
Penguin Group (Australia), 250 Camberwell Road, Camberwell, Victoria 3124,
Australia (a division of Pearson Australia Group Pty. Ltd.)
Penguin Books India Pvt. Ltd., 11 Community Centre, Panchsheel Park,
New Delhi - 110 017, India
Penguin Group (NZ), 67 Apollo Drive, Rosedale, Auckland 0632,
New Zealand (a division of Pearson New Zealand Ltd.)
Penguin Books (South Africa) (Pty.) Ltd., 24 Sturdee Avenue,
Rosebank, Johannesburg 2196, South Africa

Penguin Books Ltd., Registered Offices:
80 Strand, London WC2R 0RL, England

First published by Signet Eclipse, an imprint of New American Library,
a division of Penguin Group (USA) Inc.

First Printing, August 2012
10 9 8 7 6 5 4 3 2 1

ALWAYS LEARNING   PEARSON

PRAISE FOR *SWEET ENEMY*

"Historical intrigue and heart-pounding passion make *Sweet Enemy* a great read. Romance fans will love it."
— #1 *New York Times* bestselling author Julie Garwood

"Heather Snow combines sizzling tension, witty dialogue, and achingly raw emotions for a passionate love story you'll remember long after the last page."
— *USA Today* bestselling author Kathryn Smith

"Newcomer Snow makes a mark on the genre....The plot, with its tinge of mystery, matchmaking, and a bit of mayhem, will warm readers' hearts." — *RT Book Reviews*

"*Sweet Enemy* combines romance, history, and intrigue into one excellent read. Readers won't be able to put *Sweet Enemy* down. A fast-paced plot and captivating characters make [this] a must read for all historical romance fans. Well deserving of the Perfect 10 rating, readers, myself included, will be eagerly anticipating another novel by this delightful author."
— Romance Reviews Today

"Unlike so many other Regencies, almost everything from the setting to the characters to the suspense comes with a twist and never feels cliched . . . a wonderful, emotional, and intellectually satisfying read." — All About Romance

"Amusing, delightful, and charming. . . . The characters are well developed and the writing is highly engaging. I was vested in the characters and their goals from the start." — Manic Readers

"A solid plot, well-developed characters, and deftly drawn setting . . . an excellent first novel. Readers will be delighted to add Ms. Snow to their list of must-read authors." — *BookPage*

"Liliana was a wonderful heroine and was so vastly different than the other historic heroines that I have read before . . . a fantastic book and I still can't stop thinking about it. Looking forward to reading *Sweet Deception* later this year, and Heather Snow is definitely an author to watch." — Night Owl Reviews

"[A] refreshing romance. . . . Heather Snow has done a phenomenal job of writing characters a reader can connect with. *Sweet Enemy* is a must read for any historical romance fan!"
— Fresh Fiction

This book is dedicated to my parents, Tom and Sarah Fry. I can't thank you enough for all the extra time you spent spoiling . . . er, I mean . . . loving on your grandsons as my deadline approached. I'm forever grateful to be part of such a supportive and giving family. The example of love you've always set is one Jason and I strive to pass on to our sons.

Acknowledgments

I'd always heard second books were tough, and even then, I underestimated just how tough it would be — at least for me. There are many people who helped me through this process, who held my hand and assured me that yes, I could do this — even with a new baby and a toddler and a husband gone on business much of the year and sleep deprived within an inch of my sanity. People who read along and made me believe that I was a good writer, that I had more than one book in me. People who talked me off my ledge when I needed it. I am grateful for you: Karen King, Leigh Stites, Keri Smith, Christie Novak, Tatiana Henley, Gretchen Jones, Cindy Renshaw, Lisa Lovelace, Georgina Green, Carolyn Reece, Erin Knightley, Erica O'Rourke, Eliza Evans, Jennifer McAndrews, Ashley March, Angi Morgan, Jillian Stone and Carla Cassidy. Please, please forgive me if I've forgotten someone — I'm still sleep deprived, you know!

Also, to my editor, Danielle Perez, and my agent, Barbara Poelle — you both showed tremendous faith in me as a writer and as a person, and I appreciate you.

Finally, my sincerest thanks to Cathy, Steve and the rest of the staff at the Laclede County Library in Lebanon, Missouri, for going out of your way to welcome me, encourage me and make me feel at home away from home.

Chapter One

Derbyshire, June 1817

The medieval tower rose high and proud above the bilberry heath covering the castle's grounds, its vibrant red bricks proclaiming it a foreigner amongst a plateau of white limestone. Derick Aveline, Viscount Scarsdale, exhaled with a snort—he certainly knew what *that* felt like.

If there was one place on earth he'd hoped never to set eyes upon again, his northernmost family estate was certainly it. He supposed that would surprise most people, given the dangerous and often unpleasant spots he'd been in over the years. But these lush rolling hills and deep, narrow valleys of his childhood loomed ominous and more treacherous to his well-being than even the filthiest of French prisons that had once held him.

With a sharp tap of his heel, Derick directed his steed down the knoll and onto the lane, as a wealth of memories he'd thought long locked away assailed him. The restless boy he'd been, roaming the hills and dales of White Peak with endless summer days stretching out before him. His mother's red-rimmed eyes, looking at him

with alternating sadness and indifference. The last day
he'd seen this patch of England, the day his identity had
crumbled away like the ancient limestone the area was
named for.

Gravel crunched beneath his stallion's hooves as they
entered the stable yard, shaking Derick from his
thoughts. He'd been a fool to come back. If not for this
last mission for the Crown, he would never have returned. But he always did what must be done for love of
country.

Even when it wasn't his country to love.

"Boy!" Derick called out, throwing his leg over his
saddle and dismounting. He rolled his shoulders, stretching knotted muscles. He'd had to race to stay ahead of
the weather and felt every rough mile bone deep. If God
were merciful, a hot meal, a warm fire and a clean bed
waited within. He scanned the yard for a stable hand.

The lane leading up to Aveline Castle was in clear
view of both the stables and the main hall. It was inex-
cusable that no one waited to greet him, particularly as
he'd sent word well ahead to expect him.

Several moments passed, yet no one appeared.

"Damnation," Derick grumbled, turning his collar up
against the chilly wind. The clime this far north had yet
to recover from last summer's unimaginable cold, and
with dusk fast on Derick's heels there was little sun left
for warmth. He'd managed to beat the coming storm by
only minutes, he'd guess. He led his horse to the deserted
stable, secured the mount and promised the animal that
he would send a groom straightaway to brush him down.

Derick strode along the north side of the fifteenth-
century castle, his gait far from the languid, leisurely
manner of walking that he usually affected. He would
slip into his ne'er-do-well persona once there was someone about who might observe him.

He climbed the front steps two at a time. When he
reached the stoop, he found the massive door half open.

Had the staff lost all discipline since his mother had died? The place was drafty enough without carelessly leaving the door unlatched. He pushed it wide, the ancient carved English oak giving way with a groan.

No candlelight greeted him. Indeed, it was as if the place were deserted. Derick frowned, his steps echoing as he walked into the stone foyer. The hairs on the back of his neck rose. His trunks, which had been sent ahead and should have long since been unpacked, sat stacked at the base of the grand staircase. No fire burned in the grate. No lamps had been lit.

Where the devil was everyone?

"—take this area, from the bend in the creek to the waterfall—"

A feminine voice, full of authority, drifted to him from the back of the house.

Curious, Derick started in that direction.

"—and Thomas, you and John Coachman take from here to Felman's Hill."

Derick furrowed his brow. There was something eerily familiar about that voice, which was ridiculous given that the only woman he'd known in Derbyshire was his mother, and she had been dead two months now. As he turned into the long hallway leading toward the kitchens, light spilled from the dining hall and a low murmuring of voices reached his ears.

He slipped unnoticed into the room, melting into the shadows along the far wall. It wasn't even a challenge, as no one paid him a bit of mind. His eyes took in the whole room at once, a skill honed through years in the espionage game.

A dozen and a half people of mixed age and company hovered around the table—all servants, from their dress. Aveline Castle employed only a skeleton staff now that his mother was gone. So who were all these people whispering quietly, their faces grim?

The room smelled crisp, filled with the tang of the

outdoors carried in on clothing. And indeed, most of those gathered around were dressed for the elements, garbed in coats and hats or scarves. Several noses were red, as if they had been long out in the wind, and many boots were dirty, covered with mud.

The group seemed to be waiting for something, or someone. Derick shifted more into the corner until he found a break in the wall of people large enough to see through.

Ah, the source of the mysterious voice, he'd wager. The woman stood at the head of the table, but he could not see her face, as she was leaning over a large square of paper that was rolled out across the polished mahogany. Her position made it difficult to gauge her height as well, but there was no mistaking the ample curves her simple muslin dress couldn't hide.

Her well-tailored frock was a vibrant green, the dye not faded as a castoff would be. A lady of quality, then. One slender hand braced her as she marked furiously upon the paper. The tilt of her head and the way she held herself in determined focus niggled at his memory. Derick tried to place her, but locks of chestnut hair had slipped her coiffure, obscuring even her profile from him.

He turned his attention to the paper and squinted his eyes in the low light. That looked suspiciously like . . . A discarded frame caught his attention then, propped up against the wall. His eyes snapped back to the table, to the blotchy inked areas the mystery woman was currently drawing lines through.

She was scribbling all over an irreplaceable Burnett map of the countryside, commissioned by his grandfather over half a century ago.

He should be appalled. But Derick had long ago shed any care for the trappings of the viscountcy. Instead, he eyed the scene with detached curiosity, angling for the best way to use it to his purposes. Hmmm. Outrage would be precisely what people would expect of the "pampered aristocrat" persona he typically used for these missions. And Little Miss Map Despoiler had given him the perfect opening. All he had to do was take the stage she'd inadvertently set for him.

"What the devil are you doing?" he barked as he pushed off from the wall. His exclamation had the desired effect. A chorus of gasps registered, but Derick ignored them as he reached the head of the table in three long strides and snatched the priceless map from atop it.

He rolled the map with deceptive casualness, the dry paper making a hissing sound against his palms in the now otherwise silent room. He raised a brow and injected a supercilious tone into his voice as he turned to the woman standing frozen before him.

"Do you mind telling me just who you are"—his gaze traveled up her slim body in an intentionally arrogant perusal—"and why you are vandalizing *my* property?"

The last word caught in his throat as his eyes finally reached hers.

A flash of memory came, of a scrawny blond pest who'd trailed behind him every summer like an unwanted hound, a little hoyden with unforgettably wide amber eyes.

No longer a blonde, he noted.

And no longer a girl, his baser side chimed in. Derick pressed his lips together, hard. Damnation. The neighbor girl, Miss Wallingford.

Anna? Ella? *No, Emma*. Derick was surprised he recalled her Christian name. He'd always just called her Pygmy. She'd hated the nickname, thinking he was poking fun at her tiny stature. There *was* that, but he'd really given her the moniker because her golden eyes and tenacious nature had reminded him of the pygmy owlets that hunted these hills at twilight.

She was apparently still a pest—and one already interfering with his plans, even if she couldn't possibly know it.

Miss Wallingford's wide gaze narrowed, and her mouth flattened in what was certainly pique.

Derick waited for her answer, tapping the rolled-up map against the highly polished walnut tabletop in feigned irritation.

Well, mostly feigned. This wasn't quite the foot he'd hoped to get off on with Miss Wallingford. As sister of the local magistrate, she could prove integral to his mission. He'd intended to call on her at her home, play on their childhood friendship—if one could call it that—to gain better access to her brother. Not snap her head off in front of a room full of witnesses.

But what was done was done. Derick had learned long ago that the key to a good deception was to always go on as one had begun. He would brazen through, play his part and find a way to sweeten Miss Wallingford later.

Emma Wallingford had never felt so riveted to one spot in her entire life. It was as if she were carved out of marble, much like the statues of the Greek scholars she'd so admired on her only trip to London. *Move, Emma, you ninny!*

What was this abominable awareness? Her logical mind told her it was only Derick. Yet her stomach fluttered, forcing her to amend that thought. Yes, it was Derick, but he was also . . . *more*. His hair was still black as night, thick and unruly, yet the lines of his face were more angular now, more chiseled. His shoulders seemed wider, his hips more narrow. His eyes hadn't changed, though. They still glittered like fiery emeralds and still gazed at her as if she were the bane of his existence, sent by Hades himself with the express purpose of bedeviling him.

"My—my lord." Billingsly, Aveline Castle's aged butler, brushed past her, his stooped form cutting through her line of sight, rescuing her from Derick's hard green gaze. Emma dropped her eyes to the floor, grateful for the moment to collect herself as the chaos of stammered excuses erupted around her.

His arrival shouldn't be such a shock to her—the entire village knew he was due today. Only she hadn't intended to come anywhere near Aveline Castle while he was in residence, but then Billingsly's note had arrived and—

Emma gasped. How could she have forgotten? She, of all people, didn't forget things like that.

Taking advantage of the continued distraction, she stepped forward and plucked the map from Derick's loosened grasp, berating herself for loss of focus. She spread it out on the table and resumed drawing the border she'd started. With dusk coming, time had become critical.

The voices around her stilled abruptly, and Emma could have sworn she felt Derick's gaze boring into her more surely than Archimedes' famed screw. Which was impossible, of course, as a mere gaze had no actual physical properties.

She didn't look up from her task as she said, "I'm certain Lord Scarsdale will agree that explanations can wait until *after* we find his missing upstairs maid."

Crack!

The sharp, sizzling pop of lightning served as harsh punctuation to her pronouncement. A low rumble of thunder followed quickly behind. Emma glanced over her shoulder at the window in time to see the first fat drops of a summer storm splash against the panes. Fig! If Molly were outside and injured . . . Emma mentally kicked herself for the bit of time she'd squandered mooning like a schoolgirl over a man who obviously didn't even remember her. She returned her eyes to the table and scanned the map again.

"My missing upstairs maid?" Derick repeated, sounding dubious.

"Yes." Without raising her gaze to him, Emma held up a hand to forestall any more questions. She ran her finger over the map. If her calculations were correct, the only feasible place Molly could be that they hadn't already searched was this area to the east of—

"*Miss* Wallingford," Derick growled, in a voice that demanded her attention.

So he did remember her.

"As these are *my* resources you seem to be marshaling," he said, "I expect an explanation."

She looked up at him then, annoyed. Had he just referred to his staff, and some of hers for that matter, as *his resources*? Emma narrowed her eyes, considering the possible ramifications of ignoring him completely. She had more important things to do than appease his "lord of the manor" sensibilities, particularly when this lord hadn't bothered to grace this manor with his presence in more than a dozen years.

But Derick had risen to his full formidable height, taller even than she remembered. His glittering eyes had taken on a look of arrogant command. Emma gritted her teeth.

"Molly Simms," she explained. "The gardener's daughter. No one has seen her since she retired last evening."

His shoulder rose in a half shrug. "That's not even twenty-four hours," he said. "I would hardly consider that 'missing.'"

Emma pursed her lips. What did he know of anything? "Well, the rest of us disagree," she said. "We feel Molly did not leave of her own volition and fear her situation may be dire."

She'd given him as much of an explanation as he was going to get. Emma dismissed him and returned her gaze to the map.

"Yes, but *why* do you disagree?" he asked, plopping

his hand down in the center of the map to block her view. "Do people in this village routinely find themselves in dire circumstances? Have you had a rash of dastardly events?"

Emma pinched the bridge of her nose. The Derick she remembered hadn't been so tiresome. But then, she'd known only the boy. He had been seventeen when she'd seen him last, a whole lifetime of changes ago.

"Of course not," she said. Being situated at the south end of the Peak District, they'd had a bit more crime than perhaps was normal due to the number of strangers that passed through. Even a few suspicious deaths, but nothing like that for at least two years.

"Were there signs of a struggle?" he persisted.

"No," Emma admitted.

"And yet you suspect foul play . . ." Derick lifted his hand and crossed his arms with a slow negligence that set her teeth on edge. "The girl is young. She's probably visiting with a . . . *friend*, and lost track of the time."

The tips of Emma's ears burned with indignation. She glanced around, grateful that neither of Molly's parents was in the room.

"Or perhaps she eloped with the lucky chap," he offered.

Emma nearly gasped at his cheek. Could Derick truly have become such an insensitive boor? A lifetime of changes or not, people didn't usually transform into someone completely unrecognizable.

Regardless, she'd heard enough. She raised herself to her full height, which unfortunately barely put her at his chest level. Her cheeks warmed as she remembered that horrid nickname he used to call her as a child. Still, she gave him her fiercest glare. He was *going* to take her seriously and get out of her way, so help her.

"I suppose that in the realm of possibilities, these are all reasonable questions. However, if I may point out" — she emphasized the point with a poke of her finger right to his breastbone—"that you don't know Molly from Eve. You can credit those of us who do that we have considered all other likely scenarios and have exhausted them."

Another rolling boom of thunder sounded, ever closer. A quick glance confirmed that the sunlight was fading fast.

She turned her gaze back to Derick and narrowed it on him. "Molly is out there, somewhere, and the more time we waste chatting about it, the less chance we have of finding her before dark."

Derick regarded her. He still looked as though he doubted her conclusions, but gone were the arrogant tilt to his nose, the pinched lines around his mouth, the bored ease of his stance. "I su—"

"She tweren't anywhere, Miss Emma." Two footmen came through the door then, cutting off whatever Derick had been about to say. The taller one spoke for them. "We searched the whole spot ye told us."

Emma grimaced. The men stood in the doorway, taking great gulps of air and wiping moisture from their faces. Her frown deepened at their rain-sodden coats. She waved them toward the kitchen, not caring if Derick took issue with her directing *his resources*. "Thank you. Go on and get a hot drink, then hurry right back. We'll need you both as soon as you're able."

She turned back to the map, bracing herself on the table with her left hand and using her right to draw lines through the section the men had been assigned— another search area combed through without success. Emma scanned the darkening sky through the window, mentally calculating how much daylight remained. She'd always been able to tabulate numbers in her head faster than even her father, an esteemed mathematician, had been able to do on paper. She factored in how much area a man could cover on foot in that time, and divided the result by the number of servants available.

Rain pelted the glass in an ever-increasing tattoo.

She'd better account for that variable in her time estimations. She was doing just that when a large bronzed hand planted itself to the outside of her smaller pale one. Emma sucked in a breath, startled by the long, blunt-tipped fingers, the knuckles and skin dusted with a hint of black hair. Her entire body warmed curiously as Derick leaned over her back to see what she was doing.

"You're mapping search areas," he murmured, his voice sliding past her right ear in a hot breath.

"Y-yes," Emma answered, damning herself for the catch in her throat. What in the heavens was wrong with h—

She jerked as the inside of his jacketed arm brushed the outside of her pelissed one. His right hand reached out to run a finger down the eastern border she'd recently traced herself. Emma shivered, as if it were she he stroked rather than the vellum.

"And this unshaded portion is what you have left to search?"

Emma gave a jerky nod. "Those two footmen just finished searching here." She pointed to a marked area to the northeast, abashed to see her finger tremble just a bit. "Since their greatcoats were soaked, I can only assume it's been pouring east of here for some time, which you may remember—"

"Is prone to sudden flooding," Derick said. He straightened, pulling away from her so quickly that gooseflesh prickled her skin at the sudden absence of his heat. "Don't let me interrupt further, then."

She nodded, relieved, but whether more from the fact that he'd capitulated than that he'd moved away from her, she wasn't certain. It didn't signify—at least he would no longer interfere. Emma quickly divvied up the eastern boundary into manageable sections.

"Right." She addressed the tired servants, her middle tightening with unease. "We haven't daylight left to search the remaining area in pairs," she said, suppressing her discomfort the best way she knew how—with action. "We'll all have to take our own section."

As each man or woman came forward, Emma assigned them a small, defined boundary until only she, Billingsly, and Derick remained in the room.

"Billingsly." Emma motioned the butler to follow as she exited the dining hall and made her way toward the front entrance. The old servant was too frail to be out searching in the rain, but she knew he'd want to be useful. "As the searchers return, you and Cook do what you can to get them warmed, dry and fed. God forbid we need to continue the search tomorrow," she muttered, shoving her arms into a coat and struggling to pull it on.

The coat lifted from her shoulders, as if by unseen hands, before the heavy wool settled around her. She whirled in surprise, her elbow coming into solid contact with a hard wall—

"Ooof," Derick grunted, his black brows dipping as he winced.

—of abdomen, as it were.

"Oh! Oh pardon me . . ." Emma mumbled, though truthfully she didn't regret the accidental jab. But how had he appeared behind her? She looked down at his sturdy black boots. Certainly she should have heard a man of his size clomping down the hall after her.

Derick rubbed at the spot where Emma's elbow had speared him. The place she'd poked on his chest still smarted, too. She was quite strong for such a compact little thing. Bright, too, given what little he'd seen of her tactical mind at work, even if she was overreacting. If he remembered correctly, Emma always had been one to take things too seriously, and to infect those around her with her imaginings. He'd guess she was making a mountain out of the proverbial molehill.

She was also adept at giving orders, and accustomed

to being obeyed. Oh yes, little Pygmy had grown into just the kind of woman he'd thought she would.

Emma turned her back on him—again. Derick shook his head as he watched her struggle with the heavy oak door.

She still had more intelligence than common sense, however, since she was apparently planning to run out into a dangerous storm alone.

He reached around her and grasped the handle, stopping the door from opening. "You neglected to give *me* an assignment."

Emma turned, effectively caged by his arm and the door at her back. Those large amber eyes widened as he loomed over her. Which heightened his own awareness of how close his body was to hers, nearly touching. How fragile she seemed . . . how diminutive, and yet so uncommonly tough. He'd already been the recipient of her tart tongue and sharp appendages. Now, thinking back, he remembered that when they were children, Emma had always kept up with him, no matter how he'd tried to lose her.

As if to demonstrate that her stubbornness still remained, Emma lifted her chin in challenge. "I hadn't thought you would—"

"Wish to help?" Derick returned her challenge, raising a brow. Damn. Her assumption irked. And the fact that he'd been stung by it irked more. He'd long ago grown accustomed to not caring what anyone thought. "Feel responsible for a member of my household?"

Emma blinked. "Your household?" She sputtered. "You haven't been to Derbyshire in fourteen—"

"No, but I *am* human, Miss Wallingford." Derick stepped closer, bringing his other arm around and planting it on the door behind her, trapping her. Only so that she would listen to him, of course. Not at all because of her tantalizing scent, a heady mix of lavender and . . .

something he couldn't quite place. "I may not agree with your assumptions, but it is clear you strongly believe the maid is in danger. If there is a chance you are correct, I would like to do what I can."

A huff of exasperation escaped her lips, a gesture Derick took to mean she didn't think too highly of him or his offer. He allowed a half-cynical smile to curve his lips. What did he care if Miss Emma Wallingford disapproved of one of his many alter egos? It wasn't *him*, after all.

Besides, he doubted she'd like him any better if she knew his *true* purpose in Derbyshire.

To investigate her brother for treason.

Chapter Two

Emma blinked up at him, her eyes widening like twin full moons at harvest. Her chest rose and fell in shallow pants. Derick's blood thickened. She was as affected by their nearness as he. Her rapid pulse beat in the hollow of her throat, nearly in time with his.

Why did he react so to her? Certainly he'd been in tighter proximity to many a woman, in and out of the course of duty. But rarely did he allow himself so . . . *close* to one.

So why now? Why her?

For reasons beyond him, he permitted her perusal— held so still, in fact, that his arms ached from remaining locked on either side of her. Emma's amber gaze traveled over his forehead, swept his cheeks, settled on his mouth for a long moment, then flew to his eyes. She stared, her chestnut brows dipping in concentration. What did she think she saw?

A part of Derick's brain registered the danger of letting her see too much. Yet he still didn't pull away.

Then her full lips flattened, and before he sensed what she was about, Emma ducked beneath his left arm and darted away.

Little minx. She hadn't been caught up in him. She had been calculating how best to get back to her search. Tenacious nature, indeed. She'd barely had to dip her head to escape him, given their difference in height. He must remember to place his arms lower next time.

Next time? He had no intention of staying in Derbyshire long enough for there to be a next time. He planned only to settle his estate and discover whether Emma's brother was the last of the traitors he was hunting, and then his responsibilities to home and country would be finished. And he could finally look forward—to an uncertain future, but at least one on his own terms.

Right now, however, he'd better look behind him if he wanted to keep Emma in his sights, as her footfalls indicated a hasty retreat. Since she would be the most expedient avenue through which to investigate her brother, he intended to stick by her side. Derick pushed away from the door and turned to follow her.

Emma was more than halfway down the hallway already, her oversized coat dragging the ground behind her like the train of a gown being worn by a child playing dress-up. Did they not have decent tailors in upper Derbyshire? That coat was designed for someone much taller than she.

"Emma," he called out, his longer strides eating the ground between them. The shuffle of Billingsly's footsteps fell away. No telling what the old butler thought of his and Emma's unorthodox behavior.

"If you would like to help"—Emma's voice floated back to him—"then stay here and mark off the map when the searchers return."

"That would be no help at all," he countered, almost offended that she thought him thick enough to be pawned off by such a useless task. He shouldn't be, however. Didn't he want her and everyone else to view him as feckless?

She stopped abruptly then, without even acknowledging him, and placed her hands on a panel of wood wainscoting beneath the grand staircase.

The passageway. It had been used as an escape when the castle functioned as such in medieval times—and when he'd wanted to avoid his mother. It was a service passage now.

The panel slid away, creating an opening in the wall that Emma stepped through. The wood slid closed behind her with a *snick*.

That was rich. Not only was she barely attempting to placate him, she was trying to lose him. Well, he'd be damned before he would allow Emma to get away so easily. His intent to shadow her aside, what kind of man would he be to let her traipse through the countryside alone during a storm, no matter how imperative she thought the reason? She'd pointed out herself how dangerous that could be. The question struck him again about why he cared so much. What was it about this chit of a girl?

When he reached the panel, Derick pressed it as he'd seen Emma do. Nothing happened. The damned wainscoting bore an intricate checkered pattern and he couldn't remember exactly which squares tripped the lever. He'd been too far away to see which ones Emma had pushed.

He tried them all in turn, stewing with frustration. When he reached the last, he slammed his palm against it with an annoyed growl—which earned him nothing more than a smarting palm. He fisted his hand to soothe the sting.

Which was, of course, when Billingsly finally caught up to him. "Press these two together, milord," Billingsly suggested, not by expression or tone acknowledging that he'd just witnessed his employer acting like a petulant child. The butler's gnarled hands trembled slightly as he reached out and touched offset squares. The panel slid open, revealing a narrow but well-tended hallway.

The man nodded his head to the left. "Miss Emma's likely gone that way, to the servants' entrance at the back of the house."

"Thank you, Billingsly," Derick said. He ducked to clear the tapered beam and stepped into the passage, looking in the direction the butler had indicated. Emma must have already turned the corner.

Derick shot down the hallway, not exactly at a run, but not far from it. The irony wasn't lost on him. After ten summers trying to ditch little Pygmy, here he was chasing after her—and through his own house, no less.

Natural light greeted him at the next turn, fading as a closing door shut it out. Derick sped up, pushing through the exit. Cold rain met his face as he burst outside. Damnation.

The sky held a pinkish gray cast—pink to the west where the sun had begun its gentle descent into the horizon, gray to the east where dark, swollen clouds forced the light away. It was to the east that Derick spotted Emma, her determined steps carrying her through the stable yard and toward the forest.

He did run then, cursing as his foot slipped in the mud. He frowned, dismayed at how dangerously slick it had grown in such a short time. The spongy consistency spoke of oversaturated ground, not simply rain from this storm. It must have poured here for several days prior.

Already moisture soaked his clothing, conspiring with the brisk wind to chill him through. A little thing like Emma would be reduced to a shivering heap inside those gargantuan outer garments within moments.

"Devil take it, Pygmy," he growled, coming alongside her. "A woman shouldn't be out in this storm alone."

"No, she shouldn't," Emma agreed, her tone placid. She kept her eyes straight ahead and didn't slow her stride one whit. "Which is why I am going to find her and bring her home."

Derick stopped walking, staring after Emma. "You deliberately misun—"

"And *don't* call me Pygmy," she snapped over her shoulder.

Emma forged ahead, holding up her dress and coat as she might the skirts of a ball gown she was trying not to step on while ascending a staircase. The raised hems revealed a dirty pair of—

What *did* she have on her feet? And had she borrowed those ungainly boots from the same owner as the coat?

Derick shook his head, but despite her ill-fitting footwear and the slippery terrain, she picked her way across the yard with a single-minded dexterity that would have made any spymaster proud.

It took only four long strides to catch her once again. "At least stop and wait here whilst I fetch my horse," he requested, expecting once again to be ignored and already thinking of ways to bend her to his will.

But Emma did stop. She opened her mouth, no doubt to protest. He placed his fingers over her lips to shush her. Her soft skin radiated a pleasant warmth against his chilled fingers. Her cheeks flushed pink and her eyes widened.

Heat unfurled low in his gut. Removing his hand from her mouth, Derick slowly curled his fingers into a fist.

"I noticed you assigned the farthest and most treacherous section of the map to yourself," he said gruffly. Emma had not given the servants a dangerous task that she was unwilling to do herself. Admiration and disapproval welled up in him. She might be foolish, but she was also noble. "If you truly mean to get through it by dark, a fast steed and another warm body would not be amiss," he murmured.

Her gaze held him, assessing. Unknown thoughts flitted across her face, as if she were trying to discern his very character.

Well, that wouldn't do. Derick lowered his eyes to break the contact between them.

He mustn't forget his role. People tended to let their guard down more easily when they thought him superficial. They just assumed that a man so focused on himself didn't listen to anyone else. It made lips looser, and his job easier.

He pasted a smile on his face and regarded Emma with a well-practiced "put upon" expression. "Besides," he said, giving a wave of his hand, "since you've appropriated all of my groomsmen, my horse hasn't been properly rubbed down. He'll have to be run anyway."

Whatever favor he might have found in her eyes vanished and her face went slack. Just as well.

"Fine," she said, her mouth twisting. "But hurry."

Emma held herself stiff, not giving in to the urge to relax and settle back against Derick's warmth. The heat radiating from his hard thighs where she sat cradled sideways upon his lap caused fluttering enough.

Perhaps she should have protested when he'd pulled her onto the horse. But they would reach the search area—and hopefully Molly—faster on horseback, and as Emma wore a dress, being held thus was the only practical solution. At least the oilskin blanket Derick had procured to protect her from the storm afforded a measure of separation, and comfort. She had to admit, the relief from the wind and driving rain was welcome.

What was *not* welcome was the churning in her middle. Fig! She had worked so very hard to forget Derick Aveline. In the back of her mind, she supposed she'd expected he would return to Derbyshire someday, given that he was set to inherit the castle. What she hadn't expected was this sharp ache, as if his very arrival dug into her soul, turning over feelings long buried, exposing them to the sun like a farmer's pitchfork turning over fresh dirt for the spring planting. She had thought these emotions had been long put to rest, curse them. She didn't have the time or capacity to deal with them right now.

Usually, whenever she wished to block such disturbing thoughts, she would seclude herself in her workroom, taking chalk to her boards and losing herself in her equations or reviewing the crime statistics she'd been compiling for years and plotting them on her maps, until the unwelcome feelings passed. But with Molly missing, that wasn't an option.

Perhaps she could just block him out by closing her eyes and working familiar math equations in her head. It couldn't hurt to try. She wouldn't miss much along the way, she knew. The stiff blanket enshrouding her face blocked most of the rain, but it also acted like blinders. All she could really see was patches of endless gray sky and flashes of the sessile oaks, birch and dogwoods that populated the area anyway.

Emma squeezed her eyes shut. But that only increased her awareness of other things. She flinched at the terrible cracking of twigs and underbrush as the horse trampled the woodland. The earthy aroma of sodden peat and rotting vegetation mixed with the pungent scents of horse and hay from the stable blanket, flooding her nose. And though she should be freezing from the damp muslin clinging to her skin, inside she blazed with an uncomfortable heat, no doubt a reaction to the man whose arms held her so securely.

Her eyes flew open. *That* certainly hadn't worked.

Emma took in a deep breath, letting it out slowly. If only Derick had stayed back at the castle, had left her to search on her own. She could have used the solitude to regain her equilibrium.

Don't lie to yourself, Emma. You never had any kind of equilibrium where Derick was concerned. She pursed her lips. True, but she was no longer a lovesick girl, and she had no intention of letting herself get hurt again.

Emma pulled the musty blanket more tightly around her, as if cocooning herself in it could provide safe haven in addition to shelter from the storm. Rain drummed against the oilskin, the rapid, irregular beat drowning out all other sounds. But it couldn't drown her thoughts of Derick.

Why had he insisted upon coming along? He'd trivialized her concerns, after all. And it certainly seemed he'd grown rather spoiled in his years away. One would have thought he'd prefer to wait in the nice warm castle rather than set off into this storm with her. It couldn't be because of any desire to spend time with her, could it? Maybe—

The roaring rain ceased abruptly, dried up in an instant, as English storms were wont to do. Emma glanced around. They'd almost reached their destination. She pushed Derick out of her mind and instead forced her thoughts to finding Molly.

Now that nature had gone silent, the distant cries of other searchers echoed through the wood. Perhaps someone had already found her? Emma listened, hope deflating in her chest as only exploratory cries of "Moooolllyyyy" reached her ears.

Emma pushed the blanket away from her face, preparing to dismount. A refreshing blast of clean air cleared her senses—and opened them to another scent, one of bay and bergamot and man. *Derick.*

Just like that, she could no longer block her awareness of him. Every rolling undulation of the horse beneath them translated to a corresponding brush of Derick's hard thighs against her bottom. His nearness, his scent, his low voice murmuring to their mount, the way she sat caged in his embrace—it simply overwhelmed her. The blanket grew stifling, constricting. She had to get clear of it.

Emma wriggled her torso out of the blanket, pushing it down to her waist to free her arms. Behind her, Derick made a strangled grunt, as if her writhing had somehow injured him. She stilled suddenly.

His hands moved down her body, gripping her hips.

Emma gasped at his familiarity, but before she could upbraid him, he scooted her forward on his thighs, away from his, well, his . . . And all of a sudden she understood what that curious hardness against her hip must have been. She flushed hot.

Dear Lord, she had to get off of this horse and away from this man.

"Stop," she commanded, tugging on the blanket in an effort to pull it from beneath her. If she could kick her legs free, she could vault from the horse.

Derick's arms moved back up around her waist. "Emma. Cease. Moving."

"But we've arrived." She pointed to the fallen oak several feet ahead that marked the boundary of her assigned section. "Let me down," she ordered, grateful she had reason now to put some much-needed distance between herself and Derick. She should be putting all of her energy into finding Molly, not spiraling into a tizzy over her own confused feelings. "I suggest we split up, to cover more ground. I'll take the right side."

But he didn't release her. If anything, his arms tensed, pulling her closer. Why would he do that?

She wrenched around in his lap to look at his face, placing her hands squarely on his chest to support her twisted position.

Derick's jaw had clenched tight, his eyes showed lines of strain, almost as if her movements . . . pained him?

"We stay together," he said, implacable.

"That's ridiculous," she argued, all concern for him dissipating in the face of his illogical dictate. "How else am I to take advantage of your warm body?"

Derick's head pulled back, and his eyes scrunched together. "What?"

Had she said something wrong? She did sometimes. It was the literal way her mind worked. She tended to take things differently than most people. "You argued that I should let you come along because 'a fast steed and another warm body wouldn't be amiss.' I agree. Two will search faster than one."

"Ah." He drew the word out, eyeing her in a way that made her certain she'd made a fool of herself somehow. "Well, it's not a good idea. If we separate, chances are I'll end up searching for *two* missing women rather than one."

Emma choked. Of all of the conceited—"What makes you think—"

"I don't doubt your intelligence, Pygmy," Derick interrupted. "Nor your capabilities. But can you admit that forest rescues may not be your forte?"

She pressed her tongue against the back of her teeth. He had a point. "Oh, but I suppose they are yours?"

A sound very much like a long-suffering sigh escaped him. "Look behind us. What do you see?"

She tried, but she was too short to lever herself up enough to see over his shoulder, what with her legs still trapped within the blanket.

He seemed to sense her problem and with a tap of his heel, turned the horse.

"I see trampled grass and snapped twigs," she said, describing the clear markings of their passing.

"Exactly." Derick brought them around. "Whereas ahead of us, the ground cover is pristine. The girl has not come this way. No one has, not for some time."

Shame heated her cheeks. He was right. She would have wasted valuable time in her ignorance. "So there is no point in searching by foot here," she concluded.

"And our search will go faster if we remain together on horseback until there is evidence to do otherwise."

She nodded. Still, she had to do something to regain a sense of control. She unwrapped the blanket, shimmying and kicking her feet until she was able to pull it from beneath her. She did her best to ignore the way Derick tensed against her. Once the blanket was rolled, she settled herself as far away as possible. Yes, she still sat on his lap, but as respectably as she could manage.

"I concede," she said, indicating she was ready to set off again. "But *stop* calling me Pygmy."

Derick released a long breath, but it did little to relieve the arousal humming through him. How long had it been since a woman, *any* woman, affected him so? Maybe such a reaction was to be expected, given this was the closest he'd come to touching a woman in two years. But this was Pygmy, for God's sake. Pygmy! Where had his control gone?

It was that damnable scent, he decided. Lavender mingled with something more . . . earthy. He always had preferred earthy. Or perhaps it was that even her shapeless overcoat couldn't hide the curve of her hips or her surprisingly rounded bosom. Or maybe it was the way she moved with him, the backs of her thighs rolling with the motion of the horse, flexing and relaxing against him much as they would if she were—

Derick swallowed, hard. He'd never had a woman across his lap on horseback before, hadn't known how alluring it could be. That must be it. Not the woman herself.

He had to find a way of distracting himself from his inconvenient awareness of her softness nestled so close to his . . . hardness.

"So, tell me about this maid and why you are so certain she is in trouble," he tossed out.

As Emma shifted in his lap to look at him, her overcoat gapped, revealing a glimpse of the swell of her bosom. Dear God. Perhaps he should have left well enough alone.

"'This maid' has a name, and it's Molly," Emma said, chastening him. She waited until he'd nodded his acknowledgment. "Molly grew up at Aveline Castle. Her entire family lives in upper Derbyshire."

Derick huffed. "Sometimes family is precisely the reason to leave a place and never look back."

Emma eyed him with a quizzical frown. "Not in this case. Molly adores her family. She is particularly close to *her* mother."

Why had he said such a revealing thing? Perhaps it was a good thing he'd given up espionage when he had. Perhaps he was losing his knack. Or perhaps Pygmy just knocked him off balance. He cleared his throat, ignoring the not-so-veiled curiosity in Emma's tone even as he wondered at the note of censure. "She may have met a young man they didn't approve of."

Emma pursed her lips as if both annoyed at his dodging her and condemning him for even mentioning the possibility. "No. She's engaged to be married in a few weeks." She told him about the girl's routine, her movements of the past few days, of her own discussions with the maid's parents, her affianced, and her friends. Everything about the maid's life seemed . . . perfect. Normal. Happy, even.

"Of course, I checked with the local inns and the mail coach. But Molly is as reliable as they come. She wouldn't have just run off. Besides, none of her clothes or personal effects are missing."

Emma made a convincing case. He now had to admit that the poor maid *may* have met with an accident. He must have sounded like a total ass, which had been his intention, of course. And yet, somehow, it bothered him now.

"Detail the search for me up to this point," he said.

Emma raised a brow.

"Humor me."

She let out an aggrieved sigh. "We started with the assumption that she'd gone for an early walk and somehow injured herself," she began. Emma spoke of how she'd calculated the most likely search radius, taking into account timing and walking speed of both man and beast, the topography of the area, and a number of other variables that had near made his mind spin. He was impressed. He'd recognized, even when they were children, that her odd nature hid an unusual brightness. But Pygmy wasn't just intelligent—she was bloody brilliant.

No amount of brilliance was going to find the poor maid tonight, however. The calls of other searchers faded away, and the last gasps of sunlight filtered through the trees in foggy rays.

Emma sat tense on his lap. Derick felt her frustration rolling off of her in waves, and now shared it. Yet as much as he expected Emma to fight him, for her safety's sake he was going to have to insist that they return to the castle and start again in the morning.

"Emma, we have to turn back."

She shook her head vehemently. "But Molly," she said. "Her poor parents . . . No one should have to worry about someone they care about, to wonder where they are, what happened to them." She turned a fierce frown on him that left him feeling like she wasn't just talking about Molly Simms.

"I understand," he said softly, not sure that he did. "But—"

"Derick!" She cut him off, clutching his arm and pointing ahead.

He straightened, his body reacting to the urgency in her voice. Peering in the distance he spotted what she must have. A trail of broken branches and torn undergrowth. Someone had been through here recently.

"You're certain no one else has searched this area today?" he asked, his instincts roused.

Emma shook her head. "No one should have. Why?"

Derick assessed the damaged underbrush. The breaks were still fresh, still green, not twenty-four hours old. And leading north. Nothing lay north of here, no road, no shelter . . . just cliffs that dropped off into the deep valley below.

The same cliffs where his mother had taken her life. Derick forced his jaw to unclench.

Might Molly Simms have done the same? The maid's life sounded idyllic, but he knew better than most that one's appearance often hid something else entirely. He almost asked Emma if she thought it could be possible, but instead only pointed out, "This swath is wide, made by a horse or mule, not a person. Were any cattle missing from the stable this morning?"

"No. Billingsly said all were accounted for." A delicate frown marred Emma's face and a crease appeared between her eyes. "Besides, Molly didn't ride. She was terrified of horses."

Which meant if Molly did come this way, she was either very desperate or not alone . . . perhaps not even agreeable? Derick kept his thoughts to himself, saying only, "Anyone could have passed through here . . ."

"True," Emma said, "but I am *not* going back until I see for myself whether Molly did."

Chapter Three

From the set of her chin and the gleam in her amber eyes, Derick knew Emma meant those words.

He nodded and pulled her back to him, tightening his grip on her with one hand and on the reins with his other. He kicked his heel and his horse surged forward.

They picked up the trail and followed it, but the quaggy ground sucked at the horse's hooves, slowing them. Blood coursed through Derick, as did agitation. He suspected Emma felt the same. She leaned forward, straining against his hold in an effort to see ahead, her fists forming tight balls by her sides.

The sound of rushing water grew closer as they moved north. They must be closing in on St. William's Creek. As they had when he'd first seen Aveline Castle after fourteen years, more memories of his years here as a boy came back to Derick. He used to build dams in this creek, didn't he? Yes. He also remembered Emma "correcting" his engineering. It was normally a quiet, peaceful stream, but from the sounds echoing through the forest, today it was anything but that.

As they crested a gently sloping hill overlooking the creek, Derick pulled back on the reins. The tracks split, forking both north and northwest. Could two different people have come this way? He studied both paths. No. The path pointing toward the cliffs had branches snapped going and coming—the other's foliage was bent only one way. Someone had gone north, come back, then departed to the northwest.

Emma scrambled off his lap, turned and dangled her legs off the side of the horse before dropping to the ground.

"What do you think you're doing?" he demanded.

"*I'm* being the warm body," she said, taking the path to the north. She pointed to her left as she scurried up the trail. "You go that way."

Damn it. Derick knew the only way he was going to get Emma back on the horse was to bodily force her, and then he'd have to fight her all the way back to the castle. Or, he could take his horse northwest as fast as possible, and come right back for her.

Emma's retreating form was already yards away, disappearing behind the greenery.

"Don't leave the path, Pygmy," he yelled.

Her left hand shot up and she gave a short wave of acknowledgment. Or, knowing her, more likely dismissal.

As he turned his mount northwest, her voice carried back to him.

"*Don't* call me Pygmy!"

Derick didn't bother to restrain his grin.

Several minutes later, the trail he'd been following dead-ended into the bulging banks of St. William's Creek.

He'd never seen these waters so full, or so turbulent. They rushed past, carrying clumps of grass and earth, pushing branches that looked as if they'd been torn from their trees.

If memory served, the bend where he used to build

his dams was not far upstream. He'd loved that spot, as natural logjams regularly formed there, even when it wasn't swollen with rain.

Emma should be passing by there right about now. Derick's stomach tightened as he looked at the raging water. He shouldn't have let her go alone.

He shook off his concern and hopped from his horse. He peered across the stream, looking to see if the tracks picked up on the other side. Nothing. If Molly had gone that way, she was beyond them now . . . at least for tonight. The last of the light dipped below the tree line. He was going to get back on his horse and fetch Emma straightaway. He'd drag her back to the castle if necessary.

As he put his foot in the stirrup, an ungodly roar rent the air. His stallion whinnied and reared, knocking Derick onto his arse in the mud. He rolled, narrowly missing a hoof to the head, blinking in confusion as the horse shot away.

Derick swiveled in time to see the wall of water just before it crashed over him.

Pain exploded in his temple. He clamped down on the urge to gasp. A lungful of the frigid murky creek would do him in. He couldn't tell whether his feet were above or below his head in the churning jumble, but he knew he was underwater.

What the hell had hit him? A bloody log?

He opened his eyes. A greenish gray haze filled his vision and bits of debris stung him. He squeezed his eyelids shut again and flailed his arms in the darkness, trying to create some resistance to the tumultuous jostling as the water dragged him along.

Christ, his lungs burned. He had to get his head up. He scrabbled for traction on the muddy bed, finding none. In desperation, he jammed his feet down and pushed with all his might. His face broke the plane and he sucked in air—through his nose, through his mouth, however he could get it. But he still couldn't gain his footing.

I must relax . . . flow with the current. Yes, but first he'd need to get his legs out in front of him in case the water slammed him into any rocks. Better a broken leg than a broken neck.

His heart hammered in his chest, reverberating in his ears like drums beaten underwater as he fought to keep at least his nose and mouth above the water level. He cast a rolling glance behind him. How far had he washed downstream?

Something bumped his shoulder, sliding against his back as it moved past. Derick jerked his head around, thrashing to swim free of entanglement. He stilled as a red deer bobbed by, its large brown eyes open and unseeing, its neck twisted at a peculiar angle. Twigs and leaves were caught up like bedraggled birds' nests in its majestic antlers. Its body floated fluidly, not stiff with death—it hadn't been dead long. Poor beast must have been caught unawares upstream somewhere.

A jolt like a hoof to the chest jarred Derick.

Emma.

Had she been in the line of the flood? He kicked hard toward the bank, his arms arcing in determined strokes. He had to get to her.

At last the banks of the creek gave way, allowing the wall of water to disperse over the land. The flood slowed.

Limbs shaking and out of breath, Derick pulled himself from the water. But he was on the bloody wrong side of the creek. He stepped cautiously into the rushing swell and was nearly knocked from his feet . . . he couldn't risk crossing here. He'd be damned if he'd go farther south, farther from Emma. He'd just have to find a better spot farther upstream to ford.

Soggy undergrowth and bared roots exposed by the

sudden flood grabbed at his feet like tentacles, but he shook free of them.

"Emma?" he called out, shocked at his own hoarse rasp. Damn it. He'd *told* her he'd be looking for two missing women if she didn't stay with him.

That's not fair, he chided himself. If she had been with him, she'd have washed away with him, too.

"Emma!" he yelled again, listening for any sign of her, but little could be heard above the angry creek and his squelching footfalls. He had to be closing in on where he'd been knocked off his feet. His eyes scanned ahead. Blessedly the clouds had passed, allowing some moonlight to penetrate the canopy. The greens of the forest and the murky water blurred together in what little light filtered through. He could barely differentiate the dark edges of even the trees anymore. How would he ever—

A flash of something pale caught his eye in the moonlight, about four or five yards ahead. Derick's stomach clenched. He squinted in an effort to make it out. It was almost like alabaster—could that be skin?

His heart kicked. Whatever it was, it was unmoving. A rush of sensation flowed through him very much as it had when he'd been a spy, about to uncover a crucial piece of information from within a target's stronghold. Yet rather than the familiar excitement of the hunt, this was a terrible dread that filled his mouth with the sour taste of bile.

It could be anything, he reasoned—the clean white surface of a newly shaved rock broken open by the flooding waters, or the underbelly of a dead trout, caught up in debris.

Yet he ran, as much as the sucking mud would allow. As he drew closer, a shape took form. Feet? *Yes,* and legs, arms, darkish hair floating erratically in the lapping water . . . *a green dress.*

"Emma!" he roared, leaping from the bank to reach

her. She floated facedown, caught against a log. His mouth went utterly dry. Good Christ, she wasn't moving. *She wasn't moving!*

Derick dropped to his knees, grabbing Emma by the shoulders and yanking her around. He must get her face above water. Then he could force the water from her lungs.

Her body seemed so stiff beneath his hands. Her hair had wrapped around her head as he'd turned her, obscuring her face. His hand shook as he reached to brush the straggling mess aside. *Oh God, Emma.* This was his fault.

His consciousness plummeted when her face came into view, slack in death. Her neck was twisted, much like that of the deer from before. Her eyes were open wide, clouded over and . . . *blue?*

Derick sucked in the breath that had been squeezed from him. It wasn't her.

His shoulders went slack. Derick concentrated on breathing, on stilling his pulse.

"Derick?"

He snapped his head up, turning to the voice.

Emma. Straddling his horse, safe on the far side of the creek. *Safe.*

Relief swamped him, crashing over his body more fiercely than the raging creek he'd just survived. His eyes devoured her—every living, breathing inch. Her skirts were ruched high up on her milky thighs, allowing her to sit astride the saddle, and those ridiculous boots dangled precariously on her feet.

Smudges of mud marred the pale skin of her face and her chestnut hair hung disheveled about her, but good Christ, he'd never seen such a beautiful sight in his life.

Her brilliant eyes were wide, fixed not on him but on what he held in his arms.

"Molly!" she cried, scrambling to bring her leg around to dismount. Derick's horse whinnied and stamped in protest. Emma's eyes flared and she nearly toppled from her perch. If Pygmy didn't settle down, she would fall and break her neck as well.

"Stay put, Emma," Derick barked, then softened his voice. "She's gone. There's nothing you can do for her now."

Emma stilled. Her shoulders slumped and some of the luster left her golden eyes as they filled with tears.

His intense joy and relief at seeing Emma alive dimmed when so juxtaposed to her grief.

He hadn't even considered the possibility that she and the maid might have been friends. After fourteen years living behind enemy lines, always on his guard, Derick had nearly forgotten that genuine relationships with other people were even possible.

He glanced down at the poor soul he cradled. She looked nothing like Emma, did she? How the hell had he thought otherwise?

The moment he'd seen Emma safe on that horse, his panicked haze had lifted. Now he could see what he should have from the first. Molly was fine-featured like Emma, but taller, fuller-bodied. The dress she wore *was* green, but well faded. And she wasn't wearing an overcoat.

Mistakes like that were completely unlike him and would have meant death in his other life. Unforgivable.

Gently he ran his palm over the maid's face, closing eyes that saw no more. How had poor Molly Simms gotten to this place?

And more importantly, was she an unfortunate victim of the flood, or of something more nefarious?

A splashing noise jerked his attention to the stream. Hooves sloshed through water as Emma urged the horse into the elevated water. The steed's eyes and nostrils flared but Derick could see that Emma gripped the horse tightly with her knees and had a firm grasp on the reins. She cooed something low to the animal.

Damned disobedient woman. "I told you to stay put."

"And I might have listened had your dictate made any sense," she retorted. "However, we have to get Molly back to the castle somehow, and this horse has a better chance of crossing these waters than you would. Particularly whilst carrying her . . . body."

Derick bit his tongue on an ungentlemanly response.

Emma never looked away from the water sluicing around the horse's legs, her teeth tugging on her lower lip with calm focus.

While his bloody heart was in his bloody throat. And if she made it across safely, he might bloody well thrash her.

He didn't breathe again until Emma pulled the horse up onto the bank.

As she dismounted, Derick lifted Molly from the water, laying her out on the bank. As he knelt beside the maid, Emma's cumbersome boots came into view across from him. His gaze traveled up her as he rose to his feet.

Emma seemed unusually pale. Her fist balled in front of her middle and deep brackets appeared on either side of her mouth. Poor Pygmy must be turning in knots, as she wouldn't be used to such things.

She circled Molly, flinching when her gaze met the maid's face.

"You needn't look," he murmured. "I will carry the mai—*Molly* on horseback, if you'll walk beside." He reached out his hand, moved with the desire to touch Emma, to comfort her.

She gave a little shake of her head, and Derick snatched his arm back. He clasped his hands behind him. Just as well—he didn't see himself as the comforting sort anyway.

"Do you think her"—Emma cleared her throat—"her neck was broken prior to her washing downriver, or as a result of the flood?"

"I'm not certain we can tell. We might attempt to estimate how long ago she died by the stiffness of her joints," he suggested. "But in this situation it might not tell us much."

"Because of the cold water," she said, nodding.

Derick raised a brow, looking at her with curiosity. He waited for her to fill the expectant silence, but she didn't. She just stared at him. *Odd.* Finally, he had to ask. "And how would you know that?"

Emma winced, and nodded. "This is hardly the first death that I've seen," she replied. "I've . . . assisted my brother in his duties as magistrate for quite some time, and my father before him, so I am familiar with rigor mortis and how to calculate a person's passing from it."

Derick gaped. Pygmy was full of surprises, wasn't she?

"However," she said, "a few years ago, twin boys from the village went missing. Their . . . bodies were found in a spring-fed pond several days later. When they were pulled from the water, they were quite unrecognizable." Emma shifted on her feet, clearly uncomfortable with whatever she'd seen that day. "But though they'd been dead for days, I noticed rigor didn't set in until they'd warmed." She raised a chestnut brow of her own. "How did *you* know cold water could affect rigor mortis?"

He wasn't about to tell her that he'd been trained by both the French and the English in myriad ways to dispose of a body while throwing off suspicion as to what truly had befallen it.

He cleared his throat and dropped his gaze to the maid, deflecting the question. "Well, if she did die elsewhere, the flood would have washed away any evidence of it," he said. "And her body may have been carried in from anywhere upstream. We may never be able to tell whether her death was an accident or not."

Emma squatted, and reached her hand out to take Molly's chin. She turned the maid's head slowly, squinting in the low light. "I wouldn't say never," she murmured.

Derick came around, squatting down beside Emma.

Even in the feeble moonlight, ugly purple bruises that resembled nothing more than long fingers stood out on the maid's neck.

"Damn," Derick uttered.

It seemed he wouldn't be leaving upper Derbyshire until he'd uncovered both a traitor *and* a murderer.

Chapter Four

Early the following afternoon, Derick stood at the door of Wallingford Manor. He tugged the fine linen of his cuff so that it emerged from the sleeve of his burgundy Bath coating jacket just so and then rapped three swift clangs with the massive knocker. As he waited, he wiped damp palms against his buff pantaloons. His hands felt empty, as if he should be bearing flowers or some other pleasing gift for the lady of the house.

Good Lord. Where had that thought come from? By the time he was of an age to call on young ladies, he'd been well ensconced behind enemy lines and the only thing he'd been interested in wooing was sensitive information. That most of that information had *come* from wooing ladies, young and otherwise, was another matter entirely. Besides, he wasn't here to see Emma—indeed, hoped not to see her again at all. Emma disturbed him, unbalanced him. And he couldn't afford the distraction.

No, he needed to focus solely on the task at hand. It was unlikely that poor Molly Simms' murder had anything to do with his mission. But tragic though it was, it did gave Derick a legitimate reason to work directly with the magistrate himself and leave Emma out of his investigation altogether.

An annoying pang of disappointment twinged in his chest. He pushed it aside. This remained a mission like any other, a chess match of sorts, and Emma just a pawn. Not his opponent.

If anyone played the white king to his black one, it was her brother. Once Derick's fellow agent at the War Department, Thaddeus Farnsworth, had pinpointed a leak of military secrets to a source in upper Derbyshire, Wallingford immediately became the most likely suspect. A decorated war hero with vast military experience, he was one of the few people known to reside in the area who had the kind of knowledge that had been sold to the French. Wallingford hadn't presented himself at Aveline Castle either last night or this morning—which was odd, given the man's duties as magistrate. So Derick had come to him. It was time to get a good look across the board at his potential adversary.

The door cracked and Derick was met by the polite stare of the butler.

"Lord Scarsdale to see Lord Wallingford." He whipped out his calling card. A bit much for the country, he knew, but it was all part of the affectation.

The servant's eyes widened as he stared at the stark but finely engraved card. Derick raised a brow, and finally the butler reached out and took the offering with his bare hand rather than the customary silver tray. This being a country manor, Derick supposed the man didn't keep a salver at the ready. But being in the country did not excuse keeping a viscount waiting on the front stoop.

Derick cleared his throat, acting his part. "Lord Wallingford?" he drawled. "I have magistratorial business to discuss with him."

The statement seemed to shake the butler from his stupor. The door opened wide and Derick stepped into the marbled entry.

"If you'll come this way, my lord, I'll fetch . . . the magistrate." The butler ushered Derick into a spacious sitting room and bowed out the door.

When the door clicked shut, Derick made a quick turn about the room, taking stock. Nothing of any obvious evidentiary value lay about, but he hadn't expected it would. However, one could learn many beneficial tidbits about a home's owner just by small observations.

Derick removed to the far corner, taking in the space as a whole. While it was grand, it was sparsely decorated. There were no trappings of wealth anywhere in the room. In fact, the Aubusson rug, woven in the Oriental style, was thin in spots, the colors badly faded. The warm leather of the wingback chairs near the open fireplace showed signs of heavy use and little balls of fabric clung to the worn chintz of the settees.

He ran his hands over the frayed material of a chaise. This was the main parlor, the face Wallingford showed to the world. The man was clearly suffering from some financial distress. Telling . . . but by no means definitive. While most treason was motivated by money, not all was. He hoped, in this case, it wasn't about money. It sickened Derick to think that someone who had fought alongside the very soldiers he went on to betray would do it simply for gold. Hell, it sickened him that he would do it at all.

If, indeed, Wallingford was the traitor. Derick would have to worm his way further into the house to look for more evidence. Most likely, Wallingford would invite him into the study or library to discuss the maid's murder, which should give him a larger view. And he could always resort to a late-night exploration if he must.

His imagination flashed a vision of him happening across Emma, tucked into her bed in nothing but a flimsy night rail. What would she look like, her features relaxed in sleep, her hair down and spread across her pillow? Derick's entire body tightened like a fist as his mind emptied of all thoughts but her. Her tempting scent would alter with her skin warmed from sleep, would sweeten tantalizingly like nectar.

Derick caught himself taking a deep breath. Damnation. This was precisely why he shouldn't be around Emma. He hadn't physically seen the woman in hours and yet he was thoroughly distracted, which made no sense whatsoever. He didn't even *like* her. And he was determined to stop letting her interfere with the role he was here to play.

The door clicked, and Derick's mind snapped back to the charade at hand. He stepped from behind the chaise to greet Lord Wallingford, a droll greeting on his lips.

His mouth snapped shut as Emma, not Wallingford, strode into the room, her skirts swishing behind her. She stopped abruptly only a scant two feet from him, her eyes traveling his length.

Her sudden nearness hummed in his veins. Damn, but those eyes of hers made a man feel she could see right through him. Derick fought the ridiculous urge to step back from her frank perusal. He had no reason for concern—he knew exactly what she would see. He'd planned every detail.

Gold buttons winked in the sun that beamed through the massive windows, his burgundy-and-cream-striped waistcoat contrasted nicely with his buff pantaloons, and his black Hessians fair gleamed. While he'd never go so far as to polish them with champagne, as Brummel had so famously espoused, Derick would challenge the man himself to find any other fault with his presentation.

And that's what it was—the pretentious clothing, the intricately tied neck cloth, the close-shaven face, the precisely styled hair—a presentation. A uniform.

And today, perhaps even a suit of armor.

His mouth twisted wryly. As if he needed protection from Pygmy. "Why are *you* here?"

Emma's brows dipped and her mouth wobbled, like

she couldn't decide whether to smile or scowl. "I *live* here, Derick."

Imbecile. "Yes, of course." Really, if his superiors could have seen him around Emma Wallingford, they'd never have entrusted the country's greatest secrets to him. At least his incompetent fop act should be especially believable today. "What I meant to say was that I was expecting your brother."

Emma crossed her arms. "Yes, Perkins said you wished to speak with the magistrate. Why?"

The back of Derick's neck tingled. She was on the defensive. Interesting. Because of his desire to see her brother? Or because of him? Both were intriguing questions, but for different reasons.

A slow heat spread through him at the possibility that he might have the same physical effect on her as she did on him. He might be able to use that.

No. He was finished with those days, when seduction had been his stock-in-trade. He shouldn't need to resort to sensual interrogation. He would be able to get what he needed from Lord Wallingford—if he could get past the man's formidably lovely gatekeeper. "I should think that obvious."

"Indeed." Emma's expression turned to a decided scowl, and her foot tapped in irritation. "What is not so obvious," she continued in a clipped tone, "is why you should feel it necessary to insert yourself into an investigation that has nothing to do with you."

Oh, yes . . . she was most certainly defensive. Which meant he was onto something. The question was, what?

He had hoped that Farnsworth would have made contact last night or this morning. The last communication the War Department had received from the agent was that he was headed here. This mission would be much easier if Derick knew what Farnsworth knew, and he was anxious to talk with the man. Surely with the way word spread in small villages like this one, Farnsworth would have heard of his arrival, no matter how deep undercover he was. Until he came forward, however, Derick was on his own in sorting whether or not George Wallingford was the traitor they were hunting. And the quickest way to get to Wallingford was to stick to his story. "Because the girl was a member—"

"—of your household." Disapproval dripped from Emma's voice, landing on him like a particularly annoying drizzle. She blinked up at him with those owl-like eyes. "Am I to assume that you intend to stay in Derbyshire and take up the reins at the castle, then?"

Derick chafed at the censure in her tone. "Good God, no. This would be the *last* place I would live. I don't expect to be here more than a few weeks at most," he answered. "As if that's any of your concern," he grumbled under his breath. He swiped a hand across his forehead. She was wasting his time. Nosy, irritating chit. "Damnation, Pygmy, you are *exactly* as you were as a girl."

Derick couldn't keep his eyes from dropping to her cleavage, so lusciously pushed up by her crossed arms. "Well, not *exactly*," he muttered.

Emma's shoulders rose slightly as a tiny gasp escaped her. "Of course I'm not."

Hell. Had he actually just said that aloud? What had gotten into him?

"While I still don't care to be called Pygmy," she reminded him, not so subtly, "I've changed quite significantly in other ways." She sniffed. "I'm no longer straw-headed, for one. I speak four additional languages than I did when you last knew me and I've grown at least two hands taller."

A huff of laughter escaped him at her attempt to lighten the moment, but it quickly faded. Emma wasn't smiling.

Instead she heaved a sigh, uncrossed her arms and turned her body, as if to allow him a clear path to the door. She even extended a delicate hand in that direction, wafting her delicious lavender scent near. "Listen, while I appreciate your assistance last evening, my lord, you needn't concern yourself any further. I suggest you go about whatever . . . *business* a gentleman like yourself might have in Derbyshire. There's no need for you to dirty your hands"—her gaze traveled over him again and her lips flattened—"or your fancy clothes with the matter."

Derick pressed his fingers against his forehead, closing his eyes. This was not going according to plan. He'd never had such trouble bending a female to his will.

Except her. What *was* it about Emma that threw him off so?

She makes you forget your role.

Yes. Something about her reduced some part of him to the boy he didn't even remember being—a singular and disturbing truth he couldn't avoid or fathom. All he knew was that it was true—and dangerous—which made it all the more important for him to deal solely with her brother. It was time to regain command of this conversation. Derick straightened, crossed his own arms and leveled his gaze on her.

"*I* suggest," he drawled, looking down his nose at her in a way certain to nettle, "that you fetch the magistrate like a good girl and then go about whatever . . . *business* a country miss like you should be doing. No doubt there's a pillow that needs embroidering somewhere?"

Emma's eyes became slits, and he bit back a satisfied grin. That should send her off in a huff to get her brother.

Yet she visibly dug in her heels and crossed her arms again, pushing her delectable décolletage prominently back into view. A view, of course, that he couldn't help but avail himself of. He might be acting a part, might have chosen to remain celibate at least until he put this life behind him, but he *was* still male.

Emma clenched her jaw. The nerve of the man! How

dare this . . . this perfectly turned-out popinjay come to
her home and provoke her? The cad didn't even have
the decency to look her in the eye after insulting her so.
And what was he staring at? She followed the path of
his eyes, her chin dipping as she looked down to her . . .

Her cheeks flamed and she hastily dropped her arms.
And yet the heat from her face spread down her neck
and through her chest. She knew better than to think
that Derick actually found *her* attractive. He certainly
never had when they were younger, no matter how she'd
tried to get him to notice her. But he'd certainly *seemed*
captivated just then, hadn't he?

She couldn't resist a curious peek at his face. But the
corners of his eyes drooped along with his mouth in an
expression that could only be described as blasé. Her
face burned all the more. Had she really expected otherwise?

Blasted, confusing man. Why wouldn't he just waltz
blithely off on his merry way? "You said you have no
intention of staying in Derbyshire at all. Why won't you
just leave matters be?"

A tremble rolled through her middle as she considered what was at stake. What an ironic sort of travesty it
would be if Derick, who couldn't be bothered with this
village for an age, came back on a lark and discovered
her brother's secret. He could use it to destroy the life
she'd worked so hard to fashion for herself after her father's death, and then he would just trot back to London—
or France—or wherever he'd been for the last decade
and a half.

Derick raised his chin a notch and stared at her with
those unnerving green eyes, suddenly anything but unin-
terested. "Why do *you* so badly wish me to?"

The rolling multiplied, magnified. Emma swallowed.
That was a line of questioning she had no intention of
following.

She couldn't take the chance that he would puff up

with autocratic male pride and act . . . well, exactly like he was acting now. If he uncovered the truth about her brother, a man like him would think it his duty to take the matter to higher authorities. That was certain to bring her comfortable life crashing down around her. No. She needed to get him out of the house, none the wiser, before he had the opportunity to make trouble.

Emma fisted her hands. "No reason," she said with a shrug that she suspected made her look like a stiff puppet. "I simply expected you'd be relieved not to have to involve yourself in Molly's murder. I'm certain you had other plans in mind for your visit—"

"As much as I am enjoying your *delightful* company, Emma, I insist upon seeing your brother. Is he here or not?"

Emma snapped her mouth shut on a frown. She considered lying, saying George was out in the woods combing the spot where they'd found Molly's body, as she herself had done this morning, but deceit had never sat well with her . . . even when she was doing it for good reasons. "Yes. But—"

"Then I will have this conversation with him."

"Oh, for goodness' sake—" Emma bit her lip as Derick casually brushed nonexistent lint from his finely cut jacket. She couldn't shake the gnawing sense that he wasn't quite what he seemed. Something . . . dangerous lurked just behind his emerald gaze. Emma wondered if other people saw it, or if only she did because they had once been friends of a sort. Or perhaps she only imagined it. It was just . . . he seemed so different from the boy she'd known. She had learned, as part of her research into the behavior of criminals, that people didn't change very much once their personalities had developed. Yet her memories of the boy he'd been didn't match up with the image of a fop that he projected now.

Well, either way, she couldn't allow him to see George.

She'd just have to delay and hope he lost interest. "My brother can't see you today. He . . . isn't well."

A frown shifted the perfect angles of Derick's face. "Nothing serious, I hope?"

"Nothing out of the ordinary," she hedged. *For him,* she added silently to quiet her conscience.

"I see," he said, turning toward the door. "Very well."

Emma's stomach unclenched as she took her first deep breath since Perkins had interrupted her with that white linen card. While she regretted that Derick would leave thinking her an awful shrew, at least he *was* leaving.

"I shall expect to see Lord Wallingford at Aveline Castle in the morning, then," Derick called over his shoulder.

"That will be *quite* out of the question." She hated how the pitch of her voice rose like an aggrieved peahen's.

Derick turned on his heel, seeming every bit the autocratic nobleman she'd feared. "While *I* appreciate *your* assistance last evening," he said, tossing her earlier words back at her in a thoroughly infuriating way, "investigating murder is a business for men."

Emma bristled. *Of all the—* Her worries flew from her mind in her outrage. "I hardly see how one's gender plays into this. I have handled such matters quite well on my own over the years." How dare he come to her home, *her* village, and act as though he owned it? "And I'll have you know that—"

"You've handled *what* such matters quite well on your own?" Derick's question cut through her bluster and quite nearly knocked her off her feet.

Cold flowed from her head to her toes as quick and shocking as a spring-fed waterfall.

She'd just given up the game, hadn't she?

Perhaps not. Her palms turned clammy as she scrambled for a way to recover. "What kind of question is that?" Emma couldn't help averting her eyes, focusing on the bust of Archimedes to her left. "I do many things well on my own." She glanced back at him, pasting what she hoped was a look of confused annoyance on her face, hoping he would let the matter drop.

"Such as?"

Emma huffed. "It isn't relevant."

But one black brow cocked expectantly.

Her eyes strayed back to the bust. "I m-manage the house, assist my brother . . ." This was getting worse and worse. A pox on all perceptive people, and a pox squared on her foolish tongue.

"We've strayed from the point. A murder—or any other misdeed—in our village is a business for those of us who *live* here, who have a vested interest in each other."

A corner of Derick's mouth kicked up in . . . *amusement*? This wasn't at all funny. Who did he think he was?

"Not for some *interloper* who hasn't deigned to grace us with his presence in fourteen years," she accused. Oh, what could she say to get him to leave? "Not even for his own mother's funeral."

The half smile froze on his face, then began to twitch, hovering on his mouth like an angry hummingbird briefly before his features went completely smooth.

Emma held her breath as gooseflesh popped over her skin. Oh, she'd gone too far. Certainly she had wondered at Derick's conspicuous absence all these years, had condemned him in her own mind as she'd watched his mother suffer over her son's desertion, had been appalled when Derick had not seen fit to pay his respects even after the woman was dead. But she hadn't intended to hurl such an ugly volley. She'd just wanted him to depart, leave her and George alone with their secret. She held her breath. Guilt choked her, warring with her hope that he'd been offended enough to retreat.

"You're a terrible liar, Emma," he said instead, his

voice all smooth, dark silk, as were his movements as he advanced upon her.

Her eyes snapped to his hard gaze and she tried to escape it, escape him, backing herself up until her rump bumped the arm of a settee.

"Your lips say one thing," he murmured, standing so close that bergamot and bay tickled her nose, "but your eyes tell a completely different story." Derick leaned forward, forcing her backward as his long arms came around her in a flash. He planted them on the settee, on either side of her hips.

Emma's heart fluttered in her throat. She was trapped. No ducking to escape him this time, no matter how much taller he was. Her breath came fast and hard . . . not from fear, exactly, though there was that. But from something more like . . . excitement?

What was wrong with her? She had to put some space between them and get control of herself before this damnable attraction she obviously still felt for Derick ruined everything. Emma braced her own arms beside her hips to the inside of his and arched back until she felt her spine might snap.

Derick's gaze dropped low, melted into a green pool. It traveled up over her mouth to her eyes, holding her entranced. "Give me the truth now," he coaxed, and she felt his voice almost as if it were a warm finger brushing her cheek. It made her want to spill every secret she'd ever had. "What are you hiding, Emma?"

She wanted to give him a tart answer, but it was as if he had immobilized her entirely with some unseen energy that held her in his thrall. Emma swallowed, hard, in a desperate attempt to wet her suddenly parched mouth.

Derick leaned closer, taking in a deep breath. Emma frowned as fiercely as she could muster, but he gave her no quarter. "You know, Emma, I can stay here all day . . ."

She imagined tucking her knees and rolling backward over the arm of the settee to escape him. She might take him by surprise, but she knew better than to think she'd get far. She would only make a fool of herself and make the situation more unbearable.

There was no way around it. Now he would learn everything, and the life she'd come to hold dear would be at his mercy. Emma heaved a choppy sigh. "*I* am the magistrate," she admitted, her arms trembling from the strain of leaning away from him. But her voice didn't warble, and she took strength from that.

If she had to tell him all, she intended to do it on her own two feet. Emma pushed off from the cushion in an attempt to straighten, but Derick had pressed her into an awkward position. She had no choice but to relent and fall back again, except to—

Without further thought, she threw her arms around his waist and tried to pull herself up. Electricity jolted through her, singeing her nerves as her skin tingled and her breath strangled in her throat.

Derick tensed beneath her hands, sinewy muscle rippling beneath fine linen. He tried to pull back, presumably to bring them both to their feet, but their angle was too acute. Instead, he toppled.

Emma squeezed her eyes shut as momentum carried them over the arm of the settee, expecting to be crushed beneath Derick's superior weight.

But it never came. She lifted one eyelid to see Derick above her, holding his arms stiff on either side of her chest in an awkward, crooked position to avoid smashing her. Emma slowly became aware of where the rest of his weight had settled. Almost as if it were a natural thing, her legs had spread to accommodate him and he was pressed most intimately against her. Her blood spiked, then seemed to pool precisely where his body met hers. Her thoughts scattered as sensation flooded her mind.

"What do you mean you are the magistrate?" Derick's voice had gone raspy, but the man had at least retained his faculties. Unlike her.

Emma grunted. She wriggled, trying to dislodge him. But it was a mistake. A groan ripped from his throat, and that scratchy, vulnerable sound sent shivers through her, chills that tightened her nipples painfully and that froze the breath in her chest.

Derick clenched his jaw, but made no move to get off of her. Indeed, he lowered his chest, settling himself onto his elbows. "Emma," he said, his voice gravel, "you can either tell me what I want to know, or we can stay here like this until your brother comes looking for you. Then I can ask him myself."

Flames licked her as her traitorous body screamed to let him stay all day. How could she be of two minds like this? "Let me up," she whispered. "Now," she said more loudly. "Let me up, and I'll tell you what you want to know."

Several heartbeats pounded past. Emma felt pinned. Pinned by Derick's strength, pinned by his penetrating gaze. And yet while her insides squirmed, the feeling wasn't necessarily unpleasant. Discomfiting, yes, but also hot, inquisitive, curious . . . almost desperate to know where these sensations might lead.

"As you wish . . ." he murmured.

The breath whooshed out of her as Derick lifted himself. Though he did so gingerly, Emma felt every excruciatingly titillating press, shift, slide of his body. At last he extended a hand and helped her to her feet.

Emma pushed out of Derick's arms and took a deep breath, desperate to clear her mind. But his scent lingered in her nose like a cherished memory. "I am the magistrate," she repeated, trying to pick up the strains of the conversation they'd been having. "*Acting* magistrate," she corrected.

Derick's brows dipped into a midnight vee. "Why?"

Emma wrapped her arms around her waist to quell her

still rioting senses. She had more important issues to worry about than how Derick affected her. She well knew that the men who appointed the county magistrates would never allow a woman to hold such an important position. One word from Derick to the Commission of the Peace and her brother would be stripped of his position and she of the duties that had given her life meaning these past years. Not to mention the access to all of the magistratorial records she needed to complete her moral statistics project. If she could prove that a high percentage of criminal behavior was not a result of bad blood, but instead was due mainly to learned, environmental factors—and if she could get someone in Parliament to take notice—it could change the face of England for the better. "My brother no longer has the competence."

The vee deepened as he looked off to his right. The corners of his lips turned down. "I think you should explain."

It wouldn't take him long to find out the whole truth now that he was looking for it.

Emma released a resigned sigh. "George had some sort of apoplectic fit a few years back, brought on, we think, by a fall from his horse. He was found unconscious after one of his morning rides, a wicked gash on his head and his horse nowhere to be seen." She moved away, still needing to escape his draw on her senses. She paced about the sparsely furnished room. "As he came back to his senses, in a fashion, his wish was that no one know. He is a proud man, even now when he is himself less than a third of the time."

"When was this, exactly?" Derick said, his gaze following her intently—she could feel it almost like a ray of sun beating on her and like that brilliant star, it heated her to a splotchy red.

"Nearly six years ago," she answered. Why did it matter? Unless she could convince Derick to leave well enough alone, it was all over. "We brought in the best doctors. We thought George would recuperate and for a while, it seemed like he might. I . . . had been handling most of the administrative side of his post, as I had done for my father before him, but after George's accident, I began handling some of the more physical aspects as well."

A tightness settled in Emma's chest. What if her position was taken away from her? Assisting first her father, then her brother, in their roles as magistrate had given her life meaning in a time when she'd been floundering and facing a life of bleak prospects. She'd been a dismal failure in her one London Season, ridiculed for her oddly rational mind and for her tendency to say what was on it without veiling her thoughts. Accepting that she was destined to end up a spinster and a burden to her family, she'd been grateful for some purpose. She couldn't admit that to Derick, however. A man like him would never understand what it felt like to be searching for a place to belong.

"But then he took a turn for the worse," she went on, pushing any sentiment from her tone, "and by the next year, it had all become too taxing for him. So I stepped fully into his role." And found a life of her own, a life of being needed by the villagers and townsfolk, respected for her logical mind and straightforward approach to life and problem solving. It hadn't been easy. She'd had to prove herself to them first, but it hadn't been long until Emma had gone from being pitied to being appreciated. And now Derick had it in his power to take that from her.

Emma stopped pacing and searched his face, desperate to know what he was thinking. But she was met with inscrutability.

"And what is your brother's condition now?" Derick asked, his gaze hooded.

Emma struggled to put into words what it was like to live with George. "The closest thing I can think to describe my brother is to compare him to an aged person who suffers from dementia. There are days when George seems almost himself, and aside from his being confined to a rolling chair, I can almost believe he'd never had the stroke—although those days are fewer and further between. Other days, he doesn't know his own name." Those were the hardest times, when he stared at her as if she were a stranger . . . sometimes even acting afraid of her. "Some days, he can remember everything about our lives, but others . . . he can't remember what he had for breakfast." A sigh escaped her. "Then there are the times where he's completely unable to communicate, sometimes for days, even weeks at a time. Those are rare, too, thank God, though he's been in one of those spells for much of the last month."

"I'm sorry, Pygmy," he said softly. "It must be very difficult for you."

"Don't call me that." She didn't want his pity. She wanted him to keep her secret and leave her brother in peace. "Besides, having my brother only part of the time is better than having no one at all," she whispered.

"I see," he said as he strode toward the door. "I must think on this."

Emma followed, unable to let him just leave without knowing his intentions. She reached out and grabbed his elbow.

"Must think on what?"

He turned back, his eyes roving her face, searching for something.

Emma quickly released her grip even as she tightened her lips and straightened her shoulders, determined not to show him her worry.

"This is a highly unusual circumstance," he said, finally. "I must decide what is best all around."

How utterly arrogant! And unfair. And completely like a man. "And what makes *you* thusly qualified to make such a decision?" The words flew out of her mouth, as they so often did, and immediately she wished to bite them back. It never paid for the mouse to anger the lion who held her in his paw.

His green gaze held hers for so long, she thought she could distinguish a dozen subtle verdant shades in his glittering irises. "So very many things," he said finally, enigmatic. "I will return in the morning, at ten. I expect to see your brother then, to determine for myself the truth of the circumstances. Then you and I will discuss what is to be done."

Derick stepped through the entrance of the town's largest inn and pub, the Swan and Stag. It was the fourth such establishment he'd visited today in his effort to learn what he needed to without having to deal with Emma Wallingford.

He couldn't get her out of his mind. Even now, just the thought of her set his body on edge. Damnation. Well, at least the madness between them wasn't one-sided. Wouldn't it have been ironic, though, if the first woman he'd felt true desire for in years felt nothing for him? But Emma wanted him. Oh, she might pretend she loathed him, but he'd picked up all the signs of her attraction . . . the soft melting against him, the subtle shift of her scent, the way her amber eyes had darkened with desire. He'd wager that whatever little Pygmy was doing right now, she was doing it with him on her mind. He could take some solace in that.

He wasn't sure what to think about what he'd learned today about Emma's brother. If the man was as incapacitated as she let on, Derick didn't see how he could be the traitor. While many of the secrets had been passed prior to Wallingford's accident, the information had continued to flow long after it. He would have to reserve judgment until he met the man, of course. Emma had certainly done her best to ensure that he wouldn't get that chance today. Had she succeeded in keeping Farnsworth from her brother? Could that be one of the reasons this mission was still unresolved?

And why the hell hadn't Farnsworth made contact by now? There was always the chance he'd picked up another trail that had led him away from here. But if he had moved on, why hadn't he sent word to the War Department?

Well, Derick wasn't moving on until he had some answers. And since Farnsworth hadn't come to him, he had decided to look for the man himself.

Derick stepped up to the bar. The pleasantly earthy scents of wood fire, meat stew and spilled ale filled the air, as did murmurs of conversation and the occasional guffawing laugh. And yet, as Derick stood waiting to be acknowledged, the lull of voices died out. He could feel the curious stares heavy upon his back. He loosened his shoulders to appear casually relaxed and pretended not to notice, withdrawing a coin from his purse and lazily placing it on the surface of the bar. It clicked loudly against the scarred wood, drawing the pub owner's attention. The portly man was of middle years, and had the aches of one much older, if his slow, shuffling gait was any indication. As he approached Derick, the man lifted his chin, setting excess skin to jiggling.

"I'm looking for a man," Derick said. "He may have been in town off and on the past couple of months. Have you noticed anyone who doesn't belong?"

The owner flicked his eyes to the coin, but didn't move to take it. Then he ran his gaze over Derick. "I notice plenty of people who don't belong here." He used the cloth he held in his hamlike fist to polish nonexistent dirt from the bar. "Lots of travelers come through, m'lord, to see the sights o' the Peak District," he went on, just quickly enough that he could claim he hadn't meant any insult. But Derick knew better.

He kept his eyes on the bar owner, resisting the urge

to glance around at the other patrons. He knew what he'd see—all of them staring back at him. Some discreetly, some openly, but all of them with a distrusting bent to their expressions. The war may have been over for two years now, but as far as these villagers were concerned, he was half French and, worse, had been in France during most of the conflict.

It had been like that in the last three pubs he'd visited. He'd never experienced anything quite like it, and he had to admit it rankled. But he thought he knew the problem. Most of his missions over the years had been on the Continent. People hadn't known him, nor had they cared for anything save for the fact that he was a rich and dashing aristocrat. They'd taken him at face value, accepting whatever image he projected.

But now that he was back in England? Everyone had some expectation of him. It was probably worse here. These villagers didn't know him either, but they *thought* they did. His family had lived, at least part of the year, in upper Derbyshire for centuries. He'd spent many of his early years here, and every summer of his youth after his mother had been banished from the family seat in Shropshire to the castle. No telling what kind of stories they'd made up to explain why he'd left and never returned. They all had their own ideas of what he must have been up to in France during the war, too. While their theories might vary, the conclusion was the same: he was not to be trusted.

Most times, he found ironic humor in the fact that people suspected him of being a traitor when it had been his position for more than a decade to bring traitors to justice. But he didn't find it funny today.

"Yes, well," Derick said, injecting a heavy dose of authority into his tone. "I'm only looking for one. Now, you seem to be a man who knows this area and those who pass through it well. Can you think of any who might be the man I'm seeking?"

The barkeep lowered his eyes. The man might not trust him, but he hesitated at openly denying a viscount. His thick fingers flashed over the bar to swipe the coin. "Perhaps. There's two or three who come to mind."

Derick raised a black brow. Then he plucked another coin from his pocket and set it on the bar.

"One in particular who might be who you're after. 'Bout 'alf a 'ead shorter than you. Dark 'air."

That was the right height for Farnsworth, though the man was blond. Of course, he could be in one of many disguises, and it was much easier to darken one's hair with coal dust than to lighten it. It sounded promising.

"Is he lodging here?" Derick asked as a pretty barmaid stepped up and held up two fingers.

The beefy man shook his head at Derick and moved to pour two pints of ale for the waiting barmaid to deliver. "No. Only came in once—I wasn't even the one to talk to 'im. I just 'ear everything, you understand? I don't know where 'e might be staying, or if 'e's even still in town."

Damn. "What makes you think he's the man I'm looking for, versus the others, then?"

The man looked up from the tap and pinned him with a shrewd gaze. "Cause 'e was going around town asking all sorts of questions about Lady Scarsdale, round about the time she threw 'erself off of the cliffs."

Derick felt as if the man had poured that cold ale over his head. Farnsworth had been asking questions about *his* mother? "When exactly?" he asked, keeping his voice calm, showing no reaction. "Was it before or after she . . . died?"

The man didn't answer for a long moment, and instead watched Derick carefully. Then he shrugged and dropped his eyes back to his task—apparently recognizing that Derick wasn't going to give him any additional fodder for the village gossip mill. "I can't say. It was a couple of months ago, and like I said, I didn't 'ear it first'and."

That was a development he hadn't expected. He would have liked to know more, but he knew he wouldn't get anything else out of the barkeep today. "If you hear of, or see him again, send word to the castle right off."

"M'lord."

Derick strode away from the bar, his frustration brewing. Aside from this bit he'd heard from the owner of the Swan and Stag, he'd come up empty everywhere today. People didn't want to talk to him. All he could do now was wait for Farnsworth to come to him, if indeed the agent was still in upper Derbyshire, and visit George Wallingford in the morning to see where that trail might lead.

And he might have to accept that working with Emma was his only option if he wanted to finish this mission and get out of here.

Chapter Five

"'Tis bloody frigid in here," George Wallingford grumbled, his voice rusty with disuse. Still, it had been more than a week since Emma had heard her brother string a proper sentence together. She was so glad to hear it that she wouldn't dream of taking issue with the ungentlemanly word choice.

Emma tucked a wool blanket gently beneath George's thighs and positioned his rolling chair as near the crackling fire as she dared. The west-facing parlor was a touch chilly this morning, but even in the heart of the hottest summer, George often complained of being cold.

A bittersweet smile pulled at Emma's lips. Fiery, robust—even hot-blooded—were words she'd often heard growing up to describe George. Never cold.

Emma scoffed at that ridiculous thought. George was cold now due simply to the lack of blood flowing through his body, as he'd been bound to his chair for some years. 'Twas a physical reality, nothing more. But the contradiction still saddened her.

"There, George," she said, wrapping a second blanket around his shoulders. "You'll be warm in no time."

His unruly chestnut brows inched together like woolly

caterpillars. "Tell me why I've been spruced up and rolled out here like a display piece." The ghost of his old wry grin flitted over his face before confusion clouded his gaze again. The backs of Emma's eyes pricked at the hint of the rascal he'd been before his affliction.

She sighed. There was nothing for it but the truth.

"Viscount Scarsdale is in residence at Aveline Castle, and . . ." She bit her lip. She couldn't tell her brother the *whole* truth as to why Derick really wished to see him. He would be mortified, if he even comprehended the precariousness of their situation. But neither would he be happy with any other excuse she came up with. He and Derick had never been contemporaries, as George was fourteen years Derick's senior. But they likely *had* run in similar circles, and George hated the idea of *anyone* seeing him as he'd become. Still, she dared not put Derick off. She wanted the matter settled. She had put off looking for Molly's killer long enough. ". . . He would like to pay his respects."

She eyed George warily, waiting for his reaction.

"Scarsdale?" he said, his hands fisting in his lap. He sat straighter in his chair, glancing down automatically to his useless legs, panic flaring in his eyes before they narrowed ominously. "Send him away!"

Emma grimaced. Perhaps she should have sent a note to Aveline Castle crying off after all. Ever since his stroke, George had been prone to bouts of irrational anger. One never knew when they might strike. While his response had been perfectly reasonable, Emma knew from the light in his eyes that he could very quickly devolve. "George . . . a baron doesn't turn away a viscount, and besides, Lord Scarsdale is already aware of your . . . condition."

Her brother's face mottled, turning a deep shade of red. "Probably thinks he's a better man than I, the blackguard. Well, my body may be ruined, but at least I'm not a deserter."

"Of course not," Emma soothed, touching his hand. Still, she was taken aback by his heated accusation. Though many had whispered about Derick's mysterious choice to remain in France during the war, it wasn't something they spoke aloud. She wondered how Derick would react if her brother fired off such a charge in his presence—and he very well might. George had served honorably in His Majesty's service until he'd been pulled back to England after their father's death. If, in his mind, he'd decided that Derick had shirked his duty to England during wartime, there was no telling how he'd react. She sent up a silent plea that George not say anything too terribly untoward. Their future was in Derick's hands, after all, as much as she hated to admit it.

George hitched a deep breath and his face cleared. This storm had passed quickly, which wasn't always the case. Perhaps all would be fine yet.

"Never could understand how Scarsdale could abandon his wife," George said, his voice suddenly conversational. "Especially one as fragile and lovely as Vivienne."

Emma started as understanding dawned. George had been speaking of Derick's *father,* not Derick. But of course, the old viscount had passed only a few weeks ago. George's memory of recent events often failed him. He mightn't remember. She breathed a sigh of relief.

"If the man's come to Derbyshire at last, I expect that explains why Vivienne hasn't been to see me," he mused on a sigh.

"Oh, George," Emma whispered. The viscountess, Derick's mother, had arrived in upper Derbyshire without her husband many years past—exiled to the country, it seemed, though no one knew precisely why. She'd been a colorful addition to their village, a gorgeous if flighty woman prone to histrionics that had been gossiped about by the locals over their glasses of sherry or their port and cigars.

Upon George's return to Derbyshire, the viscountess

had become a companion of sorts to him—a situation that had waggled tongues aplenty.

But Vivienne Aveline had shocked everyone by taking her own life only days after Lord Scarsdale passed. Emma had been shocked most of all, since Lord and Lady Scarsdale hadn't seen each other, or even spoken, to her knowledge, in years. George had been inconsolable at the time, but some days—like today—he didn't even remember she was gone. It was as if he expected her to breeze in anytime, her delicate French perfume trailing behind her to look in on her "*darling Jorge*." Emma didn't care to upset him any further today, so she let the mention slide.

"No, George . . . Lady Scarsdale's husband passed away recently. It is his son, Derick, who wishes to see you."

George's brows dipped, as if he were concentrating mightily.

Just then, Perkins' balding pate popped through the door. "Lord Scarsdale has arrived, Miss Emma." The butler issued that warning before dashing off to the entryway to greet Derick.

Emma's stomach suddenly went all aflutter. Her gaze flew to the settee, remembering their tumble over its arm. She could almost feel Derick's muscled frame pressed against her, the hot slide of his body as he removed himself from atop her.

Could a mere memory engage one's senses like that? Apparently so, because she flushed warm.

None of that. She already detested the idea that her way of life was at Derick's mercy. To acknowledge, even to herself, the vexing hold he seemed to have over her senses, too—always *had* had, even before she knew what it meant—would be too much. It was embarrassing enough that those old longings still existed. No, she was here only to convince Derick that she was capable to remain magistrate. She had a murderer to catch, and this delay was only slowing her down.

Emma crossed to her brother, coming to stand with a protective hand on his shoulder. Murmurs of greeting floated in from the hallway, followed by the click of heels against marble.

"Derick?" George seemed to fight to place him. "Do you mean Aveline? That young rascal you once set your cap for?" he asked, and rather loudly, in that annoying way only older brothers could manage.

Emma darted her eyes to the open door of the parlor. "I was fifteen, George," she whispered furiously, bending low so her mouth was right by his ear. Thankfully, Derick was too far away yet to have heard. How mortifying that would have been! "I hardly knew what a cap was." Nor did she appreciate the reminder that she'd once been foolish enough to fancy herself in love with Derick Aveline. "And he's a man of one and thirty, hardly a 'young rascal,' as you say."

An image of Derick kneeling by the creek two nights past, his face dark and grimly determined, passed through her mind. No. The description certainly didn't suit now, if it ever had. And as it had before, the image bothered her, being so at odds with the man he now seemed to be.

"Lord Scarsdale," Perkins announced then. Quite formally and with a bit more . . . well, *snoot* in his voice than usual.

Derick strode into the room, and immediately Emma forgave Perkins his small defection. Even she had to fight the urge to automatically usher Derick in and give him anything he wanted.

Emma's chest suddenly felt too small for her lungs. She'd entertained the notion of having this meeting in the much smaller study, thinking her brother might be more comfortable with his lameness obscured behind his desk, but she was suddenly glad she hadn't. She was having enough trouble adjusting to Derick's presence in this vastly larger space. It was as if he took up an entire room when he entered it, as if something within him pushed the very atmosphere to the farthest corners.

Today, Derick was resplendent in blue, the cut of his jacket superb in how well it displayed his wide shoulders and lean frame. His buff pantaloons seemed almost the color of bone when set against a rich cream and sapphire striped waistcoat dotted with pearl buttons. Fashionable — but completely impractical — ruffles adorned his sleeves.

In comparison, her staid morning gown, which she'd chosen to convey the seriousness with which she took her post, made Emma feel like the drabbest peahen next to the more vibrant male of her species. Only what were the chances this preening peacock sported his finery in an effort to impress her? None. He must just dress so as a matter of course, because men never went out of their way to entice her. Emma hated to admit it, but that knowledge ruffled her brownish gray feathers.

"Lord Wallingford, thank you for seeing me." Derick gave a nod to her brother. "Miss Wallingford." His eyes slid away, and Emma swore he glanced at the settee . . . Perhaps he, too, was remembering their last encounter?

"Ah, Scarsdale," George said in greeting, drawing Derick's attention back to them. "I've only just learned of your father's death. My condolences."

Emma was torn by George's cogent welcome. On one side of the equation, she was grateful that he wasn't incoherent, or spouting insults at Derick about letting down his country. On the other, a lucid George presented an unknown variable that could upset her plans. She needed Derick to see her brother as he truly was most of the time. That was the only way he would see reason and agree to leave her and George to their comfortable, quiet lives.

"Thank you," Derick returned politely. He raised his brow to her, though, clearly confused by the discrepancy between her description of George's mental state and what he saw before him.

A slight frown pulled at the corners of Derick's mouth, and Emma felt an answering tug in her stomach.

But then she gave a light shrug. What did Derick have to frown about? She hadn't lied to him. And part of her was beyond grateful to have her brother truly present after such a long time. If she could predict when George would have days like this—if she'd ever seen a pattern, a trigger—she would do everything in her power to make it so *every* day. Alas, she knew from experience that it wouldn't last.

"How is your mother dealing with the loss?" George asked, an absent smile lifting his cheeks.

Derick's brows shot up, and Emma experienced equal parts relief, sadness and alarm. She waggled her own brows and gave a short, negative shake of her head, willing him not to upset her brother.

"As well as can be expected," Derick replied, recovering nicely, yet Emma could almost hear the unspoken *"given that she's dead."*

"I would visit the castle to pay my respects, but . . ." George's shaky hand passed over his lap. His face turned red and Emma could see him struggling with the shame of being seen so by another peer. Her heart ached for her brother.

"Of course." Derick gave a crisp nod. "I shall convey your thoughts at my first opportunity." His voice was smooth, his face congenial, as if he hadn't just promised the impossible to a confused soul. And Derick's expression . . . it was somehow different than what she was accustomed to seeing on the faces of George's few visitors.

Emma pondered what that difference might be, her brow knitting in puzzlement, when it suddenly hit her.

Unlike others who had visited George these past years, not by expression or tone did Derick show that he saw her brother as anything other than the baron next door.

The ache in Emma's chest eased, to be replaced by a strange, warm, melting sensation. People who had known George his entire life—neighbors, servants, even the vicar and his wife—usually couldn't hide their pity when faced with his new reality. She would never have expected such perceptive kindness from Derick—a man who'd all but abandoned his family, his country even, when they had needed him most. But there it was. She supposed she must thank him.

After, of course, he agreed to let her carry on with her work—*without* his interference. She didn't need it. This was her home, not his. She was the one who'd given herself in service to the people of her village, not he. Filling her brother's position had given her life purpose. It called on her strengths—her level head, her highly logical mind, and her ability to detach her emotions to see things clearly. She may have failed at catching a husband—what most would say was the true merit of a woman—but she didn't fail at her duties as magistrate. And she wouldn't now, if Derick would just get out of her way.

Emma straightened at that reminder. Right. Certainly Derick had seen enough to know that George, even on his best day, was non compos mentis. Now, all that was left to do was detail her competence in George's stead so that she could get back to solving Molly's murder. She had barely been able to sleep since the maid's death, no matter how exhausted she'd been when she'd found her bed. Her mind wouldn't rest, sifting through years of conversations and observations. Who in their small village might actually be a killer? If she was up nights worrying over it, she was certain others were, too. The sooner the man was caught, the easier everyone would rest.

Emma stepped behind her brother's rolling chair and gripped the wood-and-wicker frame, intending to see him settled in the gardens for a bit of sunlight so she might deal directly with Derick outside of George's hearing.

She planted her feet, preparing to push the unwieldy chair toward the French doors.

"What brings you back to Derbyshire after all these years?" George asked Derick.

Emma stilled. Despite herself, she found herself listening with an eagerness quite unlike her. She was suddenly more curious about that than she was about the elusive mystery of the prime numbers.

"Just refamiliarizing myself with the family holdings," Derick answered with a nonchalance that fit his relaxed stance. "Now that I am Scarsdale."

Emma let out a breath. Much as she'd expected. So why this feeling of deflation? *Emma. You ninny-hammer! You didn't think he'd returned because he had any interest in seeing* you *again, did you?*

She frowned. Well, of course not. Just because the girl she'd been had dreamt of seeing *him* again, nearly every night for *two* years after his unexplained departure, that didn't mean he'd ever spared her another thought. When she thought of how childish she'd been then . . . how she'd begged her father for a Season in London just in hopes of dazzling Derick with her newly acquired charms . . . how she'd applied herself every day in an effort to obtain said charms even though her father assured her she was neither attractive nor wealthy enough for a husband to be willing to overlook her bookishness . . . how he'd been right. Her face heated, even now, as she recalled the snickers behind painted fans, the empty dance cards, the way even on the rare occasion a gentleman engaged her in conversation, his eyes would soon glaze over and then he would wander away as soon as she said anything she found remotely interesting.

What a disaster it all had been. And worse, *Derick* hadn't even been in London at all, so the entire humiliating experience had been for naught.

"Ah." George nodded. "And I assume now that you *are* Scarsdale, you'll be looking for a nice, *sensible* English miss—from a good family, of course—to be your viscountess." George shifted in his seat to waggle his brows at her before turning back to Derick.

"Can't go wrong with strong Derbyshire stock, you know," George intoned, and then further appalled her by tipping his head toward her with no subtlety whatsoever.

"George!" Emma exclaimed, her face afire now. "I am certain Derick's—" She winced. "I mean, Lord Scarsdale's marital intentions are none of our concern."

But George's brows just dipped in that innocent incomprehension that sometimes marked those whose minds were slightly addled.

Emma touched a hand to her burning cheek. When she'd worried over how George might boggle her plans, she certainly hadn't envisioned him thoroughly embarrassing her this way.

"Well, it's been a lovely visit," she said, detesting the singsong quality her voice had taken on. "So lovely to catch up, isn't it?" Fig! Singsongy *and* she'd used "lovely" twice in as many seconds. Like "lovely" squared, only it wasn't.

She gave a great heave, swinging George's rolling chair around and aiming for the French doors. She felt only a momentary pang of remorse at his surprised grunt of pain as she clipped the side of an ottoman with what was most likely his leg.

She looked behind her, narrowing her eyes to communicate to Derick to stay put and wait for her return. A horrible creaking made her cringe as she pushed her way out the doors. It was time to order Perkins to have them oiled again.

Emma settled George outside in the warmish sunshine, with a maid as companion, promising him she'd join him for luncheon. She hated to deprive herself of time with her brother when he was so much himself, so rare it was these days. But she wouldn't be able to enjoy herself with George until she was assured that Derick wasn't going to upset their world.

"'Can't go wrong with strong Derbyshire stock, you know.' Gracious, George," she mumbled to herself as she hurried back to the parlor. Emma fanned her face in time with her brisk clip. She knew too well that her fairish skin blotched with any little untoward thought. She didn't wish to appear like a schoolgirl when she spoke with Derick. If she was going to persuade him to take her seriously and agree to leave matters as they were, she needed to be cool, calm, collected, as a capable woman—a capable *magistrate*—would be. She needed to assure him that she could well handle anything that happened in her corner of upper Derbyshire.

Emma took a calming breath and stepped through the doors.

Derick was sprawled on *the* settee, one ankle propped negligently on the opposite knee, one arm stretched out over the back of the piece, his long fingers drumming idly on the fabric. His green gaze glittered and a smile spread across his face, as lazy as the rhythmic beat of his fingers.

Emma stopped suddenly. She cleared her throat, hoping to cover the tiny catch in her breathing. *Come now, girl! This won't do.* She straightened her shoulders, wondering if she'd ever noticed before that the critical voice in her head sounded so much like her late father. Regardless, the voice was right. It *wouldn't* do for her to react like a lovesick girl every time Derick Aveline so much as looked at her. He hadn't known she existed when she *was* a lovesick girl, and he certainly didn't now. It was ridiculous, really. *She* was ridiculous. And it was time she got this conversation started on a proper foot.

"As I'm sure you must agree, my brother—"

Derick stood abruptly, cutting off her line of thought. He unfolded his lanky form and gained his feet with a speed and masculine grace one wouldn't expect from a man of his height. Then, almost like the contradiction he seemed to be, he took a languid step toward her. The odd light that entered his eyes made Emma's belly go all aquiver with foreboding, and something else.

"Did you *really* set your cap for me, Emma?"

Emma gasped, and it was all Derick could do not to grin at the way her eyes widened and her lips spread thin in horrified affront. Her poor cheeks turned the color of succulent late-summer cherries.

"H-how did you hear that from all the way out in the hall?" she sputtered.

In retrospect, it mightn't have been the wisest thing to tip his hand as to how very observant he could be, but he hadn't been able to resist. Her reaction was better than he'd expected, and truly, he hadn't had this much fun baiting someone in—well, since he used to bait her as a girl.

A lot of memories had surfaced last night as he lay in his bed at the castle. He'd never slept well in the drafty old pile. The recollections were inevitable, he supposed, given that he was here. Luckily, most of them had been pleasant. Many about Emma, actually—and how ridiculously easy she'd been to tease—always taking everything so literally, even for a child.

He ignored her question, of course. "Well, did you? Set your cap for me, that is? You were all of twelve, Emma."

"I was fifteen!" she exclaimed, flustered, and then those amber eyes widened even more, if such a thing were possible, as she realized what she'd just admitted. "And what does that *mean*, anyway? Granted, I'll be the first to agree that most things in the world can be explained through numbers, but I never did understand at precisely what degree of angle one sets one's cap to attract a man. And why that should . . . matter . . . anyway." Emma curled her lips around her teeth, clamping her mouth shut along with her eyes.

She was so easy to fluster, this one. Which should make her equally easy to read. Hell, when agitated, Emma blurted out her every thought, which was a good thing for him, particularly since he'd sworn off using his tried-and-true method of seduction to get information out of women.

Still, he really should stop teasing her. He reached out a hand, curled his fingers and gently lifted her chin. Her eyes flew open at his touch.

"Well," he murmured, "you really shouldn't have. I wasn't worth it." He'd meant the words offhandedly, but the undeniable truth of them echoed in his mind.

Emma's head tilted, pulling her chin from his grasp. Her eyes narrowed, just slightly. "No, you weren't."

Derick took a step back, his arm dropping to his side, as lame as her brother's lower half. While he wholeheartedly agreed with her, Emma's words still felt like a gut punch. He had to remind himself that he didn't care. He'd done far worse things than breaking little girls' hearts since he'd left Derbyshire so many years ago. If little Pygmy knew even the least of his dark deeds, she'd likely heap more than condemnation on his head.

He cleared his throat in the awkward silence. "Your brother—"

"I'm sorry." Emma rushed the apology out. "That was badly done of me and I—"

Derick held up a hand to forestall her. "Think nothing of it," he said. In truth, he'd rather deal with this tougher Emma. He'd felt dirty after intimidating her in this same parlor yesterday afternoon, no matter how much he'd also enjoyed the press of his body against hers, the sensual hitch of her breathing, the liquid melting he'd glimpsed in her amber eyes.

No, he much preferred her prickly.

"Your brother," he began again. "I—"

"Surely you see I speak the truth," Emma interrupted, rising up on the balls of her feet as she self-consciously smoothed that awful, matronly dress she wore. So transparent, Emma was. She probably thought that the plain clothes and tightly scraped-back hairstyle would help her cause.

"Yes," he said. "About that—"

"And surely you also agree, what with Molly's killer waiting to be caught, that bringing in another person will only slow the investigation down."

Derick could almost see Emma mentally ticking off the tenets of her argument in her head.

"Yes," he drawled. He nearly smiled as her shoulders relaxed in relief, along with her exquisitely formed features. "And no."

Her body snapped to attention nearly as stiff as the foot guards who stood sentry at St. James's Palace. "No?"

"While I agree, *for now*, that you should remain de facto magistrate," Derick said, crossing his arms in front of him, "I insist you bring another alongside to assist you until the killer is found."

"But I don't—"

"If you refuse, I will send a messenger to the Commission of the Peace this very afternoon."

Emma huffed an aggravated breath. Her right hand fisted by her side, and Derick noticed that her same leg tensed, as if she barely restrained herself from stomping her foot in vexation.

"And just who do you propose I 'bring alongside' to assist me?"

Derick let his smile flash quick and wide.

"Me."

Chapter Six

"**Y**ou think I'm incapable?"

Damnation. Standing there with her amber eyes aglow and her ample cleavage rising and falling with her aggravated breaths, little Pygmy was stunning in her righteous indignation. Derick couldn't resist provoking her further. "I have no way to judge that, Emma. Are you?"

She huffed, and the most darling touch of color turned the skin above her scooped neckline a splotchy pink. He wondered if she would be as passionate in bed as she was about what he thought of her—

Good God. Where had that thought come from?

"Of course not!" she fumed. "I am incredibly competent. Ask anyone." She huffed. "You're probably one of those men who thinks women are good for nothing aside from looking pretty," Emma grumbled under her breath. But of course, he heard.

"On the contrary, Emma," he murmured. His hardening body intimated that Emma would be good at *many* things. Derick struggled to rein himself in. He'd never had such a difficult time keeping his focus. What had he been saying? Oh yes. "I am well aware of how brilliant

women can be. Indeed, I find the wife of my friend the
Earl of Stratford, to be an amazingly capable woman.
She's both a chemist and a healer whom I respect im-
mensely," he said.

While he spoke the words as a means to unruffle Emma's feathers, he meant every one. He'd met Liliana,
Lady Stratford, when she'd been simply Miss Claremont.
He'd been sent to investigate the man who was now her
husband as a traitor, much as he was currently investigating George Wallingford. His time spent in her company, as well as observing her loyalty, devotion and
protectiveness toward Stratford, had given Derick pause
regarding his views on women. Views he'd developed
first from his abominable relationship with his mother
and then from his experiences with the women he'd
come across in the world of back alleys, back ballrooms
and back bedrooms of the espionage game.

Emma, however, stared at him as if he'd said something particularly out of character.

Well, maybe he had. Out of character, at least, for the
man he'd projected to her. Whether or not it was out of
character for the man he actually was, he couldn't say.
After spending nearly half his life intentionally being
someone else, Derick could no longer say who or what
he was with any clarity. That was one of the many reasons he was anxious to make contact with Farnsworth,
finish up this mission and leave England behind him for
good. He would never be able to find himself if he stayed
here.

Still, until that day he needed to do a better job of
playing his part, even if every day the caricature grew
more and more tiresome.

"Then what are you about?" she demanded, a deep
vee forming between her eyes. "You can't possibly care
about Molly. If you'd ever even met her, she would have
been but a babe."

Derick opened his mouth to speak. "Tru—"

"And don't start that rubbish about her being a member of your household," Emma said, pointing an accusatory finger in his direction. "You have nothing at stake here. If you truly think I am capable, that I should remain as magistrate, why this farce of assisting me?"

It took years of discipline not to grimace. God save him from intelligent women. They *thought* about things. They asked *questions*.

He couldn't very well tell her that she was now the only viable source available to him regarding George Wallingford and his activities over the years.

Wallingford may look less likely to be the traitor Derick was hunting, but with the man's military experience and access to sensitive information, there was just too much smoke for there not to be fire—or at least kindling. If the man wasn't a traitor, Derick needed to uncover who else might have taken advantage of Wallingford's state of mind to wheedle sellable tidbits from him.

It would be much quicker to parlay Emma's trusted position with the villagers than to take the time to establish his own contacts and inroads as he searched for a new suspect. At least until Farnsworth made contact, *if* he was even still here in Derbyshire.

Derick cocked his head just so, lifting one cheek in a half smile that he knew displayed a deep dimple to his best advantage. He lowered his voice charmingly. "Come now, Emma. We had great adventures as children, you and I. It will be quite a lark."

Her frown deepened.

He raised the brilliance of his smile accordingly. "Just think. This time it will be me following *you* around."

The overt eye roll told him he'd missed his mark.

Damned woman. He knew she wasn't immune to him. So if sentimental charm didn't appeal, what did? Logic, he decided. "Have you ever investigated a murder before?" he asked, thinking to use the two-heads-being-better-than-one argument again.

"Not exactly," she said.

"What do you mean by that?"

"The only murders I've dealt with have been drunken disputes, with the killer easily identified. There *have* been a few suspicious deaths over the years. Nothing that could be called outright murder, but certainly deaths that no one was able to explain."

Derick's ears perked up at this. "Suspicious deaths" could often be laid at the feet of people like him, people who'd been trained to dispatch others without leaving a trace as to how or why. Though he hadn't been specifically fishing for information, he intended to reel it in.

"How many of these 'suspicious deaths' would you say you've encountered, and over how long?" His heart sped up. Finally, he was getting somewhere. He'd bet anything she meant the Crown's missing couriers. After Farnsworth had alerted the War Department of the traitorous tie to upper Derbyshire, someone in the agency had made the connection that two men carrying sensitive information had gone missing, albeit years apart, while on missions that would have brought them through Derbyshire or the Peak District. "Do you remember approximate dates and places where the bodies were found?" If he could establish—

"What does that have to do with anything?" Emma's head had tilted slightly and she squinted at him, speculation shining in her amber eyes. "Least of all Molly's death?"

"Nothing, of course. I was just curious about your work." Damnation. He'd been so close to learning something about the couriers. He knew it, but he couldn't press further now without raising Emma's suspicions.

He'd learned one thing, though. Emma might know even more than he thought, which made it all the more important to stick by her side. "You don't have a choice, Emma. You *will* allow me to assist you or I will be certain a new magistrate is appointed within a fortnight."

She stared mutinously at him. The storm flashing in the depths of her eyes gave Derick the unnerving feeling that he might soon be struck down by amber lightning. But then Emma took a deep breath.

He released his breath in turn.

"You *were* rather useful in the search for Molly," Emma admitted. "And I can see where having you beneath me could prove quite satisfactory."

Derick felt his eyebrows rise, along with another part of his body. Had she meant . . . ? But no, Emma stood before him looking quite serene. He knew, given their previous encounters, that if she'd meant that the way it had sounded, she'd be blushing red all over.

She must have meant "beneath her" in a more literal sense, such as him being below her rank as a mere assistant.

"I suggest we return to where we found Molly's body and see if any evidence can be found now that the water has receded a bit," Emma stated. She turned on her heel and quit the parlor, leaving him to follow or not. He followed, of course, knowing he should be pleased that he'd won her acquiescence with relative ease.

But something told him that naught else in this partnership would be easy.

If Derick thought she was just going to sit back and let him dictate every step of "their" investigation, he was sadly mistaken. Their search of the forest yesterday afternoon had turned up nothing new, leaving them both frustrated. But there was no way she was going to allow him to re-question Molly's friends and family this morning. Not at the girl's funeral.

"I refuse to upset them more than they already are," Emma whispered fiercely. To speak any louder might draw attention from the mourners who'd come to the castle to pay their respects before Molly Simms was laid to rest later in the day.

"There is no *need*." Emma finally did raise her voice

just a bit when Derick didn't respond, though she knew from the way the dratted man seemed to hear every little mumbled whisper—especially those most likely to embarrass her—that he was far from deaf. "I have a particular memory for these things. I can repeat verbatim what each person said to me."

As seemed to be his way, Derick ignored her statement and instead drawled a question. "Verbatim. Really?"

Emma huffed, but in spending the better part of two days with the infuriating man tagging along as her *oblige* assistant, she'd learned that it was quicker just to answer his myriad questions. "Yes. I've always had a peculiar memory. As a very young child, I would watch my father work, scratching equations and formulas on his boards. One day—and I don't remember it myself, but I've heard the story many times—I snuck into his rooms and wrote a series of numbers out on his boards long after he'd erased them.

"My father was furious that I dared play in his workroom, of course, until he looked closer. Apparently, I'd regurgitated a rather complex theorem precisely. So he began to test me. No matter how detailed of an equation he'd write out, I could study it for a few moments and duplicate it exactly."

It hadn't been long before she could expound logically on what he'd given her. It's what finally convinced Emma's father to deign to teach her, even though she was female.

Emma swallowed against an unpleasant tightness. Her father had been dead nearly nine years now, yet anytime she thought of those years spent at his side, she was left with a sad, sort of anxious knot lodged in her chest. She'd always known that while her father sometimes seemed reluctantly pleased with her abilities, he'd resented her at the same time for not being a man. A son. Much as he'd reviled George for not having her abilities.

But that wasn't relative now, was it? "I've found I can do the same with spoken words. They have a certain lyrical cadence, a pattern, which my memory seems to inherently latch on to."

Derick stiffened. Emma glanced over to find him looking fixedly at her. "You can remember anything said to you?" he asked.

"Yes, as well as anything I've read or written."

Derick shot her a disbelieving glance. "What were the first words I spoke to you?"

Emma closed her eyes and focused her attention, rubbing the thumb of her right hand in circles against the pad of her middle finger. What *had* he said? She opened her eyes. "'You look like a deerfly.'"

"I never said—"

"You most certainly did. The first time we met. You were seven and I, five. The very next thing you said, by the way, as your mother reprimanded you, was, 'But she does! Her eyes are too big for her face. And they're *yellow*,'" she repeated, perfectly mimicking the sneering tone of a young boy.

She rather enjoyed the combination of awe and embarrassment on his face.

"I can dredge up any conversation we've ever had. But perhaps you were thinking the first words out of your mouth the other night? They were 'What the devil are you doing?'" she intoned, trying to sound as ridiculously pompous as he had, "and 'Do you mind telling me just who you are and why you are vandalizing *my* property?'"

If she weren't mistaken, didn't his eyes narrow a fraction, almost as if in speculation? But just as she was certain they had, the impression vanished, so quickly that she might have imagined it.

"That's one hell of a gift, Emma," he mused.

She huffed. "Sometimes. Other times it's a curse." At that thought, hurtful words assaulted her, in the voices and spiteful titters of her past: her father. *"Why would God squander such talent on a damnable female?"* The not-so-subtle whispers of London society. *"How gauche she is. Simple. Country. Unsophisticated. Odd."* Her one-time affianced, Mr. Smith-Barton. *"I only asked you to marry me because your brother pressed me to. I thought I'd solidify his friendship by taking you off his hands and that there would be money in it for me, but now? His friendship isn't what it used to be and I've found someone who will be a proper wife to me, not one who thinks and acts more like a man than I do."*

She took a deep breath. "There are many things that have been said to me that I wish I could forget."

Her voice trailed off at the pitying look Derick gave her and she wished she could bite back the words. Why did she always blurt such intimate thoughts? It was as if her brain could contain only so much, and therefore couldn't hang on to her actual words once she formed them. Emma pressed her lips into a thin line, as if by exerting enough force she could seal them in a way that could never be breached.

"Can you remember only conversations you've had?" he asked, gratefully letting the moment slide. "Or do you think if you'd overheard things, you might recall them?"

Emma frowned. "It depends on how closely I paid attention. I've also noticed that I don't recall as well when I'm with my intimates. It's almost as if when I'm with someone I trust, my brain . . . relaxes, I suppose would be the right word. That's hardly the point, however. I only told you about my memory so that you'd see there is no need to upset Molly's poor loved ones right now."

Derick looked down his long, straight nose at her. "I disagree. I prefer to speak to them myself."

Emma gritted her teeth until her jaw ached. She turned a glare on him, but Derick had already resumed watching the mourners who milled about in Aveline Castle's drawing room, nibbling funeral biscuits or sipping burnt wine as they waited for the procession to the church.

"What could we possibly gain?" She continued to keep her voice low. She'd hate anyone to overhear. They might find her and Derick's conversation tasteless, given the occasion. "I spoke with each person within hours of Molly's disappearance. Do you suppose their memories have gotten *better* over the past two days?"

"Do *you* suppose Molly's murder was random?" he asked, rather than answer her once again.

Emma scoffed. "Of course not. That's impossible. Random selection implies that all options are given equal weight. The killer would have had to have considered each and every potential victim in Derbyshire."

Now why was Derick looking at her with that confused frown? She reconsidered his question. "Oh. I think you must have meant 'arbitrary,' which is very similar in meaning but would take into account human . . . bias . . ."

The vee between Derick's brows had deepened and his lips had quirked into an amused twist.

Emma's cheeks heated in embarrassment. She was being literal again, wasn't she? "You were asking if I thought Molly *knew* her killer," she said, a bit sheepish.

"Yes."

"Statistically speaking, she must have."

Derick shot her an odd look. "Statistically speaking? Who would keep track of such things?"

"I would," she said. "I've compiled years of magistratorial and other parish records from all over England."

"You're not going to tell me you have all of those memorized, are you?" he said.

Emma shrugged. "Not *all* . . . There are reams of them."

"Why would you—"

"It doesn't signify," she said. "We were discussing Molly's *murder*."

Derick eyed her for a moment as if he were a school-boy and she were a geometric proof he didn't quite understand. "We were," he said finally. "Given what a close community this is, the person who killed her is most likely in this room."

Emma's own gaze shot out over the crowd, to her friends and neighbors. Nearly the entire village was here. Surely . . . But she knew Derick was right. She shivered, looking around at the grim faces. "I can't imagine anyone in this room as a killer. I've known these people my entire life."

Derick slanted his eyes to her, and Emma couldn't shake the feeling that he viewed her as naive. "I'd wager the person who killed Molly knew her very well," he said. "We start with those closest to her and work outward from there."

"But if one of them is the killer, they're not going to tell us, just because we ask nicely," she said, frustrated. "*Now* who's being naive?"

Derick huffed with amusement at her loose tongue. "They may not tell us with their mouths, Emma, but they very well may with their bodies."

"With their bodies?" Emma scrunched her face. "How in the world would they do that?" she asked.

Emma waited for Derick to answer. Instead, he ignored her, his gaze taking in the small group of villagers hovering around Molly's parents. She pinched the underside of his jacketed arm. Not hard enough to hurt, but just enough to show her displeasure.

"Damnation, Pygmy!" he growled, rubbing at the spot, his face almost comical in his shock and indignation. "If you were a man—"

Emma snorted. "Well, I'm not," she said, not even taking him to task for calling her Pygmy this time. "And what's more, Derick Aveline, I've known you since before *you* were one. Just because you have the advantage right now doesn't mean you have the right to treat me as though my opinions and questions are a bother to you. I demand you start answering them when I ask—with real answers, not another question. You owe me that respect."

Derick sighed. "People talk with their bodies all of the time, Emma. More than they do with their mouths. I'm amazed you've been successful as magistrate this long without knowing that," he said.

She lifted her chin. "I've been successful because I'm thorough and I analyze things logically," she argued. "And you still haven't answered my question sufficiently. Do you have any evidence that what you say is true?"

"The way you just pinched me tells me you're angry with me."

Emma rolled her eyes. "The words that accompanied that pinch told you that."

"True," he said, and a strange light glinted in his emerald gaze, "but your body is also telling me that, while yes, you are angry with me, you also want me."

"W-want you?" Emma sputtered, drawing herself away from him. He couldn't possibly know that, could he? She'd been trying so hard to hide her inconvenient feelings.

"Yes. Want me. Shall I tell you how I know?"

His voice had dropped into a raspy baritone that made Emma's mouth go dry. She found herself nodding, as if her body did *indeed* want to know how he knew such a thing, even though her mind rebelled against the idea. Did her traitorous body truly communicate secret private desires to him?

"Well, the first tantalizing cue is your shoulders," he said, dropping his lips closer to her ear so she might hear him better. She tried to focus on his words, but his warm breath dancing across her skin proved a mighty distraction.

"See how they are angled just so, open to me, facing me squarely so that all you have to do is open your arms to welcome me to your bosom?"

Emma instinctively crossed her arms. She didn't miss Derick's quick, flashing grin.

"Next is how you tilt your head toward me when we speak," he said, "as if placing your delectable lips as close as you can to mine, hoping I'll bridge the gap and touch my own to yours."

Emma jerked her head back. "That's outrageous," she said. "I only lean closer so that you might hear me." She pursed her lips on a frown. "Fat lot of good that does me," she muttered, "since you refuse to answer five-eighths of the time."

She nearly jumped out of her skin when he brought a hand up behind her back and ran a finger lightly over the soft nape of her neck. Her eyes immediately sought the crowd, but no one was watching them. Derick's hand was behind her, anyway . . . It was unlikely anyone would have seen that he'd touched her so.

But oh, did she feel it. Gooseflesh popped out in waves over her skin, only to be chased away by a rolling heat.

"But what really gives you away," Derick murmured, "is the way you stroke your neck after you've tilted your head. It's as if your body is begging me to do the same." One long finger stroked her neck then, as if on cue, starting just below her earlobe and running down the side, stopping to caress that raised freckle she so hated just above her collarbone. She couldn't control a shiver. "You don't even know you're doing it, do you?" he murmured.

Emma swallowed, mesmerized. No. She'd had no idea.

"Your neck is one of the most vulnerable places on your body. It carries your breath to your lungs, your blood to your brain. It can be easily broken," he whispered. "When you expose your neck to me so, your body also tells me that you trust me—"

Emma jerked away from his touch, from him, taking

a step back that brought her backside up against the wall. "I absolutely do not trust you."

"Yes you do. You may not think so, but your body doesn't lie."

"No. Numbers don't lie. I'm sure bodies lie all the time," she said, feeling a bit inane. But was he right? How she detested this feeling that he knew her better than she knew herself. It was rubbish, wasn't it? How could she trust him? She didn't know him . . . not anymore.

Something in her proclaimed that thought a lie—as infuriating as he'd been these past days, she had found herself more and more comfortable with him, despite the fact that she still suspected his true personality was at odds with who he was being.

Her protest brought a warm chuckle that sent her receding gooseflesh back to full prickle.

"And what's more, Emma, you're relieved I'm here."

God help her, she was. For so long, she'd been handling everything on her own. While she relished the sense of accomplishment and responsibility, it was also a burden. It might irk her to have him question her at every turn, but she had to admit that Derick had proven to be more insightful than she'd expected. And didn't he tend to have his own sort of logic behind his arguments, even if he wasn't forthcoming in sharing it?

Derick dropped his hand from her neck so swiftly she felt the cool breeze. "Now that that's established, let's go question Molly's affianced first, shall we?"

Chapter Seven

Derick was reeling as he crossed the crowded parlor—and not just from the unexpected pleasure still rippling through him from his whispered interlude with Emma in the corner.

Her memory astounded him. Oh, it would need to be tested, but if she truly could do what she said? He would have to be much more careful what he said around her, for one thing. He also knew spies in droves who would kill for such an ability, himself included. What he could have done with a mind like that. Which begged the question . . . could *Emma* be the traitor he was looking for?

Something within him balked at the very idea, though he didn't know why it should. Certainly not because she was a woman. As a spy, he'd crossed—and sheathed— daggers with many a cunning female counterpart. Derick knew all too well how deadly, and deceptive, women could be.

There was no question that Emma had the mental agility to decode the messages the missing couriers had been carrying, and to code the ones that had fallen into Farnsworth's hands in France—the ones that had ultimately led the agent, and finally Derick, to upper Derbyshire. And she would be the one with the best access to her brother, if that was indeed where the information sprang from.

The object of his consideration fell into step beside him only a couple of yards before he reached the gathered mourners surrounding Molly Simms' parents. Actually, Emma kept a toe just ahead of his, as if unconsciously communicating that *she* was the one in charge here.

Derick couldn't resist a soft snort of amusement.

As they drew close to the group, Derick whispered, "Which man was Molly's affianced?"

Emma pointed out a short, stocky man, probably five or six years their junior, with a surprisingly square jaw that matched his blocklike fists. Hands capable of taking life, Derick noted. But would the man's fingers prove long enough to match the bruises on Molly Simms' neck?

"James Marwell," Emma whispered. "He's apprentice to the butcher. He and Molly had been—"

"Say no more. I'd prefer to get the particulars from Marwell himself."

She reached out and grabbed his arm, bringing them to a halt. "I can see you intend to go through with your interrogation against my wishes. Fine. I can't stop you." Her eyes shifted in a way that he was fast coming to recognize precluded one of her under-the-breath mutters.

He waited for it.

"No matter that I've spent years acting as magistrate and you've spent them acting as . . . well, as God knows what," came her barely audible grumble.

The urge to grin took Derick by surprise. Accustomed as he was to those around him carefully veiling their thoughts, this habit Emma had of spouting hers was quite refreshing.

"A man of leisure, of course. A complete libertine," he lied, enjoying the rush of color that infused her face and upper chest.

It was the primary reason he had trouble believing she could be a traitor. She blurted out any little thing on her mind, no matter the cost to her pride. And was duly mortified by it. That sort of embarrassment wasn't easily faked.

He'd just have to unnerve her randomly—er, *arbitrarily*, he corrected himself—to see if her behavior remained consistent.

Rather than acknowledge that little exchange, Emma gamely went on. "You say you can get information that I did not. I say this is a waste of time. I propose we put our currency where our mouths are."

Currency? "You mean 'money,' Emma. Money where our mouths are."

"Money," she said with a brisk nod, as if filing it away for future metaphoring.

"How is it that you claim to remember long-ago conversations with complete clarity, but you can't keep your idioms straight?"

Emma shrugged. "It's just a tic in how my mind works, I suppose. Probably because most idioms are so ridiculous, they don't bear remembering."

"Hmmm. Well, what did you have in mind?" he asked. "For your currency?"

"Oh. Well, if, as I believe, your questions lead to nothing more than I learned when I conducted my own interviews, then you will agree to step back and let me run the investigation the way I wish to from here on out. Alone."

"Alone. Hmmm." He'd be a fool to take that bet. If Emma won, it would set his investigation back days, maybe weeks. And yet, he was confident he could get *something* out of conducting interrogations that she hadn't. Perhaps he could think of information she could give him as forfeit that would make the gamble worth it. "And what do I get from this bargain if I do discover a new lead?"

"An apology, of course," she said, as if the word itself were worth its syllables in gold.

"An apology?" Derick scoffed. "Since you are *such* a capable woman, I'm sure an apology from your lips is a rare and coveted thing indeed." A dozen erotic images involving her lips and various parts of his body flitted through his mind like a fairy nymph bent on teasing. And before he'd even given the words any thought he murmured, "However, I'd rather have something else from them. A kiss would do nicely, I think."

"A kiss?" she said, her own brows now winging toward her forehead.

What the hell had he just said? He'd meant to bargain information, not bloody temptation. Yet he couldn't very well back out now that the offer was made. "A kiss. It will be much more pleasurable for me, and I'm fairly certain, less painful for you to give."

"But why on earth would you want to—" Emma clamped her lips shut on the question, her eyes darting away. One hand went up to self-consciously sweep a lock of hair away from her face, while the other splayed across her stomach.

Those two tiny movements sucked the air from Derick's chest. Because they told him two things.

First, Emma had no idea how beautiful—nay, how breath-capturingly desirable—she was. Which, strangely, made her all the more so.

And second? That the mere idea of kissing *him* set off tremors of excitement in her belly.

His gut clenched with a warm heat. He didn't even want to try to name the emotions those two bits of knowledge sent ricocheting through his own body.

"Well, what say you, Emma? Are you willing to place a kiss on the line? Mind you, I'd demand a real kiss—not just a quick peck. I wouldn't want either of us not to get our . . . currency's worth. In fact," he said, warming to the

idea now that the offer had been made, "I would demand full discretion as to the kiss' duration . . . and *thoroughness*."

Emma visibly swallowed at his emphasis. "There are
degrees of kissing?" she asked with a slight cocking of
her head that said she really had no idea what he meant.
The darkening of her amber eyes told him, however,
how very much she wanted to know.

Good God. He couldn't wait to demonstrate. After
all, it was just a kiss. It couldn't hurt anything. And he
wasn't using the kiss as a means to get anything out of
Emma, so he wasn't really breaking his vow, was he?

He waited for her response.

Her tongue darted out to moisten her lips, before she
tugged the lower one between her teeth and worried it.

In the end, she gave him one short, decisive nod that
sent heat rushing through him.

He turned his attention to Marwell, determined to
get some new bit of information out of the butcher.

As Derick and Emma approached the small group
surrounding Molly's grieving parents, the conversation
quickly lulled. Likely because of his presence. While he,
by title and association, was a part of this community, in
reality he wasn't. He knew it. And they knew it.

"My lord." Molly Simms' father stood to greet him.
"Sarah and I—we want to thank you for your generos-
ity." The gardener waved a shaking hand to encompass
the parlor and the refreshments that had been laid out.
"You honor us and our Molly."

"Think nothing of it," Derick murmured.

An awkward silence followed. He didn't show any reaction to the curious stares. Just like the villagers he'd
encountered while searching for Farnsworth, even those
on his own estate didn't know what to make of him. In
fact, they would probably afford more trust to a stranger
than they would to him. He was glad to have Emma at
his side to ease the way.

"I've asked Lord Scarsdale to assist me in my investigation," Emma began, her voice confident, assured. Calming. So much different than when she spoke with him.

Derick noticed the way the group turned to her as one. She was well respected among them. And while there was a raised brow or two, there were no signs of protest. It seemed that if Emma trusted him, the villagers would accept her judgment. Perfect.

"I understand the timing is not ideal." She flicked a glance at him, betraying her annoyance at his insistence. "But I'm sure you'll agree that finding whoever did this to Molly is of utmost importance. We can't waste a moment."

Everyone nodded, but Derick didn't watch their heads. He watched their feet. In his experience, the farther one got from the head, the less control people had over how their unconscious mind used their body to communicate. Lies were often given away first by the feet.

He saw nothing that gave him pause.

"Mr. Marwell, we'd like to speak to you first," Emma said. "In the study, if you please."

The man's eyes darted around the rest of the group, but he quickly nodded his assent.

As the trio discreetly made their way across the parlor, Derick considered his strategy. Emma was sure not to like it. It was not the way a woman would handle an interrogation.

He turned on the man as soon as the door was closed, not even giving Marwell a chance to be seated.

"I know why you killed her, Marwell," Derick said in his best man-to-man voice. "Hell, I might have killed her, too, when I found out she was spreading her legs for another man."

Surprise flicked over Marwell's boxy features an instant before his jaw tightened to granite and his dull eyes turned bright with righteous anger.

Derick ignored Emma's delayed gasp, noting only a moment of amusement that her literal mind had finally worked out what he'd been implying. He'd bet she'd had to picture it first.

Instead, he focused on Marwell.

"You bastard," Marwell spat, his fists clenching in rage as he took an ominous step toward Derick. "I don't care if you are a bloody lord of the realm. You deserves a beatin' for talking 'bout my Molly so!"

Derick held his ground. It wasn't Marwell's rage that interested him—it was the surprise that had skittered over his features *before* the anger set in. Over the years, Derick had learned that surprise was the hardest emotion to fake. Oh, guilty people *acted* surprised all the time—it was the logical emotion to show first. But they usually held the expression just a mite too long when it was consciously done. True surprise was there and gone in an instant, an honest reaction.

"Derick!" It seemed Emma finally found her voice. "How could you—"

"Molly was strangled, Marwell," Derick said blandly, knowing he was pushing the man, but it was when men were pushed that they showed their true character. "The life choked out of her with bare hands. A personal death, a passionate one. One committed by a lover, not a stranger."

The man blanched.

"What? Did you find out your girl had a bit on the side and snap? Couldn't blame you if you did." Derick coaxed the man, looking for that hint of relief he'd seen on many a traitor's face when they thought he understood them. It should translate to anyone guilty of wrongdoing.

But Marwell just crumpled in anguish like Jack's giant falling from the beanstalk. "I didn't. I c—" He choked on a sob. "I couldn't have."

Derick relented. If he were in the field and had to make a snap judgment, he would bet Marwell wasn't their man.

He moved toward the younger man and placed a hand on his shoulder, leaning close. "I'm sorry to put you through that, but I had to know."

Marwell's head snapped up. Brown eyes glittering with unshed tears pinned Derick and an unspoken promise passed between the two men. Marwell straightened, his jaw firming with the knowledge that Derick would be ruthless in his pursuit of Molly's killer. The butcher's apprentice nodded once and gathered himself.

When Marwell closed the study door behind him, Emma whirled on Derick in fury.

"How dare you say such horrid things?" she cried, her skirts still twisting around her ankles from the haste of her spin. "We have no evidence that Molly was . . . was . . . Well, you know, what you said. What kind of a man are you?"

"The kind who does what he must to get to the truth."

"Including lie?" she sputtered.

"Without question."

The look of shock that froze Emma's features definitely wasn't faked. She was appalled. Derick cursed under his breath. He hadn't meant to say anything like that, even if it was true. He needed Emma to trust him, damn it.

"I don't understand how you could impugn Molly's character in such a way." Emma's shoulders slumped.

Derick heaved a breath. "What I said about strangulation being a crime of passion is true," he said. "Particularly when it's done face-to-face, as Molly's was." Indeed, people in his business would typically garrote a victim from behind. "The killer is almost always a husband or lover, so it was a logical assumption—one I wouldn't be surprised if it bears out yet. As jealousy is a prime motive, I had to see how Marwell reacted to such a charge."

"You were fishing . . ."

"Yes."

"And?" Emma challenged.

"And I'm pretty sure he didn't do it."

"Well, I was certain he didn't do it days ago." Emma shook her head. "I would never have agreed to let you upset Molly's family and friends if I'd known you planned to—to badger and insult them!" She squared her shoulders, aiming them directly at him as if preparing herself for battle. "I will not allow you to do so again."

It was high time for little Pygmy to learn that he had no intention of always letting her be the boss. It would be easier for her in the long run. "You labor under the misapprehension that you can stop me, Emma."

Her amber eyes flashed a warning and her fists clenched by her side.

"Besides—" Derick was quick to defuse the situation. "I have no intention of using the same methods on Molly's parents or girlfriends. It's doubtful that one of them could be the killer, anyway. Strangulation takes almost brute strength. No, I'll try instead to coax information from them."

Emma huffed. "Well, if you think I'm going to keep to our bargain, you're mad. It was made in bad faith. You said nothing about badgering—"

Derick took a quick step forward, bringing his right hand up to cup Emma's face, his thumb brushing over her lips. He gave her a hard glare, capturing her amber gaze, enjoying when her eyes widened in alarm. "Oh no, Emma. I said I would glean information you hadn't—I said nothing about how. And believe me"—his other hand came up, tracing along her jaw—"when I do, you *will* be kissing me. Hard. Hot. And long."

Emma's lower lip trembled and Derick felt an answering tremor deep in his gut.

"Now go out and fetch Molly's parents," he ordered, surprised at how gruff his voice had gone. "I'll wait here." He needed the space to cool himself.

Emma backed away, fleeing the room as if her skirts were on fire. And by God, if she burned as hot as he did, they probably were.

An hour later, he had thoroughly cooled. After interviewing Molly's parents and most of the household staff, who had known her best, Derick had learned absolutely nothing new. Emma's posture, he'd noted, had become more and more smug with each failure. Oh, how he'd love to kiss that superior little smirk off her face—but he wouldn't be getting the chance if he couldn't learn anything new from this last interview. Maybe it was for the best, despite how much he'd found he wanted that kiss. He didn't need the complication.

Three housemaids stood nervously before him, eyes downcast. So far, they hadn't been able to tell him anything he hadn't heard before. "Think back to the night Molly disappeared," he said. "Was she acting oddly? Was anything out of the ordinary?"

"No, sir," the three of them chimed, almost in unison.

Damnation. Derick dropped his gaze, thinking.

And then he saw it.

The maid in the middle had her feet pointed toward the door.

Adrenaline shot through him. She was lying!

"So none of you knew Molly was planning to go out that night?"

Three capped heads shook vehemently, but one set of toes strayed farther toward the exit.

Got you.

Derick eased back, pulling his shoulders into a completely nonthreatening stance. "Thank you, ladies. You may return to your duties."

Emma nodded her agreement and moved to usher the girls from the room.

"Except you, Agnes."

The little blonde froze, her hazel eyes darting first to Emma, then back to him.

Emma's eyes narrowed on him for a long moment, but finally she said, "It's all right, Agnes."

The maid's eyes implored her friends to stay with her, but the other two girls scampered from the room without looking back.

"Please." Derick indicated the settee before him. "Sit."

Agnes did, tucking her skirts nervously beneath her.

Derick dragged an ottoman over, positioning it scant feet from the settee, and lowered himself onto it, his knees spread so that he could lean forward and prop his elbows upon them. He kept his voice soothing, like conversational velvet. "Molly was going somewhere that night, wasn't she, Agnes?"

The maid swallowed audibly.

"You know where, don't you?"

Emma, he noted, was leaning in as well from her position at the side of the settee, her gaze fixed on the maid. "Please, Agnes, if you know something you must tell us."

"B-but she'd be so ashamed, Molly would," Agnes whispered. "If'n everyone were to find out."

"Shame is for the living, Agnes," Derick said. "Molly would want justice now."

The maid covered her face with shaking hands, pinkened from hard work, that muffled her soft sobs.

Derick leaned back, giving the girl some space. He glanced up. Emma was staring at him, her lips pressed in a grim line. He stared back. Her eyes shone with admiration. And concession. He'd impressed her, finally, and it felt ridiculously satisfying.

"She went to be with her lover." Agnes' voice broke the connection between Derick and Emma.

"Marwell, you mean?" Emma asked, her brows dipping.

Agnes cast her eyes down, giving a slight negative shake of her head. "'Twas Thomas Harding, m'lady. Fr-from Wallingford Manor."

Emma gasped.

"Your footman," Agnes finished.

Chapter Eight

"We wanted to marry." Thomas Harding stood stoically in the drawing room of Wallingford Manor, his hands clasped behind his back. Emma watched him carefully. A head shorter than Derick, blond where Derick was dark, soft where Derick was hard. When she compared the two, Harding appeared . . . slight, young.

He did not, however, appear to be giving anything away that she could tell.

Emma turned her attention to Derick, trying to see where his eyes were focused. What was *he* looking for? Because clearly there was something to this body-communicating nonsense, and it was a language Derick understood. And one she desperately wanted to learn. She detested this feeling of inferiority.

Emma wondered just how Derick had learned it—it certainly wasn't something routinely taught at Eton, she'd wager.

"If you wished to marry each other so badly," Derick said in his blasé drawl, "perhaps you might explain why Molly was betrothed to Marwell?"

The footman's blue eyes flickered for a moment, but

otherwise the young man didn't move a muscle. Unless she missed it?

"Her parents pushed her toward the butcher," Thomas said. "Wanted her out of service. Marwell already has a nice cottage in the village. He'll have his own shop soon. Me, I'm just a lowly footman."

"Did Molly's parents know about you?" Emma asked. She hated to think she'd missed that, too.

"No. Molly and me, we knew they'd never give their blessing. So we tried just not to think on it, to enjoy every day as it came and not worry about the future."

"And when she married?" Derick asked casually.

Thomas shrugged. "I don't know if she would have gone through with it."

Derick's nonchalance vanished, his voice and stance suddenly hard. "And now you'll never know, will you?"

Emma flinched at the harsh statement, but Thomas didn't so much as blink.

She remained quiet through the rest of the interview, relieved for once that she wasn't required to say anything. Hearing that Molly's last hours were spent beneath her very own roof turned Emma's stomach.

Just as shocking was the change in Derick. Coldly relentless, he drew out the details of Molly and Thomas' liaisons with skill and efficiency. He was nothing like the fop he'd been these past few days. Emma had the eerie feeling that she was finally glimpsing the *real* Derick. Had he been playing a part all this time? Why would he do such a thing?

Thomas held up well throughout the whole ordeal. She would have been in tears ages ago under Derick's onslaught, and she rarely cried. But Thomas showed no more emotion than the Elgin Marbles. He admitted nothing more than the affair, no matter how hard Derick pressed him.

"I kissed Molly good-bye, and she slipped out of my

room to return to the castle just before dawn, like always," he repeated, nearly word for word for the fourth
time.

"If you say." Derick moved to stand directly in front
of the footman. "Hold your hands out in front of you
like so." Derick raised his own hands, palms facing forward, fingers splayed.

At that, Thomas blinked. "W-why?"

"Just do it," Derick growled.

Thomas brought his arms around. His hands were
pale but powerful-looking, his fingers long. Emma
couldn't stop an involuntary shiver. Long enough to
have easily wrapped around Molly's throat, leaving the
marks they'd found.

Derick must have thought so, too. A tic formed in his
jaw. "Pack your belongings, Harding. I want you gone
from this house. Immediately."

Emma's eyes flew to Derick. While she didn't relish
having a potential killer in her employ, Derick had gone
too far. She stepped forward and put a hand on his arm.
"May I speak with you in the hallway?"

Derick's head turned and he narrowed his eyes. His
features seemed carved from limestone and he stood as
hard and immovable as it, too.

"Now."

Derick followed her without protest, though the dark
expression that flashed over his face suggested he was
holding one back . . . barely. When they reached the hall,
he ordered Perkins into the drawing room. "Don't let
Harding out of your sight."

The butler glanced at Emma, a worried frown tugging
at his lips, his brows rising as if asking for her approval.
She gave a sharp nod.

When she and Derick were alone, Emma crossed her
arms over her chest. "What do you think you are doing?"

The tic in Derick's jaw jumped even more noticeably. "I am removing a threat from your home."

"*That's* not for you to decide."

A sharp inhalation made Derick's nostrils flare. "You think not?"

Emma couldn't help drawing in her own breath. The very air around Derick hummed with an energy that caused her skin to tingle. What on earth had him so incensed?

"Someone has to watch out for you, Emma." The concern in his voice coated her in an oddly delicious way.

Worry for her had wrought this remarkable change in Derick? A slow heat took Emma by surprise. No one had ever shown such upset on her account.

His next words doused the pleasant warmth before it could spread too far.

"As your brother isn't capable and *you* clearly don't have the common sense the good Lord gave a flea, I suppose it will have to be me."

Emma gasped and thumped her hand against her chest. "I'll have you know, Derick Aveline, that I have intelligence in clubs."

"Clubs?" Derick shook his head slowly. "That's spades, Emma. You have intelligence in spades." A low chuckle rumbled his chest. "Unruffle your feathers, Pygmy," he murmured, his voice laced with a wry amusement and something else. Affection? "It's not an insult. Intelligence and common sense are far from the same thing."

Emma rolled her eyes. "Don't call me that. And I'm not going to just toss Thomas out. I shouldn't have to point out that he may very well be innocent."

"He may," Derick agreed, but his voice had gone frigid again. "He may also be a cold-blooded killer. So either he leaves"—Derick rose to his full height and actually flung an arm out to point toward the grand staircase—"or you march yourself upstairs and order *your* things packed, because you are not sleeping under the same roof as that man."

Emma scoffed. "Oh?" She planted her hands at acute angles on her hips. She had no patience for his high-handedness. "And just whose roof would you have me sleep under, then?"

Derick closed the remaining distance between them faster than she could rattle off the square root of pi. Emma backed away, bringing her hands in front of her in a halting gesture—but not quickly enough. His arms closed around her, hauling her tightly to him. Her thighs crashed against his as she found her hands pinned against his chest.

"Mine."

Derick's heartbeat thumped erratically against her palms and a shiver coursed down her body in counterpoint to his hands, which skimmed upward to capture her face.

The lips that met hers were hard, demanding. Hot. Emma whimpered, not in distress but in sheer overwhelmed sensation. Derick surrounded her. His size dwarfed her, as usual, but it was as if she were also wrapped in his being, his experience.

He backed her against the flocked wallpaper, using his body to anchor her for his kiss. Thrills shot up Emma's center, and her breath caught in her throat. The only coherent thought in her mind was *Finally*. She'd been kissed before, of course—she'd been engaged, after all. But *finally*, after years of dreaming about it, she would know what it was like to be kissed by Derick Aveline.

But he seemed to want something far different from the chaste pecks she'd experienced with Mr. Smith-Barton. And she wanted to give it to him, only she wasn't certain what "it" was. She pressed her closed lips against his with as much frantic energy as she possessed, but all it seemed to do was frustrate him, if the groan that ripped from the back of his throat was any evidence.

His thumbs moved to her chin, tilting her head back as he gently parted her lips. Emma had a mere fraction of a second to wonder at that before he sealed his mouth over hers. Shock rippled through her as his warm tongue slipped between her lips and rubbed along her own. Shock and heat, then chills. More heat. A curious string pulled longitudinally through her middle, tugging at her breasts and a lower, more sensitive spot that turned her legs to pudding. She thrust her arms up and around Derick's neck, using him to steady herself.

She opened wider, giving him more access, sending her tongue on a foray of its own.

Her enthusiasm seemed to incite him further. His kiss became rougher, his breathing more ragged. Emma reveled in it, reveled in the fact that somehow, some way, something in *her* had effected this change in him.

"Christ, Emma." Derick groaned, pulling his lips from hers to burn a fiery trail down her neck. Oh, it was so much better than she could ever have imagined in all those hours, days, months she'd dreamt of being in his arms. Her chest hitched. It became increasingly hard to draw breath, and when his hand cupped her breast, kneading it with firm, rhythmic squeezes, she stopped breathing altogether.

When she did draw air again, it came in a harsh, hiccuping gasp that echoed off the cold marble floor. It was the equivalent of a dousing in St. William's Creek in early spring. Emma's chest constricted, and her mind cleared in an instant. She was acting the trollop in the middle of her own foyer. Oh God. The servants. George. What would they think if they saw her? What would they say?

Derick's lips continued downward in hot licks, his mouth nearing her scooped neckline.

"Derick, please." She pushed at him. "Anyone might see."

He lifted his head and a strange light flickered in the emerald depths of his eyes, as if that very possibility excited him. His gaze dropped to her mouth and he leaned in to capture her lips once more.

Emma turned her face away, ducking her head to bury it against his heaving chest.

After an endless moment, she felt his hands leave her body, sensed him brace them against the wall behind her. All the molten heat that had pooled low in her body now rose to her chest in a seething ball of mortification. What had she been thinking?

What had *he* been thinking? Was there a chance he held some feeling for her?

"Why did you kiss me like that?" she whispered, her lips brushing against the fine linen of Derick's shirt.

His chest leapt beneath her, as if he'd huffed in disbelief at what he'd done. "I wanted—" Fast, choppy pants ruffled her hair. "The bet," he rasped finally, his voice deep, full of gravel. "You owed me."

The ball in her chest burst, flinging hot moisture to sting the backs of her eyes. Of course. It hadn't anything to do with her charms. He'd just been caught up in the heat of their argument and had seen a convenient way to vent his frustration with her and to collect his due at the same time.

She shoved harder at his chest, ducking below his arms when he wouldn't budge. She stiffened her spine as she put several paces between them, counting them off to calm herself. *Four. Five. Six. Seven.* "Consider my debt paid, then."

With Emma's back to him, she was unable to see him blanch. Derick was glad for it, because at this moment he didn't think he could hide anything from her. If she only turned to look at him, he was certain she'd see all.

His lust. His confusion. His regret. Maybe even his secrets. They had to be written all over his face, as clear as covert messages scrawled in invisible ink after having been revealed over a hot flame. He tunneled his fingers through his hair as blood slowly returned to his face.

Never had he been so undone.

He hadn't meant to kiss her. Not now, at any rate. And not like that, for God's sake. He'd meant to tease her, coax her, slowly introduce her to the "degrees of kissing," as she'd so quaintly put it. Somewhere comfortable, somewhere private, somewhere they wouldn't have been disturbed for a long, long time.

Instead, a protective rage had fired his blood. As Harding had stretched out his fingers, all Derick could see was the ugly purple bruising around poor Molly Simms' neck and her blue eyes washed whitish in death. Then, in his mind's eye, that eerie blue had turned amber—and Derick had seen red.

When Emma had insisted on allowing the blackguard to remain in her home, something primitive in Derick had roared his dissent . . . and demanded her submission. Still, he shouldn't have kissed her to gain it.

"Emma, I—"

"Don't," she said, the word shooting from her lips like a lead ball from a dueling pistol. The wounded quality of her command pierced him as surely as a bullet would have. He heard a suspicious sniff that twisted his gut. What in the hell did she have to be hurt over? Angry, yes.

Derick tensed, waiting for her to turn so he could see exactly what she was thinking. If he knew the nature of the wound, he could repair the damage.

But when Emma faced him, her expression and posture were cool, collected. "Do you truly think Thomas killed Molly?"

It was all Derick could do not to gape at her. If her

lips hadn't still been swollen from his kiss, and her hair mussed from his touch, he'd have thought that kiss had been a figment of his imagination.

Or an erotic dream.

"Back to business, Emma?" he said, still trying to wade out of a fog of lust. Damnation. Had their kiss not affected her at all? How could she stand there, so proper, her spine straighter than a ramrod while he felt the need to lean against the wall until he was certain he was steady?

She pressed her lips together tightly, probably miffed that he'd not answered her question. But God's truth, he couldn't think about Harding right now. How the hell could she?

"Because I think we should discuss what just happened between us," he found himself saying. Where the devil had *that* come from? And what would he say should she agree?

Emma cocked her head to the side. "Oh? Was my payment not satisfactory, then?"

Good Christ. Had it been any more satisfactory, she'd have found her skirts tossed up and her legs dragged around his hips—and he'd have a lot more to apologize for.

"Did the exchange not meet your standards for 'duration and thoroughness'?" she continued.

"That's not what I—"

"Good. Because *I* think we should discuss why you've been pretending to be someone you're not, instead."

Derick went very still.

Pretending to be someone you're not . . . That could mean so many things, couldn't it? Vague things. It seemed little Pygmy was a quick study—now she was the one fishing. The question was, what exactly was she angling for?

Emma stood before him, tapping her foot as she

waited for his response. Derick nearly smiled. Silence was a tactic he used to great effect on others. It never bothered him, so he'd have no difficulty waiting her out.

Indeed, Emma broke first. "Where were you all of those years?"

Hmmm. The question was an easy one, even when he wasn't certain what she was seeking. He gave the same answer he always did—one that was quite factual, but far from the whole truth. "Here. There," he said in an intentionally bored singsong. "The Continent, mainly. France, Vienna, Belgium. Wherever my fortunes took me."

Emma frowned, clearly unsatisfied with his answer. Crossing her arms, she demanded, "Tell me where you learned to discern what people are thinking by how they carry themselves."

An uneasy frown pulled at the corner of Derick's mouth. He didn't like the direction she was heading. He quickly turned his lips up into a smile of masculine arrogance before she could notice his discomfort. "Why, the ballrooms of Europe, of course," he bluffed, waving an idle hand. "I was as hot-blooded as any young buck in my youth, always with my eye on one attractive woman or another. Experience taught me which ones were worth . . . pursuing, and which weren't." Again, another half-truth. The best lies were filled with them. Though women were often his targets, he hadn't been pursuing them for their charms.

Emma's eyes narrowed further. "While I can certainly picture you as some youthful Lothario, I must say—I don't believe you. Where did you learn to interrogate people?" she pressed. She held out her right hand in a staying motion. "Don't deny it. You do it too well."

Ah, hell. He shouldn't have gone after Harding so hard. But the bastard had just stood there. No remorse. No feeling. Just an emotionless recitation that spoke of indifference. It had made Derick's blood run cold, then hot. Harding may or may not be Molly's killer, but either way, Derick still wanted to put a fist through the man's face for his callous attitude.

"And how do you sneak up on people without them hearing a sound? No one even noticed you slip into the dining room at the castle the other night. We didn't know you were there until the precise moment you wanted us to." Her amber gaze leveled on him. "And how is it that you hear every little thing I say, even when I know I said it under my breath?"

Damnation. He needed to deflect her. Now. He forced a light chuckle. "Don't be ridiculous, Emma. A little overzealousness on my part, and you're imagining all kinds of nefarious things."

She actually snorted. "You're the ridiculous one if you think I don't see through you. In fact, I don't know how I was so blind before."

Emma cocked her head, and the golden gleam in her eyes, along with the self-satisfied press of her lips, told Derick he wasn't going to like what she was about to say.

"You were a spy, weren't you?"

Chapter Nine

Derick barked a laugh, doing his damnedest to inflect it with just the right mixture of scoffing disbelief and innocence. "Really, Emma," he drawled. "You *must* get out of Derbyshire more often. I knew, of course, the place was deadly dull, but it is worse than I remember if you must entertain yourself by concocting such ridiculous scenarios. Believe me"—he lowered his voice, deliberately trying to embarrass her out of this dangerous line of thinking—"there are . . . diversions aplenty to keep a man in his prime quite satisfied to remain on the Continent." He added a slow wink, to make sure she grasped his meaning.

A flicker of doubt clouded Emma's face.

He hoped to hell his bluff worked.

Her eyelids fell briefly and Derick noticed her thumb moving in a rapid circle against the pads of the fingers on her right hand. She'd done that before, hadn't she? When she was trying to recall something. A focusing maneuver, perhaps?

Emma opened her eyes, settling her feet as if preparing to literally hold her ground. "No."

Son of a bitch. He knew only too well how tenacious

Pygmy could be once she'd sunk her talons into something.

"No," she repeated, clenching her fist and bringing her curled fingers to tap against her lips. "If you were the pompous ass you pretend to be—"

"Pompous ass?" Derick sputtered.

"Yes." She colored, but she didn't demure. "Unruffle your feathers, Derick. It's not an insult," she said, tossing his earlier words back at him with a chestnut eyebrow cocked at a jaunty angle. "I'm certain you've worked very hard at affecting the perfect degree of pomposity."

Well, yes, he had actually. But he didn't appreciate her pointing it out. Or noticing that it was an affectation, for that matter.

"However, if you *were* the skirt-chasing ne'er-do-well you want me to believe you are, you wouldn't be here," she said. "You would care naught for finding Molly's killer or for"—she averted her gaze—"watching over me, as you say." Her eyes returned to him and she pointed a delicate finger directly at him. "You'd still be traipsing around the Continent sowing your wild seeds."

Something between a choke and a cough closed his throat. Derick huffed twice to clear it. "That's oats, Emma," he murmured. "Wild oats."

"Whatever. The point is," she said, turning slightly as she paced a tight circle in front of him, "something about you has been bothering me since the moment you arrived at Aveline Castle the other night and I've finally figured out what it is."

He had to throw her off, give her another explanation—a convincing one, a heady one. "You've got it all wrong, Emma. It's the attraction between us that has you bothered," he said, stepping ever so slightly closer to her. He bent his head toward her and inhaled her lavender scent. Satisfaction stole over him when she unconsciously leaned in. This could work.

"You so much as admitted you've carried a torch for

me all of these years, and now . . . here I am." He reached out a finger and brushed it against her cheek, feeling the cad for using her girlhood infatuation against her. "In the flesh. It's only natural you'd be . . . bothered."

Her lips parted as his finger caressed the corner of her mouth and her gaze held his for a long moment.

Then she pulled her head back smartly. "That's not it."

"Damnation, Pygmy!"

Rather than take issue with his use of her nickname, in vain even, she actually smiled at him, a Cheshire-like grin that made him feel like kicking an entire family of cats. "You wouldn't be trying so hard to convince me otherwise if I weren't right, you know."

"I wouldn't be trying to convince you at all if you had a lick of sense," he growled, going for the one sure thing to dig at her.

"That's not going to work this time," she said, wagging her finger at him and despite his immense irritation, he burned with the urge to kiss that smug little smirk right off her face.

But it disappeared on its own as Emma chewed at her lower lip. "You forget, Derick. I knew you well. Once."

His annoyance unexpectedly burst into true anger, all dissemblance forgotten. "You know nothing!" Derick tunneled his fingers through his hair, spinning away from her. She'd never known him. How could she have? Even *he* hadn't known the truth then. Who he really was. What was in his blood. What he was capable of.

Appalled at his lack of control, he turned back to face her. Emma's amber eyes had gone wide, and it seemed she held her breath, waiting for him to explain his outburst. Well, he had no intention of enlightening her, so he said instead, more gently, "I was just a boy, Emma. I've lived an entire life since then." He hoped to God his voice didn't sound as weary as he felt in this moment.

She swallowed. "Yes," she said cautiously, her head

dipping in the affirmative, "but while modern philosophy disagrees about whether our personalities are inborn or whether they are a product of our environment, it does suggest that it is very rare for a person to grow to be the polar opposite of how they were as a child. Rather, it suggests our personalities are set at a young age. That's why you've seemed such a contradiction to me. The boy I knew never could have become the man you pretend to be."

Derick veiled his eyes. She couldn't understand unless he told her everything, and that he would never do. "This conversation grows tiresome." And it had. In fact, this *life* had grown tiresome. How he longed to start fresh. While he couldn't change what was past, he could leave it all behind. Forever. And as soon as Molly's killer was caught and a traitor unmasked, he would.

"You know, I could give you a dozen reasons why I know I'm right about you," Emma said.

"Don't waste your breath."

"Then just admit that I am right, and I'll drop it," Emma said.

Derick snorted. She'd drop nothing.

"We didn't come out into the hallway to discuss me," he reminded her. "I believe your intent was to take me to task for tossing your murderous footman out on his arse?"

Emma heaved a very unladylike sigh, her shoulders slumping in resignation. "Do you truly think him murderous?"

Thank God. She was letting the spy talk drop.

"Knowing now that you have *experience* in such things, I am willing to defer to you in this matter," she continued.

Derick nearly growled aloud.

"What do your finely honed instincts tell you?" she pressed and he knew—just knew—she was taking some sort of perverse delight in this.

He heaved a sigh of his own. It seemed now that Emma was convinced that she'd blown the lid off of his own personal box of secrets, he had two choices. He could continue to deny, knowing she wouldn't believe him and would consequently dig deeper and deeper. Or, he could control what she thought and how much she found out by leading her in the direction least dangerous to his mission.

He just needed a little time to decide exactly what direction that was.

"I'm not sure," he said finally, his face and posture relaxing as he dropped the pretense. Had he ever noticed how tightly he held himself when acting a part? He did his best to ignore Emma, who was trying very hard—and failing—to conceal a triumphant smile. Superior, nosy little chit.

"Some people are simple to read. Harding, however, is a cold fish," he continued. "He gave nothing away, which typically means one of two things. He is either one of those few people who lack genuine emotions, or he is highly trained to hide them. Since it's doubtful a footman from Derbyshire would have had that kind of training . . ."

Or was it? Harding would certainly have had easy access to Wallingford—could have easily been the one to wheedle Wallingford's secrets from him. Could the footman be the man he was looking for? "How long did you say Harding has been with you?"

"I didn't. Thomas joined our staff just after my brother's accident. It was actually your mother who sent him to us. She insisted that we needed an additional servant to assist with the extra care George required."

"My mother?"

"Yes. It was very kind of her. At the time, coin was very dear to us. She even paid Thomas' wages until we could absorb them on our own."

That was a disturbing connection. First, he'd learned

that a stranger, who could be Farnsworth, had been asking questions about his mother, and now he discovered she had placed a member of her own staff close to George Wallingford? It might be best to keep the man underfoot after all.

"You know, Emma, I've decided you're right. It would be unjust to toss Harding out with no real proof of his guilt." Derick thought quickly. He couldn't allow Harding to sleep in the same house as Emma—he wasn't certain why not, since the man had lived at the manor for several years and Emma had never come to any harm. But he couldn't. Wouldn't.

"Do you have faith in your stable master?" Derick asked.

Emma blinked, frowning. "McCandless? Of course."

"Until Harding can be proven innocent, I will not allow him to remain in your home."

He waited for Emma to fight him, but she remained silent. Perhaps there was some silver lining in this bloody situation of her pegging him as more than what he pretended to be—it seemed now she knew he wasn't some wastrel, she put a little faith in his judgment.

"Therefore I propose a compromise. I suggest he remove to the stables, under the watchful eye of your man." Of course, he would interview McCandless himself, to take his measure before he left Harding in his custody. He'd also give a few orders as to how the man should be accommodated.

Emma tapped an index finger on her bottom lip. "That sounds reasonable—just until his guilt or innocence is established."

Derick didn't kid himself. She might trust his instincts to a point, but he knew if she felt she knew better than he did, she'd override him in an instant. She was that kind of person.

Still, he nodded. "Good. That's settled, then."

He spun on his heel to return to the parlor, and Harding.

"*That* may be settled, but the rest is far from it," Emma called. "If you think I'm letting you escape without a full accounting, you're mad."

He turned at the door, raising both hands in mock surrender. "I concede, Emma. But this is not the time. Now that we know Molly spent many of her nights here, we need to see if anyone outside of Harding knew. We need to interview your entire staff this very afternoon, before word gets out, before they have time to think about or confer with each other over their answers—if they haven't already. We need to determine if there were any witnesses who saw her leave, that last morning or any before. This may be our best—and last—lead."

"And after that?" Emma raised an eyebrow, tapping her slippered toe against the stone floor.

"Come to the castle tonight," he said, hoping that would give him enough time to work out the most convincing and advantageous mix of truth and fiction. "We'll discuss my . . . past then. Over dinner."

Emma smoothed a hand down the delicate lace of her overdress as she viewed herself in the beveled glass mirror with a critical eye. Her hair, as always, hung a little too limply. And she was certain that if Derick looked too closely, he'd notice the slightly asymmetrical bent to her face . . . every feature on the right side was just a fraction larger than on the left. She knew. She'd measured. Twice. But at least the cream lace of her gown contrasted nicely with the green silk satin beneath, she thought as she tugged on matching satin gloves. And the colors complemented her skin, even if the fashion was a few years out of date.

She smoothed her hand over her middle again, as if the motion could also smooth the nerves within.

It was just dinner, for goodness' sake. A meal. One of three a day, not including tea. Nothing to be so nervous about.

And yet . . . she hadn't felt such jitters since her first

blush of infatuation with Derick so many years ago. Not even with Mr. Smith-Barton. With her onetime affianced she'd felt only a comfortable warmth—interest, yes, but nothing compared to this jumble of twisting excitement. Perhaps it was a blessing the bounder had jilted her.

And left her free to explore possibilities with Derick. *Or be devastated by him again.* Emma pushed the thought away. She'd been a foolish girl then. And Derick hadn't *meant* to hurt her—he'd been a young man who had no idea of the dreams she'd carried in her heart. A heart she knew better how to protect now.

"Oh, Emma. You are ten to the tenth times a fool if you think he would ever want you," she firmly told her reflection. But the stern admonishment didn't dampen her hopes as it should have. He may have kissed her this afternoon in a temper, but that kiss had reawakened feelings she'd fought years to extinguish. It had also opened her eyes. There had been an underlying current of need there—hadn't there? After an afternoon's reflection, she was fairly certain it had not just been on her part.

Not that she was any expert, of course, but the desire between them was . . . promising.

"You look lovely."

Emma turned, startled, to find her brother in the doorway to her rooms. A footman stood behind George, his hands gripping the sides of the rolling chair. It was odd seeing someone besides Thomas accompanying George. He'd been such a fixture at her brother's side since his stroke. She just couldn't believe that he'd been the one to kill Molly. But those were thoughts for another time.

"George." A warm smile of welcome creased her face as she took in his pressed shirt and freshly shaven jaw. "Whatever are you doing about?"

"I was feeling oddly chipper this evening," he said, stretching his arms out before him. "Up to dining *en famille*. But when I rang to be dressed for dinner, I was told you were expected at the castle tonight instead?"

"Yes, I was . . . but—"

A burst of disappointment shot through Emma, followed quickly by guilt. Quality time spent with her brother was such a rarity. How could she squander a good moment with George just to assuage her curiosity where Derick was concerned? "But of course, I'd much rather dine with you. I shall just send a message to the castle conveying my regrets."

Emma straightened her shoulders, fighting not to let her deflation show. She had no wish to hurt George's feelings. Now that she was aware that bodies communicated without words, she was determined to be hypervigilant about what she revealed. She would do even better once she persuaded Derick to teach her the language.

"Nonsense," George said. "I'll just go along with you. It won't be the first time I've showed up unannounced at Vivienne's table. Indeed, it has been far too long between visits. She'll be delighted to see me."

Emma stilled, careful not to wince at her brother's inability to remember that Vivienne Aveline had been dead for several weeks now. "Lady Scarsdale . . . wasn't scheduled to dine with us tonight, George. It was only going to be Derick and I."

Her brother's eyes widened, then sharpened in on her. She squirmed beneath his regard. "But it wasn't important, of course. We can do it another time."

"Hmmm," George murmured, snagging her hand as she made to brush by him on her way to send Derick a note. "You know, it's been years since I've seen you made up so. Were you visited by your fairy godmother, then?"

She scoffed. "It's just a dress. Besides, you know I don't believe in fairy tales."

"More's the pity." George squeezed her hand gently. "But you are quite stunning this evening. Am I to assume you've gone to such effort because you have hopes where Scarsdale is concerned?"

Emma forced a light laugh, even as she felt the blush heating her face. "Of course not." And yet, she couldn't deny the part of her that wanted to shout, *Yes. Yes. Unwisely, impractically yes.* Ever since she'd realized Derick was playing a role, it was as if all the feelings she'd once had for him had come rushing back with a vengeance. And when he'd confirmed that he'd not just bandied about the Continent all these years, that he'd been gone from England for the most noble reasons, that girlish infatuation had been strengthened with respect. Admiration. And a woman's longing. Foolish hope had welled up in her and even her most critical self-barbs couldn't squelch it. After all, the war was over now. Which meant Derick would be looking to settle in at home—perhaps with a wife. Why couldn't that wife be her?

She shushed her mind before it could give her dozens of answers to that question.

But to George she said only, "We're merely two neighbors who decided to dine together." At George's raised eyebrows, she added, "To discuss the case he's partnering with me to solve."

"Yes." George nodded sagely. "Because it's like you to share your work with someone else. And even more like you to discuss magistratorial business in your best evening gown."

"George . . ." she intoned.

"You should go, Emma. Keep your plans. It's not often that such an eligible bachelor graces our fair village, and God knows I've tried to push you to London often enough without success." He grasped her other hand, now holding both of hers tightly. "I won't always be around to offer my protection, such that it is. Not in my condition. Where will you go when the title and lands pass on to our distant cousin?"

"You needn't worry about that. I shall be fine."

"Em." George tsked. "I know you ply me with platitudes so as not to worry me. But I also know the money

Father willed you was not much. You must have used it all up to keep this place from falling down around us. How do you expect to get by?"

"I don't *need* much." She hesitated, knowing the fact that Father willed all monies to her rather than George had always been a sore spot. Still, she wished to put her brother's mind at ease. "And I've more than quadrupled what Father left since I implemented the new farming techniques." Indeed, most of the farmers in the village were now using her calculations to increase their harvests. In the past few years, the production had gone up and up, of which Emma was very proud. "I expect that to increase exponentially. So you see? I should have plenty enough to purchase a tidy cottage and live out my days, if I do so frugally. So I truly mean it when I say you needn't worry."

"Truly?" George gave a great sigh. His skin, though, had turned a shade pale. It seemed as if he was tiring. "I am glad of it. For I am convinced my time is waning."

"Stop talking nonsense, George," she said, not liking the emotion pricking her throat. She gave her brother's hands a squeeze. "Let's away to the dining room and see what Cook has to tempt us, eh?"

But George released her, slumping into his chair as if suddenly very exhausted. "I've changed my mind," he said, looking away from her. "I'd prefer a tray in my room."

Emma stood there, sadness and concern warring with the anticipation she'd felt since Derick's invitation this afternoon. Concern won out. "Let me join you there, then."

George shook his head, but when he turned his face back to her, it was lit with a warm smile. "No. Off to the castle with you, dear sister. Your *partner* awaits." He made a shooing motion when she continued to hesitate. "I won't brook any argument. Go. Discuss . . . whatever it is you said you meant to."

Emma stared at him a moment longer, but then dropped a quick kiss on his leathery cheek, knowing how useless it was to fight him when he had his mind set. A half smile lifted her lips. In that way they were very alike, even though they had been nurtured so differently due to their gender and age difference. She supposed it must have something to do with having the same overall environment and opportunities in life.

She quit the room, promising to be home before midnight.

"I don't see why," George called after her. "It's not as if you'll turn into a pumpkin."

She could hardly sit still in the short carriage ride over to the castle, expectancy causing her hands to tap an irregular rhythm on the squabs. She felt a little like that fairy-tale princess George had teased her with. Only she wasn't going to the castle to catch the eye of a prince. She was going to learn the truth about a viscount's past.

But what she truly wanted to learn, God help her, was what he had in mind for his future.

Chapter Ten

Derick was glad he'd given Billingsly the night off, for the absolute vision that greeted him when he opened the door would surely have sent the old servant into heart seizure. As it was, Derick's own heart beat madly, forcing blood to tingle through all the wrong places. He needed to use his head tonight—the one on his shoulders, that was.

"Emma." He had no other words. Good God. He'd never imagined Pygmy thus. With her hair artfully swept up around her face, she stole his breath. Gone was her staid colorless day gown. Delicate lace caressed her bosom, which was accentuated by some sort of shiny green trim, while the rest of the dress floated around her figure, only hinting at the curves he knew lay beneath. How in the hell was he going to keep his mind on the half-truths he planned to weave?

"Please, come inside." He offered his arm, which she accepted gracefully. Her satin slippers made no noise alongside the clicking of his booted heels on the stone flooring as they made their way toward the dining room but even had he been blind, deaf and dumb, he would have known she was beside him—his entire body hummed with awareness.

"I hope you don't mind, but I had the staff lay out a cold supper for us before excusing them for the evening," Derick said as he guided her across the threshold with a hand to her lower back. He felt her shiver at his touch, felt the tremor through his own body. He hastily removed his hand.

Derick's eyes lingered on Emma, dressed in all her finery. Then he glanced at the simple fare of meat, cheese, fruit and bread with a touch of regret. "While you deserve a feast served by footmen in full livery, the fewer ears to hear our conversation, the better."

"I understand," Emma murmured as she lowered herself into her chair. He'd placed it diagonal to his own at the head of the table, so that they might hear one another without shouting.

"Let me serve you." He turned to the buffet to make selections.

Emma waited quietly as he filled plates and wineglasses for them both. Derick was glad of it. Most women would be blathering on about one thing or another. He was particularly impressed that Emma wasn't. Knowing her, he was sure she must be brimming with questions, practically biting her tongue to keep them in.

As he bent over her shoulder to serve her, the heady scent of lavender warmed by flesh filled his senses. It stayed with him as he settled into his place. Sitting so near, Derick couldn't miss the way the candlelight glistened on Emma's exposed skin, how it glowed in her amber eyes. He swallowed a gulp of wine to alleviate the sudden dryness in his throat. He hadn't anticipated the intimacy of such seating, thinking only of the practicality. Damnation. He was in for a long night.

He looked away as he took a bite of the smoked meat, focusing on his strategy. Emma's curiosity would be to his advantage. If he set himself to only answering the specific questions she asked, he would be both feeding into her preconceptions and ensuring that he didn't give away anything more than he had to.

Although "had to" was a relative term. He didn't *have* to tell Emma anything. At this point, it was more like taking a measured risk. The more she believed he confided in her, the more he hoped to gain her trust for his purposes.

"Well, then," he said, turning in his chair so that he faced her as best as the table arrangement allowed. "What say we skip the small talk and get right down to why you've come."

Emma, who'd just taken a sip of wine, coughed as she gave him a startled nod. She hastily set aside her goblet.

Measured risk or not, opening this door could place his current mission in jeopardy, so he'd best do what he could to minimize it. "Before you begin your interrogation," he said, "I must insist on complete confidentiality. I wish no one to know of my past. It is my own personal affair."

Emma nodded her understanding.

He leaned ever so slightly toward her, pinning her with his gaze. "I require your word, Emma, that you'll speak of this to no one—not your brother, not your servants." Derick smiled to ease his demand. "Not even your priest."

Emma returned his smile with a tentative one of her own, but said solemnly, "Of course."

He nodded. Living a life of deception, he found it ironic that he demanded—and trusted—her word. But some people took vows very seriously. He had a feeling Emma was one of them. It was the best he could hope for and still move forward. "Good." Derick opened his hands, spreading them like an open book. "What would you like to know?"

Emma placed her napkin on the table, pushing her plate aside without having taken a bite and leaned toward him in her eagerness. Derick suppressed a wry grin. He imagined she'd have rubbed her hands together if it wouldn't have been completely rude.

"Had you already been recruited as a spy when you left England for France?"

Derick nearly laughed. "You do get right to the point, don't you?" At Emma's blush he murmured, "It's a trait I find I appreciate."

The smile that peeked at the corners of Emma's mouth was both shy and a touch alluring.

He considered her question and decided to answer truthfully but simply. "No."

Emma waited for him to continue. When he didn't, she pursed her lips. She dipped her chin and widened her eyes as she crossed her arms in front of her. "If you're going to give one-word answers, we'll be here all night," she warned. "Believe me, I can ask the most minute and tedious of questions if you force me to."

Derick did laugh then. He couldn't help himself. "Touché." He leaned back in his chair to convey complete ease and openness, though in truth he guarded his words carefully. "I left for France only with the intention of seeking out my family."

Emma frowned. "But . . . didn't your mother's family come over from Paris along with her?"

"Most, but not all," he hedged. It hadn't been his mother's family he'd been seeking, though, had it? A shameful truth that he intended would never see the light of day. "I was young." He shrugged lightly. "I had an overwhelming urge to see where I'd come from."

"So you were already in France when the Treaty of Amiens broke down . . ."

He nodded. "Common knowledge," he said, knowing it would irritate Emma. "You ask questions like a girl, Emma." He made a waving motion with his hand. "Just floating your suppositions out there instead of coming out and asking what you really want to know." He gave her a lazy grin. "You'd have made a terrible spy."

He found he liked that about her.

Emma huffed and her amber eyes narrowed on him speculatively. "Fine, then. You were detained, along with the rest of the British tourists in the country at the time. But you weren't released with the majority. What happened?"

Derick cocked his head. "That is *not* common knowledge. How did you—"

Emma's shoulders raised, ever so slightly. "Your mother told me." She blinked, looking away. "After I hounded her for information about you, night and day," she mumbled.

Derick leaned back in his seat, slowly, the controlled movement masking his shock. "How did my mother know what became of me?" He'd certainly never told her. Nor had he expected the viscountess would have cared a whit what had happened to her son. She certainly hadn't paid him any mind when he'd been right in front of her all those years.

"She made inquiries, of course." Emma frowned at him. "I assume she still had connections in France—and you *were* her only son, Derick."

His skin prickled with unease. What kind of connections might his mother have had that would have known such potentially sensitive information?

Emma had noticed his hesitation. That wouldn't do. He'd worry about his mother later. Tonight was about deflecting Emma's curiosity regarding his past. And the best way to do that was to put her on the hot seat a bit, too. He leaned forward again, giving her a slow grin. "You say you *hounded* Mother for information? About me? Why ever would you do such a thing?"

Her blush made it obvious. Her childish infatuation with him must have run very deep. How had he not seen it? He nearly snorted. He'd been seventeen, that was how. And he'd seen her as little more than an adolescent pest. But now . . .

Emma cleared her throat. "We were discussing what happened when you were detained," she said pointedly.

Now she was an adult pest. His eyes raked over her. An incredibly distracting one.

"So we were." Satisfied that the subject of the viscountess was closed, Derick considered. He hadn't realized Emma knew of his detainment. Damn. He'd have to reveal a little more. "With my darker coloring—and this nose, of course—my French heritage was obvious."

"Half French," Emma corrected.

He let her believe what she would. "As you can imagine, tensions were high. Many of us, particularly young men, were held apart from the others. Loyalties were . . . questioned." He nearly shuddered. That was as close as he would come to discussing those weeks of "interviews" that turned to interrogations—followed by extreme . . . intimidation.

"I was approached by the French. You see, they knew of my family connections. They also knew of my position in English society—that I would inherit a viscountcy one day."

They'd thought it a great lark, hadn't they? A coup of sorts, to have a full-blood Frenchman accepted as British aristocracy—a truth they'd learned courtesy of his sire's brother, who'd become a high-ranking official in Napoleon's government. "It made me the ideal candidate to spy for the French."

"You refused, of course," she said staunchly.

Derick blew out a breath through his nose, and yet her unwavering faith in him soothed a place inside of him he hadn't even known still hurt. He hadn't missed the snide insinuations and distrustful stares whenever he returned to England. People usually assumed the worst. After all, everyone knew his mother was French, and he *had* been in France most of the war.

So why was Emma different? "What makes you so certain? Do you forget I have French blood flowing through my veins?"

Emma stared at him as if he were a prize idiot. "Well, for one, you wouldn't be admitting it to me now. You know very well there's no leniency for traitors, no matter how much time has passed since the offense was committed. You couldn't expect me, as a magistrate—as an Englishwoman—to keep my vow of confidentiality if you'd betrayed our country."

Ah. It was logic that convinced her, not any faith in him. What had he expected? Still, disappointment nettled.

"Besides," she said, "blood doesn't matter. It's how we are raised that determines who we are."

"Blood doesn't matter? What rot. Just look at the successions of kings and nobility for ages. Or how some families are bad to the core." Like his. "Blood matters above all."

"*That's* rot," she said. "But that's not what I meant. I meant that it doesn't matter whose blood runs through your veins. It's what you're exposed to that makes you who you are. There's great debate about the subject, of course, but I am a firm believer that John Locke is correct with his tabula rasa theory."

Derick translated the Latin. "Blank slate?"

Emma nodded. "Precisely. He says each of us is born a blank slate, and our personalities, who we are, develop not because of who sired us but because of where and how we are nurtured. There's no such thing as 'bad' blood or 'good' blood, only bad and good choices. So no matter what blood runs through your veins"—she pointed at him for emphasis— "you were raised here. You love England, the same as I do. The same as any Briton. You would never betray her."

He scoffed. "How would you know such a thing?" She'd spent a few summers with him at best. Even the man who had raised him, the old viscount, had doubted his loyalties. "My own . . . father died thinking me a traitor," he uttered, his voice harsh. Unexpected pain sliced through his chest, stealing his breath. God, he'd thought he'd dealt with these feelings, accepted them as a tolerable sacrifice for the choices he'd made. Emma's gloved fingers slipped over his where they rested on the table. He tried to pull away, but she grasped tight, infusing his cold skin with her warmth. "Then he was a fool."

Derick stared at her. Her face was open, her amber eyes bright with moisture—his pain reflected in her eyes. Christ.

"Stop looking at me so." He pulled harder, this time successfully extracting his hand from hers. He shifted in his chair, putting distance between them.

Emma fisted her hand, slowly moving it back to her side of the table. After a long silence she said, "You asked how I know you love England?"

"Yes," he said gruffly, glad the awkward moment had passed.

Emma leaned back in her own chair, seemingly lost in thought. Derick noticed her thumb moving against her fingers again. "When we were young, all you talked about was your home in Shropshire, the land, what you intended to do with it once you inherited. Every game we played featured you as a lord of the realm, the protector of hearth and home." She shook her head and her lips twitched with a wry smile. "It was rather annoying, actually, and terribly unimaginative."

He huffed. "Thanks."

She shrugged. "As we got older, you would often speak of what you wanted to change when you took your seat in Parliament."

Had he? He brought a hand to his temple, pressing.

He hardly remembered, hadn't *wanted* to remember. So much had changed since then.

"But more than that," Emma continued, "there was so much pride in your bearing, because you knew your place. When we were playing on Aveline lands, it was as if you treated it with reverence. As if you breathed it in. Much as I feel when I'm riding Wallingford lands. That's how I know you love England. It's a part of you. That's how I know you would have died before serving the French."

Throughout her recitation, Derick's chest had tightened painfully. Emma remembered a boy he'd long forgotten. Had he ever been so innocent, so . . . deluded to the realities of the world? He brought his hand down hard on the table. "Well, you'd be wrong," he said harshly, taking a perverse satisfaction in her sudden shocked gasp.

He was angry now—unreasonably so, a distant part of himself whispered. He struggled to rein it in, which was more difficult than it had ever been. It seemed as if his control over his emotions frayed more and more every day. It must be this place.

He glared at Emma. Or this woman. This girl who knew nothing about him but thought she knew everything.

"D-do you mean to say—" Emma swallowed, her amber eyes wide and her face gone pale. "Do you expect me to believe you agreed to spy *for* the French?" Her tiny hands had curled into fists on the table and she looked a bit shaken.

Hell. He hadn't meant to say anything of the sort. It had just burst out of him, the truth. Because he'd wanted to disillusion her noble ideals of him? Because he couldn't stand the way she'd been looking at him, all soft and admiring?

Derick pushed back from the table, the wood legs of

his chair screeching a high pitch against the floor. He paced away, leaving Emma seated there staring at him as if he'd suddenly shrunk a foot and a half and morphed into Napoleon himself.

"I did," he said quietly, the weight of his words falling dully in the room. "I won't explain my reasons, so don't ask." How could he explain that angry young man, who'd just learned his entire identity had been a lie? That he *was French*, through and through, thanks to a cuckolding, faithless mother and her French lover? That he was an impostor, a bloody British aristocrat without a drop of English blood in his body. He'd been lost, broken, confused—easy prey for the persuasive tactics of the French. "Nor do I regret it," he said softly.

He turned to face Emma, expecting to see disgust marring her beautiful face. Instead, she gaped at him, her brow furrowed and her gaze calculating—as if she stubbornly refused to believe she'd been wrong about him.

And that blessed Pygmy stubbornness lightened his heart, lifting the cloud of anger and darkness that had settled over him. Derick sighed. In a way, she *had* been right about him.

"I don't regret it," he repeated more forcefully, "because had I not gone over to the French, I never would have become as useful to the British as I did."

He waited for Emma to work out his words. The stark relief that crossed her face when she did caught at him. Did she want to believe such good about him? Why did it matter to her?

"You became a *double* agent, then? But for *our* side?"

"For England's side," he demurred. He was no more British than Fouché. "It took only a matter of days for me to come to my senses, to realize I could no more betray the country of my birth than I could change the blood flowing through my veins."

He lowered himself back into his chair, taking a deep swallow of wine. Well, this discussion hadn't quite gone as he'd intended, had it? He slanted his gaze to Emma, who was now looking at him with a mixture of pity and understanding that both set his teeth on edge and filled him with an absurd relief at the same time.

He'd never spoken of that time in his life. For some unfathomable reason, it felt right to be sharing it with the closest thing he'd had to a childhood friend. Now, before he left England and this life behind him forever.

"The French thought it best to leave me rotting away with the other British prisoners for a while, so as not to alert them of my change of allegiance. Sent me back, eyes blackened, lips split and bleeding, body bruised and broken." He snorted. "A hero of British resistance." Derick's lips twisted in recall. "Smart of them, really. Within a week, I'd been welcomed by the leaders of the British rebellion. I was meant to uncover their secret plans and report back to the French, but instead, I told them the truth of my situation and offered my service to England."

"They accepted you at your word?" Emma asked shrewdly.

"Not at first," he admitted. "For many months I was tested sorely by both sides." He shuttered his eyes, refusing to open himself to discussion on that front. "But in the end I won the trust of each. And I used it."

Silence fell once again between them. While he didn't care for the contemplative gleam in Emma's eyes, the stillness wasn't uncomfortable. Until he began to wonder what, exactly, she was thinking. Then his body tensed, as if he were a garrote wire pulled tightly, waiting for the right moment to take an enemy by surprise.

It seemed an hour before she finally spoke, though in truth it was likely less than a minute.

"So, now that your wartime service to our country is behind you," Emma said, "what are your plans?"

Surprise flickered through Derick. He'd expected Emma to bury him under a barrage of inquiries now that he'd opened the door. She had to be curious about what he'd done, how he'd done it. Not that he would have answered her truthfully, but he'd certainly thought she'd ask. "No more questions about my past?"

But she just shook her head in a slow side-to-side motion. "No," she murmured, her face serious, somber. "I know everything I need to know."

Now what did that mean?

"Will you be settling in Shropshire, then?" she persisted. "At your seat?"

"I haven't decided," he lied. There was nothing to be gained by telling her the truth in this instance. That as soon as this last mission for the Crown was completed— and now, Molly's killer brought to justice—he intended to depart for the Americas. To make a life for himself where his birth, *his blood*, truly *didn't* matter. For now, it was best just to let her believe what she expected of an English viscount.

"You have no particular loyalty to that property?"

He shrugged.

"I imagine after years of such . . . intrigue, the life of a viscount must seem tame indeed," she mused.

"On the contrary," Derick murmured. "I grew tired of the deception. I would embrace a quiet life." Indeed, he looked forward to losing himself in the vast, untamed wilderness of the Americas.

Emma's gaze dropped to her lap.

Derick frowned. It wasn't like her to go all shy and wilting. "Mmm." She nodded. He knew Emma better than to think she asked idle questions. And he had a suspicion he knew where she was going with this.

Her gaze rose to him. "You could make your home here," she said, confirming his fears. She took a deep breath before saying the rest. "In Derbyshire."

Chapter Eleven

"**D**erbyshire . . ." Derick repeated. Damnation. That kiss between them today had been a mistake. Now that he knew Emma had carried a *tendre* for him, he could see why she might think there was hope, given how out of control their kiss had gotten.

"Yes." She nodded. "It would be *very* quiet, and yet you could lead a useful existence." Emma's normally calm, sedate voice rose in speed and pitch in her enthusiasm. "Heroic as you are, you must be looking for new ways to be of service."

"I must, must I?" He grew more awkward as the conversation went on. He really should disabuse her of any romantic notions. *Heroic.* He fought the urge to snort. If she only knew what he'd done to accomplish his great successes as a spy.

But that way of life was behind him. Or was it? He'd vowed to himself at the end of the war never again to use a woman's desire for him solely to get information from her. Given how Emma had responded to his kiss, Derick knew it would be easy to exploit her in that way and he intended under no circumstances to do so. But now he was faced with a new dilemma. Her feelings for him apparently ran much deeper than desire. Since there could be no future between them, if he allowed her to hope there might be to suit his purposes, wouldn't he still be breaking his vow, if not technically, then at least in spirit?

"Well, I know that the Earl of Stratford holds the magistrate position near your seat, being the highest-ranking nobleman," she went on, oblivious to the ethical turmoil going on in his mind. "But if you made your home here, you would outrank my brother, and therefore be his logical successor."

"Don't you mean *your* logical successor? Why ever would you wish that?"

"I don't, exactly. Nor would I expect you to just waltz in and usurp me." She fixed him with a stern gaze. But after a moment it softened. "I was thinking more along the line of a . . . business partnership."

"A business partnership . . ." Hell. This unexpected development was both the best and the worst at the same time. When Emma had voiced her suspicions about him being a spy this afternoon, he'd been certain that his mission was shot. He'd taken a risk being truthful with her, but he'd expected that she would become wary of him once she knew the truth, forcing him to try to win her trust anew. And yet, here she was, attempting to draw him further in.

"It would be perfect," she said with a growing enthusiasm that stabbed him with guilt. "If *you* were the official magistrate, I would no longer have to worry about my and my brother's secret being discovered."

Ah. He supposed that particular fear was a burden for her to carry.

"I won't be able to hide it forever," she said simply, confirming his thought. "At least you would be the demon I know."

"Demon?" Derick protested, even as he lifted one corner of his mouth in a wicked half-grin. "I do believe you mean 'the devil you know.' Though I can't say I care for being likened to the Prince of Darkness any more than I do one of his minions."

She shrugged, as if to say "if the sock fits."

He snorted to himself. He'd been around Emma too much—he was now mangling her metaphors for her.

"Besides"—Emma reached across the table and grabbed him again, not in comfort but in her bid to persuade him. A sizzle of heat shot through Derick as he imagined myriad ways he would rather have her try to persuade him, despite his best intentions—"we've proven we work well together. You have skills that I desire to learn, and I have superior knowledge of the people and the area. We would make a formidable team."

"A team, eh?" In the terms of his mission, he'd be a fool not to take advantage of what she was offering, for as long as necessary. Of course, he would never make his home in Derbyshire. But Emma didn't have to know that. He could accept her "partnership" as a trial. The more closely they worked together, the more natural his other questions would seem. And the less obvious his nosing around would appear.

But what of the other concern? Well, it wouldn't be breaking his personal vow, he decided, to go along to a point—it wasn't as if he was going to sleep with Emma to get what he needed, and he would be extra-careful with her tender feelings now that he was fully aware of them.

He would also do what he could to help her. He could try to leverage what connections he had to make sure she didn't have to worry about being replaced as magistrate. The government owed him much. He could also talk to his friend Geoffrey, Lord Stratford, about Emma's situation, see what the influential earl could do for her—if any peer understood how capable a brilliant woman could be, it was Stratford, who was married to a lady chemist. And, the earl's political star was rising fast.

Derick nodded to himself. Yes, that could work. Once he'd done what he'd come to do and departed England, Emma would be no worse off than she was right now—she might even be in a better position. That would make up for any small heartache she might feel upon his departure.

"It's an interesting proposition, Emma," he said. "One I must think on."

"Of course," she said, gaining her feet. "I've given you much to consider." She made a quick curtsy and Derick understood she meant to leave him to his contemplations. That wouldn't do. He'd made the calculated move to confide in her. Now he'd try to exact his quid pro quo.

He rose to his feet as well, to block her exit, and placed a hand at the small of her back to guide her back to her chair.

"The night is still young," he chided as she lowered herself into her seat, "and you haven't touched a bite. Besides, your curiosity about me has been assuaged and yet . . ." He couldn't resist skimming his finger along her exposed shoulders and the back of her neck as he crossed behind her chair to return to his own. "I find myself burning with a desire to know the woman you've become in the long years since we last saw one another."

Emma shivered at his touch, and Derick flushed as he yanked his hand away. Old habits died hard, he supposed. Even as the adage flitted through his mind, he knew it to be a hollow excuse. He hadn't touched her pale skin out of the habits of seduction, but because he simply had to know if she was as soft as he imagined. She was.

He didn't even want to fathom where the words had come from, though he couldn't hide from their truth. He was burning.

Still, the mixed message he was sending Emma was unfair. He cleared his throat and affected a businesslike tone as he moved to refill her wine goblet. "If we're going to consider working together, I'd like to know more about you, too." Most importantly, all about her brother and who might have been using him for information. "It's only fair."

Emma quirked a dubious smile at him. "I can't imagine what about my quiet life might interest you."

"Indulge me," he said. He topped off his own glass and took his seat catty-corner to hers. He leaned back in a relaxed pose and steepled his fingers atop the table. It might seem strange to jump immediately to questions about George Wallingford, so Derick decided to start with a personal one that would likely lead the discussion there naturally. "I was surprised to find you still in Derbyshire. Why did you not marry and leave this place?"

"I—" Emma dropped her eyes from his to the table-top and cleared her throat. "Well, George, of course," she said, her voice tight. "I can't leave George." When she looked back up at him, her face had smoothed to a blank expression, but she'd crossed her hands over her stomach in a protective gesture that told him the topic he'd chosen made her feel vulnerable.

Damnation. Here she was giving him the perfect opening to turn the conversation to her brother, as he'd hoped, and yet . . . Derick could see that something from her past pained her, and it sparked a deep curiosity, an empathy even, that had nothing to do with his mission. He hadn't intended his question to cause her distress, but he'd clearly brought some emotion to the surface with it. If he chose to brush right past it and move on to discussing her brother, as he should, she'd likely bury it again. But he would feel like a cad. Since he'd pushed her into her shell, it was only right that he talk her back out of it, but to do it, he needed to get at what really bothered her.

"You were three and twenty when your brother had his accident," he pointed out gently. "Did you not debut in London?"

"I did, but—" Emma pursed her lips, shaking her head. "I wasn't a fit."

The emotions that rippled over her face told several stories in the space of a second. He could imagine the girl he'd known, that blond waif with too large eyes, a pert tongue and a keen intelligence that she wouldn't have even tried to hide. No, she wouldn't have been a smashing success on the marriage mart, he supposed. But she'd clearly had hopes that had been painfully dashed. "Then they were fools, Emma," he said, giving her the same answer she'd given him about his father.

A cryptic smile creased her face before she waved a dismissive hand. "It doesn't matter. I only wanted—" Her eyes widened and she snatched her wine goblet and took a healthy sip. "There was no one there who interested me."

Derick furrowed his brow. "And there hasn't been since?"

Her amber gaze flew to his. Derick stopped breathing as he glimpsed unconcealed longing in their depths—a yearning that ran deep, a desire that gave the impression of long standing. But then Emma blinked and it was gone. "Not particularly."

Derick searched her face. Had he only imagined the look he'd seen in her eyes?

Emma shrugged. "Unless you count my former betrothed."

Betrothed? A fierce stab of irritation jerked his train of thought from whatever he might have seen in Emma's eyes. "You were engaged?"

"For nearly five years," she confirmed.

"Five years?" What the hell? And why the hell did the idea of Emma as another man's wife bother him so? "What kind of horse's arse leaves a woman waiting five years?"

She actually laughed. "As opposed to a cow's arse?" Emma shook her head. "Is there any wonder I can't

SWEET DECEPTION   141

seem to keep colloquialisms straight when they make so little sense? Horse's arse," she mumbled. "Well, I suppose Albert is that. But in Mr. Smith-Barton's defense, our original wedding date was scheduled only three short weeks after George's accident. We originally postponed the ceremony because we hoped that George would recover, but then . . . he never did."

"So, this Smith-Barton resented your having to care for your brother?"

"Oh, no. Albert and George were great friends. That's how we met, actually. He was a fixture in our household when George returned home, and we developed a friendship that I thought had the potential to be more. But in the end, it didn't." Emma's shoulder lifted in a shrug that he knew she meant to be light, but spoke of insecurity. Derick damned the man for making her feel that way. "I may laugh now and agree Albert is an arse, as you say, but he was a great support to my brother in the years following his accident."

"You say he spent a lot of time with your brother before *and* after his accident?"

Emma nodded. "Yes."

Smith-Barton was a potential suspect as well, then.

"Until he broke our engagement, that is."

Derick calculated. Wallingford's accident was in 1811, so assuming the engagement had been a few months old by then, five years would put the association ending right around the end of the war . . .

"And we didn't see him much after that," she said, her voice artificially light.

Derick reached out and covered her hand with his. "I'm sorry, Emma."

A self-deprecating smile turned her lips up. "Don't be. I must admit to having been shocked when Albert proposed. Not so much when he called it off. As the years wore on, neither one of us seemed in a rush to stand up at the altar."

Derick sensed he wasn't getting all of the story. He squeezed gently. "Still, it must have hurt."

Emma's eyelids fluttered down. "Only but a moment."

He experienced a strong need to plant his fist in Smith-Barton's face.

"Without him, Thomas and your mother, I don't know how I would have made it," Emma continued quietly. "I will always be grateful to him for that, at least." She sighed and speared a piece of cheese with her fork. "However, I no longer wish to discuss Albert," she declared as she took a bite.

Well, damn it all, he did. And not just because he wanted to find out more about the man's dealings with Wallingford. No, Derick wanted to uncover what Smith-Barton had said to cause the self-doubt that had crept into Emma's voice. What he'd done to cause the sadness that turned her perfect lips down just at the mention of his name. But he couldn't press now. He'd send a dispatch off to London in the morning to have the man found and investigated. Derick pressed his own lips into a grim smile. He might even pay Smith-Barton a visit himself. But for now, Emma had just given him an even wider opening to discuss who else had had access to her brother.

He let her eat in silence, sensing that she was desperate to leave the uncomfortable topic of her former affianced behind. After a few moments, her shoulders relaxed and some of the tension from their conversation seemed to leave her. Now would be the time to float out an open-ended question, counting on her relief from the subject change to give him the information he needed without thinking. It was basic human nature, in his experience. "It is fortunate you had people around to support you and your brother through such a difficult time . . ."

"Yes." She nodded. "Albert, as I've said. And then your mother sent us Thomas."

He would certainly be investigating the footman further.

"A few friends from the village came by at first, and the vicar, of course," Emma went on, as expected. "Though most faded away over time. The only other person who didn't was a dear friend of ours, Mr. Stubbins, who still visits George regularly."

"Stubbins?" Derick thought for a moment. "I don't recall any local family of that name."

"No, Mr. Stubbins hails from Leeds. However, he's a frequent visitor to the area. He fell in love with White Peak when he first visited several years ago and passes through every couple of months. He always makes it a point to spend time with George when he's in town."

Now *that* sounded promising. A nonlocal who took interest in an invalid ex-soldier? Derick made a mental note to find out what he could about Stubbins from the local innkeepers. He'd also send a dispatch to Geoffrey. As it happened, the earl was currently *in* Leeds, attending the surprise wedding of his wife's cousin, Lady Penelope—the daughter of a marquess who was marrying down despite the protests of her mother. Stratford would likely relish the opportunity to escape the tense festivities for a bit and do a little investigation on Derick's behalf.

Derick sat back in his chair and took a satisfying sip of wine. He couldn't believe how well this conversation had turned out. He now had three very viable suspects to look into and he hadn't so much as had to kiss Emma's hand to get them.

"Still, the person who was the greatest help to George and me over the years was Lady Scarsdale, of course."

The rich wine in his mouth seemed to take on the taste of vinegar, souring as his thoughts often did when they turned to his mother. "Because she helped with Harding, you mean?" Derick had a hard time picturing his mother being generous. He'd been surprised when

Emma had told him his mother had actually paid Harding's wages herself for a time.

"Well, yes, but . . ." Emma's pearl white teeth tugged at her lower lip. "Her friendship with my brother was . . . deep. I suppose there's no delicate way to put this," she said, "but your mother and my brother were lovers in the years before his accident."

Derick shot straight in his seat, setting the goblet back on the table with a clink as crystal met wood. Droplets of the red liquid sloshed over the side, where they beaded on the finish. "Lovers?"

Emma winced. "I can see it shocks you. It did me at first, too, but then I realized that they were, in truth, barely six years apart in age. They were also both worldly people stuck in the country for reasons of their own, and they found each other. They seemed to make each other happy, at any rate."

"Lovers," Derick repeated. It shouldn't surprise him. His mother must have been a woman of strong passions, to throw her life, her marriage, her *son* away over a man who wasn't her husband. "It makes sense, I suppose, she and your brother. Mother was rather elitist. Who else would she have taken up with, tucked away here in the country, but the closest available nobleman?"

"Perhaps she was a bit haughty," Emma conceded, "but she was good to George. And as much as I got the feeling that George cared more for her than she did for him, in the end I came to respect her. She didn't abandon him after his accident. She spent many hours talking or reading to him, or strolling with him in the garden as Thomas pushed his chair along. In truth, she was his closest confidante. Closer even than I was."

Derick pushed away from the table and rose, walking a few feet from the table, needing to veil his thoughts from Emma. What a mess. *His mother had been sleeping with George Wallingford.* Derick knew better than most that was often the simplest way to uncover someone's secrets.

Which made her the most likely suspect of them all. If he combined this new information with the knowledge that someone, most likely Farnsworth, had been asking questions recently about her . . .

A sickening irony slammed into Derick's gut. He had to face the possibility that his mother had done to George Wallingford the exact same thing he'd done to scores of women, only for her own traitorous purposes versus his so-called patriotic ones. But why would she do such a thing? Rationales aside, it made them more alike than he could stomach—just further proof that his blood was black as sin.

Behind him, Emma's chair scraped against the floor. The swishing of her skirts told him she approached tentatively. "I can see that I have given you even more to consider now," she said. "So I will take my leave. We can discuss more of my past later, if you wish it."

Derick turned to her, noting the curiosity brimming in her eyes. She had to wonder what had caused the schism between him and his mother. As far as he knew, no one in England, aside from his superiors and the late Scarsdale, knew. Sensing his discomfort, Emma probably thought their conversation had stirred up unpleasant memories. It was best to let her continue to think that.

"Thank you," he said as he offered her his arm.

As they neared the front entrance, Emma's gloved hand squeezed his forearm gently. "Thank *you* for confiding in me. You have my word, your secret is safe with me."

She turned to face him at the threshold, waiting as he retrieved her wrap.

Derick returned with the hooded cape, swinging it around Emma's shoulders.

Her head tilted to the side and her nose scrunched in thought. "One thing still bothers me, though."

Derick's gut clenched. He'd known things had gone too easily. He decided to make light, letting his mouth rise in a half smile. "Only one thing?" he asked silkily as his hands settled upon her shoulders.

Emma raised her eyes to the ceiling, in an abbreviated eye roll, before settling them back on him. "I can understand you not wishing your . . . history to be common knowledge. But why do you keep up the pretense of being . . . well, a useless fop? I assume that is one of the personas you've used throughout your . . . career. But why use it now? Why not just be yourself?"

Damned smart woman.

He couldn't very well tell her he'd acted such because he was currently hunting a traitor—who he was now afraid might have been his own mother—and had thought it the best way to proceed, now could he? He searched for an answer. And then the words just came, and they were the most honest words he'd ever said.

"I've been pretending to be someone else my entire adult life, Emma," he murmured, swallowing against the sudden scratching in his throat. "I couldn't tell you who I truly am anymore."

Chapter Twelve

Emma whipped her head around as a firm knock fell upon her private parlor door. She glanced at the ormolu clock on the mantel. 'Twas already ten in the morning? She had been so engrossed in studying her maps, she'd lost track of the time.

She jerked to her feet, smoothing back a lock of hair that had pulled free from her loose chignon. She pinched the apples of her cheeks, too. Four quick, firm tugs. There.

"Derick." She smiled as she pulled open the door, even though flutters set off in her middle. He loomed large in the doorway, his lanky frame filling the space. "Thank you for coming so early," she said. It was early, for callers anyway. She'd been up working for hours, however.

The slow grin that crept over his face sent a frisson of warmth skittering down her body. "It looks as though you've been hard at work already."

Emma couldn't help an answering smile, although she wasn't certain what had caused his. "I have." She cocked her head to the side. "But how would you know that?"

Derick reached a long-fingered hand out, gently cupping her jaw. Emma sucked in a breath and held it at the unexpected contact, at the soft heat his touch evoked. His thumb ever so gently swiped across her cheek in a long, slow motion that she felt all the way to her toes.

When he pulled his hand away, he held it before her face. His thumb was a powdery blue.

Emma's own hand flew up to her other cheek. "Oh, no!" she exclaimed, scrubbing at skin that burned with mortification. As expected, her palm came away blue, too.

Derick was rubbing his thumb against his fingers. "What is this, Emma? Chalk?"

"Yes," she muttered, swiping her hands on her dress. How embarrassing. She hadn't even thought about the fact she'd been shading her maps with chalk—and then she'd gone and pinched her cheeks! Argh. She'd been trying to look fresh and attractive for Derick and ended up looking like a blueberry tart.

He raised his hand to his nose and sniffed. "What is this earthy scent?"

"It's probably the oil I use when I mix the chalk. I make my own colors, as I need more shades than I've ever found for purchase." She grinned at him. "There's certainly no shortage of limestone around here to use as my base."

"Ah," he drawled out, nodding as if she'd answered a question he'd long wondered about. He also continued to stare at her in such a contemplative manner that she squirmed beneath his gaze. Then she realized they were still standing in the doorway.

She stepped back and extended an arm into the space. "Please, won't you come the rest of the way in?"

"Thank you," he said and stepped past her, and she caught his scent of bergamot and bay rum and breathed deeply. Derick, she noticed, was different this morning. She tried to place what it was. And then it hit her—gone were the frilly lace cuffs and the brightly striped waist-coat, the flashy buttons and extravagant colors. It seemed that now she knew he was not the fop he pretended to be, he dressed more casually, more simply.

A pleasant warmth filled her chest. She liked that he felt comfortable enough around her to be more himself.

"I am an early riser, too." Derick's voice broke her train of thought. Her eyes snapped from the sleek cut of his jacket to his face. "If it's amenable to you, we could meet as early as you like on days we work together."

"Of course." Inside she wished to crow. He had just as much as accepted her "partnership," hadn't he? She'd been a jumble of nerves last night when she'd mentioned it, had been certain by the way he had hooded his eyes and by the troubled expressions that had crossed his face, that he would refuse. Yet here he was. Part one of her plan to win Derick was falling into place.

Last night, she'd hardly slept a wink. It hadn't just been thoughts of Derick that had kept her up. George had had one of his more difficult nights, and even though he hadn't known who she was during the course of it, she'd sat with him anyway—only feeling a little guilty that her mind had been more occupied with how she might win Derick's affection than with her brother.

It was a simple equation, really. $A + B + C = D^2$. $A = $ **A**ccepting her partnership. Done. $B = $ **B**oyhood, or Derick rediscovering who he was before he'd become a spy—with her help, of course. Something told her it was vital, in order for him to heal from the wounds she'd seen in his eyes last night at Aveline Castle. And he would need to heal properly before they could move into $C = $ **C**ourtship—she pursuing him or he pursuing her, whichever seemed the most natural when they got to that point. She wasn't picky. And finally $D^2 = $ **D**erick, staying in **D**erbyshire. With her.

Emma smiled at Derick but his green gaze had strayed as he stood, taking in the room. He studied it intently, and Emma's chest tightened just a bit. She'd had this upstairs parlor made into her own personal study after the downstairs study had been converted to a bedroom for George. It was the only practical solution so that servants didn't have to carry her brother up and down all day long. But she'd rarely allowed anyone into her private space. In fact, she had never invited Mr. Smith-Barton, not once in their nearly five-year engagement. And yet she hadn't thought twice when she'd sent the note last night asking Derick to meet her here this morning.

Because she wanted to show him her work, she realized. Knew he was keen enough to understand. Hoped he would want to partner with her on it, too—insomuch as to consider taking her research to Parliament one day, after he took up his seat.

"Emma, what *is* all of this?"

She followed his line of vision, trying to view her work as one who was seeing it for the first time. Her study was quite cluttered to the naked eye, she realized, with scores of rolled records piled pyramid-like on the floor and reams of paper on nearly every available space, leaning towerlike in the corners, stacked stairlike against the walls. Of course, everything had a very precise place.

One wall was completely covered in blackboards, which were in turn covered in colorful scrawl, equations chalked in various shades in seemingly nonsensical order. Another was filled with bookshelves, which were themselves filled to overflowing with volumes on all subjects related to math, geometry, and crime.

The last two walls were plastered with maps. Mostly maps of England, broken down into counties and shires—collectively and individually. Each map was a kaleidoscope of colors, shaded by her own hand to represent the various statistics she'd collected so that she could see them visually and look for patterns.

"My project," she said, recognizing the tinge of pride in her own voice. Rarely did she have anyone with whom she could discuss her work. Some days, George could converse with her intelligently about it, but most not. "I'm compiling a map of sorts, a moral statistics map of England."

A frown insinuated itself between Derick's brows, his words coming out in a slow drawl. "A moral statistics—"

"Map. Yes. As I've said before, numbers are everything. They make up everything, and can explain everything in a perfect, clean language unbiased by human experience. But they can *define* human experience."

"How do you mean?" Derick asked, moving away to peruse several maps hanging on the wall opposite them.

Emma paused before answering, taking a moment to appreciate how he moved with a natural grace. He nearly prowled along the edges of the room.

"Well, the idea is nothing new," she said, following. She stopped when Derick did, standing behind his right shoulder as he scanned one map in particular. It was a challenge to keep up her line of conversation, not to be distracted by his nearness, his scent, his overwhelming presence. "Political arithmeticians have been using population data since the seventeenth century to analyze raw numbers. They look for comparisons related to wealth, taxes, population growth, mortality and the like in order to inform their policy making."

Derick nodded. "Yes, I've seen similar reports that help the War Department judge their ability to raise an army."

"Just so. It's the same thing as I'm doing. I simply thought to put the numbers to a different sort of use."

"You're collecting crime statistics?" he asked, running a hand along her scribbles. "Charges, age, sex, occupation of the accused . . ." he murmured.

"Exactly. Over the years, I kept detailed reports of every incident that happened in my father's or my brother's—" Emma stopped herself. She didn't have to pretend with Derick anymore. An odd lightening sensation filled her chest. "That is, within *my* purview." It felt extraordinary to say the words aloud without worry. "One day, I realized that if I kept such things, other magistrates might do the same. So I wrote to them, using only the Wallingford name, of course."

"You wrote to every magistrate in England?"

"It took weeks, but yes. And most responded. Many continue to send me reports quarterly. It would be much simpler if England had a national system of crime reporting, as they do for births, deaths, mortality and such."

"Hmmm. I'm sure the policy makers see no monetary gain to be had in such an endeavor."

She shrugged. "They're wrong, of course. If we can spot patterns amongst types of crimes, find out who is committing them and more importantly *why*, we can address those core problems to reduce crime. Which will have immense monetary benefits. And all of those answers lie in the numbers."

He turned his startling green gaze on her. "You were making some sense, Emma, but how can numbers tell you why a person committed a crime?"

A pleasant flush warmed her. His interest invigorated her and she found herself relishing the challenge. "Well, once I'd gathered the criminal statistics, I started comparing them to other numbers that *are* available nationally." She ticked them off on the fingers of her left hand as she named them. "Such as the number of inhabitants of an area per condemned person, the number of boys in primary school in that district, the type of industry and wealth in the area. And I've seen some startling patterns." She pointed to the map he was currently scanning and its array of blues and purples. "See here? Property crimes tend to happen in areas of *higher* education, for example, suggesting a more sophisticated criminal without the motivation of survival for his or her crimes."

Derick peered at the map, scanning the numbers jotted alongside. "I'd have expected the exact opposite."

"Exactly!" Emma clasped Derick's upper arm with both of hers, pulling him along to the next map to the right, this one colored with reds, yellows and oranges. How right it felt, having him beside her, showing him her passion. "And it's not just who is committing the crimes that is of interest, but *when* they are committed. For example, this map shows that crimes against persons occur most often during the summer months. Is it the heat? Longer daylight hours? Crimes against property tend to happen in the winter. What could we do to combat those phenomena?"

She tugged him along to another one of greens, grays and golds before relinquishing her grasp on his arm. "Other important factors are 'where' and 'how many.' This map proves that both personal and property crimes occur not just in higher numbers in urban areas — as we would expect — but also in higher *percentages* per capita versus rural areas. So what is it about city life that makes people more disposed to crime? Is it geographical? Are there moral variables? And if so, can we make policies to address them? Better education, religious instruction, improved diet — there's so much room for research. And if I add in more variables — illegitimate births, for example, or age — "

"This is fascinating, Emma, but what is it you're hoping to accomplish with it all?"

She turned away from her maps and faced Derick. Numbers and variables were all well and good, and she could talk them all day long. That's what she understood. But she wasn't nearly as proficient with people. If her work was ever going to actually help mankind, she'd need someone like Derick to take her ideas and help her make others understand. "Most people, policy makers in particular, simply assume it is the poor and uneducated who commit most of the crime. Yes, there is more crime amongst the lower orders, but statistically speaking, that's only true because there are more *people* amongst the lower orders. When you look at the picture as a whole, crime mars all classes . . . the only difference is the type. My research is proving that the way we look at crime and how to stop it is flawed. We have to stop blaming lack of proper breeding or bad blood, as some claim, and face the real issues."

Derick frowned at her. She knew from their discussion last night that he might be on the other side of that argument. Still, if she couldn't convince him, she'd have very little chance convincing anyone else.

"I believe all persons *are* born blank slates, and it is more the circumstances we are born into that shape who we become, the opportunities and examples we are given. I intend to discover exactly what circumstances tend to breed what type of crime so we can figure out how to combat it. We can *change* what becomes written on someone's slate. *Before* they become criminals."

Derick's hand came up, his thumb and forefinger cradling her chin. Energy crackled all around Emma, stilling her breath and tingling in forbidden places. His eyes squinted slightly as an enigmatic half smile lifted his mouth. "My little Pygmy," he murmured. "Are you planning to save the world?"

"Yes," she whispered, caught in his gaze. Her hand came up to grasp his wrist, and she absently stroked the soft inner skin with her thumb. Something sad and cynical crept into his eyes, coloring the green—a shadow of the pain she'd glimpsed last night. She wanted to banish it for him. Something in her knew that even more than she wanted to make the lives of Britons better, she wanted to help heal Derick Aveline. She reached her other hand to his face, cupping his jaw. "Yes," she said again, aloud, more firmly than before. "I *am* going to save the world."

And I'm going to start with you, her heart whispered.

She stretched up on her toes and pulled his lips to hers.

Chapter Thirteen

He should have turned his face. He should have yanked himself from her grasp. His mind commanded him to do just that, to turn on his heel and walk away from her. Run, even. But his body wouldn't obey.

Instead, every muscle, every nerve clamored for her, yearned for Emma to touch him—not with the gentle grip she used now, but with hot, needy tugs, frantic gropes, overtly carnal clutches. To have her stroke him with even a taste of the passion he saw whirling in her eyes. God, how he wanted her.

His lips burned where she'd pressed hers against them. He held himself stiff, tried desperately to resist as her tongue licked along the seam of his mouth, begging for entrance. He shouldn't allow this. Shouldn't encourage her. Shouldn't let her open herself to the inevitable heartbreak he would bring. He breathed harshly through his nose, fighting to control his unreasonable desire.

And then she breathed his name. "Derick." Just a sweet sigh of frustrated longing. And the fight left him, his thoughts flying away in the face of their mutual desire. Christ, had he ever burned so hot, so fast? Certainly not since sex had become a tool of his trade, a way to get information that he—and the War Department—needed.

But he wasn't using her for information, was he? This was strictly about a different kind of need, only her need and his. That was all right, wasn't it? His body sagged into her hold, and Emma moaned in relief, throwing her arms around his neck and nearly climbing up his body to get closer.

A moan of his own ripped from Derick's throat as he obliged her. He scooped his arms around her bottom and lifted her so that her face was even with his, their mouths locked in a desperate kiss. Her breasts flattened against his chest and even through the layers of their clothing he could feel how soft, how supple they were. The need to bare them—to taste them—made his hands shake.

Emma's legs parted to settle around his hips. She broke away from the kiss, gasping at the contact. Her eyes widened for a brief second, then became heavy lidded, turning a deep molten gold as she moved tentatively, with innocent wonder, against his arousal.

"Oh God, Emma," he groaned, unable to hold back the answering thrust. Sparks such as he'd never felt in his life burst through him, raining down tingles upon every inch of his skin. What was this madness? He trembled like a green boy—even his legs threatened to give out on him.

Good God. He had to find something stable before he collapsed in a heap on the floor, taking Emma with him.

He wasn't given much time to consider, however. A brilliant smile wreathed Emma's face before she renewed their kiss with an untutored fierceness that stole his breath. Her next undulation was anything but tentative and wrung a moan from them both.

From the corner of his eye, Emma's desk caught his attention. He shuffled toward it, still clasping her tightly to him. He had just enough restraint not to sweep the surface clean. He doubted Emma would appreciate her meticulously shaded maps being flung to the floor. With one forearm, he nudged aside some papers and settled himself on the corner of the desk with Emma draped in his lap, her legs still straddling his hips.

He pulled back and stared at the woman in his arms. Damnation. Had he ever seen such an arresting sight?

And what a sight she was, her skirts pooled high around her thighs, her chest heaving as she struggled for breath, her lips swollen with his kisses. A fierce possessiveness flared.

"Derick?" Emma's shy inquiry should have brought him to his senses, but then she reached for his hand, taking it in hers and pressing it against her breast. "I ache," she said simply.

"I know," he murmured, reveling in her gasp as he squeezed her firmly. And in this moment, that was all he did know—her need, and how to fill it. His mind emptied of any other thought than how to bring the most pleasure to them both. His other hand followed suit on her neglected breast until he was caressing them both in rhythmic rotating tugs that culminated with the simultaneous rolling of her clothed nipples between his thumbs and forefingers.

"Oh. Oh!" She squirmed in his lap, instinctively grinding against him in a movement that hurled him even further into the madness.

Derick released her breasts just long enough to tug the lace fichu from her bodice. Better, but not enough, not nearly enough. He yanked the muslin down and her breasts popped free of her dress. He cupped her once again, pressing them together as she was bared to his eyes, his hands. His mouth.

He lowered his head, rasping his tongue against her pebbled nipple. Emma nearly shot from his lap. He had to exert pressure on her thighs with his forearms to keep her in place. "You liked that, didn't you?" he murmured against her breast, his voice gone rough with his own building need. "Let us see what you think of this."

He drew her into his mouth, suckling hard, then laving soft licks to soothe her before drawing upon her again.

Her fingers tunneled into his hair, squeezing, tugging spasmodically as she held him tightly against her chest. "Please," she panted. "Please. More."

"More what?" he asked as his mouth skimmed to her other breast.

"More anything," she groaned, ending on a jagged inhalation as he sucked her in again.

More anything. He wanted to give her more *everything.* To take everything from her. His hand delved beneath her skirts, finding the soft skin of her thigh. It felt as supple beneath his fingers as her breasts did beneath his tongue. He wondered briefly if she would taste as sweet between her thighs as she did between the valley of her breasts. He burned with the need to know.

Later. Now, it was his questing fingers that found her silken folds. Hot. Wet. Swollen. She moaned against the top of his head as he fondled her gently, circling the nub of her pleasure with the pads of his fingers in a way that had her clenching her thighs tightly around his hips.

How he burned to release himself, to thrust into her beckoning heat. And he would, as soon as he was certain she was ready for him.

He lifted his head, straightening as his other hand found its way through her cascading chestnut curls, winding around her hair and pulling her head back so that he could take her lips in a voracious kiss. His tongue swept into her mouth at the same moment he pressed a hard finger into her dew-slickened body.

She stiffened with a moan. Damnation, she was tight. Exquisitely, deliciously . . . *tight.* A frigid chill burst through Derick's belly as cold reality returned him to his senses. Of course she was tight. She was a *virgin.*

And not just a virgin. She was Emma. Pygmy.

His hand stilled as his eyes raked her. Her hair fell in wild disarray around them, her chest heaved, passion-splotched breasts spilling free over her neckline, glistening with moisture from his own mouth. Her legs were splayed, her skirts tossed above her waist, his bronzed hand stark against her pink skin where he touched her intimately.

Self-disgust ravaged him. Look what he'd led her to. Look how close he'd come to ruining her. What a bloody ass.

He knew she wanted him, knew how vulnerable she was to him. And he'd nearly taken her atop her own desk, in her brother's house, for Christ's sake.

Derick trembled all over, no longer with passion but with the effort of holding still with a writhing woman in his lap.

She must have felt the change in him because she grabbed his forearm with both of her hands, just above where his hand still rested between her thighs. "Derick?"

She was so beautiful with her eyes clouded, her muscles tight and twitching with her need. "Please," she said, her voice shaking. He knew she didn't even know what she was asking for. She only knew she needed it. Badly.

Tension coiled in him, pushing away every conflicted thought save one. *This was his fault, not hers.* Still, there was no way he could consummate what they'd begun. But neither could he leave her like this.

"Shhh . . ." he crooned, gentling her. He opened his hand over her mons again, his fingers returning to their swirling movement on her clitoris. His other hand left her hair, skimming down her spine in a soothing motion. "I know what you need, Emma. Trust me to give it to you."

He had tupped scores of women in the name of duty, never once losing his head like this. Now he called on this other self. The one who wrung pleasure for a purpose. Only this time, his purpose was simply to give Emma the release he owed her.

He brought her down gently, then helped her start a slower climb, bringing to bear every bit of experience he'd gleaned in all of those years of seducing women for their secrets. He knew precisely how to shift his touch when her pearl quivered beneath his fingers, how to gently suck her tongue into his mouth to give her a point to focus on when the sensations wracking her body became unbearable. He knew when to spear his fingers into her body, when to plump her breasts and when to pinch her nipples to push her just to the very edge.

But what he didn't know was how to stop his own body from climbing with her. Derick gasped for breath, when by all accounts his only exertion at the moment was with his hands and mouth. Alarming bursts of pleasure sporadically rocketed through his body. Damnation. He'd never had this problem with any other woman. He'd always been able to wring from them whatever he needed, without becoming any more engaged than necessary to be able to complete the deed. But with every gasping moan from Emma's lips, Derick was strung tighter and tighter. He hoped to hell she came soon, as her every cry of pleasure twisted him.

"Derick!" she cried out as she crested.

Thank God.

She clenched his hand tight between her thighs, clasping his head to her chest with a strength that screamed the power of her climax. She jerked in his arms, moaning in hiccuping little waves.

Derick's breath strangled in his chest as a fierce burning started in his spine. What the hell?

Emma shuddered again, her bottom notching against his still-clothed arousal.

Pleasure exploded through him, shocking him, spasming through his cock in hot violent spurts. "Ah—ah—ah—ahhhhh!" Derick shook, mindless, grinding Emma's hips against him until every last bit of him was spent.

As their cries died out, only their harsh panting echoed in the room. Derick buried his face against the humid skin of Emma's throat, and he couldn't help himself from licking her, tasting her salty sweetness.

She slumped, boneless, in his arms. Derick let his hands skim over her back, her hair, in long, soothing strokes. But the more she relaxed, the more tense he grew. By all rights, he should be as languidly sated as she. Instead, tension grew to alarm.

He'd just been undone, popping in his trousers like a lad during his first slap and tickle. He, whose longevity and sexual prowess had been whispered about throughout countless ballrooms on the Continent. And even though Emma had never actually touched him, it had been the most wrenching, wringing, intense climax of his life.

It was unthinkable, what he'd done. He'd lost control.

An even more disturbing realization struck him.

He'd *liked* losing control.

He was in serious trouble.

Emma struggled to catch her breath. Not just her breath, but her thoughts. Words danced into her mind, jumbling together in combinations that made no sense. Much like others saw her equations, she imagined. She let them go, too tired, too . . . blissful to try to hang on and make sense of them.

Unfamiliar physical sensations flitted in next. An odd moisture between her thighs. A humming, tinglingly raw pulsing there as well. A twinging in her breasts. A full-body ache, as if she'd climbed one of the great hills White Peak was named for the day before and had the sore muscles to prove it. And yet, it was all overlaid with a golden honeyed glow. What had Derick done to her?

Her eyes popped open. Derick. He was . . . beneath her, would be the best way to describe it. And yet between her, and around her, too . . . and fully clothed, while she—*dear God*—was half naked.

She stared down her body as if it were someone else wantonly splayed in a man's lap in the middle of the morning, on top of a desk, no less. Her breasts spilled out over her dress, nipples darkened and throbbing, a dark head nestled between them. And—and her thighs were bare. Heat flooded her once again, this time from embarrassment. Thank God Derick's body blocked the rest of what she knew she'd see—her most private of places, bared and pressed tightly against him, pinkish white skin against the dark brown material of his pantaloons.

She tensed, the urge to reach down and yank her bodice up and her skirts down overwhelming. And yet . . . This was Derick. The one man she'd always wanted. She relaxed a little, comforted, and breathed him in again. Were she ever to do . . . well, whatever they'd just done, he was the man she would have chosen. And that had to make it all right, didn't it?

Because he'd chosen her, too.

She stroked his silky black hair as a contented smile lifted her lips.

Derick flinched beneath her. The harsh jerk reverberated through Emma, sending her heart into her throat. Her smile dipped. Why would he flinch at her touch?

He pulled back from her. The sudden loss of his heat against her bare chest sent a chill through her and left her feeling cold. And strangely alone, which was ridiculous, as she'd never been *less* alone in her life, still seated as she was, so intimately on his lap.

As he straightened, his hands moved to tug her dress up over her chest. Emma shivered as his hot palms delved beneath the lace of her neckline, efficiently shifting her breasts back into place. Efficiently . . . and almost impersonally—nothing like how he'd touched her before. Why?

When she was decently covered, Derick's hands moved to grip her upper arms. "Can you stand?"

"Of course," she said automatically, but could she? She didn't know. She didn't want to. Emma searched Derick's face. His expression had gone blank—firm and emotionless. Confusion twisted in her belly. "If you wish it . . ."

"I do," he said in a clipped tone, and Emma's throat constricted painfully.

She hadn't pleased him.

Shame flooded her. She turned her face away, unable to look at him as she braced her hands upon his shoulders so that she could gingerly slide her legs from atop his. Derick gripped her waist, standing to assist her glide to the floor. Her legs trembled and ached as she gained her feet, but she ignored it. She stepped back, pushing his hands away when he tried to help her smooth her skirts down. She focused her gaze on the patterned rug as she finished the task herself.

Derick's booted feet disappeared from her view, leaving only her discarded fichu crumpled on the floor.

Emma rubbed her forehead with the fingers of her left hand. She had no experience in these things, but she'd thought for certain he'd found the same unnameable bliss as she, given his throaty cries there at the end. Hadn't he shaken with the same pleasure she had?

"What did I do wrong?" The question flew from her lips, and at once she wished she could call it back. And yet she couldn't stop the torrent. "Was I too wanton? Too eager?" She braved a look at him. "Or am I the opposite? Too . . . boring? Not worldly enough?"

Derick stood only feet from her in profile, his darkly clothed form in stark relief against the light color of the door. His chest lifted and fell with a heavy breath. Emma drank in his sleek angles, the perfectly formed lines that defined his face, the precise balance of sinew and bone from head to toe.

And then she knew. Derick was beautiful—perfectly proportioned, physically magnificent. One of those beings graced by the Divine, without flaw. Whereas she . . . Emma winced, hugging her arms around herself. She was not. Her breasts, she knew, were disproportionate to her small frame, her hips a degree too wide while her waist dipped too narrowly. He would have seen all of that, felt it. He must think her severely lacking when compared to what he could have, what he deserved.

"Do you find my form distasteful?" she whispered, ashamed. But she had to know.

A choke emerged from his throat as his face whipped around. He pinned her with his glittering gaze. After several long seconds, the strained lines around his eyes softened. "You don't actually believe that, Emma," he murmured. He squinted at her a moment longer. "Do you?"

She certainly did. She was so tightly wound, she couldn't utter a "yes," though. She could barely manage a shrug.

In three long strides, he stood directly before her. His long-fingered hands delved into her hair on either side of her face and he pulled her toward him. Emma was so surprised by his suddenness, all she could do was uncross her hands and bring them to rest, palm down on his chest, before his lips took hers.

She welcomed his tongue as if it were as natural to her as long division. He groaned at her easy acceptance, and the sound pushed away the ache of tears that had been threatening.

"God, Emma," he whispered when at last the kiss broke. Still, he pressed tiny kisses around the corners of her mouth as he continued. His hand left her face and spread out over one of her own atop his chest. "Don't you feel the way my heart pounds when I touch you?"

Beneath her hand, beneath the cambric of his shirt, beneath the heat of his skin, she felt his pulse racing. "Yes," she whispered, her own heart threatening to leap from her chest. "Like mine."

His hands skated down her sides then, fanning out when he reached her hips to cup her bottom. He pulled her tightly to him and a hot thrill swirled up Emma's middle as his unmistakable arousal dug into her. "Believe me, I don't find you distasteful," he growled before taking her lips once again.

A warm glow infused her with every slide of his tongue, with every caress of his hands, with every hitch in his breathing. When, at last, Derick gentled the kiss and set her away from him a few inches, they were both panting for air.

"But we can never do this again," he said.

"What?" Perhaps she hadn't heard him correctly through the rush of blood still pounding through her ears. "Why?" She reached for him, intending to protest his ridiculous pronouncement with a rash of fresh kisses, of heated touches.

He blocked her, taking both of her hands firmly in his own, holding her at arm's length. A pained expression crossed his face and his emerald eyes darkened. "You made me lose my control, Emma." His voice scraped, as if he'd confessed some dire sin.

Emma tugged at his hands, her shoulders dropping in frustration even as the feminine side of her rejoiced. She'd made Derick lose control? She? "But you made me lose mine as well." Sensation arced through her as she remembered that moment, that feeling of flying apart, of not being able to stop herself from shattering into more pieces than even she could count. It *had* been terrifying, but also exhilarating. Unlike anything she'd ever known. And she desperately wanted to feel it again. And again . . . to infinity. Didn't he? "Isn't that a welcome thing?"

His eyes shuttered and he released her hands. "Not to me." Derick stepped back from her, and she let him. "This never should have happened. I'm . . . sorry, Emma."

"I'm not," she said simply. Nor did she glance away from him, refusing to grant him the easy way to escape her gaze. Her blood raced faster the longer their eyes locked.

Derick broke first. He turned his face toward the door. "I'll just let myself out, then."

She nodded, not trusting herself to speak.

Only when the door clicked behind him did she allow herself to consider what had just happened. But rather than regret or tears, it was hope she felt.

Derick had fled the room. She knew he wasn't a coward. How could a man who had served his country behind enemy lines, the threat of discovery looming over him at all times, be a coward? And yet he'd been fleeing just the same.

You made me lose my control, Emma.

She walked over to her desk, snagging a piece of chalk from the leather-topped surface before continuing on to one of her boards. Absently she picked up the corner of her muslin skirt and used it to wipe the bottom of the board clean.

Then she set to it, the familiar clicking of chalk on slate a welcome balm.

$A + B + C = D^2$

She stepped back, staring at the simple equation, which was turning out not to be as simple as she'd expected.

You made me lose my control, Emma.

Derick hadn't thought that a good thing, had he? She supposed he must prize it, his control. It had likely saved his life countless times over the years. And yet, something told Emma that *that* was the key. The integral integer that her equation was missing.

She stepped back up to the board thoughtfully and added in a pair of parentheses and a multiplier.

$S (A + B + C) = D^2$

There.

"**S** equals seduction," she said into the empty room. Because for reasons she couldn't fathom, something about *her* touch had driven him to losing his vaunted control. If she were going to win him, she'd need to push him to it again and again, until he finally broke.

Her fist squeezed around the chalk. That could be a challenge. Neither of them had expected her to reach up and kiss him today. He might very well be better prepared next time, since he was so adamant that it not happen again. So how *was* she going to go about seducing him?

She glanced woefully at her bookshelves. Plenty of material about murder and mayhem, but nothing about how to tempt a man beyond his reason.

Well, perhaps she could send off for a volume or two that might shed some light for her. But it would be days, maybe a week or more, before she'd receive them. Something told her she couldn't allow Derick that kind of time to erect his defenses. No, she had to act now, while whatever magical momentum she had over him held sway.

She tried to think back to their encounter, to pinpoint the exact moments that had so affected Derick, so she knew what to do again. Well, let's see . . . She'd kissed him. He'd resisted at first, but then she'd whispered his name. Yes, then he'd lifted her up and . . . And . . .

Emma closed her eyes, rubbing her thumb and fingers together, searching for the memories.

They wouldn't come. Her lids flew open. Though it had only happened moments ago, she couldn't recall the specifics. All she could bring forth were the echoes of ecstasy. Not how she'd gotten there. Not how she'd driven him there, either.

That was a first. She always remembered everything. It was as if the pleasure had muddled her brain, made her memories foggy.

Fig.

Well, she was an intelligent woman. She could figure this out. She was just going to have to rely on her instincts.

Obviously she'd need to endeavor to get Derick alone, as much as possible. She could dovetail that in nicely with her plan to help him remember his boyhood by revisiting some of their childhood haunts.

She'd need to touch him, of course—that went without saying. She wasn't certain yet how she'd accomplish that without being transparent, but she'd figure that out when the opportunities arose.

She glanced down at her chalk-dust-streaked dress. It couldn't hurt if she made up a little, either.

That didn't help you in London, did it, my girl? No one wanted you then. What makes you think Derick will want you now?

Emma frowned. Her memory might not be working properly, but it seemed the negative voice in her head was as strong as ever.

"He wants me already," she argued aloud. For whatever reason, by whatever miracle, he did. Physically, at least.

And she planned to take full advantage of it. Then the rest would come.

Chapter Fourteen

He was being a coward. He knew it. But he wasn't prepared to do anything about it just yet. He'd been away from upper Derbyshire for three days now, but it wasn't enough time to cool his growing need for Emma Wallingford—a need he couldn't act upon. All right, couldn't act *further* upon.

After that scorching interlude in her study, he'd had no choice but retreat. In an effort to keep himself from going back for more, he'd set out to interview innkeepers not only in the village but in a few neighboring towns about the tourist Emma had mentioned the other night, Stubbins. Then he'd discovered where Smith-Barton, the man who'd jilted her, had moved and paid him a visit. She was well shot of the smarmy prig, who'd gone on and on about how he'd dodged a bullet by not marrying her. Just the idea of Emma as Smith-Barton's wife turned Derick's stomach. What the hell had George Wallingford been thinking, introducing his sister to such an ass? She deserved a man who appreciated how unique and extraordinary she was. A man like—

Derick wouldn't allow himself to complete the thought. Smith-Barton remained a strong suspect. Not only did he raise Derick's hackles—usually a good indicator, though Derick admitted they could well be raised on Emma's behalf—but Smith-Barton lived rather opulently for a mere mister, though he'd claimed he'd gained his fortune through his recent marriage.

Derick had then sent an inquiry to the War Department, asking them to dig deeper into the backgrounds of Harding, Stubbins and Smith-Barton. But he wondered if it was for naught, given what he'd learned about his mother. He hated to think the traitor he hunted was actually his own flesh and blood, but he could believe it, given the faithless way she'd lived her life—an ability she'd passed on to him. Not to mention the circumstantial evidence that was piling up. Before leaving the castle, he'd had disturbing discussions with various members of the staff. His mother, it seemed, had been hastily packing in the days before her suicide. She'd been preparing to run. From what? Justice? Had Farnsworth's asking questions about her spooked her? Had she been guilty and feared the agent was onto her?

And then Derick had found her journals. He'd known she'd been unhappy in England, but he'd had no idea how much his mother had detested this country until he read it in her own words.

Would it be such a bad thing if the traitor did turn out to be his mother? After all, the only person's reputation that could be hurt was his own, and he'd be long gone from these shores. Yes, it would confirm that his blood was tainted even more than he'd known, but that was just by degrees, wasn't it? It would merely give him all the more reason to put England behind him.

Emma might be able to enlighten him further about his mother and her actions. But he didn't quite trust himself to be around her yet and not ravish her. She'd haunted him these past few days and nights, keeping his body on a knife's edge of desire, the memory of her just as tenacious as the actual woman herself.

When he'd returned home, Billingsly had informed him that Emma had come to the castle all three days, looking for him.

She must have learned he was back, because a note had arrived this morning inviting him to discuss their investigation over breakfast. He'd sent back a polite refusal, claiming estate business.

'Twas a perfectly legitimate excuse. After all, that *was* one of the reasons he'd agreed to take this last mission in Derbyshire—and regardless of whether Farnsworth ever showed himself or not, Derick still had to make certain everything was in order with the castle and its lands before he left for the Americas. He intended to hire a local steward. As Derick wouldn't be available to oversee the estate as a whole from abroad, he wanted a separate man managing each of his properties who would in turn report to his newly hired man of business.

That was the excuse he was giving himself, anyway. Derick looked over the list of possible applicants. There were five names on it, men local to the area who'd come highly recommended. Emma would probably have some sort of mathematical equation to determine which one of them would be best—

Damnation. She intruded even when he was doing the most mundane of tasks.

He turned his focus back to his list. He recognized two of the names as boys he'd known in his youth. Interviewing them would give him at least a couple more days of respite before he had to face Emma again—

"I hope you don't mind that I let myself in."

Derick's head jerked up at the sound of Emma's voice. He nearly snapped the leaded pencil he held in his hand, so tight was his grip on it.

Good God. Just one glance and he knew he was going to have to keep a tight grip on more than his pencil, because the woman standing in the doorway to his study presented one hell of a temptation.

Gone were her colorless plain dresses and mismatched footwear. Instead, a green riding dress molded to her curves—curves he would know by touch alone now—complemented by chocolate kid boots. Her rich chestnut hair ringed her face in a more intricate coiffure than he'd ever seen her wear, yet his mind's eye conjured how it had looked only days ago, rippling down her back in wild abandon. His hands itched to feel the silky strands slipping between his fingers again. Her skin glowed soft against the fabric of her dress, making his mouth water for a taste. It would take nothing, just a tiny movement and he could be out from behind his desk and have her in his arms, his tongue skimming down the sweet valley between her breasts—

His eyes widened as they reached her neckline. Derick cleared his throat. "Did you lose your fichu on the ride over?"

Damnation, he could practically see to her navel in that low-cut vee. Well, that was an exaggeration. The dress was actually rather modest compared to some of the European styles he was used to, but there was certainly more of Emma's bosom on display than was practical. Or advisable, given his demonstrated lack of control where she was concerned. Derick swallowed.

"I've decided to stop wearing them." She shrugged. "I find this fashion much more . . . freeing. Don't you?"

A not-so-innocent smile tugged at Emma's lips. Derick narrowed his gaze. So *that's* what she was about. He'd suspected that she was entertaining hopes in his direction, but he hadn't counted on her active pursuit. Perhaps he should have. She'd clearly been plotting in his absence. But now that he was onto her game, he would just have to discourage her.

He shrugged in return, slipping on a mask of nonchalance. "It's a matter of taste, I suppose," he said, returning his gaze to the list of possible stewards before him.

Emma didn't say anything for a long moment. Finally,

he couldn't resist a quick glance. She still wore a smile, but it seemed a little too wide, and her right fist was clenched by her side. Ah, hell. He'd injured her feelings. He shouldn't care. If this were any other mission, any other woman, he wouldn't care. But this was Emma, and he had no desire to hurt her. He would have to be gentler in his rebuffs. "The look is very becoming on you, however."

"Thank you." Her smile turned self-deprecating, but at least it was genuine. She took a deep breath. "I warn you now, I've come to tempt you."

"What?" The pencil in his hand did snap then, the crack harsh in the room. He knew subtlety wasn't one of Emma's many talents, but still.

A small line appeared on her forehead and her brows dipped in confusion. "I remembered how you used to filch Cook's blackberry pastries when we were younger. She was pensioned off a few years ago, but I found her recipe and tried my hand at them. I thought I might tempt you into taking a break from your accounts for a nice picnic."

Of course. He needed to remember that Emma didn't always mean things the way they sounded, or always take things the way they were meant. Still, his body didn't care how she'd meant it. His nerves had gone on alert the moment she'd walked into the room, and when the words "tempt you" had crossed her lips, they'd gone wild.

"That *is* rather tempting," he murmured. "But I still need to finish up these books."

Rather than leave him be, Emma came farther into the room. He felt her movements as if he and she were connected by some unseen force. The closer she came, the more his body tensed in anticipation.

"You have to eat sometime," she cajoled lightheartedly, "and I don't cook for just anyone. In fact, I've never cooked for anyone before." She stopped between the chairs that fronted his desk, and tilted her head toward the window, where pleasant summer sunshine streaked in. "It's a glorious day outside . . ."

He felt like the stodgiest curmudgeon disappointing her, particularly when she was trying so hard. And something told him Emma didn't try in this arena. Indeed, her vulnerability spoke to him through the slight tremor in her otherwise light tone, through the over-brightness of her amber eyes. But the best course of action, for his sake and for hers, was to keep their interactions as businesslike as possible.

"Would that I could," he said, aware that at least part of him meant that, "but I really must finish. And then I must arrange to interview potential stewards."

A frown settled on her face. "Stewards? For your other properties?"

"No. For the castle."

"Oh." She chewed her lip as a soft sigh escaped her. "I thought you would oversee it yourself."

When he came to live here and became the magistrate—and her "partner." She'd left it unsaid but he heard it anyway.

"I haven't decided to stay, Emma." He needed her cooperative, though, so he left open the possibility even as guilt niggled at misleading her. "But even if I did, it would be some time before I could make such a move. There are many improvements a steward could get started making right away."

Emma nodded. "Oh, I agree. In fact, I've long thought your land could benefit from some of the farming techniques we've been using at the manor. I'd love to spend a few days giving you a detailed tutorial on how I like my fields plowed."

Derick felt his eyes go wide. He pressed his lips together tightly in an odd combination of lust and amusement.

"Or I could instruct your new man—if you'd rather,"

she rushed, misunderstanding his expression, he was sure.

His amusement fled. The idea of her showing any man how to plow her anything balled in his chest like a hot fist. If he didn't know better, he'd think the tightness in his gullet was jealousy—of a yet-to-be-hired steward, no less. Absurd.

"I'm assuming you'd wish to engage someone local. Did you have a specific person in mind?" she asked.

"Yes. I have five names here." He cleared his throat, having a hard time not thinking of the men on his list now as licentious field-plowers, and not liking it one bit.

"Fine. If you won't come out for a picnic with me . . ." She held out her hand across his desk. When he just stared, she gave an imperious little snap of her fingers. "Let me see your list. I know everyone around here. I can give you my impressions." She took the list from his hand and had a seat across from him in a scalloped wingback chair. "Although pastries and a bottle of wine would have been much more enjoyable," she murmured beneath her breath.

Her quiet grumble restored his good humor.

As Emma settled her skirts around her, an uncharacteristically whimsical thought struck him. Sitting against the pearly bisque fabric, her green skirts hugging her thighs before flaring around her ankles, she looked like a mermaid queen upon her throne.

The image brought with it more old memories. Emma had often pretended to be a mermaid princess when they used to swim in the deepest part of the creek, hadn't she? The one that pooled near the old cave close to the eastern border of Aveline lands. Yes. He'd forgotten all about that, but now . . . Recollections came rushing back, of the sun hot on his skin, his belly full of stolen pastries, Emma refusing to play one more game of King Arthur and the Knights of the Round Table until he pretended to be her merman servant. How he'd pouted and fussed, but had dutifully brought her make-believe food and drinks, or flowers, or whatever else she commanded until she was finally tired of that silly girl-game and relented. Then they'd be back off, running through the fields, playing *fun* games.

"Why are you smiling?" Emma's bemused voice yanked him out of the past.

"I—" He hadn't known he *was* smiling. "No reason," he said, shaking off her question, but he couldn't shake the feeling of lightness that remained. It had been years since he'd remembered something pleasant about his childhood. About the boy he'd been. How long ago that had been, how far he'd come—and gone.

He was a grown man, now. A man with years of false identities and dangerous, ugly memories. A spy. A fake.

He hadn't always been, though, had he?

Emma's words from the other night rang in his mind.

There was so much pride in your bearing. Because you knew your place.

Derick sat back in his chair, suddenly feeling off-kilter. He pushed his shoulders flat against the tufted leather, as if the ancient chair could ground him. Christ. He had no place. He'd *never* had a place. He just hadn't known it back then. Hadn't known he was a blood impostor to the viscountcy he was meant to inherit, to the country he loved.

But oh, how he wished he could recapture that pride, that feeling of knowing who he was, where he belonged. He could never un-remember all that he knew, but could he uncover that seminal part of himself that Emma once saw? If his childhood were laid out before him again, could he find it? Capture it? Take it with him to build upon in an unknown future?

Everything in him told Derick that if he didn't find himself here, he never would.

It was a foolish thought. Hell, he could hardly even remember those days.

His gaze went to Emma, who was still studying his list of stewards, unaware of his intense regard.

He couldn't remember, but *she* could.

She chewed on her lip for a bit, then handed the list back to him. "I'd skip interviewing Smalls . . . he's a drunkard. And Ogleby is horrible with figures—not at all what you want in a steward. Any of the other three should do nicely."

"Thank you."

"You're welcome."

An awkward silence drew out between them. Emma's eyes flitted to the door, but she pulled her bottom lip back between her teeth. It was clear she didn't want to leave. Derick was no longer certain he wished her to, either.

Finally, she cleared her throat. "Well, since you've decided we're to be all business this afternoon, I've learned something new in our investigation."

"You mean about Molly's death?" He frowned. "You still don't think it's Harding?"

"It could be, of course. But I wasn't entirely convinced. So while you were gone . . ." She paused, rampant curiosity on her face, perhaps hoping he'd offer up where he'd been. He didn't. Thankfully, she gave up. "I went back into town and asked more questions, dug a little deeper. And guess what I discovered."

He shook his head, waiting.

"There's been a stranger hanging about the past few weeks."

Oh hell. He did not want Emma stumbling upon Farnsworth, or learning why the agent—and by extension, why he—was really here. "A stranger?"

"Yes. A drifter. Several people have seen him, yet no one knows where he's staying or why he's here. Perhaps *he's* the man we're looking for." She shivered. "I'd much rather believe that than to think someone I've known for years did such an awful thing. I haven't had any luck finding him the past couple of days, but since you've turned me down for the afternoon"—she stood, brushing her skirts out—"I suppose I'll go back into town and continue my search."

Derick rose from his chair, as well. He was glad to hear Farnsworth might still be around, though the agent better have a good reason he'd yet to contact him. Regardless, he couldn't have Emma coming across the man before he did. "You know, I've decided that a picnic would be just the thing."

Emma's head snapped up. "Truly?" Her delighted smile gave him pause as he remembered his intention to discourage her. He weighed it against his need to distract her. He didn't want Emma caught up in this mess any more than she had to be.

"I've got to eat sometime," he said, using her argument. "I have one request, however."

A bemused smile crossed Emma's face as she cocked her head. "Yes?"

"I'd like to take our picnic up to the old cave we used to play in. Do you remember it?"

Emma laughed. "Of course . . ."

"Good. Now run home and change into something more adventurous," he said. *And less alluring.* "Maybe even a bit scruffy. Suitable for climbing about. I'll do the same and meet you at the manor in an hour. You can tell me more over those pastries and that bottle of wine."

Emma slid a sideways glance to the man riding on horseback alongside her mare. In simple buckskin breeches and a plain cotton shirt, Derick seemed more . . . rugged. She liked seeing him without his cravat, the muscled column of his neck swarthy against his white collar. She noticed his lustrous black hair wasn't so precisely styled as it had been, either. It was as if every day he let go of a little more of the masquerade, became a little more like the young man she'd known.

She loved it when a plan came together. The fact that Derick was falling so neatly into her schemes further convinced Emma of the rightness of them.

Oh, she'd had a few moments of doubt when he'd turned down her invitations. And when he'd not responded to her attempted flirting. But he'd come around, hadn't he?

"What changed your mind about our picnic?"

A smile lifted the corner of Derick's mouth that she could see in profile, though he didn't look at her. "I remembered how much I loved those pastries," he said.

She resisted a grin. She'd known those were a good idea. And so was the *two* bottles of wine she'd brought. She was thrilled that he'd changed his mind, as she hadn't really looked forward to another fruitless afternoon of searching for a stranger who very well might not even be in town anymore. She'd been excited when she'd first heard of the man, hoping she could solve Molly's murder without having it be her own footman. But she'd had no luck finding the mysterious stranger, and it had frustrated her to no end. This afternoon with Derick would be a much-needed respite.

Though the cave was on Derick's lands, it was not far from the border of Wallingford Manor, which had made it an ideal play spot for them as children. The lane was overgrown now, taken over by the short-leafed, slender-stemmed primrose with its basal rosettes of pale yellow, guelder rosebushes with their little red cranberry-like berries and pretty lavender four-petaled mezereon. The flowering shrubs formed a beautiful carpet. Emma thought it almost a shame to let the horses trample upon it.

"I remember a time when this path was well worn," Emma said. "By *my* feet."

Derick turned his head to look at her then. "Yes. You always did seem to turn up at *my* favorite spot."

She laughed, and gave a little shrug. "It was the one place I could be almost guaranteed of finding you."

His deep chuckle joined hers. "You *were* quite the pest, you know."

Emma harrumphed. "As much as you grumped and complained, you were still there every single day." She aimed for a jaunty raise of her eyebrow. "I would say you wanted to be found."

Emma couldn't keep the smile from her face. Just like he'd wanted to be found then, she was certain he did now, too. She couldn't have envisioned getting him so thoroughly alone as the cave on her first try—and it was his idea. It was as if he were scripting his own seduction. On some unconscious level, Derick must want to be compromised. Because deep down, he wanted what she had on offer . . . a partnership—based on business at first, yes, but she suspected more would follow once he got accustomed to the idea—purpose, a place to belong.

Derick's expression had smoothed into one both thoughtful and intense. One that warmed her thoroughly, even though they had entered a deeper, shadier part of the forest. "Perhaps you're right," he said.

They rode in companionable silence, their horses edging closer to each other as the lane narrowed. The low canopy of trees above them grew together in this part of the forest, forming a natural tunnel, one that smelled of wild orchids and crisp, dense greenery—a heady feast for the senses.

As the shadows enclosed them, Derick's voice drifted across to her. "I know why I was always running these woods, Emma. I was trying to escape my mother." He paused and she looked over, caught by the curiosity and the . . . the empathy in his gaze. "What were *you* running from?"

Emma's stomach knotted at the unexpected question. She could tell herself she'd just wanted to be near him, a girlhood infatuation, but the lie would sound false, even to her own ears.

"Was it your father?" he asked boldly. "I remember

hearing that he was a harsh man. Demanding, with little patience for anyone."

"He was that," she admitted. "Exacting as well, and always obsessed with whatever mathematical theorem he was working on at the time. He had little left for anyone else, and he didn't suffer fools." *Or daughters.*

"You've never been a fool, Emma."

"No, but I was a disappointment, if only because of my gender. And he never let me forget it, even if he didn't say a word." She shrugged off the familiar ache. "It was worse for George, really, because he was the *son.* The man who should have been able to carry on Father's legacy. But George's mind simply doesn't work the way Father's did . . . the way mine does, and Father was always bitter about it. George had left the house before I can really remember, but I heard things growing up about the animosity between the two of them."

"Mmmm . . ." Derick said thoughtfully. "Did they ever reconcile?"

"No. George rarely came home when my mother was alive. Never, after she died. Not until he came back to take up the reins after Father's death."

"It must have been lonely for you, living in that house."

Emma's chest squeezed. She never talked about her father, having done her best to bury her feelings with him. But somehow, here in the shadows with Derick, it felt . . . freeing to voice them. "It was. I know my father wanted more children before I was born . . . another son, one who hopefully took after him. But fifteen years passed before my mother fell pregnant again, and then only with a useless girl."

"Emma . . ."

"No, I know I'm not useless," she said. "And my father eventually came around, in his own way. He recognized my talents and fostered them, but always with an overtone of . . . resentment."

"Did you resent him for *that*?" he asked.

"Yes," she whispered, and it felt good to say it. "I resented trying to live up to what he wanted and knowing that I never would. That he would always consider me inferior."

"You could never be inferior."

She huffed. "Good of you to say," she said lightly, trying to ease the moment. "I suppose that's why I always followed you around all those summers. You treated me like a pest, yes, but . . . you also treated me like an equal. You taught me things, not begrudgingly, but because I was there. With you, I could simply be . . . there."

She couldn't believe she'd admitted that to him. As the silence grew, she worried she shouldn't have.

"I'm glad, Emma," he said, finally. "I . . . think it was the same for me with you."

And then they emerged into the sunlight again, and the surreal interlude was broken. Emma took a deep breath of the clean forest air. What had he meant by that? She looked over at him, but he was staring straight ahead. Still, something had . . . changed, had grown between them there in the shade of the forest.

But the moment was gone. Rippling sounds from the creek now reached their ears, as did the warbling cry of the pudgy little dipper birds who so loved the fast-moving water.

"My God," Derick said, his voice soft with wonder. "I feel as though I've just passed through an enchanted tunnel and been transported back in time."

Emma looked over at Derick, grateful that he seemed willing to forget their recent conversation. She wished to simply enjoy this afternoon with him as they were now. It seemed he felt the same. His gaze fixed on the landscape before them, on the babbling creek that wound through the vegetation until it pooled at the mouth of the cave, some thirty yards ahead of them. He leaned forward in his saddle, as if most eager to get to their destination.

Derick turned to her then and Emma caught her breath. The afternoon sun hung in the sky behind him, casting its light around his head in golden rays. The black of his hair shone in dark relief, the rays lending a glow to his skin and casting shadows that highlighted the chiseled beauty of his features. But it was the boyish grin that had stolen the air from her lungs. Yet at the same time, her heart expanded in her chest until she felt like bursting. *This* was the Derick she knew, the Derick she'd always loved. Emma had to look away lest she blurt the words too soon. While *she* knew what was best for him, she expected it would take him some time to come to the inevitable conclusion.

"Then you're glad you let yourself be tempted?" She phrased it as a question, but it really wasn't.

His smile faded and his eyes darkened a little, as if he'd been reminded of something he'd rather not think on. When his smile returned, it didn't seem as genuine as it had a moment before. "Depends on how good those pastries are," he said, then urged his horse ahead to the cave.

Emma allowed Derick to secure her mount alongside his as she spread out the blanket and basket she'd brought. She picked the softest ground she could find that wasn't damp from the abundant rains—a soggy blanket seeped through with cold water wouldn't be at all a good spot for seduction. She had to settle for a rockier patch than she would have liked, closer to the mouth of the cave but it was still near enough to the creek to enjoy the soothing rhythm of the running water.

When she had everything arranged just so, Emma closed her eyes and raised her face to the sun, basking for a moment in the perfection of the day.

"It's more lovely than I remember."

Emma's eyes flew open at Derick's low voice, just near her ear. His emerald gaze was fixed not on the picturesque scene around them, but on *her*. Those eyes, always so sharp, that seemed to take in everything at once, roved her face, her body. They grew heavy-lidded. A feeling like gooseflesh, only hotter, skittered over Emma.

Unprepared for the intensity of the moment, outside in the brightness of day no less, Emma stammered. "It—it is." She took an involuntary step back, then stopped herself. *Quit being a ninny, Emma. Isn't this what you wanted?* Yes. Yes, it was. She took in a breath, and resolved to play this coolly, as if they were just two old friends having a picnic—at least until she got up her nerve to kiss him.

"It couldn't be more perfect," she said brightly. "Only it's a shame that it's too cool this summer to swim, as we used to."

Derick blinked, a slow dip of his lids followed by several rapid ones. He, too, took a step back. "Yes." And then he laughed, though it sounded a little forced to Emma's ear. "Although if you think I'd be so easily badgered into merman service these days, you'd be disappointed."

Emma blushed, remembering the imperious commands she used to give him. "It was only fair, given how often I had to play Lancelot." She hadn't minded so much when they were very young, but as they'd approached their teens. "When what I really wanted was to be your Guinevere."

Derick's head tilted, his eyes contemplative.

Emma felt her own eyes go wide. Dear God, had she said that last bit aloud? Damn her loose lips. She grabbed his arm and pulled him toward the picnic blanket before he could comment on her blunder. "No worries about merman service, today, however," she said. "In fact, I intend to service you."

Derick's step faltered and his muscled arm went tense beneath her hands. A strange choking sound reached her ear.

Had she said something wrong? The way Derick bit his lip as if trying mightily to keep in a guffaw or two certainly indicated she had. She thought back.

"Serve you, I mean." A wry smile twisted her lips. In her nervousness, she'd magpied the incorrect verb tense.

Laughter burst from Derick's lips, but his eyes sparked with something more than amusement. "What?" she asked, her smile twisting down a fraction. So she'd bungled a verb. Was it truly that funny?

But Derick only laughed harder, placing his hand over hers on his arm and resuming their walk to the blanket. "Nothing," he said, still snorting a bit. "Service away."

Emma left Derick to get settled on the blanket while she knelt before the basket. As she pulled out two crude cups, one of the bottles of wine, wooden plates, a round of cheese and the pastries she'd wrapped in cheesecloth to keep them warm, she was acutely aware of Derick's regard. Although she wasn't facing him, it was as if she could feel his gaze on the sensitive skin of the back of her neck. It set off a slow burn.

When she turned with her bounty, however, Derick's face was raised to the sun much as hers had been earlier. Seated on the blanket, leaning back on his hands, one long leg stretched out before him, the other bent at the knee, he . . . lounged. He seemed relaxed. At ease. And yet . . .

Emma had a sense that he could spring to full alert at any moment. Just like his ability to move so quietly that she rarely heard him before he reached her, she imagined he'd acquired the facility of constant readiness as a means to survive during his years as a spy.

Her gaze traveled over him, taking advantage of the view while his eyes were closed. There was so much about him, about the time he was away, that piqued her curiosity. Who was this man? She remembered what he'd wanted out of life as a boy, but given the much dif-

ferent life he'd led since then, what was important to
him now? What drove him? How had he changed, beyond just the raw physicality that had erased any soft
lines from his body? Beyond the natural maturity that
comes with age?

Part of her itched to pepper him with questions, to
learn all. But she had years to rediscover Derick, a lifetime. For now, it was enough for them to have an afternoon out of time.

"Your pastries, good sir."

An easy smile crossed Derick's face as he pushed off
of his hands and leaned toward her. He accepted a pastry with ill-concealed delight and Emma moved to pour
him a cup of wine.

"If these taste half as good as I remember, I shall
soon be in raptures," he said, turning the sweet so that a
corner was poised near his mouth, ready to be devoured.

The look of pleasurable anticipation on Derick's face
made every bit of her fumbling about in the kitchens
this morning worth it—even her burnt finger. She
soothed that finger with her tongue nervously, waiting to
see what he thought of her efforts.

Derick's even white teeth bit into the crust, and his
jaw moved to chew. The movement slowed, as if he were
savoring the taste in his mouth. And yet . . . if he were
savoring, why had his lips just pursed into an almost grimace? And why had his eyes widened? And why did his
hand fly up to his mouth to cover a choking cough?

"You don't like them?"

"No, I—" His words dissolved into a fit of coughing.
"I mean, yes, of course I do. They're just—different than
I remember."

Emma frowned. "You don't like them."

He choked again, frantically motioning for the cup of
wine in her hand. Emma handed it over, and he took a
great swallow. Then another.

"No," he said when he'd drained the cup. "No, I don't

like them. In fact"—a chuckle rumbled in his chest—
"I'd rather eat the mud pies with kelp filling you used to
make from the creek floor."

"But you used to love them!" she cried, dejected.
Had she gotten them wrong?

His brows waggled with an amused sort of sympathy.
"Maybe I liked them so much then because they were
filched. Ill-gotten gains always taste much better than
ones that come honestly." The look on his face told her
he was scrambling to spare her feelings.

"They should be perfect. I followed the recipe precisely." She reached out her hand. "Give me that." She
took the pastry and raised it to her lips, taking a generous bite.

"Argh." She gagged. She didn't even bother trying to
swallow. Instead, she turned and dove back into the basket, snatching a square of linen so that she could discreetly spit the offensive dessert out of her mouth. "I
must have mixed up the salt and sugar."

Derick's laughter boomed, sending a white-bibbed
dipper flying from his perch on a rock in the middle of
the creek with an indignant *zit-zit-zit*.

"What? The kitchen is not where I am most skilled.
And they do look alike," she insisted, in her own defense.

"Oh, Emma. The look on your face. Didn't you taste
them?"

She wrinkled her nose, sitting back on her heels. "I
didn't need to. I measured every ingredient twice, just to
be certain. It should be like plugging numbers into an
equation. They *should* have turned out perfectly."

"Oh, they did," he said, rising to his own knees to
reach for the bottle of wine. "Perfectly horrid." His
chuckles had become mostly silent, but they still shook
his chest in irregular spurts.

Emma couldn't help sharing in his amusement. It
was . . . infecting. She'd never been good at laughing at

herself, but somehow she wasn't able to berate herself with him looking at her so. Still, she tried. "I suppose I've spoiled your day, now, haven't I?"

He sat back on his own heels, facing her, both of them on their knees. In one hand, he still held the wine bottle, but the other reached out and cupped her cheek. She leaned her face into his palm . . . she couldn't help it.

"No, Emma," he whispered, his voice and expression gone soft and serious. "You've made it."

Chapter Fifteen

The loud growl from Emma's stomach saved him. She, of course, turned red as a guelder rose berry, likely cursing her tummy's inconvenient interruption. But for Derick, it was a godsend.

He'd nearly kissed her. Again. He'd come so close earlier, lost in some sort of damnable nostalgia, but luckily for him, she'd shied away. She hadn't been going to shy away this time, however, and he wasn't certain he could have stopped himself.

"We'll need to do something about that," he said, grateful for the chance to pull away. "Did I see a round of cheese over there?" He rose and walked over to the food arranged around the picnic basket.

"Yes," she said, moving to rise herself. "I'll just—"

"No, no, my mermaid princess." He waved her off. "Let me serve you this time."

Derick welcomed the mundane task of slicing through the large chunk of cheese, using the controlled movements to regain a handle on himself. But he could feel the grip slipping. He was tempted to just let it go. Hell and damnation, it was exhausting having to grasp so hard for it.

He had to, though. For Emma's sake. He supposed he could retreat to the castle, but he was loath to leave this place. Since he'd crossed into the valley, he'd felt . . . bathed. Coated in some magical balm he didn't understand. All he knew was that he felt a sense of peace that had eluded him for years, forever maybe. Whatever it was, he hadn't expected to find it here—not in Derbyshire, not in England. Not with Emma.

Who just might be the *noisiest* person in all Britain. Behind him, she fidgeted, rustled the blanket, sat, groaned, fidgeted some more. A grin creased his face. What on earth was she doing? When he turned back with wine and a wooden plate of cheese, she was sitting rather awkwardly. Her legs were bent at the knees, but she was twisted at the waist so that her hip and bottom were partially off of the ground. "Rocks," she said by way of explanation.

After handing her a cup and plate, he settled himself on the blanket as well, though he was careful to keep a respectable distance. He moved experimentally, but felt no rocks beneath him, only the cushion of the fabric.

"*I am* sorry about the pastries," she said after swallowing a bite of cheese. She looked so shocked, so affronted that her attempt hadn't turned out that he had to laugh all over again.

"Don't be. They were . . . memorable," he said, sipping his wine. "Besides, I find it rather relieving that you can't cook," he teased. "No one likes someone who's perfect."

"Me? Perfect?" She snorted, scooting to her left as if trying to find a comfortable, rock-less spot. She wiggled her bottom to test out a new position. He swallowed, trying not to watch. "There must have been something more in those pastries than butter, blackberries and all the wrong spices if you think something *that* deluded," she said.

"I'm quite serious," he protested, and realized that he was. Hell, when had he gone from finding Emma an annoyance to defending her virtues to the woman herself? "Emma, you are beautiful in so many ways."

She huffed, shaking her head as she looked down at the cup of wine in her lap.

Derick took another bite of cheese, hardly tasting it, so lost in thought was he. What a contradiction Emma had turned out to be. From her words and actions over the last few days, he knew that she had both a very high opinion of her abilities and a very low opinion of herself. He also knew that she placed a high value on his estimation of her.

Maybe she needed him in the same way that he needed her. Except rather than her helping him see himself as he *used* to be . . .

"I wish that you could see yourself as *I* see you," he murmured.

Her head snapped up, a frown tangling her brows. Yet along with the vulnerability he glimpsed in the amber depths of her eyes, Derick saw a spark of what? Hope? A desire to believe?

She shifted again, scooting away, twisting her legs to the other side. Whether it truly was the rocks beneath their blanket making her uncomfortable, or the sentiment behind his words, Derick made a decision.

He set down his wine and plate, stretched his legs out in front of him and extended a hand. "Come here, Emma."

When she only cocked her head and stared warily at him, he flexed his fingers in a come-hither motion and patted the ground beside him with his other hand. Though it would be risky to his control to have her so near, what he had to say was important for Emma to hear and he wanted her close, where he could look her in the eyes. And he wanted to be able to throw his arms around her if she tried to get away when it became uncomfortable for her. "King Arthur wouldn't have let Guinevere sit upon pointy rocks, and neither shall I— not when I have a softer seat to offer."

She hesitated, chewing her bottom lip between her teeth as she considered. But she rose, walked the few steps that separated them, and placed her hand in his.

Something charged flowed between them, something . . . trusting, something significant. He started to pull her down beside him when Emma shifted course and sat directly on his lap, and fiery arousal burned out everything else.

Damnation. He hadn't intended to have her *that* close. But now that she was, he couldn't just toss her off. Nor did he wish to. He could control himself . . . This moment was for her.

He settled her sideways across his legs and interlaced his fingers loosely around the outside of her hip. He couldn't resist tightening his grip, though, resting his open palms against her supple curve.

Emma tensed.

"Look at me."

She turned her head and squarely met his gaze with her amber one. Brave girl.

"Now, as I was saying. You are *beautiful*, Emma. Uh-uh—" He squeezed her in his arms when she opened her mouth to protest. She stayed silent, though she pressed her lips so tightly together he knew it must be difficult for her to.

"I hadn't expected that when I saw you again. I remembered an awkward little hoyden with eyes too big for her face," and no figure to speak of, even as a girl of fifteen, but he wouldn't say that. The fact that Emma was nodding her agreement told him she still saw herself that way. "Poor darling," he murmured. "You have no idea how desirable you are, do you?"

Her eyes squinted her disbelief, but never left his. By God, he wasn't letting her off of his lap until she was convinced. "When I first saw you again, Emma, you . . ." He struggled for the right word. "You captured me. You've grown into the kind of woman men fantasize about."

Emma snorted.

"Oh, don't doubt it." He unlaced his fingers, bringing one hand to her face. "Your lips are full, yet delicately bowed." He gently rubbed his thumb across them and they parted on a breathy intake. "They beg to be kissed."

He cupped her face more fully, his thumb continuing its foray. "Your cheekbones are high and strong, your nose pert and adorable and your eyes . . . Your eyes, Emma, swim with a thousand different thoughts, secrets, memories." He lost himself in their amber depths for a long moment before murmuring, "When a man looks into them he wants to dive in and explore. Stay a while." *Stay forever.*

Emma's breathing had gone shallow. His had too. "A man, Derick?" she whispered. "Or you?"

Oh God, me! he wanted to shout. He wanted to claim, to possess. But he couldn't. He grabbed his mental leash and yanked tight.

"As delectable as your physical charms are, however," he continued, ignoring her question, "they aren't what make you truly beautiful."

"I know," she said. "My mind does."

Derick huffed, unable to contain a half-grin at her confidence, at least in that realm. If only she believed the rest of herself worthy. "It does," he agreed. "Your brilliance is incredibly alluring. But I was talking about your soul. You're full of passion, Emma. Of *compassion.* You care about people—villagers, your brother, complete and total strangers."

His hand had moved into her hair. He brushed a stray tendril away from her brow and tucked it behind her ear. His body vibrated with need. Sexual need, for certain, but even stronger was the need to get across to her how spectacular she was, so that she believed it. Really believed it.

"That's what *truly* captured me. I see it every time I'm with you," he said, his voice low and fervent. "People admire you, Emma. Rely on you. Appreciate you. *Love* you. Can't you see that?"

"I do," Emma whispered. And she did. Her heart fluttered against the cage of her chest as if it wanted to burst from its confinement and fly free. She didn't ask him whether he was referring to "people" or himself this time. She didn't have to—she could see the answer in his eyes, feel it in the way he tenderly brushed her hair back from her face and in the hard insistence of his arousal pressing against her hip.

"Do you?" he murmured. His eyes, which usually glittered so sharply green, had dulled to the shade of the deep moss surrounding them.

She moved her arms, sent them traveling up his chest so that her hands might caress his face as lovingly as he did hers. "I do," she said again as she pulled his lips to hers.

"Emma," he groaned, sounding almost as if he were in pain. She tensed. Had she misunderstood?

But then his arms crushed her to him and his lips opened over hers.

This was perfection. Her blood sang in her veins with the mathematical precision of a Bach concerto. Her body remembered vividly the peak that she was capable of, that Derick had shown her, and she raced for it.

Only she couldn't breathe. It was as if every nerve was afire, sucking up more oxygen than she could take in to keep them burning. God, why were the sensations exponentially stronger than they were last time? Because she now knew what to expect? Or was it because her emotions were so raw from his tender words?

She didn't know. She only knew that she wanted Derick to burn like she did.

She broke from the kiss. Derick's chest heaved with harsh pants, and she smiled. He seemed to be having the same issue she was, and that knowledge filled her with a wicked satisfaction. Emma pulled herself up, using his shoulders to brace herself as she maneuvered her legs from across his lap to straddle him. She used one hand to yank at her skirts, pulling them high enough so that her legs weren't trapped as she settled herself across him.

"Ah," she groaned before she captured his lips with hers once again. Strangely, his hardness against her mons was as soothing as it was igniting—as if letting her body know that she would soon be getting everything she wanted allowed her to relax and slow down a little.

Derick's hands grabbed her bottom, pressing her tightly against him with a groan of his own. She felt him shift, his body tensing. One arm left her body and then suddenly, they rolled.

Emma clung to him, gasping against Derick's mouth. But she needn't have worried. He cradled her back, settling her gently against the blanket before settling himself between her thighs, his muscled arms now planted on either side of her. She felt deliciously pinned and she reveled in it.

Then he planted his knees astride her hips and raised himself, pulling her to a semi-reclining position between his legs. "Must. Get. This. Off," he muttered, tugging at her muslin dress.

Emma's tummy fluttered. He'd claimed he found her beautiful, but would he still if he saw her completely unclothed? In the bright sunshine?

"Emma," he growled, as if he sensed the reason for her hesitation. She swallowed and raised her arms, helping him pull the dress up over her head. His long fingers went straight for her stays, tugging at her laces until only her chemise stood between her complete nudity and his greedy gaze. Emma stared at him for a long heartbeat, then removed her chemise herself with shaking hands.

"My God, Emma," he breathed, the catch in his voice sending a pleasurable thrill that cut through even her embarrassment. "You're *better* than a fantasy."

And for a brief moment, hearing the wonder in his voice, Emma believed him.

She relaxed back against the blanket. Derick didn't move. Instead, it was as if he feasted on her with his eyes. Emma let her own eyes close so she didn't have to watch him watch her.

But he wouldn't allow that. "Open your eyes, Emma," he commanded.

She squeezed them tighter and shook her head.

Warm heat engulfed her nipple as Derick suckled her into his mouth. Emma gasped as his tongue swiped and pressed, circled and whorled. As he nibbled and sucked. She was panting with the pleasure of it when it abruptly ceased.

"Open your eyes or there will be no more of that," came his arrogant voice.

She blinked, then narrowed her gaze on his sexily smirking face. "Wretched man," she grumbled, bringing a quick, flashing grin that melted her.

But then the grin slid away, and a look of pure sensuality took its place. "I want you to see yourself as I see you, Emma. I want you to see what you do to me."

She stared for a long moment into his jewel-like eyes, and then she nodded.

His gaze left her face, but she kept hers on his. She knew he was looking at her chest, and a tingling tightness grabbed her lungs. What was he was thinking?

"Your breasts are amazing," he murmured. "High, firm."

She let out a breath. "Disproportionate for my body type," she muttered.

He frowned, just a quick flash before he palmed her in both hands. "Just right." He plumped, squeezed, his fingers and thumbs working in tandem. "See how they fill my hands perfectly?" He worked his forefingers and thumbs over her nipples, rolling, testing. "See when I touch you like this, how your blood flows to your nipples, swelling them, turning them deep rose, pebbling them like luscious berries?"

She couldn't stop herself from looking. Moisture pooled between her legs at the sight of his darker skin against the milky white of her breasts and the deep pink of her nipples as they were rolled between his fingers. Watching intensified the sensation a hundredfold.

"They make my mouth water to taste them," came his scratchy voice just before his dark head dipped and he took her between his lips.

She couldn't keep her eyes open, so strong was the sensation. But then a sharp pleasure/pain snapped her gaze to her chest. He'd nipped her! She met Derick's glittering gaze, which he narrowed in warning even as his mouth soothed the sting. She was to keep watching, or else.

When she nodded her understanding, he dropped his eyes back to his sensual task.

Every suckle, every squeeze only made her breasts feel heavier, achier. Then, he sucked her in deep, his cheeks hollowing as his mouth worked. Pleasure burst in her center—not the peak she'd reached before, but something akin to a precursor. It must be, because she kept climbing higher.

After he'd treated her other breast to the same pleasure, his mouth left her. Emma couldn't take her eyes away from her own chest, heaving, glistening with moisture from Derick's tongue, nipples tight and swollen, a deep rose now.

But Derick had moved down her body. He straddled her knees now, his hands skimming her narrow waist before flaring over her too wide hips.

"Not a word," he said, raising a brow as if he knew what she'd been thinking. "You have the hips of Venus," he murmured, his palms running over the bones and skin almost reverently. "Perfect to grip as I—"

He clamped his mouth shut on whatever he'd been

about to say, but Emma remembered his hands gripping her hips as he had before, grinding her down upon his hardness as she'd sat upon his lap and she knew what he'd been imagining. More pleasurable bursts shot through her.

She squeezed her legs together, seeking relief but only causing more tingles. She tried to open her thighs, but his knees blocked her. She raised her hips with a protesting moan.

His eyes flared. "God, Emma. Everything about you makes me burn to—" Derick moved up her body in a flash. He rubbed his clothed member in a long stroke against her as she got her legs fully opened. Molten heat shot through her body as the rough fabric of his trousers dragged against her over-sensitive skin. But as delightful as that was, she had no intention of being the only one without a stitch. She wanted him naked. Now.

She pulled at his shirt, tugging it from his waistband. "I want to see you. After all, turnabout is fair game," she murmured.

Derick shuddered, his chest heaving. "Play, Emma. Turnabout is fair play. However . . ." He looked for a moment as if he would deny her. Emma's stomach clenched. There was no way she would have that. She ran her palm over the hot skin of his stomach beneath his shirt, then boldly caressed his arousal through the fabric of his trousers, pressing her palm hard against him.

Derick's eyes closed and he gasped, pressing himself against her as if caught in something he couldn't control. Emma thrilled, knowing she did that to him. "Now, take your shirt off," she ordered, heady with the sense of power she felt all of a sudden.

Together they got the shirt over his head. "Oh my," Emma whispered as the expanse of his chest came into view.

Muscles rippled beneath his skin, not bunched or

puffy but lean, sinewy. His skin was smooth, with only a smattering of black hair dusting the surface. A thin line of hair trailed down his stomach, a dark vee that disappeared beneath the fabric of his trousers, leading to . . . Emma felt a fresh warmth of moisture between her thighs. She needed to see more, see all.

She reached for the fall of his trousers, frantic now to get them off. Derick seemed equally frantic, their fingers fumbling over each other's in their haste. Finally, the fabric was pushed down around his hips and Emma stilled as he sprang free, her eyes fixed on what she'd only been able to feel recently.

Derick kept moving, pushing the trousers down his thighs and pulling his legs and feet free, but Emma couldn't drag her eyes from his thick manhood, which jutted proudly from between his thighs.

Her center ached, an empty sort of longing, even as trepidation set in. She wanted to look her fill, and yet she couldn't wait to touch him without the barrier of cloth. She could look later.

She opened her hand on him and he stilled. Positioned above her as he was, it was easiest to run her palm along the underside of his arousal. She gave him a long stroke, pressing upward with her palm. "You're like hot satin against my skin," she marveled, squeezing him, testing him, amazed at the dichotomy of hard and soft that rested heavy against the inner skin of her wrist.

She looked up at Derick. His head was leaned back, a look that could be pain but could also be pleasure riding his face. His eyes were closed.

"Not fair play," she said, squeezing his shaft in a quick, sharp grip much as he'd nipped her for the same crime.

His eyes flew open, and the hot look he gave her strangled the air in her chest. He'd liked that. She squeezed him again—

"Enough," Derick growled, grabbing her wrist. He

lifted her arm away, maneuvering it above her body while he laid her back against the blanket. Then he pinned her wrist above her head.

Emma had but a moment to feel any worry before his mouth crashed down upon hers. His tongue breached her lips boldly and she sucked him in with a keening moan. She automatically raised her other arm to rest next to its sister. The movement eased the heavy ache in her breasts a little, lifting them high.

Derick nudged her legs wide with his knees and the crisp hair of his thighs rubbed against her skin as he settled himself once again between her thighs, this time with nothing separating them.

Emma vaguely felt the pressure of his finger as it entered her, was barely aware when he added another. She was too awash in the feeling of having her naked body covered entirely by his—hot skin and coarse hair, hard muscles moving against her softer ones, her aching breasts smashed deliciously against his chest, his intimate heat insistent against her folds—

Derick flexed his hips and pressed into her. Not far, but enough to center every single one of her nerves on the spot. Her skin burned, stretched and yet somehow ached for more.

His other hand skimmed up her body, up her arm until his fingers entangled themselves in hers. He released her wrist with his opposite hand and did the same, still pinning her but palm to palm now. Hands entwined intimately.

He broke their kiss, and pulled his face back from hers.

"Look at me now, Emma."

She did. His eyes glittered with heat as he fought for breath, turned dark with satisfaction. He flexed his hips again.

But this time he didn't stop. His jaw clenched tight as he filled her, stretched her. Emma couldn't breathe at all, every bit of his intimate invasion overwhelming. An odd pressure stretched, then burst with a pinch and suddenly he slid all the way in, his pelvis bumping against her in a way that set off trembling little quakes of sensation.

She kept her eyes on his the entire time. Neither one of them seemed to be able to look away. Even when he began moving. He pulled himself from her, a tugging glide that both relieved and left her feeling empty. She moaned at the loss, pulling her knees up to try to keep him with her.

He surged forward again, hot, huge, filling her with force and purpose. He seemed to go even deeper than before now that her knees were raised higher. He stroked again. Again. Again. Steady, even thrusts that drove her mad. She sensed there was more, could be more. She *craved* more as the tightness within her grew. And still he kept his thrusts relentlessly controlled. Again. Again. Again.

All the while, she held his gaze. She longed to touch him, but she couldn't with her hands pinned by his. So she squeezed him between her thighs as tightly as she could, spurring him forward with her heels to his buttocks.

A groan ripped from Derick's throat and he slammed into her. He dropped his head, forehead to hers and bucked again.

"Yes!" she cried out as his rhythm devolved into irregular, jarring surges. And suddenly one of her hands was free as he sent his between them, bringing his thumb against her in circling rubs. She threw her arm around his neck, holding him tightly to her as he pounded into her—holding him to her heart, wishing they could be even closer. She closed her eyes, now able to focus only on the fire licking her body.

And then she flew, clenching and grabbing at him as if he were the only anchor that kept her lifeline tied to the earth. Her body hummed, her ears rang—she heard his harsh shouts of pleasure as if they were somewhere far below her, though in truth he was above her. She felt him shudder between her thighs, felt a hot gush of warmth within her even as she floated . . . floated . . . floated back down to where, in actuality, she lay beneath him. Surreal. Perfect.

Emma gradually became aware of Derick's heavy weight upon her. He'd released her other hand, his head had dropped atop her shoulder, and his hot breath rushed against the side of her neck. She brought her other arm around him now, cradling him to her much as she still cradled him between her thighs.

She opened her eyes, almost surprised by the blue sky above her. Sounds and sights of the forest gradually filtered back into her consciousness—birds chirping, the creek gurgling, the bursts of color that stood out from the greenery. "Dear me," she mused with a sudden bit of humor, "deflowered amidst the wildflowers. For shame."

But rather than shame, she was filled with a peace and happiness unlike any she'd ever known. A euphoria almost. Derick loved her. Oh, he hadn't said the words, but he'd shown her with other words, with his body.

Emma hugged him tighter to her. How many times had she sat in this very spot, dreaming of this moment? Well, not this moment exactly, because she hadn't had the worldly knowledge to imagine anything *close* to what had just happened between them. But dreaming of Derick and herself, together. In love.

Emma idly stroked her fingers through his hair. He stirred. He lay against her for a moment, then shifted his weight, moving his hands to brace himself above her. Emma smiled as his face rose above hers, but it froze upon her lips as she registered his pale complexion, his features twisted with regret.

"Oh, hell. That was a mistake."

Chapter Sixteen

Emma flinched, her head falling back and her eyes widening with shock, much as if he'd slapped her. And damnation, he may as well have.

"Oh, Emma." His voice sounded raw to his ears, yet slurred with the languid satiation that battled with his self-disgust and with a bone-deep fear he could not name. "I'm so sorry. I didn't mean that."

Hell. *She* was the one who blurted her deepest thoughts, not he. He was supposed to be in control of himself—his actions, his emotions, his words. And yet, lying here with Emma, still buried between her sweet thighs with her satiny skin surrounding him, with her lavender scent mixed with the heady smell of sex and woman still arousing him, he was in control of nothing.

A tremor passed through him. Damnation, he was shaken to his core. Sex had never been like that for him. Never once had he so completely lost himself in another person. He wondered vaguely if he'd ever find his way back—if he even wanted to.

Her hands left him slowly. She slid her arms under his where he'd propped himself above her, and crossed them over her breasts, putting a barrier between them that squeezed something within him.

"Didn't mean the words, Derick?" Emma's voice sounded small, yet surprisingly strong. "Or didn't mean to make love to me?"

Gooseflesh popped over his skin, cold now in the absence of her warmth. He felt her withdrawing from him, even though they were still intimately joined. With one slip of the tongue, he threatened to undo every bit of the self-worth he'd been trying to build up in her. Well, that and one monumentally foolish slip of control.

"Emma . . ." He didn't want to answer her. Didn't want to see the pain his words would cause, whether he told the whole truth or just part of it.

Her lower lip trembled, that lip which he'd so recently praised. Had taken between his teeth and nipped, suckled, and soothed. Looking down at her now, his chest ached. He'd known Emma was vulnerable to him—and by joining with her, he'd made her even more so, heartless cad that he was. All because he'd lost his damned head, because he'd been unable to resist *her*, been unable to stop himself—a reality he couldn't fathom, yet it was there just the same, looming with unknown consequences he wasn't prepared to face.

Still, he owed her the truth, even if it wouldn't make things better for her. In the short run, that was. In the long run, it was for the best. He heaved a great breath.

"Neither. I didn't mean the words, but I shouldn't have . . ." Derick swallowed. He couldn't bring himself to say "used you so." That was too callous and cold for what had flared between them. In his many years as a spy, he *had* used countless women—mostly for the secrets they possessed, though sometimes there was pleasure in it, too. He had been used for the same just as many times. But Emma was as different from those women as he was from a blue-blooded Englishman.

However, neither could he utter the words "made

love to you," the idea too foreign and disturbing for him to countenance. "I shouldn't have touched you," he finally said.

Emma's chest hitched and then she shoved him, hard, successfully dislodging him. She scrambled from beneath him, coming to her feet while he was still catching his balance. He rose to his knees as Emma snatched her chemise and dress from the blanket where he'd tossed them. She yanked them over her head in harsh, jerky motions, forgoing the stays.

"That doesn't add up, Derick," she said as her head popped through the neckline of her bodice. She shoved her arms through the armholes next. "If you believe you shouldn't have *touched* me, then you *did* mean the words." She smoothed out her skirts, her amber glare turning watery. "You just didn't mean for me to hear them."

Her voice broke on that last, and a single tear slipped from her eye. That silent trail of moisture cleaved him in two. Derick dropped his head, unable to look at her pain. His eyes sought the blanket, the green, blue and yellow plaid blurring as he knelt naked before her, unsure what to say, unable to move, damning himself for a coward.

In all of his encounters over the years, he'd never stayed to see this part. He'd always left women happy, departing their beds with glib lies upon his lips — whatever he'd known they wanted to hear. Had he hurt any of the women he'd screwed for king and country? He must have, at least a few of them. But he had been gone long before he'd have known it.

Blessedly, Emma was the one to walk away. When he looked up, she had turned her back on him and seemed to be struggling with her boots. Though he heard no sobs, her shoulders were shaking and he was certain that not all of it was due to her efforts to dress.

He rose to his feet and gathered his own clothing,

slipping his trousers, shirt and boots on as he'd done a hundred times after sex. And yet, even after every stitch of clothing was perfectly righted, he still felt naked. Exposed. Bare as he had never been before in his life.

When he looked again to Emma, she had straightened, though her back was still to him. She looked so stiff and so . . . small. Smaller than her usual compact stature, as if she'd withdrawn into herself. Damn it, this wasn't her fault. He crossed the distance between them, stopping silently behind her. He couldn't let her think . . . What? He didn't know, he only knew he couldn't allow her to blame herself. To think it was she who was lacking. "Emma, I —"

She turned to face him then, her cheeks dry now, though her eyes were lined with red and her nose had gone puffy. "You didn't mean any of it, did you?" Her voice held a flat, resigned note that ripped at him.

Then her face crumpled and she fisted her hand. "Why would you *say* all those things?" she cried, striking him in the chest. He welcomed the sharp pain, would gladly stand and let her whale upon him until her strength gave out. "Why would you try to make me believe I was beautiful? That you cared for me?"

Each word flayed him worse than the lashes he'd received in the early days of his imprisonment by the French. He knew they flayed her, too.

"Ah, Emma," he groaned and reached for her. He crushed her to him, perhaps meaning to comfort her, perhaps meaning to alleviate his own guilt and pain. He buried his nose in her hair, breathing in her scent — breathing in his own scent upon her, and a primitive longing like he'd never experienced permeated every inch of him. "I meant all of it," he whispered.

The truth of those words pierced Derick. He couldn't deny them. He could blame his lack of control until Napoleon stopped lusting to rule the world — even from exile — but he would be lying to himself. He wouldn't have taken her if deep down, some part of him hadn't wanted Emma more than he'd wanted anything in his life. He couldn't let her believe otherwise, even if there was no hope of a future for them.

He pulled back and cupped her face. "Every word, every kiss, every touch."

Emma's eyebrows dipped, the corners of her lips quivered, as if they couldn't decide whether to frown or tip up in a tremulous smile.

"Which is why you should hate me." He might be able to admit to himself that he wanted her, but if she knew who he truly was, what he'd done, what he might yet still have to do . . .

"Hate you?"

"You have every right," he pointed out, absently rubbing a thumb along her cheekbone. "I took your innocence, Emma. It can't be undone. And I can offer you nothing in return." She needed to hear at least that much of the truth, mission be damned. "Nothing that you'd want."

Emma stilled and pulled away from his embrace. And though he'd expected that reaction, hoped for it and worse, the loss still ached. She didn't look at him, instead stared at some point behind his shoulder, rubbing her thumb against her fingers.

She looked him directly in the eye. "You didn't take my innocence, Derick. I gave it to you."

"Gave it to me . . ." he repeated.

"Planned it, even. Warm pastries . . ." She winced, followed that with an endearingly wry grin. "Though admittedly, those didn't have the effect I'd hoped. *Two* bottles of wine," she added, holding up the corresponding number of fingers. "A secluded picnic . . ."

Derick gaped. *Planned it, even.* He knew she'd been trying to entice him, but he hadn't expected such aggressive pursuit. He should have, though—after all, Emma was nothing if not tenacious. Still, he should have stopped her. He wouldn't have her believing the fault lay with anyone but him.

"Well, if that's true, you gave it under false pretenses," he said. "I know you'd hoped I'd come to live in Derbyshire, that we'd become partners initially, more eventually."

Her lip quivered again . . . just minutely, but he saw. She didn't deny it.

"But that will never happen, Emma," he informed her gently. "It can't. Therefore I never should have taken . . . something of such value from you. Something that wasn't mine to take. *That* is why I said what I did, not because I regretted one second in your arms. *That* is why you should hate me. Because even though I can give you nothing, I took you anyway."

Her chest rose and fell on a deep sigh. "I'm not a child, Derick. I'm nine and twenty—my virginity a long ago devalued commodity, worth nothing save to the man I chose to give it to." She stepped toward him, laying her open palm against his chest, where it seemed to burn his skin, even through the cambric. "And that man is you. It has *always* been you."

Derick stopped breathing. He clapped his hand over hers, pressing it harder to his chest. "Emma." He swallowed, struck by a fierce possessiveness that wasn't his right to feel. He wished to hell he were worthy of her, but he was so far from it. "You undo me," he whispered.

She placed her other hand upon their joined ones, her skin warm and soft on either side of his hand now. Her eyes locked with his. "You undo me, as well." She shifted on her feet, her tongue coming out to wet her lips. "You say you can offer me nothing that I want. But what if all I want is you?"

Derick pulled his hand from between hers. "Emma, you don't want me." He turned from her. "You want the boy I once was. The man you *think* I am. You know nothing of the man I truly am—if you did . . ."

She wouldn't let him turn away. She followed, placing herself squarely in front of him. "If I did, I would still want you." She reached out and grabbed his hand, pulling it to her own heart this time.

A part of Derick longed to believe. Believe that in spite of everything he'd done, people he'd hurt, people he'd sent to their deaths—either by his own hand or by the information he gathered about them—that he deserved the love of someone like Emma. But he didn't. His soul was black, his blood even blacker, and he could change neither.

And that didn't even take into consideration the fact that he was leaving England behind as soon as this mission was complete. Emma would never consider leaving her home for the wilds of America. Nor would he wish her to.

"No, Emma," he said tenderly. "You wouldn't." He could see she didn't believe him. The hope in her eyes, the earnest press of her lips, the tremble in her hand where she still held his against her told him so.

If he wasn't already going to burn in hell for all he'd done in his life, he surely would now for tainting such an innocent. Such an angel. And for breaking her heart, for disillusioning her—which was what he was about to do. He consoled himself with the knowledge that it was the kindest thing he could do for her.

"All right, Emma. I'll tell you what kind of man I am, and then we'll see how you feel."

A shiver went through Emma at the ominous tone in Derick's voice. And yet relief coursed through her as well. She'd been shocked when he'd shown such remorse after their lovemaking. Hurt, angry, not to mention rejected.

But then she'd seen the pain in his glittering eyes, had heard it in his broken voice and knew it wasn't she he was rejecting. There was something else behind his renunciation. So she'd suppressed her own pain and tried to think logically about it.

Sometimes when working with complex equations, it was necessary for her to break the components down, remove them if she had to, solve them one by one and then put them back together again. She'd decided to try that method here.

He'd admitted he wanted her, which had gone a long way toward assuaging her feelings—one part solved. She could see his guilt over the fact that she'd been an innocent, so she'd done her best to remove that from the equation by telling him she'd intended to give herself to him—another part solved. Now, she needed to get at what really held him back from her and see what she could do to solve that.

Derick tugged his hand away and walked over to the spread blanket. He picked it up and shook it out, then carried it a little farther up the hill, away from the creek. He doubled it over, then quartered it before placing it on the ground in front of a massive sessile oak, so large that the span of her arms wouldn't reach around a quarter of its trunk if she tried to hug it. Derick motioned for her to join him.

When she reached him, he held out a hand. Emma placed hers in his, amazed at the jolt even that simple touch sent through her. She lowered herself to the blanket, using his grip as support until she was settled.

The corner of his lip curled up. "No rocks this time, my little mermaid princess?"

She smiled in return, though she felt her cheeks pinkening as she remembered throwing herself into his lap, and everything that had happened after. But she couldn't regret it. "No. Nor any peas, for that matter."

Derick's mouth spread into a half grin then. But when he was seated beside her, with his back leaned up against the trunk, feet flat on the ground, legs bent with his hands resting on his knees, the smile faded from his face.

Emma scooted herself until she was perpendicular to him, near his thigh. She crossed her own legs, folding them toward her body and hooking them at the ankles tailor style. She leaned toward him, just slightly.

Derick turned his head to look at her then. He seemed to stare at her face for an endless moment. "You must realize, Emma, that I'm no saint. I've done things . . ." He turned his face forward, and his hands stretched out, though his palms remained on his knees. His jaw tightened and his face became hard, wiping away the man she knew and showing her someone else entirely. Emma held her breath.

"As an agent for the government, my superiors found I had a knack for ferreting out secrets. Over the years, it became my primary mission to uncover traitors, and other double agents like myself." He slid a glance at her. "Occasionally I was called upon to terminate them . . . and those who'd divulged England's secrets."

Emma pressed her lips tightly together, doing her best to show no reaction. She'd expected something like this—after all, she knew that true spy work would be ugly, not a childlike game of cloak and dagger.

"I've taken lives," he said more loudly, as if she hadn't understood. When she said nothing, he returned his gaze to his outstretched hands. "By my own hand. Men's lives, women's lives. So many that I've lost count."

Emma swallowed. Somehow she knew from the bleak look on his face, from the way he stared at his hands, that his words weren't completely true. He remembered every one.

She turned her gaze to his hands as well. Lean, elegant, long-fingered. Strong hands. She realized her own palms had gone clammy and her heart had sped up. Even though she'd known he would say something like that, the reality of knowing that the hands that had touched her so tenderly, that had brought her such pleasure, had also snuffed out life—lives—shot a cold shiver through her.

Would she ever be able to look at him the same?

Emma swallowed again, trying to wet her dry throat. "You did what you had to do. It was war, Derick. And those . . . people were betraying our country. It's not as if you took innocent lives."

The ghost of an expression that wasn't quite a smile flitted over his face, which was still in profile. "Most likely not."

"M-most likely?" she asked, bewildered.

He looked at her then. "In the majority of cases, the evidence was irrefutable. But there were times, in the field, when things weren't so clear. When I had to go with only what knowledge I had and with my gut. With instinct and probabilities."

"But probabilities are just that," she said, shocked. She wasn't one to rely on instinct, so she couldn't speak to that, but as a mathematician she understood probabilities. And knew they weren't always accurate.

"Just so," he said grimly. "You're appalled now, aren't you?"

"I . . ." Emma gathered her scattered thoughts. "No, I'm just taken aback." The more Derick spoke about his past, the paler his complexion had grown. Brackets had appeared around his lips, which had thinned. He clearly suffered over things he'd done—most likely more than he'd told her, or might ever tell her. Only a good man would agonize so. She knew in her heart Derick hadn't taken anyone's life lightly.

She reached a hand out and placed it on his forearm, squeezing gently. Muscle flexed beneath her fingertips, rippled as if seething emotion roiled beneath his skin. "I can't imagine having to make such a decision. Having to carry out such an act. But I am certain that the things you did saved British lives, and if you think I would condemn you for that—that I wouldn't want you because of it, you are wrong."

Derick let out a harsh breath, his shoulders slumping,

his gaze sliding to where her hand rested upon his arm in support. "I can see I shall have to tell you more."

Emma involuntarily squeezed him harder. She wasn't sure she wanted to hear more. But his words confirmed her suspicion that he was trying to drive her away. She firmed her jaw as she released his arm. Well, she would hear anything he had to say, but nothing would sway her.

"Most spies, the best ones anyway, are the ones who don't stand out in any way. Average height, average build, no distinguishing features," he said. "People who can slip in and out of places unnoticed. Who are forgettable."

"Then you must have been terrible at it," Emma said, only halfway joking. If ever there was a less average-looking person, it was Derick. His superior height alone made him stand out in a crowd, and that was before you took into account his thick black hair, his stunningly perfect features and his arresting emerald eyes. She couldn't imagine anyone, male or female, who would forget seeing him.

A dark smile touched his lips. "No, I was a very good spy. I was just given a different type of mission than most." He scrubbed a hand over his face then, as if he didn't wish to tell her the rest.

"I told you that the French noticed me because my heritage was obvious, and because of my position as heir to a British viscountcy. That was true. Part and parcel with that was my ability to move in and out of very elite circles throughout Europe. Where some of their other operatives might have to spend weeks working their way into a household as a servant or such, I would be welcomed right in because of my wealth and status. An agent in plain sight, one no one would expect."

"That makes perfect sense," Emma said, wondering what could possibly be so terrible about that.

"Yes, well, what else made perfect sense was to use the other thing people notice about me."

Emma waited for him to elaborate, tapping on her thigh with her fingers.

Derick cocked a raven brow and gave her a sardonic smile. "What most *women* notice about me, then."

"Oh!" Emma exclaimed, understanding practically smacking her in the forehead, much as it did when she'd stared at an equation so long that she missed the obvious answer.

"I see you begin to comprehend," Derick murmured. "My role was that of the dissipated young rake, suffering from ennui, sleeping my way through the ballrooms of Europe. A life of gambling and drinking, with a different woman in my bed every night. Some I seduced because they actually had secrets I was commanded to get from them—their own or those of someone close to them. Some I took to my bed just to maintain the facade."

Emma opened her mouth, but could think of nothing to say. Derick had . . . slept with women all throughout Europe for their country? What's more— "You lived that way for *thirteen* years?"

"More like ten—ten and a half," he said. "I didn't start truly spying for either country until '04, and there wasn't much need for that kind of . . . activity after Waterloo."

A different woman in my bed every night. For ten and a half years? Emma struggled with the idea of that, her mind automatically extrapolating. Even if he exaggerated, even if it was a different woman in his bed every *month*, that would be a hundred and twenty-six different women. A different woman every week? Five hundred and forty-six women. A different woman every night?

"That's three thousand eight hundred and thirty-two women! Thirty-four if I count leap years." Emma felt the blood drain from her cheeks. For the first time in her life, she wished she didn't know how to multiply.

His lips quirked and a peculiar light lit his emerald eyes. "I may have overembellished a tad." He snorted with grim amusement. "Still, the point is the same. What think you now, Emma?"

What did she think? She thought "a tad" was not a very precise number. "How could you have done what—what we just did with so many different women?" Emma scrambled to her feet, unable to sit so close to him. She walked a few paces away, her back to Derick.

She could never imagine allowing another man to touch her the way he had touched her. Could never dream of holding another man close to her heart as she had held him. What she'd felt when he'd been moving within her had been profound, deeply personal. And yet to him, she had been just one of dozens? Emma's stomach roiled.

"I've succeeded in shocking you." Derick's breath brushed past her ear. She whirled to find him standing behind her. Emma cursed his damnably silent spy footsteps. "But have I succeeded in convincing you that I am not the man you want?"

No, her heart cried even as her mind rebelled. "I . . . I don't know," she said. "I don't understand any of this." She looked at him standing there before her, so handsome. A thick lock of his black hair brushed his forehead, hair she'd so very recently run her fingers through with tenderness. At his Lothario lips that she'd kissed with such earnest, innocent passion. How many other women had done the same, and likely better than she had? Had any of those women loved him, as she did? And more importantly . . . "Didn't any of them mean anything to you?"

Derick's face went oddly still, blank in a way she'd never seen as he stared somewhere past her shoulder. "No, Emma," he said finally, his gaze returning to her. "Sex with them was a means to an end, a tool of my profession, a way to get what I needed from them, be that information or continuation of my cover."

"And with me?" Emma was amazed her voice didn't wobble, so much did she fear the answer.

Something blazed within Derick's green eyes and a look she could only describe as two parts stricken and one part longing flashed over his face. The sight stilled her heart, which then pounded doubly hard and fast in an effort to get back into rhythm.

He opened his mouth. His throat worked almost violently, but no sound emerged. His shoulders dropped, as if in defeat. "Emma," he said hoarsely. "I—"

"Miss Wallllliiiiiiiingford?"

Emma startled at the exploratory shout of her name, coming from somewhere behind them. She jerked toward the sound. Someone was looking for her? She could see no one. Yet.

"Miss Waaaaaaaaallingford?" Closer now. Panic squeezed her throat as her hands flew to her tousled hair. She looked down at her rumpled dress. Fig! She wasn't even wearing her stays.

Derick stepped protectively in front of her, his head turned toward the voice as well. "Grab your things and run into the cave. Right yourself as best you can." When she stayed frozen in her spot, he barked, "Go!"

"Right." Emma hurried toward the mouth of the cave, stopping once to retrieve her stays from the ground, and again to grab the small bag still tied to her saddle.

She squinted her eyes, trying to adjust to the darkness after walking out of the fading sunlight. Being alone was a relief, but the chilly damp of the cave did little to cool her agitation.

She struggled with so many feelings at once. Anger, certainly. Confusion. Desire. Disgust. Shame. Love. They flew at her, bombarded and overwhelmed her, much as the bats that had once swarmed her when she'd disturbed them in this very cave as a girl.

The overriding emotion was pity, though—for him or

for herself, she wasn't sure. Maybe both. Emma's groan echoed off of the cave walls as she fought her tears and her uncooperative stays.

What had Derick been about to say?

Would it have mattered? *Could it matter?* She didn't know.

"—just over in the cave, sketching fossils or some such thing." Derick's voice floated to her, reminding her that she must hurry.

She dug in the little bag, retrieved her brush and started pulling it through her hair. Her coiffure had gotten so disturbed during their kisses in her study the other day, she'd had to sneak to her rooms. So when she'd decided to seduce Derick on their picnic, she'd come prepared to repair her appearance should she succeed.

The brush stilled and an ache welled in her chest. Well, she had succeeded all right. But it hadn't turned out a bit like she'd wanted, had it?

"Let me just see what's keeping her." Derick's voice was clearer now, closer.

She returned the brush to her bag with shaking hands and wound her long hair, twisting it round and round before tying it in a knot that rested against the back of her neck. A simple style that people were accustomed to seeing on her. She sniffed, fanned her cheeks and pasted on a smile that felt horribly brittle on her face. She only hoped it hid the tumult of other things she was feeling. She walked to the entrance and affected an easy stroll, hoping to preserve her reputation at least.

"You really should come see these, Aveline," she called out as she exited the mouth of the cave. "The sea lilies are particularly well preserved . . ." She let her words drift off and feigned surprise when she noticed their visitor. "John Coachman? What brings you here?" Her stomach knotted with actual fear—why had a servant been sent to find her? Unless— "Is everything all right with George?"

"Yes, miss." The servant's head bobbed and Emma started to breathe again. "But ye've got to come back to the manor now. They've found a dead man in the woods."

Chapter Seventeen

Derick paced impatiently in the back kitchens of Wallingford Manor, waiting for Emma to change her clothing. Shouts and the clinks and clanks of metal and wood rang through the open back door as out in the stable yard, men gathered the cart, lanterns, ropes and tools that Emma had ordered before dashing upstairs. Given that the sun had been fading when John Coachman had found them, they would be conducting this recovery in nearly full dark.

Hurried footsteps came from behind him. Derick turned as Emma burst into the room, dressed once again in a plain, colorless frock. The mere sight of her, even in the drabbest of garb, sent lust rocketing through him. Over the past days, he'd become accustomed to the fierce desire that gripped him every time he saw her. But now that he'd actually tasted her fully? It twisted within him in exquisite torture. Damnation. How could he live without having her again?

Bitter regret burned in his gut. He'd made certain that would never happen, hadn't he? Why couldn't he have just kept his fool mouth shut and enjoyed the strange magic he'd known in her arms for as long as he could have held on to it?

Derick released a tight breath. He knew why. Because Emma deserved more than a few days' romp in the bed sheets. But knowing it was for her own good didn't make the reality taste any less like ash in his mouth.

"Almost ready," she said as she shuffled past him into a cloakroom, without meeting his eyes. She hadn't looked at him once during their trip back to Wallingford Manor. Had, in fact, kept John Coachman between them the entire way. She'd tried to be subtle about it, but he'd known.

Thank God John Coachman's call had interrupted them when it had. He'd been perilously close to breaking down and begging Emma for . . . what? Forgiveness? Absolution? Derick scoffed. Only one of those was hers to give, and at any rate, it wouldn't change anything.

The sooner he left for America, the better.

The sense of relief that usually accompanied the thought of his impending escape didn't come. Instead, an insidious longing crept into his chest, a desire to stay with Emma, to let her love him. A desire for something that could never be.

When Emma emerged, she'd been swallowed by another giant greatcoat. Not the one she'd worn that first night—indeed, this one might be even larger. Derick glanced down at her feet, frowning at the oversized boots, which were caked with dried mud. "Do you not own your own boots, Emma?" Before he left Derbyshire, he was going to have at least three styles of coats with matching boots made up for her.

She still wouldn't look at him. Instead, she gestured absently toward the cloakroom. "I do. Somewhere in there. But in an emergency, it's quicker just to grab what's nearest." She'd almost reached the back door when he snagged her elbow, pulling her up short.

She gasped at his touch. She must have felt the same charge he did. She turned and finally looked at him. Caught in her intense, wounded gaze, Derick felt shame ooze over him. Confusion swam alongside the hurt in her golden eyes. Words of contrition, of supplication, of remorse hovered on his tongue. However, all he said was, "The man is dead, Emma. He can wait for you to find some proper-fitting boots."

She looked about to argue, but Derick cut her off. "I won't have you tripping in the dark and breaking your pretty neck," he murmured.

Emma shook her head, but disappeared back into the cloakroom.

Fabrics rustled and a series of thuds echoed from the doorway before she reemerged, wearing a somewhat shorter coat and horribly mismatched boots. Derick rolled his eyes. At least they fit properly.

"I don't need a keeper, Derick. And as you've made it clear you won't be a suitable partner, I don't understand why you're still here," she said, her voice tight. "I am more than capable of handling this on my own. Just go home."

Inside, he ached that he'd caused such a rift between them, but outwardly, all he did was raise an eyebrow. There was no way he was staying behind, and she may as well accept it.

Emma turned and left in a huff. He was glad of it. He'd rather have her angry with him than confused and hurt. When he left England, she'd get over anger faster than she would a broken heart. He followed her outside.

Emma rode on the cart next to her driver as they made their way into the forest, with Derick alongside on his charger. Besides John Coachman, the stable master and three other able-bodied men joined their group, including the hunter from the village who'd found the remains.

The sun had dipped below the western horizon, though

a shadow of light remained. Only the snorting of horses, the creaking of the cart and the snapping of rolled-over twigs filled the air.

Derick scanned the landscape, easily seeing the trail of tramped-down grass the hunter had made before his gruesome discovery, as well as his hasty track out. The paths were closing in on one another—they must be getting close.

He wondered if the body they were going to recover could be that of Farnsworth. Emma's report of a drifter had given him pause, but many times in the past week, Derick had wondered if the reason the agent had failed to make contact was that he'd met with a foul end. If that were the case, Derick would know that his mother had had an accomplice who was still here in upper Derbyshire. And if this body wasn't that of Farnsworth, maybe it was time to move on. Without knowing exactly what evidence Farnsworth had uncovered, he had no proof of anything.

"Not far now," came the man's shaken voice a few moments later, but Derick didn't need to be told. The cloying rotten/sweet smell of death hit them like a wall, permeating the air and hovering like a noxious cloud.

"Just there," the hunter croaked, pointing a few yards ahead with the hand that wasn't shielding his nose.

Derick reined in his mount, and his rioting senses. He vaulted off the horse and tied him to the cart. Emma, he noticed, had slipped down from the box and was busy gathering a lantern and a small bag that she'd brought. He was relieved to see that her wounded look was gone, replaced with the efficiency she normally exhibited.

"Gentlemen." She motioned to the rather green-looking men hanging back from the cart as if they wished to slink into the darkness falling behind them. "Each of you grab a lantern and form a perimeter of light around the man. I'd say a circumference of twenty-eight feet would do nicely." She turned and dug into her satchel, leaving the men scratching their heads.

When she realized they hadn't moved, a wry expression stole over her face. "My apologies. That would be a
circle with approximately three yards in diameter,
please."

She went back to her digging, pulling out a pair of
worn gloves, a polished stick that resembled nothing
more than a wand, and a dark scarf, which she proceeded
to tie around her nose and mouth.

While she prepared herself, Derick discreetly directed the still-confused men to stand cross points from
each other at the correct distance, pretending not to notice when one of them retched into the bushes.

Derick stepped into the circle of light and looked
down at the remains. His first thought was that there
wasn't much left of the man—insects and carrion animals had done their worst. His second was that while
this very well *could* be Farnsworth, he might not be able
to tell, given the amount of damage to the corpse. Most
of one arm and both lower extremities were missing,
likely dragged off by hungry beasts. And there were no
personal belongings around the body to speak of.

"You seem rather prepared," he commented as
Emma came alongside him, looking more like a bandit
than a gentle lady. She gave him a withering glance, and
he thought she might ignore him. He couldn't blame her
for reverting to how she'd treated him when he'd first
arrived back in upper Derbyshire. Not after the way he'd
hurt her today.

Then she sighed, the bottom edge of her scarf fluttering with her breath.

"Thn-in-th—" came her muffled voice. She reached
up and pulled the scarf down past her chin. "This isn't
the first dead person I've encountered, you know." She
pulled a leather work glove onto one hand, flexing her
fingers before repeating with the other hand. "Besides, I
got the idea to keep a bag like this at the ready from one
of the magistrates that I correspond with. Although, I

think I am going to have to write back and recommend he add some sort of ointment laced with peppermint or menthol to block the nose."

Derick thought that would be a fine idea indeed.

She pulled her scarf back up and stepped closer to the body, squatting down beside it. Derick hung back, letting Emma take the lead. She gingerly used her stick to prod and poke or lift as she made her examination. He wasn't certain what she thought she'd be able to tell, given what little she had to work with.

She stood after a few moments, stretching her back and shoulders. She tugged the scarf back down. "I see nothing that indicates how the man died," she said, apparently deciding that since Derick had insisted upon coming, she may as well include him. "Of course, even without so much of him carried off by animals, it would be hard to tell. But I would guess he's been out here around three weeks."

Derick glanced at the body dubiously. While he had more experience in death than he would like to admit, he'd never seen this part of it. "How can you be certain? It looks more like months' worth of decay." And if it *were* months' worth, the body couldn't be that of Farnsworth.

"Yes, well, it's been very wet of late, which would accelerate the process. Not to mention the insect and animal activity," she said. "But, his teeth and nails on the one hand we have are just beginning to loosen, which indicates three to four weeks."

He didn't even want to know how she knew that. His expression must have indicated he did, however, because Emma said, "I read a lot."

And retains it all, he remembered. Still. "What on earth have you been reading where you would learn something like *that*?"

She shrugged. "There are several volumes that detail what coroners should look for when investigating murders and otherwise suspicious deaths. Farr's *Elements of Medical Jurisprudence* comes to mind. Although I must say I've found it largely imperfect and in some places, not even logical." She wiped her stick clean with a cloth and placed it back into her bag. "However, George Edward Male's *Epitome of Juridical or Forensic Medicine* was published just last year, and it's fascinatingly helpful."

"As are you," he murmured before he even thought about the words. Emma's eyes flew to his and she frowned. Derick cleared his throat and sought to cover his gaffe. "You know, Emma, your gifts are wasted here in the country. Have you ever considered moving? Say to"—*New York*—"London, or some other large city, where your knowledge could be put to better use solving crimes?"

Good Christ, where had *that* thought sprung from? Had a little sex after two years of celibacy addled his brain?

"I don't want to leave Derbyshire," she said. "My brother needs me and it's peaceful and lovely here. It's my home. Besides, I don't want to solve crimes, though I do so out of necessity on occasion. I want to prevent them. The best way I, as a woman, can do *that* is to complete my study of moral statistics and find a peer willing to present it to Parliament in my stead."

"Of course," Derick said, still shaken by the radical leap his mind had made and feeling guilty that he couldn't be that man for her when he knew she'd been hoping he would. He couldn't stay in England, pretending to be a nobleman when he knew he was not.

Nor could he ask Emma to come to America with him. Even if she would, it wouldn't change who he was. What he'd done. He still wouldn't be worthy of her. Nor would he want to take her from her work. "It's a very admirable project, Emma."

She just gave him a short nod and turned away, and he knew he'd disappointed her greatly. Again.

Derick scrubbed a hand over his face. *Get your mind back on the business at hand.* Right. Emma said the body had been out here three to four weeks—the timing certainly fit for this body to be that of Farnsworth, then.

Emma strode back to the cart, returning with a stable blanket and a handful of burlap sacks. "Leave two lanterns here with me," she ordered the men. "Take the rest and spread out, looking for the rest of this poor unfortunate. Clothing, belongings, bones—whatever animals may have scattered. Perhaps we'll find out who he is yet."

The men stared at her, gaping with horror, but Emma didn't notice. Instead, she spread the stable blanket on the ground beside the body and began to gently transfer what was left of one to the other.

Derick grabbed a lantern and a sack, glaring the others into doing the same. Maybe one of them would find something of use. They fanned out.

Derick, however, considered for a moment before setting off. If the body *was* that of Farnsworth, whoever killed the man had likely taken his bag and anything else the agent was carrying, but they may have overlooked his boots. And those were exactly what Derick hoped to find.

It would have taken a largish animal to make off with legs still encased in heavy boots. Derick spotted a promising set of animal tracks that led off to the south. He decided to follow those.

He held the lantern out in front of him, swinging it left and right, arcing the light to see as much as he could in his path. It had gone full dark now, so that wasn't much.

After following the tracks for several yards, his toe kicked something hard in the tall weeds. Derick halted, lowering the lantern to get a closer look. Brown leather peeked through the greenery, surrounded by scratching claw marks and an area of smashed-down grass, as if the animal had extracted its feast and then rolled around for a bit before carrying off its spoils and leaving the boot behind.

Derick reached down and pulled up the empty boot. It was the left foot, too—a stroke of luck, for that was precisely the one he needed. He turned the footwear upside down, trying very hard not to think about how it had gotten here. He ran a gloved finger along the base of the heel . . . searching . . . feeling for—there! He tripped a small catch and twisted the heel, revealing a hidden compartment—standard issue for the agents and couriers who worked in his department.

He squeezed his index finger and thumb into the small space and pulled out the tiny rolled paper. A tiny glass vial also rolled out into his palm. Farnsworth's vial of last resort, a fast-acting poison that all of the agents carried just in case. He pinched it between his fingers so as not to drop it while he very carefully placed the boot in his burlap sack.

Anticipation buzzed through him, the thrill of the hunt still as strong as ever, even after all his years as a spy. Maybe even more so because he knew once this job was complete, he could leave. Could start his new life. He unrolled the message.

Derick exhaled a harsh breath and the tops of his shoulders twinged as he forced muscles that had tensed in expectation to relax. Damnation. All he'd learned was that the body they'd found was indeed Farnsworth. The paper had been nothing more than identification and a listing of common ciphers to aid with deciphering or encoding messages. It seemed the man had taken the traitor's identity with him to the next life.

Hell. He was no better off than he'd been the first night he'd arrived. Actually, he was worse off, now that he'd so thoroughly alienated Emma.

A vision of her horrified face when it had finally dawned on her how exactly he'd served her country raked him over the coals once again. But then he snorted with sudden amusement. The look that had come next when she'd multiplied out what a woman a night would be over ten years . . . It had been priceless, and so like Emma.

God, he found her adorable. Whereas she must find him revolting now. His amusement fled.

Well, whether or not she wanted to spend time in his company after what she'd learned today, she'd have to. Now that he knew Farnsworth had been killed in Derbyshire, he'd have to work even more closely with her. Someone had murdered a man to keep their secret hidden. Derick needed to find out more about Emma's other "suspicious deaths." Perhaps she could account for the missing couriers, and give him insight into who in this area had the best opportunity to silence them.

Just how he was going to do that and keep his hands off of Emma, he didn't know.

He was tucking away the paper he'd found when her voice came out of the darkness, somewhere in front of him.

"So, who is the man, Derick?"

He jerked his head up, searching for her. A moment later, she stepped into the circle of light cast by his lantern.

Damn. "How did you—"

She wiggled her bootless toes. "I don't have your superior stealthy spying skills, so I took off my boots to move more quietly and picked my way without a lantern so you wouldn't see me coming," she said.

"Ah. But why would you—"

"Because those lessons you gave me on how to read people paid dividends. I wondered why you held back from the others. Watched as you searched for something, noticed how you straightened *ever* so slightly when you spotted whatever you were looking for, saw how determinedly you set off after it."

Damned smart woman. And looking quite proud of herself, wasn't she, with her raised eyebrow and the confident tilt of her head. Hell, he was proud of her himself, if annoyed as well. He'd thought she'd been thoroughly engrossed in collecting Farnsworth.

Emma stepped closer, more into the light, and the glow of the lantern flickered over her face, shadowing the brackets around her mouth that were deepening by the second. "You didn't hesitate when you picked up that boot. You knew exactly what you were looking for, as if you expected to find it. And that there would be something hidden in its heel."

Damned, damned smart woman. If she'd reasoned that much out already, it was only a matter of time before she—

"You're still working for the government, aren't you?" A wrinkle of consternation formed on her brow before her eyes widened. "You're on an assignment here in Derbyshire. *That's* why you came back." She narrowed her gaze on him.

"That's why you're still here."

Chapter Eighteen

"**I** should have known it," Emma muttered. And she should have, too! She paced around Derick in a fluid circle—as if together they were one of Galileo's ingenious geometry compasses she used on her maps, with Derick the sharp pointer in the middle and she the pencil. And a dull one, at that.

"I thought it odd when your missive arrived at Aveline Castle saying to expect you after all of these years." She scanned her memory, trying to look at everything with fresh eyes—rather than ones blinded with girlish infatuation. "Especially when you hadn't bothered to return only two months earlier when your mother died. But then I, like everyone else, just assumed you'd finally gotten around to inspecting this part of your new inheritance."

Derick stood still as stone in the wavering light from the lantern, not bothering to deny her accusations—for which Emma was grateful. She felt stupid enough without him trying to patronize her. Her mind was awhirl, struggling to recalculate all she'd thought she knew.

"Then when you arrived, you were acting so self-absorbed and pompous . . ." She remembered how relieved and delighted she had been when she'd learned he wasn't some feckless wastrel but instead had been a spy for England.

And then she recalled the night his secretive past had come to light. She spun on her heel and glared at him, pointing a finger. "I *asked* you why you kept up the pretense of being a fop," she reminded him, "as I was taking my leave after our dinner at the castle. And you *lied* to me!"

"I didn't lie to you, Emma." Derick pinned her with his emerald gaze, which seemed such a murky green in the weak light of the lantern—or maybe it just seemed that way because she was rapidly learning that everything she knew about *him* was murky.

"I told you that I'd been pretending to be someone else for so long that I didn't know who I was anymore," he continued, his face and bearing solemn. "That is true."

The same tender pity she'd felt when she'd first heard those words threatened to undermine her pique. Emma wanted to tug at her hair. After all she'd learned today and she still wished to take the blasted man into her arms and comfort him? "Well, it certainly wasn't the whole truth, was it?"

Derick had the good sense not to answer her rhetorical question.

Emma sighed. She supposed he couldn't have told her the whole truth, could he? Not without giving away his cover. The question was why did he need a cover here, now?

"But the war's been over for more than two years, and it isn't as if upper Derbyshire is a hotbed of international secrets. What assignment could you possibly be on here?"

Tiny lines appeared along the outsides of his eyes and mouth, as if he were suppressing the answer, dreading giving it to her.

His words from earlier today came back to her. *It be-came my primary mission to uncover traitors, and other double agents like myself.* Shock drained the blood from her face.

"You think there's a traitor living in Derbyshire?" In less than two weeks, her peaceful village had had to contend with a murderer and now a traitor, too?

Derick's jaw clenched, and his eyes became hooded. "Not anymore."

Not anymore? Emma glanced at the burlap sack that held the dead man's boot. "Do you mean to say the body we found is that of the traitor you're hunting?" Relief lightened the weight on her chest. She had asked if there was a traitor *living* in Derbyshire, after all. This man was most certainly dead. Nor was he from around here. She'd have known if a local man were missing.

She was glad to know that they hadn't been living with a traitor in their midst. It was difficult enough to accept that a man who had lived in her own household for several years was most likely a killer.

Derick gave a quick shake of his head. "No. The man we found tonight is—er, was—Thaddeus Farnsworth, another agent with the War Department. He'd been investigating rumors of a traitor operating out of this area whilst I finished up another case. But he stopped communicating with us a little over two months ago, so I was sent to find him."

Emma's unease returned. Her brow knit as she tried to puzzle out what he'd meant. Getting a straight answer from a spy was proving more difficult than solving a Diophantine equation. "Then are you saying you no longer believe there was a traitor? And if so, what do you think befell your Farnsworth?"

"No. I said 'not anymore' because I believe the traitor to be dead," he said. "However, there must be an accomplice. One who learned that Farnsworth was onto him and was able to catch our agent by surprise. I need your help figuring out who that might be."

"Wait a minute," she said. Something wasn't adding up. "How do you know the traitor is dead? Because you know who he was? And if you needed my help, why didn't you just tell me the truth when you first arrived and ask for it then? You have to know I would have given you every manner of assistance."

If possible, Derick's eyes became even more shuttered, which sent a frisson of alarm bubbling up from her middle.

"What matters here is that we catch the accomplice. Now that he knows the government has agents sniffing around, there's no telling what he might do. The rest is strictly the business of the War Department."

The unease in Emma's chest expanded until it burst into anger. "War Department, my derriere," she said, even as her cheeks heated up at her crass language. "What matters is that *you* stop being evasive. All of this time, you've been keeping this from me?"

What a ninny she'd made of herself . . . trying to coax him into working with her, thinking she could help him find a new purpose for his life. How he must have chuckled to himself at her naivety.

"If you want my help, you can start by telling me everything," she demanded. "As you should have from the beginning."

"Do you forget that with one word to the Commission of the Peace, I can—"

"Go right ahead," she said recklessly. She didn't fear his threat anymore. In fact, she had feared it only because he'd been acting like a typical chauvinistic male—a spoiled aristocrat who didn't believe a woman capable of tying her own bootlace. But she now knew he didn't really feel that way . . .

Emma stilled, her anger going cold. He hadn't felt

that way then, either. And yet he had threatened her anyway. Bullied her into letting him "assist" her. Why would he do such a thing? Why would he antagonize her, force himself into her investigation?

"You don't think Molly's death was part of this, do you?"

Derick was watching her carefully. Too carefully.

"No," he said. "I think Molly's death is what it seems—a lovers' quarrel gone wrong."

"Then why were you so interested in her? So insistent to be included?" She dropped her gaze to the ground, barely conscious that she was rubbing her fingers and thumb together as she tried to remember everything about their early interactions. "Unless you were trying to get close to me, but that makes no sense unless you thought I knew something . . ."

She gasped, snapping her head up to look at him. "You didn't think *I* could be the traitor, did you?"

The briefest flicker passed over his face. Someone who didn't know Derick might have missed it, but the tiny wince stunned her.

"But that's ridiculous! I never leave Derbyshire. The only contact I have with people outside of my little sphere is the occasional Peak District traveler who comes through, and even that's limited, as they tend to stick to the sights or to the inns—with the exception of Mr. Stubbins, of course."

"I only thought it for the briefest of moments," he murmured.

"You shouldn't have thought it at all." She waved her hand in an irritated swipe. "Aside from what I read in the papers, the closest I've ever come to knowing anything about the war or military goings-on is what I've learned from—" The words died in her throat. She stared at him, unbelieving. "My . . . brother."

Her hand dropped listlessly to her side, the ugly truth

dropping into her mind like a missing integer she needed to solve a complex problem.

"You used me to get close to my brother?" Her voice didn't even sound like her own to her ears.

Emma saw the truth in Derick's tight stance, his stoic expression, recognized the pitying tenderness in his gaze.

Fury was the first emotion to hit her. At him. At *herself*. If she hadn't been so childishly lovestruck, she might have recognized his attention for what it was—or at least questioned it more.

But no, she'd seen him only the way she'd wanted to. As the boy she'd once known, now grown into a noble, wounded hero who needed her to heal his soul. She'd made assumptions and justified his every word and action to fit into her stupid little equation so that she could dream of a happily-ever-after with him.

A sharp ache burst in her chest, stinging her throat and nose and pricking the backs of her eyes.

"At first," he allowed, and the pain in her heart grew acute. "Your brother *is* the most likely source of the kind of military secrets that were passed to the French."

"My brother was a war hero, for goodness' sake!" she cried.

"Yes, he was. And I was just a dissipated young rake, trolling the ballrooms of Europe . . ."

Oh God, what a fool she'd been. And him! She turned a glare on Derick. He'd been . . .

I was a very good spy. I was just given a different type of mission than most.

His words rang in her memory.

Some I seduced because they actually had secrets I was commanded to get from them—their own or those of someone close *to them.*

Emma's world started to spin. She reached out and tried to grasp thin air, as if it would keep her steady.

"Emma?"

She heard his voice from far away. She startled when he appeared by her side, reaching out to support her. His mere touch sent warmth streaking through her, but that sensual heat quickly flamed into fire of a different kind. She shoved him away, hard.

Derick stumbled backward, amazed at the force of Emma's vehemence. He'd known she wouldn't be happy if she ever learned the truth, but he hadn't expected she'd react this strongly. What was going through her brilliant little mind?

He couldn't see her face to tell. After she'd pushed him, she'd hunched her shoulders, pulling her arms across her middle as if she were a boxer trying to protect herself from another gut punch. She'd also drifted out of the circle of light, leaving him eerily alone even though he knew she was only feet from him, across the border of darkness. He could hear her tight exhalations of breath.

"You seduced me because you thought I might be able to give you evidence against my brother." Her wounded voice drifted to him through the light fog that was rising from the ground now that the night temperature had cooled around them.

At first, Derick couldn't speak. *That's* what she believed of him? *Of course that's what she thinks, you ass.* Hadn't he extolled his sins to her just hours ago in an effort to drive her away?

But then righteous indignation fired his tongue. After all the pains he'd taken to resist her . . . "I did no such thing. *You're* the one who kissed *me* in your study if you remember."

A huff came out of the darkness, followed by a suspicious sniff. "Oh, and who was it that proposed that very first kiss as a wager? You knew I'd have risked anything to be rid of your intrusion."

Her arrow hit its mark. He was the one who had

started them down this path, though it hadn't been his intention.

"Yes, well, how do you explain today, with your sultry dress? *Sans* fichu," he reminded her. "And your pastries and your *two* bottles of wine?" After all of his agonizing, his resolve—his selfless resolve, he might add—to leave her untouched. While she'd done her utmost to tempt him beyond reason. And she had the nerve to accuse *him*?

"You knew what I thought! I thought we would be partners. I thought you would stay here. You said—"

"No, Emma. I never agreed to either of those things. Use that perfect memory of yours. I may not have corrected your misassumptions, but I never lied to you. And I never tried to seduce you."

Derick's chest tightened in the long silence. He imagined Emma, there in the dark, her thumb working furiously against her fingers as she tried to remember.

She stepped back into the light, and Derick felt himself pale at the sight of her tear-ravaged face. Though she'd wiped it mostly dry, her eyes, cheeks and nose were red and splotchy. Her arms were wrapped tightly around herself.

But the bitter laugh that emerged from her lips wrenched his chest. It was a sound unlike any he'd ever heard from her. Part angry, part hurt, part defeated.

"Then it's no wonder you are the premier womanizing spy of the century," she said tonelessly. "You even got me to do the seducing for you."

He closed his eyes, just briefly, as if he could blot out his guilt and her pain if he just didn't look at her. But it was useless. Hell, he'd made a mess of things. And like Emma was wont to do, she was taking it all on herself, withdrawing into her shell. Only maybe this time, she would retreat so far inside that she wouldn't venture out again. He couldn't let that happen. Trying to put his sincerity into his eyes, into his expression, into his voice, he said, "Emma, it wasn't like that."

Pain slashed over her face. "How you must have laughed yourself silly at my clumsy attempts at seduction."

"Laughed?" He'd been undone, charmed by her innocent enthusiasm in a way he'd never been by any other.

"Indeed. In fact, I'm sure it was an awful trial to bring yourself to do the deed with one so inexperienced as myself. But then, you did it for your country, I suppose. Closed your eyes and thought of England, and all that."

"That's quite enough!" he roared, surprising them both.

Emma jumped back and stared at him with wary eyes. He immediately regretted making her start like that, but at least she was no longer hugging herself protectively.

"Damn it, Emma, you are going to listen to me and get this foolish notion out of your head. Yes, I coerced you into letting me act as your assistant, but it wasn't to get into your drawers. I just needed you to ease my way with the locals. Lend me your experience and insight. Provide me with a cover for any questions I might need to ask."

She pressed her lips together in patent disbelief. "So you weren't after information about my brother?"

He raked a hand through his hair in frustration. "Yes, I was. But I had no *need* to seduce you for that. You'd already told me about your brother and the people who interacted with him on a regular basis."

She turned her face away from him. "Then I guess that just makes me easier than most."

Her words fell between them like stones.

"Ahhhh," he growled, starting toward her. He was finished with her self-flagellation. "Hell and damnation—"

But she held up a hand in surrender, and that fragile gesture stopped him cold. The broken look in her eyes when she looked directly at him sent that cold sluicing through his body.

"Just stop," she said quietly, and turned away, walking back toward the darkness.

"Where are you going, Emma?" he asked, quickly gathering the lantern and burlap sack from the ground, set to follow her.

"I'm going to collect the rest of Mr. Farnsworth," she said, her words floating back to him. "And then I'm going home."

Emma eased into the door of the back kitchens, not wishing to wake the servants, and turned the lock securely behind her. It had taken a couple more hours to thoroughly collect all that they could find of the unfortunate War Department agent, and another hour to bring him back to the manor and place him in the cold cellar, where she could conduct a more thorough investigation tomorrow.

Blessedly, she'd had no more time alone with Derick. When she'd tromped back to the cart, John Coachman and the other three men had been waiting for them and had accompanied them back to Wallingford Manor. She didn't think she could have listened to any more of Derick's lies anyway.

She waited for more pain to pierce her at the thought of his deception, but instead she felt strangely numb. Numb was good, however. It would allow her the capacity to think and remember, unhindered by wretched feelings.

She removed her coat and mud-stained boots and walked them wearily over to the cloakroom. Well, someone's coat. Could have been her mother's for all she knew, as she didn't recall buying it. The boots were hers, though. Derick had insisted.

I won't have you tripping in the dark and breaking your pretty neck. A surge of irritation cut through her numbness at his high-handedness. As if he truly cared.

She tossed the boots to the floor harder than was probably necessary. They bounced, tumbling in opposing directions but both landing near a pile of similarly mud-covered boots of all sizes. Hers, her brother's . . . some maybe even her father's and mother's. She'd probably worn them all in the last year or so, grabbing whatever was most convenient. She really should clean out the cloakroom, pass on all of the too big greatcoats and ill-fitting footwear to those less fortunate—after she cleaned the dirt off of them.

Why in the world was she thinking about a pile of blasted boots? *Maybe because you don't want to face the rest, my girl—your gullibility, your foolishness.*

"Oh do be quiet," she told the negative voice in her head, almost surprised to hear it. It had been largely absent these past few days, days when she'd been so happily thinking of and being with Derick instead.

Well, it would be back with a vengeance now, wouldn't it? Emma heaved a weary sigh. It normally came out in times that she was anxious or tired and this day's events had left her both. Her body ached in all sorts of places. Some of the twinges were from bending and crouching all evening as they meticulously collected Mr. Farnsworth's remains. But shame swamped her when she realized the soreness in unusual places must be a result of making love with Derick.

Making love. Could she really call it that? It had just been government-condoned sex for him, hadn't it? Or had it? He had made the painful point that he hadn't needed to seduce her to get what he needed from her.

Emma didn't know what to believe. But she decided one thing. She would always remember her time in Derick's arms as making love, because for *her* that's what it had been.

A shard of anguish sliced through her numbness and she let it. The sooner the hurt ran its course, the sooner she could forget. Then she snorted. No, she would never forget, not a single word, not a single moment. It was her gift and her curse.

Tired as she was, she didn't think she would be able

to sleep. Maybe a glass or two of sherry would help. She lit an oil lamp from the fire in the kitchen. Padding down the hallway in her stockinged feet, she made her way to the parlor.

A loud creak reached her ear just before she reached the open parlor door. She frowned. That sounded like the French doors. Was Derick sneaking into the house to finish their conversation? The dark look he'd given her when she'd left the cellars without saying a word to him promised that their conversation was far from over. Perhaps he'd decided not to wait until morning to have it out.

Fig! From inside the darkened parlor, he'd have to have seen the advancing ring of light from her lamp coming toward the doorway, which meant there'd be no sneaking off and hiding now.

"I hardly think this is the time or place for this discussion," she snapped as she fully entered the room, her eyes searching for him. A cold breeze swirled around her ankles and the flickering reflection of her oil lamp in the glass door panes shone back at her from odd angles in the still-open French doors. But Derick wasn't there. No one was. Her brow knitted as she cautiously started toward the doors.

A light snore startled Emma so much that she shrieked. The snore turned into a harsh snort.

Emma jerked toward the sound, holding her lamp out in front of her as if its feeble flame offered protection as well as light. Within three steps, the shadowy image of someone seated near the fireplace came into focus against the negligible embers of a dying fire. But there were no chairs there. They always left that area open as it was a favorite spot of— "George!" Emma exclaimed, rushing over to where her brother was indeed ensconced in his rolling chair.

"Wh-what? Who?" came his sleep-groggy reply. He blinked up at her. "Em?"

"What are you doing here in the dark?" she asked,

placing the lamp on a nearby table. "And at this hour?" Emma grabbed a spill from the jar atop the mantel and returned to the lamp. She removed the glass chimney and turned the knob on the brass burner to give it more wick. The ring of light grew. She held her spill in the flame and then used it to light the wall sconces on either side of the fireplace.

When she got a look at George in the light, he was rubbing the sleep from his eyes with one hand and clutching the lap blanket tightly around him with the other. She hurried over and placed a hand on his face. "Oh, George, you're freezing. Why are you sitting here alone with no fire?"

Emma grabbed a heavy poker, the brass chill to the touch. She stoked the embers until they glowed red before placing another log on the fire.

"I'd heard whispers from the staff that a dead man had been found in the woods," George said, his voice still gravelly from sleep. "I decided to wait up for you to find out if it was true. I must have fallen asleep and let the fire die out."

Emma added one more log as the first caught fire. "Yes, well, Perkins will answer for this. Why didn't one of the servants check on you?"

"You'll not say a word to Perkins, or any of the other servants, little sister, for none of them knew I was here *to* check on me." George frowned at her, reminding her more of a sullen youth than a man in his middle years. "I'm not a complete invalid. I *am* capable of rolling myself to the parlor after the staff is abed." His lips flattened as he added, "At least on days I'm feeling well."

Emma moved behind George to position him even closer to the now roaring fire. "Well, I don't like the idea of you moving about without someone knowing. What if you'd have fallen?"

"I'm fine, Emma, so quit your worrying," he grumbled petulantly. "Now, who was the dead man you went after, then?"

She'd given her promise to Derick to keep his business private. Was breaking your word to a man who lied for a living truly breaking it? Emma released a breath through her nose. Yes, it was. And just because Derick was a dishonest cad didn't mean she should be.

"Just a poor unfortunate," she said. "He was so badly decomposed that I can't even tell what happened to him. Could have been an accident, I suppose."

She had never before lied to George. *That wasn't technically a lie,* her conscience whispered. *Farnsworth was unfortunate, you don't know what happened to him precisely, and it could have been an accident. Like, a three percent chance, but still.*

Great. Now she sounded like Derick.

"Well, accident or no," George said, "the maid's death was no accident, I hear. I don't want you out in the woods alone."

She waved a hand. "I wasn't alone, George. I had three burly servants with me, plus a hunter from the village. And Derick, of course."

"Aaaah," George said with an annoying-older-brother inflection. "The budding partnership. How goes that? You've been gone so much lately, I'm left completely in the dark."

Now that the adrenaline was wearing off from the fright George had given her, Emma suddenly felt very tired. She allowed her shoulders to slump. "There will be no partnership."

George's eyebrows came together over the bridge of his nose. "What do you mean?" His eyes narrowed and the fist still holding the blanket tightened, twisting the fabric in his lap. "You look sad, Emma," he said, his voice growing deep and louder. "Did Aveline do something to upset you?"

Emma placed a calming hand on her brother's shoulders. The last thing she wanted was to send George into one of his rages. Nor did she have any intention of discussing what lay between her and Derick with her brother. "No, George. Of course not. I just decided we wouldn't suit as partners. Besides, I don't think Derick intends to settle in Derbyshire at all, and I have no intentions of leaving here."

George's face smoothed, and Emma released a quiet breath.

"Because of me?" he asked quietly.

"What?"

"Do you not want to leave Derbyshire because of me?" George's frown came back, only darker. "If you're thinking a match between you and Aveline won't work because you would have to follow him to his seat or to London . . . I don't want you throwing away a chance at happiness because of your loyalty to me."

"Oh, George, that's not it at all," she said, leaning down to hug her brother around his shoulders. She gave him an extra-tight squeeze before she pulled back from him, to convince him that she meant the words. "There are many reasons Derick won't suit, the least of which would be geography."

Have you ever considered moving? Say to . . . London, or some other large city, where your knowledge could be put to better use solving crimes? Had Derick been hinting that he wanted her to come with him? He'd called her fascinatingly helpful right before he'd said those words, and the way he'd looked at her—

Emma mentally smacked herself. What in the heavens was she doing? Assigning imaginary intentions to his words again? *Ninny.* How quickly she'd forgotten that she meant nothing to him outside of his blasted assignment.

A cool breeze curled around her ankles and snaked beneath her skirts, sending a shiver through her.

And how quickly she'd forgotten the open French doors once she'd been startled by her brother. She started over to shut them, looking over her shoulder to ask, "George, were the French doors open when you came in here?"

"I . . . I don't think so." Her brother's eyes blinked slowly. "Are they open? I would have noticed . . . wouldn't I?"

Emma frowned as she pulled the knobs toward her until the doors clicked. The creaking she heard could very well have been the wind pushing the doors around, but how had they gotten open in the first place? Perkins always did a walk-through of the house before finding his bed.

The wind couldn't have blown them open because the doors opened outward. How about a faulty latch, then, allowing them to crack just enough that the outside wind could have caught them? Emma pressed against the doors hard. Harder. But the latch held.

Someone had deliberately tried to come into Wallingford Manor through the parlor doors. But who? Derick? Or someone else?

Your brother is *the most likely source of the kind of military secrets that were passed to the French.*

She'd been so upset tonight that she'd never pressed Derick on the identity of the traitor, or indeed much else about his true reason for being here. All he'd really told her was that he believed the traitor to be dead and that he must have had an accomplice.

A horrible thought occurred to her. What if the traitor *had* coaxed information from her brother? His accomplice would surely know that. What if the man saw her brother as a loose end, one that needed tying off?

Her heart pounded furiously, as if it could break free of the grip of her sudden fear.

Get ahold of yourself, Emma. You're jumping to conclusions. Besides, Derick had said her brother was the most *likely* source, not that he actually *had* been the source. She'd learned a hard lesson tonight, and that was that Derick was very specific in his word choices.

Occasionally I was called upon to terminate those who'd divulged England's secrets.

Emma's blood ran cold in her veins, chased by a shiver. No. No. No! She refused to believe that Derick had any intention to harm George. After all, hadn't he said the actual traitor was dead? If her brother was involved, it was because someone else had taken advantage of him, not because of any malfeasance on his part. Surely Derick saw that.

Still, she wasn't taking any chances with George's life. She locked the French doors, then hurried back to George, who seemed to be dozing off again. She wheeled him around. "Come, George. Let's get you back to your room."

She woke Perkins, who was duly mortified when she explained how she'd found George. She ordered the butler to assign their burliest footman to stand guard outside her brother's door. Then she asked him to wake the housekeeper and canvass the house to ensure that all doors and windows were secure. She couldn't give him an explanation, and Perkins—bless the man—didn't ask for one.

Hopefully the stable master wouldn't ask for one either when she demanded that her horse be readied at near midnight.

She intended to demand some explanations of her own, from Derick—lateness of the hour be damned.

Chapter Nineteen

"What do you mean, Harding's not here?" Derick glared at Wallingford Manor's stable master. Sweat glistened on the older man's prominent brow in the yellow glow of lantern light.

McCandless stood rigid, his forearms and the muscles where his neck met his shoulders bulging defensively. "I said I'd keep watch over him, but this ain't no jail, m'lord. Only so much I can do. He must've slipped past me head groom while I was with you and Miss Wallingford out in the woods. Took 'is belongings and everything."

"Damnation," Derick muttered. Harding was looking more and more like the man who'd assisted his mother in her traitorous scheme. After all, his mother had been dead before Farnsworth was killed, so she couldn't have done it. But if Farnsworth had been onto her trail, he may also have learned of Harding's involvement and become a threat to the footman. Now Derick had to wonder if the poor maid, Molly, had been his victim not because of jealousy but because of something she might have known, since she had been a maid in his mother's household in addition to being Harding's lover.

"Do you think Thomas was the one that killed that

man?" the servant asked. For all his bulk and bluster, McCandless looked pale and shaken. After their gruesome errand in the forest, Derick couldn't help but sympathize with him.

"I don't know," Derick said, but let his voice imply otherwise.

The stable master's lips thinned into a grim line. Let McCandless think what he would. Word would spread through the town now, probably long before sunrise. Derick needed to question Harding again and that would only happen if the footman was caught and turned in. The villagers would keep a closer eye out for the escaped servant if they truly considered him dangerous—as he very well might be.

Now that Derick knew Farnsworth *was* dead, and had been killed here in Derbyshire, this entire mission took on a sharper edge. Someone had committed murder to protect himself less than a month ago. Whether the killer was an accomplice or the actual traitor, his crimes were no longer in the distant past. The situation had become imminently deadly.

"If Harding shows up, or if anyone sees him, be sure to send word to Miss Wallingford and myself right away," Derick instructed McCandless as he strode out of the stables and into the night. He headed toward the manor. Harding could be a potential threat and Emma would need to be informed of the danger. Besides, he wanted to get to work solving the rest of this mess. He doubted she'd sleep much anyway, after the day she'd had. He knew he wouldn't.

God, he'd never forget the way she'd curled into herself and staggered away from him, out of the light, like a wounded animal. He hated that he'd done that to her— hated that he'd probably make things worse for her by disturbing her yet again tonight. She must still be reeling. If only he could give her more time—time to use that remarkable memory of hers to sift through everything that had happened, every word spoken between them since his return—maybe she'd see that his intentions had never been to hurt her.

Derick snorted. As if that mattered. He knew better than most what the road to hell was paved with, and it wasn't the gravel crunching loudly beneath his boots. He *had* hurt her. Terribly. The best thing he could do for Emma now was to finish this and leave her in peace.

Rather than wake the household, he decided to enter through the back kitchens and search her out. He quietly stepped onto the stoop and reached for the door. He turned the knob, but it wouldn't give. Damnation. He jiggled the knob again, to the same result. He bent down to examine the lock. It didn't look to be too complicated. He supposed he could pick it—

The door jerked open, and Derick stumbled backward, nearly slipping off of the low lip of the stoop as he tried to straighten and right himself all at once. Who—

"Emma?" Silhouetted in the low light from the doorway, she looked absurdly beautiful, given that she still wore the dirt-smudged coat she'd been wearing in the forest and that several locks of her hair had slipped from the simple knot she'd tied it in. She also looked exhausted as hell.

And furious.

"So it *was* you!" Emma took an aggressive step out onto the stoop, leaving Derick no choice but to retreat further. Fire flashed in her amber eyes, but relief did as well. He wasn't sure what to make of either reaction.

"Pardon?"

"Why are you trying to sneak into my house?" Her hands fisted by her sides and she shifted on her feet. If he hadn't known better, he'd have thought Emma was preparing to do battle.

"I was being *courteous*," he replied defensively. "I needed to talk with you and didn't wish to wake your entire household. Nor did I think you'd appreciate me coming in your bedroom window."

"If it was me you wanted to talk to, why didn't you stay in the parlor just now instead of running away when I came in?" Her eyes narrowed on him ominously, as if she'd caught him in a lie. "Or is it really my brother you're after?"

It seemed Emma had picked up on his interrogation tactics well. But he hardly heard past the first part of her accusation. "There was someone in your parlor?"

Unease focused his senses when she nodded, putting his instincts on alert. Had it been Harding? The idea of a potential killer anywhere near Emma made his mouth go dry and his blood boil. "It wasn't me, Emma. I've been at the stables, talking with McCandless."

Emma had relaxed her combative stance, but apprehension quickly clouded her expression and she worried her lower lip between her teeth.

"Tell me exactly what you saw," he commanded.

Emma's nose scrunched. "It's more what I heard," she said. "I was heading for the parlor for a nightcap, when the French doors creaked."

Derick relaxed a little. She hadn't actually seen someone. Emma had been through a lot today. In fact, now that she'd lost some of her earlier steam, he noticed that her hand was trembling. She could just be overwrought.

"I assumed it must be you," she said, "wanting to finish our discussion from earlier." She shook her head slowly. "My mind making order out of chaos, I suppose. But when I entered the room, the doors were wide open."

"They were probably just left—"

But Emma was shaking her head. "No. Perkins routinely locks up at night. Nor could the wind have blown them open. I tested the latch myself."

Damn it.

"I did call out, to who I thought was you, before I entered the room. Maybe I frightened him away." She was nodding now, her voice stronger. "Or he could have already gone and just not closed the doors behind him."

Or have come earlier and still be in the house. Derick

didn't wish to frighten Emma any more than necessary. However, he'd heard enough. He moved past her and into the kitchen, heading for the parlor. He snagged her hand as he brushed by, pulling her along with him. "Come." He'd be damned if he let her out of his sight until he was certain she was safe.

"Derick!" She yanked her hand, trying to pull away from him, but he didn't relinquish his grasp. She huffed behind him. "Do slow down, at least," she grumbled.

He didn't, but he did shorten his strides to accommodate her shorter legs.

He found the parlor empty but well lit by a bright fire and flickering wall sconces. Oddly, Emma no longer tried to pull her hand from his, even when they stood before the closed French doors on the far side of the parlor. If anything, her grip tightened. After all that had happened between them today, it humbled Derick that she found comfort in him. He squeezed back.

Which must have broken the spell, because Emma snatched her hand away, curling her fist and tucking it against her middle. Derick's palm chilled, leaving a cold ache from the loss of her touch. He cleared his throat against a peculiar tightness.

"Well. Let's see if we can find any evidence that someone was here." He unlocked and opened the doors, stepping out into the night. He examined the doors first. He didn't see any pry marks near the handles, but he knew from experience that the locks on doors such as these were child's play. He scanned the ground. A small courtyard flanked the parlor, the stone thwarting his efforts to find any footprints.

As Derick reached the edge of the stone, the shadows of the night made it too difficult to see anything else. "Emma," he called behind him. "Bring a lamp."

Moments later, she joined him. When he explained what he was looking for, she bent to hold the light low as they walked the perimeter of the courtyard.

"There," she said, pointing at a dark spot on the stone in the far corner. As they drew closer, the spot morphed into part of a muddy footprint. Definitely a man-sized print, and not completely dry. In these cool temperatures, though, it could have been made anytime in the last few hours. It pointed toward the house.

Emma held the light farther in front of them. A stride behind the first print was another, better-defined one, as if the mud had worn off the boot the closer the wearer got to the house, but the prints disappeared completely long before he'd reached the door.

When they came to the edge of the courtyard, two very definite sets of footprints—one coming and one going—were visible in the damp ground just off the stone.

"It seems as if whoever it was went back the way they came," Emma said.

"Yes."

Derick looked out over the dark lawn. They certainly could have come from the stables, but a few yards away was the gravel drive, which would obscure any direction the intruder might have gone past that. Derick would try to follow the prints later, when Emma wasn't with him, but he doubted they'd be of any use.

He took the lamp from her and squatted to get a better look at the prints. They appeared to be those of an average-sized man, which Harding was. Or possibly—

"You're certain you haven't come this way today? Tromping around in your men's boots?"

Emma shook her head. "No. I tend to exit from the kitchens. But you make a good point. It could have been anyone. We should be careful not to jump to any misguided conclusions." Her voice dipped, and he had to strain to hear what she said next. "A painful lesson I'm only recently learning."

Whether she'd aimed that dagger at him or herself, it pierced Derick just the same. When he glanced up at her, she wasn't looking at him at all, however. Her gaze was fixed off in the distance. In the darkness he couldn't be sure, but it seemed more like she was lost in thought. Or memory.

An unfamiliar longing bade him to rise to his feet, to encircle Emma in his arms and pull her into his embrace. To rub his hands soothingly over her back, to tuck her head beneath his chin and simply breathe her in.

But he did not. Any tenderness on his part would be a stopgap at best, a temporary balm that she might not even welcome anymore. No. The best thing he could do for Emma—hell, the best thing he could do for himself— would be to get her mind back on their investigation. Because once it was finished, he would leave. And with every mile farther he got from England's shores, this awful ache would lessen until it faded away entirely. For both of them.

He handed the lamp back to Emma and stood. "It could have been Harding." He filled her in on the footman's disappearance.

Emma grimaced, placing her fingers on her forehead as if to press away the beginnings of a megrim. "George was asleep in the parlor when I got there. Do you think this intruder—Harding or otherwise—could have meant to harm him?"

"It's possible. I'm sure word has already spread that we found a body in the woods. If the man sees your brother as a liability . . ." Or, worse yet, what if the man now saw Emma as a threat because she would be investigating the murder? The thought chilled Derick. Damnation. Well, he'd just have to send to Aveline Castle for a few of his things. He wasn't going to leave Emma here unprotected.

For her part, he could see her mind whirling, the thoughts churning in her amber gaze, the questions tumbling about. He waited for her to voice them.

But for once she didn't. The silence grew, awkward in

a way it had never been between them. It left him ill at ease and self-conscious, like he hadn't felt since he'd been a callow youth, or at the least since his unseasoned early days as a spy.

Then Emma gave a decisive nod and turned on her heel, striding back toward the parlor.

Derick followed, but she didn't stop once they reached the house. Instead, her step quickened as she hurried through the parlor, down the hallway and toward the staircase. Derick caught her elbow as she reached the third stair. "Where are you going?"

She half turned on the step and stared down her nose at him. 'Twas disconcerting for a man of his height, even though the third step barely put her half a head above him. Still, he hadn't been at this particular disadvantage since he was a boy. It was more than just their positions that made him feel so on edge, and he knew it. His hand fell away from Emma's arm. Everything that had happened between them today, everything that had been revealed, everything that had been touched . . . That was what truly left him out of sorts.

"I am going to my study to pore through my files," she said, her voice like he'd never heard it. Devoid of emotion. Not matter-of-fact, as she often was about things, but strangely . . . detached.

It saddened him and filled him with envy at the same time. Emma, it seemed, had donned the cloak of efficiency, much as she had earlier in the forest. It was a garment he knew well, having masked himself behind it many a time to get through a mission. So why did it elude him today, leaving him feeling so exposed? So raw and uncertain?

"Had I found Farnsworth on my own, not knowing what I do now, I would have classified your agent's death as 'suspicious,'" she said. "I think it's time that I pull the records of other such deaths and see whether I can find any similarities between them that might point us in a definitive direction."

Derick nodded his agreement, relieved she'd said "us." He'd been afraid he would have to force her cooperation after all that had happened between them. But his little Pygmy was proving to be made of sterner stuff, wasn't she?

Still. If he, as a more experienced man in matters such as these, was struggling with how he felt . . . "You'll be all right, Emma?" he asked softly, as much for his own sake as for hers. "Us working together, after . . . ?"

Her chin trembled. It was barely noticeable, a tiny ripple in an otherwise calm sea, but Derick saw it. Felt it deep in his gut. Wished he could comfort her. Hell, comfort them both. Standing as they were, with her three steps above him, she was at the perfect height for him to clasp her about the waist and drag her to him. The desire nearly overwhelmed his resolve to let her be.

But then her delicate chin firmed. "I will be more than all right. My brother is in danger, and I refuse to let him come to harm—whether from some traitor's accomplice or as a victim of your duty and your *probabilities*."

Her look dared him to refute her. But Derick said nothing. She had him dead to rights. If her brother had turned out to be the traitor, he would have done what he had to. He still would, if it came to that.

But for the first time in more than a dozen years, rather than pretending to be someone else, he wished he *were* someone else. Someone who had not seen what he'd seen, not done what he'd done. It could only be for one reason—because he cared what Emma thought of him. Because he wanted her to love him.

Good Christ, when had that happened?

The object of his newly discovered realization squared her shoulders and lowered her head just enough so that their eyes were of a level with each other.

Anger blazed from hers. But behind it he saw her desire. To be with him. To have him for her own. Derick stopped breathing.

"I may have been easily taken in by you. I may have allowed myself to see only what I wanted to see . . ." Her voice cracked just a little, but he felt it as if it were something within him that split. Because he knew her pain came not from what he'd done, but from her knowledge that in spite of it, she still wanted him. "But if you think I'll let anything keep me from solving this case now, you know me even less than I know the real you. Which is not at all."

She turned her back on him then and ascended the stairs in purposeful strides. Derick stood where he was, unable to move, unable to do anything but watch her go. With every step that pulled her away from him, it was as if she pulled away the last vestiges of his facade without even intending to, leaving him standing at the bottom of the stairs unable to hide from the truth.

Emma, of all people, knew the real him. Better than any other person, maybe better than he did himself.

And she might have loved him anyway.

Knowing what he could have had, if only things had been different, broke his heart.

Emma wiped a rag over one of her chalkboards, erasing formulas and scribbles until only black slate remained. She'd fixed an unmarked map of the area onto the wall beside it, as well. She wanted to look at everything with fresh eyes.

Preferably ones that didn't sting with unshed tears.

Derick had followed her up the stairs. She'd been afraid when she heard him behind her that she would break. For a moment there out in the courtyard, and then again at the bottom of the stairs, she'd seen something in Derick's eyes that made her want to throw open her arms to him and make a blessed fool of herself. But after searching her study to make certain that no one lurked in it, he'd left to search the rest of the house. She was grateful for the respite. She would just have to use the time he was away to shore up her defenses.

She'd done an admirable job of keeping her inner turmoil from him, but not without paying a price. Every part of her ached, from either strain or just a deep-down pain that she knew wasn't actually physical. It only manifested itself that way.

The only way to keep it all at bay was to get to work. *Think, Emma.* If mathematics could answer every question in the universe—which she was certain it could—how could she manipulate it to find a killer? She had precious little to go on at the moment. She'd have to get Derick to fill her in on everything he knew, but perhaps once he did, she'd see a pattern that would point them to the man. In the meantime, she would revisit her reports on the three suspicious deaths that she'd discerned might be germane, which now lay spread across her desk.

Twenty minutes later, as she was placing a mark on the map where Farnsworth's body had been found, Derick slipped into the room. Emma didn't hear him so much as sense him, her nerves suddenly alert and tingly. It was as if her body, now so intimately familiar with his, simply knew he was near.

"The house is clear," he murmured from behind her. "With the help of Perkins and your staff, every door and window is locked up tight. Not that that would deter someone with a modicum of skill if he was intent on getting in, but it's better than doing nothing at all."

"Mmmm," she acknowledged absently. There. Four locations where bodies had been found were now dotted on the map. She stepped back and stared at the seemingly random markers. They had to mean something. If only she could figure out the language that would tell her what.

Derick came up beside her, obviously interested in

what she was doing. The hairs on her arms raised, as if he was a magnet and they tiny filaments of metal. Drawn to him. Like she was.

Oh, do quit being ridiculous. She turned to look at him, certain that seeing his deceptive face would remind her why she should feel nothing for him but scorn. But it was a mistake.

A lock of his black hair had fallen across his forehead. It made him look younger, and somehow vulnerable—and yet devastatingly handsome in a tousled sort of way, as if he'd been thoroughly tumbled out-of-doors and had enjoyed every moment of it. She flushed with heat as her traitorous body reminded her that indeed, he had. As had she.

And despite everything, she wanted to be again. Emma pursed her lips. So much for shoring up her defenses.

"What is this?" he asked, eyeing her map and the equations she was tinkering with on the chalkboard.

"I'm not going to tell you," she answered. "Not until you explain exactly what is going on. Every bit of it, from the beginning." She turned back to look at her equations. "Not that I will be able to tell if you lie to me," she grumbled, for once not caring if he heard.

Derick moved in front of her in one fluid step, his large body blocking her view of everything but him. "Damn it, Emma," he said, his voice low, pitched somewhere between frustration and earnestness. "I haven't lied to you. I was not forthcoming, but I was not openly dishonest, either."

"Oh." She tossed her head back, spoiling for the fight. This was what she needed to remind her heart why he was so wrong for her. Because apparently the foolish organ hadn't caught on yet. "That's rich. A rather fine line to walk, don't you think?"

"When you're in my position, sometimes a fine line is all you have," he shot back. "I will admit that I've crossed it many times over the years. I wouldn't have survived if

I hadn't. But whether you believe me or not, Emma, I need you to know—I never crossed it with you. And I won't."

She scoffed, angry at the seeming sincerity in his glittering gaze. She stepped back from him. "You expect me to believe that I can trust you? That you'll answer me honestly, no matter what I want to know?"

He followed, a slow, deliberate step with a lean that brought his face close to hers. "Yes, you can trust me."

If only she could believe him. It was so tempting . . . until—

"Aha!" She spun away from him, turning back only when she'd put some much-needed space between them. "But you *won't* answer me honestly." She wagged a finger at him. "I'm onto your tricks. You just avoided my second question by only answering the first, so you can tell yourself you're not a liar."

A long, irritated breath escaped him. "I'll always answer you honestly, Emma," he said. "Just be certain you really want to know the truth of what you ask."

Something charged hung between them, something she didn't quite understand. She knew that some kind of emotion seethed beneath Derick's skin—she'd seen it when they'd been standing on the stairs. Whatever it was, it seemed even stronger now.

The question she'd asked him just before John Coachman interrupted them at the cave hovered on her tongue. Had their lovemaking meant anything to him or had she been just another woman seduced for duty?

She opened her mouth, hesitated. She didn't want to know the answer, did she? She didn't think she could take knowing the truth, either way. Because if he said she was just like all the rest, it would devastate her. But if he admitted any kind of feelings for her, that might be even worse . . .

In the end, she lost her nerve. "Fine. Right now, I just want to know what exactly is going on."

He looked disappointed somehow, but he simply nodded. "All right." He started a slow pace in front of her boards—a sleek, banked sort of prowl that reminded her of a caged lion she'd seen once in the menagerie at the Tower of London. "You already know I hunted traitors during the war. I'm sure you've now deduced that my work continued even after hostilities ended. Understandably, the War Department doesn't take kindly to those who betrayed England, and has no intention of letting them live to do it again."

His voice had gone dark and was tinged with just a hint of danger—but enough to make her shiver.

"Understandably," she said, simply because it seemed as though she should say something, and really . . . what did one say to that?

"For the past two years," he continued, "I, along with a select other few agents, have been tracking down the last bits of intelligence we've been able to gather about potential traitors who operated during the war. Rumors, mainly. Farnsworth was attempting to back-trace the trail of some sensitive military information that had been fed to the French over a period of years. About two months ago, he sent word from France that he was closing in on the source. With some cooperation from the French and a bit of interrogation, Farnsworth concluded the most likely source of the leak was somewhere near upper Derbyshire."

"So he's the one who accused my brother?"

"No. He didn't name any one suspect. When at all *possible*," he said with a raised eyebrow, letting her know her crack about probabilities had struck home, "we are very careful not to implicate a person without absolute proof. Farnsworth would have been chasing that proof. But then my commanders didn't hear from him again. Since last they knew he'd been headed here, they decided this should be the first place we should look for him."

"So you volunteered to come."

"No." He huffed once. "I had just retired not three days earlier. But since I had property here, and therefore a legitimate reason to show up unquestioned, I was the logical choice. I could be here very visibly and be established quickly. No matter what guise Farnsworth was hiding behind, he would undoubtedly hear of my arrival, since it was bound to be gossiped about, given I hadn't been here in so very long. If Farnsworth were here, and able, it was assumed he would make contact. Then I could assist him if needed."

So it was just an awful coincidence that had brought Derick back? "Would you have ever returned were it not for this mission?"

His eyes shuttered. "No."

Further proof that theirs was not a relationship that was meant to be. As if she needed more. She wanted to curse fickle fate, but she couldn't bring herself to do it. Because despite everything, a part of her was fiercely glad that Derick had come back into her life. However briefly. However painful it turned out to be. *Oh for goodness' sake, Emma. You are one sick individual.*

Still, she wanted to understand. And he had promised to answer any question she put to him. "Why not?"

His lips firmed and he shot her a glare, as if accusing her of exploiting his promise. Perhaps she was. She didn't care. He at least owed her that. She raised both of her brows in expectation.

Derick closed his eyes. "The day I left Derbyshire, I had an awful row with my mother. I swore then that I would never set foot here again. I—" A ripple of some repressed emotion passed over his face, bringing his eyes open again.

Emma was dying to ask what the fight had been about. She'd always wondered, but that truly would be taking advantage right now. Something told her just to let him speak.

"I don't know if I would have tried to make peace with her before I le—" He coughed. "I mean *after* my work for England was complete."

What had he been going to say?

"As it was, I never got the chance," he went on before she could think of a way to press him on the matter. "I was in France, on what was supposed to have been my last assignment, when my mother took her life," he said quietly. "She'd been interred for weeks before I even heard the news."

Her thoughts were forgotten as she flushed with guilt, remembering how she'd accused him of missing his mother's funeral when he'd first arrived. He hadn't defended himself, but now she could see why. She was never supposed to find out he'd been a spy—among other things. And even though she still didn't know what was behind his anger at his mother, she could clearly see now that it pained him greatly.

"It's just as well," he said. "No matter what grudge I've borne her all these years, I would not have relished turning her in as a traitor."

Chapter Twenty

Emma gasped. "Your *mother*?" She shook her head in denial, more of her burnished chestnut hair coming loose from its knot. Despite all that he should be focused on, Derick found himself imagining it all down, spread around her as it had been this afternoon—wishing to see it that way again. For a moment, he thought she must have heard his unspoken desire because she tugged at the knot irritably, letting her hair fall in waves around her. But she quickly gathered and twisted it, tying it all back up again.

"Let's back up a bit," she said as she pulled the knot tight. Efficient Emma had returned. "Someone passed military secrets to the French." She held out her thumb, as if ticking off a point. "After Farnsworth traced them back to upper Derbyshire, he went missing." Out popped her index finger. "You came looking for Farnsworth," she said as her middle finger joined the others, "even though you weren't certain he'd made it here. Am I right thus far?"

Derick blinked away his Godiva-esque fantasy. "Yes. We hadn't actually heard from him since just before he was supposed to have left France, but that's not unusual when an agent is on the hunt. However, when Farnsworth's silence dragged on, I was sent here to find him."

"Why here? Why not France? That was his last known location."

"True. Another agent was assigned there, just to be certain, but there were other things that pointed here."

"Such as?"

While securing the house, he'd made the decision to tell Emma everything he knew about his mission. She'd pieced together much of it already anyway. If he wanted to put her great mind to work fitting the rest together, she would need all the pieces of the puzzle.

"Once we turned our eyes to upper Derbyshire, we realized that two couriers, both of whom were thought to have traveled through this area, never made it to their destinations. Unfortunately, no one in the War Department had made that connection before. The couriers' deaths were years apart, for one, and it is a sad reality that many a good man was lost over the course of the wars. And like Farnsworth, they could have been killed anywhere between where they'd started and where they should have ended up. But to suddenly have three possible missing men who worked for the War Department, all tied to an out-of-the-way area like Derbyshire?"

Emma had crossed her arms and was tapping an index finger against her lips as she listened. "That does sound significant—statistically speaking." She dropped her hand and turned to him. "Wait. *That's* why you were so interested when I first mentioned the deaths I'd classified as 'suspicious.' And I'd thought you were just challenging my capabilities."

"I was doing that, too," he admitted. "But I should have remembered better than to doubt a brilliant woman like you."

A sad smile flitted over her face, when only yesterday she would have beamed at his praise. Now she didn't trust even a compliment from him.

Perhaps he had made a mistake in not asking for Emma's help earlier on. It had seemed prudent to keep the Crown's business to himself when he wasn't even sure that Farnsworth had made it to Derbyshire. But now . . . could some of the heartache he'd foisted on her today have been avoided if he'd just enlisted her aid once he'd decided she wasn't at all connected to the treason? Or had he been right not to take the risk that she would alert her brother?

He didn't know. Nor could he change the past. He could only move forward. "I think your unsolved deaths might be our missing couriers."

Emma nodded. "I've pulled out three files that might fit." She waved her arm toward her desk. "Now that I know more of what I'm looking for, I will see if I can determine anything that might link two of them together."

"Good." That was exactly what he'd been hoping for.

"You said other *things* pointed you to Derbyshire. Plural," she reminded him.

"So I did," he answered, bracing himself. She wouldn't like this next part. "There was also the matter of your brother living here. His reputation as a war hero was well known, of course. He was also one of the few who would have the experience and type of knowledge that the French had received. Naturally, when we learned that military secrets had been passed to the enemy, he was an obvious suspect. When the Derbyshire angle came in . . ."

"I see," she said, only a bit tightly. "And exactly when were these secrets allegedly passed?" He could see she was struggling to keep her own emotional bias out of the situation, and instead trying to apply her logic—a trait he found he appreciated more and more in her.

"As best we can tell, the first in 1808, not long after your brother arrived home. The stream of information continued right up until the end of the war. And before you ask, one of the couriers went missing in 1809, but the other not until 1813."

"Then how could you have suspected George?" Her voice and her color rose a bit as she lost, if not the battle with her emotions, at least a skirmish. "His accident would have made it impossible—"

He raised a hand to halt her protest. "We didn't know any of that, Emma. There was no reason for the department to look into your brother's life outside of the military before now. I'm sure if he was given any thought at all, it was assumed that he preferred rusticating in the country since inheriting his baronetcy."

She nodded, seemingly satisfied by that explanation.

"Once I got here, it only took me observing him for a short time to realize he hadn't the faculties to perpetrate such a long deception given his condition, nor physically could he have been the one to dispose of the second courier."

"Well, neither could your mother have! If she weighed eight stone, then I'm ten feet tall." Emma had risen to her tiptoes as she spoke.

"I don't think she did any of it alone. And I think whoever helped her is now trying to protect his own arse. If your estimations are correct, Mother was already dead when Farnsworth was killed."

"I've been thinking about that," Emma said. "When I mapped where we found Farnsworth's body, I realized it is very near the cold spring that feeds St. William's Creek. I'm not sure we can assume anything. If his remains had been in the spring and were only washed to where we found them by the recent flood, he may have been dead longer than I estimated."

"Because the cold would have slowed his decomposition . . ."

"Just so." Emma sighed. "Look, I understand now why you were so interested in who spent time with George, but even though Lady Scarsdale was his closest . . . confidante," she said tactfully, "you can't really think she was the traitor."

He pinched the bridge of his nose, his own feelings threatening. He'd have thought she would be happy to know that someone other than her own blood was his primary suspect. He knew he would be—the idea that his mother was likely the traitor gnawed at him. Not that it surprised him, given what he'd made of *him*self. Deceit was apparently in his blood. "I have my reasons."

"Well, explain them to me, because in all of the time I knew her, I can't remember her discussing much outside of herself. Certainly not anything remotely related to the war. No patriotic statements toward France, or even disparaging remarks about England, for that matter."

"No good traitor would draw attention to themselves, Emma. Not if they wanted to stay alive."

"But do you really think she was capable of—"

"Is it really so hard to believe? My mother seduced secrets out of your brother just as I did to scores of women," he snapped. "It must run in my family."

Derick immediately regretted his outburst, but damn it all—couldn't she see this was hard enough for him to discuss without her stubbornly defending his mother? That he didn't enjoy admitting his family's shame? His shame? He heaved a deep breath.

Emma stared at him, wide-eyed. Then her shoulders slumped. "Is no one around here what they seemed?"

Only you, he wanted to say, but didn't.

Instead he said wearily, "I've found evidence to corroborate this scenario. You can look it all over yourself later if you want, but it would appear that my mother was growing very paranoid in the weeks before her death. I also had reports that an unknown man, who must have been Farnsworth, had been asking questions about her—*investigating* her. I think she may have known that she was close to being discovered, and that's why she threw herself from that cliff."

Emma winced. Her eyebrows dipped, as if heavy with the weight of compassionate sorrow. "She must have hated it here, to do such a thing," she whispered. "To do either of those things. How could I not have seen—"

"There was nothing you could have done, Emma." He could see he was going to have to tell her all. He hadn't intended to share the rest—the awful secret he'd carried since that long-ago day when his mother had hurled the truth at him in a fit of tears and rage. The last day he'd set foot in Aveline Castle before his duty to England brought him back here. But it was only fair that he lay it all out in the open, not just so that Emma understood this but so that one day she might understand everything else. Why he became what he had. Why he would walk away when all of this was through.

"Mother did hate it here. She was a very bitter woman who viewed England as a prison," Derick said. "And to her it was. She longed to return to France, particularly after she was banished here to the castle, but Scarsdale would never allow it."

"Why not? It's not as if he cared about her, and I never got the sense that she cared for him either. As far as I know, they hadn't seen each other or spoken for over twenty years."

"They hadn't. But you see, as much as my mother hated England, Scarsdale hated her. He wanted her to rot away here, to punish her."

"Like locking her in a tower? That's barbaric," Emma said. "What could she have possibly done to merit such treatment?"

What she and I are both best at. "She deceived him. At her family's insistence, she agreed to marry Scarsdale to escape the deteriorating political scene in France. It was advantageous to both families. Scarsdale's coffers needed filling and my mother's family needed refuge, but at the same time wanted their aristocratic blood to mix with other nobility, even if it had to be English. But unbeknownst to Scarsdale, my mother brought her French lover with her when she married, and she carried on with him behind Scarsdale's back for years."

Emma's amber eyes had gone wide, but he could see she had not reached the obvious conclusion yet—which was just as well. He needed to tell her the worst himself.

He'd never spoken of it to anyone, and it seemed right that if he ever would, it should be to Emma. Emma, who knew him better than anyone else, and after this, always would. He couldn't see himself ever uttering the truth again. Still, knots formed in his middle, twisting his insides from his stomach to his throat. "Perhaps her adultery could have been forgiven if she had done her duty to Scarsdale first, but instead Mother bore him an heir that wasn't his . . . an heir that wasn't even English." He swallowed, his gazed fixed on hers. "Me."

"Oh." The whispered word fell quietly from Emma's lips. Despite the whirling thoughts he could see in her eyes, no other words followed, as if shock had stunned her mind out of the ability of forming more than a two-letter response.

Just as he'd lost the ability to breathe. He turned away from her. He didn't want to know what she was thinking, after all. Didn't want to see her work through the implications, to hear polite placations or assurances that she didn't view him any differently, or that his blood didn't matter. He just wanted this to be over, to move on to a place where no one knew even his name.

"I've uncovered dozens of traitors over the years," he said, feeling more tired than perhaps he ever had. "I've found that people commit treason for as many different reasons as there are traitors, but they usually fall in one of four categories: allegiance to another country, ideological convictions, money and, very rarely, revenge. But I think my mother just hated being forced to live in England against her will. Maybe she thought that if she helped France to win the war, she could go home."

Emma cleared her throat, as if coming out of a daze. "Well, she did grouse all the time about how much she detested the food here."

Derick couldn't help a snort of amusement at that, whether Emma had meant it as levity, or in her own adorable way, had taken him quite literally. It didn't matter. The pall around them had broken, and for that he was grateful. "Well, after several years on the Continent, I must agree with her in that. Traditional English fare *is* rather lacking in flavor and imagination."

"Do be serious, Derick," she said sternly, but the lines around her mouth eased and threatened to turn up.

"Oh, but I am," he replied, enjoying the bit of humor and the ease that could almost pass as camaraderie between them—a small miracle after everything else that had passed between them today. "Never once in my years abroad was I forced to endure blood pudding." He affected a shudder for good measure, just to see if he could bring a smile. "Even French prison food is better than that . . ."

"Hmmph." He could see her trying to hold on to her severe expression, and then she said rather loftily, "Well, I find it quite tasty." She lifted her nose in the air, but humor glinted in her eyes and lifted Derick's spirit.

"Oh, Emma." He affectionately tipped her chin up with the crook of his finger. "You have *got* to get out of Derbyshire."

He almost snatched his hand back when he realized what he'd done, but she didn't flinch from his casual touch. Indeed, if he read the brief hesitation, the way she held her eyes closed just a bit longer than a blink called for, he would say that she savored it.

His heart thumped hard in his chest as he slowly lowered his hand. Could it be that all of the horrid things she'd learned about him today didn't revolt her? His deception, how he'd carried out his duties as an agent, his parentage?

"Oh yes?" she murmured, her amber eyes turned smoky, like the color of expensive brandy warmed over a flame. "Where would you have me go?"

A completely misplaced feeling akin to hope burst inside his chest as the insane thought he'd had in the forest returned, resounding in his mind. *Would* she come with him?

No. No. It was madness to even think it. He was a tainted soul, by blood, by deed. Even if she would settle for a bastard like him, in every meaning of the word, someone of Emma's innocence and grace deserved so much more.

"A good French restaurant would be a start," he said lightly, though he had to force the carefree tone. He stepped away from her then, walking over to the map on the wall that she'd been marking up when he'd come back from securing the house.

"Now I've told you what I know," he said. "It's your turn to explain all of this." He moved his arm in an arc, nodding toward the board and map.

Emma couldn't move for a long moment. He'd told her much more than "what he knew," hadn't he? The barrage of today's revelations was almost too much for her to bear. So many pieces, memories, and thoughts seemed to make a new kind of sense now and yet make no sense at all. It was as if she'd been looking at Derick through a kaleidoscope that blurred his edges, but it hadn't mattered because he'd been such a beautiful, dazzling thing. But now, with a turn of the wrist, the lenses had aligned and he'd come suddenly into sharp, stark view with all of his faults on display.

And she found him even more beautiful.

Dear God, she was a crazy woman. Her emotions had careened from one end of the map to the other today and back again. Not that she could trust them, anyway, especially not where Derick was concerned.

No. She needed to push them out entirely and focus

on what he asked of her. She could analyze what might or might not still lie between her and Derick later.

"Um . . . This," she said as she moved to the map, "is the location where each of the bodies was found. Three of the suspicious deaths, though we'll need to remove one of the markers once we determine which body was least likely to be one of your couriers, and Farnsworth."

"I see," he said in that way people did when they really had no idea what she meant. "But what exactly is it that *you* are hoping to see?"

"Well, I've been thinking . . . what if we can use the locations of the murders to pinpoint where the killer lives?"

He stared harder at her map. "If you could do that, I don't think you'd have to worry about losing your position as magistrate because you're a woman. They'd probably promote you to head of Bow Street." He laughed as he glanced over at her, and then his eyes tightened. "You're serious, aren't you?"

"Yes." She tried to think of a simple way to explain what she had in mind. "Let's say I told you to take a mouthful of water and spit it out all around after I left the room. When I came back, if I measured the location of where every droplet fell and put it into a formula, I could then prove the point of origin, or in this case precisely where you were standing when you spit it."

"That makes some sense, but it's not as if a killer stands in one spot and tosses bodies as far as he can throw them," he pointed out.

"Of course not. But I do think that a person who kills more than once would leave behind *some* sort of pattern. We can argue until someone adequately defines the concept of infinity about whether humans truly are a blank slate at birth or whether personality traits are inborn. But it is thought that once our personalities are set, we are creatures of habit. Do you agree, at least, with that premise?"

"Absolutely. Many times that is how a traitor is eventually caught. He reverts to form, repeats an action or behavior I've previously observed."

Excitement charged her blood. She might really be onto something. In her research she had learned that motivations for crimes were often very similar. Could the way they are carried out be, too?

"Well, perhaps killers do the same. Perhaps a man will kill the same way each time, because it worked for him and he's comfortable with it. Or perhaps he only kills in a certain area, because it is within easy walking distance of his home—I don't know. I would need to compile a lot more statistical data from actual killers themselves, much as I'm doing in regards to the crime statistics maps I'm working on now, to be able to set the kind of rules that would allow for a true analysis—"

"You are *not* going to personally interview murderers."

Emma huffed, caught off guard by his rather authoritarian statement. "I am speaking theoretically, Derick. However, should I decide at some later date to conduct research of that nature, it wouldn't be your business anyway, would it?"

She'd asked the question rhetorically, but now, seeing the conflicting expressions pass over Derick's face, she found she really wanted to hear his answer. He looked as if he dearly wanted to assert some authority over her, but the only person who would have that right would be a husband—and he knew it. She watched as stubborn protectiveness turned to contemplation, which turned to longing, which turned to . . . regret.

"No, I suppose it wouldn't," he murmured, and Emma experienced a fierce pang of regret herself.

She blew out a pent-up breath. "Regardless, since this is such a small, isolated area without a huge population to consider, the principles of my theory might hold up without the additional data," she said. "First, however, I need to determine which two of my three suspicious deaths are most likely to be your couriers."

She walked over to her desk and settled herself behind it, picking up the three sets of records. It took her less than five minutes to decide which of the three to remove from her map, though she did find it difficult to focus with Derick's intense gaze on her the whole time. She felt it like a living thing, warming her skin.

"This man had personal belongings on his body." She rose from her desk and moved to the map, erasing one of the marks. "Nothing that would identify him, but still. Like Farnsworth, the other two had been stripped of everything but their clothing, though neither had been left to the animals as he had. We can, of course, exhume the bodies in the morning to see if they have the same hidden boot compartments, but I feel safe in my assumption that these remaining two are your couriers for our purposes tonight."

"Makes sense."

"Now I just need to assess the geographical characteristics of the crimes." She moved back to her desk and pulled a geometry compass and a measuring stick from the drawer. "The simplest method for what I have in mind would be to draw a circle, being certain that the points of the two most distant crimes are both on the line." She stuck the compass in her mouth and used the stick to measure the distances between where the bodies were found, calculating the approximate center. Then she placed the point of the compass there and rotated it, letting the pencil flow into a great circle, making adjustments as needed. "By this method, the circle would represent the area within which the killer has killed, making the midpoint the most likely location of his residence."

When she was done, she pulled the compass and stepped back. Both she and Derick peered at the map. "Hmmm." The midpoint was directly between Aveline Castle and Wallingford Manor, almost precisely at the cave where they'd played together as children. Well, and as of this afternoon, as adults, too. The heat that accompanied that reminder had nothing to do with embarrassment.

She looked at the map a little more closely. No, not at their cave, but at another, smaller one, not far from it, but still—not where a killer would be expected to live.

"Hmmm," Derick repeated her assessment. "Unless there's a traitorous cave-dwelling hermit who has squatted on our lands for the past decade, I would say that didn't work."

"Well, that was too simple a method anyway," she said. She grabbed a piece of chalk and walked over to her board. "I wonder . . . if I plot the crimes with x and y coordinates . . ." Chalk clicked against slate in rapid staccato as she quickly drew out a graph and converted the locations on the map into coordinates.

"Perhaps the mean will tell us where the killer lives." Emma jotted the equations she would need and got to work.

But strangely, as part of her mind became engaged in the math automatically, it left another part free to think about today—about Derick, about herself, about *them*—unfettered by emotion. The highly logical part that allowed her to see past extraneous detail and get to the heart of the matter—if one *could* get to the heart of a matter without using emotion. A paradox, that.

So what *had* changed between yesterday, when she'd considered herself so in love with Derick, and today? Well, she'd learned that his role as a spy had been much . . . different than she had imagined. Pushing aside the natural insecurities that arose at the thought of forever being compared to those many women who had come before her, did it change the fact that Derick was still a hero? And given all else that he'd admitted to her tonight, an even more wounded hero than he was before? Was he any less in need of the love she would give him?

So she'd discovered that his entire reason for being in Derbyshire was a deception. But was deception for a noble purpose necessarily wrong? Or intended personally against her? Didn't she, in a way, deceive the government herself by pretending that her brother was capable of acting as magistrate because she knew she would do the best job of it?

She also realized that she believed Derick when he said he hadn't purposely lied to her. Not that it made it right, but to a man who'd lived as he had these past many years, it was at least honorable in its own way. When she put her hurt feelings aside, she could also see that he hadn't tried to seduce her. He must have known she'd have been perfectly willing. It would have been the easiest course of action for him, in truth, and yet he'd not taken that avenue. Out of respect for her? Because she was different from any other target he'd had?

After long moments of concentration, her answer pointed to yet another area in the middle of nowhere, both literally and figuratively. Literally, her equation still indicated an area between Aveline Castle and Wallingford Manor, though closer to the castle. Figuratively, she still wasn't sure what she wanted to happen or not happen between her and Derick. She sighed with frustration.

"Perhaps I should try the median rather than the mean," she mumbled, clicking away again, this time focusing on nothing but the math.

Her results simply reversed themselves, moving the point closer to Wallingford Manor this time.

"Emma." Derick reached out and clasped her hand, gently prying the chalk from her fingers. He used his thumb to press circles against her palm, massaging the ache from where she'd been gripping the chalk so tightly. His touch was tender, soothing, incredibly erotic—and dear to her. "Don't fret yourself," he murmured. "You've done more than enough, more than I could have asked."

"I'm just not sure I have enough points of data." She closed her hand around his, turning hers slightly so that it rested palm to palm against his. "Nor do I think my equation is complex enough. I need some time to think and I'll need to make some assumptions . . ." She dropped his hand, and turned her gaze from his face. Instead, she stared at her board. At a safe place. "But I'm not ready to give up."

As she spoke the words, she realized they applied not only to the problem at hand but to how she felt about Derick as well.

Everything she'd thought she knew about him had been challenged today, stripped away like childhood fantasies when faced with the stark realities of life. She didn't have enough data to be sure of him anymore. And her silly little Derick equation? She snorted. It wasn't nearly complex enough to take into account everything he was, and wasn't.

She did need time to think about all she'd learned, time to process it and yes, she would have to make some assumptions from all of the new information she hadn't known before. Assumptions about his past, assumptions about his present . . . maybe even about his future. But she wasn't ready to give up on him. Maybe she would be in the morning, but not yet.

"I'll just keep mulling it over," she said, knowing he would think she meant her murderer equation.

"Perfect. I'd like you to put your mind to work on something else, too. My mother kept journals, but the woman wrote like a damned gossip columnist, never inscribing a person's name, just listing characteristics or situations to describe who she was talking about. Perhaps if you read them, you will be able to recognize people she wrote about at strategic times and we can see if she had any close associations outside of your brother who might have acted as her accomplice."

"All right," she agreed.

"For my part, I'll oversee the exhumation in the morning. Maybe one of the couriers had something of value to the investigation in his boot compartment. At the very least, their identities should be confirmed so that they can be put to rest properly. Give their families some peace, perhaps.

"Then, I'll revisit all of our possible suspects. Our priority shall be Harding. He had the best access to your brother, an association with my mother, and he was clearly here in Derbyshire during everything. Not to mention that he ran the first chance he got. We'll conduct a search in earnest for him first thing."

Derick had paced away from her, and now seemed all business. She was glad of it and did her best to follow suit.

"You know, if it *was* Harding and he *did* kill Molly, what if her death wasn't what it seemed? Nothing else has been."

Derick was already nodding. "Yes. I had that same thought."

She looked over at her map and her equations. "Perhaps I should plug where we found *her* body into my formulas to see if that makes any difference?"

"If you think it will help, by all means. While I'm out hunting Harding, can you discreetly re-question the staff here and at the castle, then, regarding her murder? See if you can unearth anything new?"

Pleased that Derick had faith in her to do so after he'd shown her up at it last time, she answered, "Of course."

"Good. Now, as to our other two suspects. Several days ago, I sent off a dispatch to have a friend look into the tourist you mentioned, Stubbins. As a frequent traveler through the Peak District, he could easily have been the man responsible for the couriers' deaths."

Emma frowned, trying to reconcile the kindly Mr.

Stubbins as a killer. Yet, he certainly had the physical strength . . .

"Can you remember if he was here during the time you estimate Farnsworth was killed?"

"Well, I am no longer certain precisely when Farnsworth met his end," she reminded him, "but Stubbins *was* here at some point in the past couple of months, though without a conversational or written record, I can't be positive exactly when." She thought back, trying to remember anything she and Mr. Stubbins had talked about that might point to a specific date. "I can't say—no reference point comes to mind.

"Although," she continued, just remembering, "he *was* here the week before your mother killed herself. I know because we were discussing how cold it was again this year. Stubbins made the point that it had been two years to the date that Mount Tambora had erupted halfway around the world, and grumbled that the weather should have righted itself by now. That would have been April tenth, and your mother was found April nineteenth. He may still have been in town, for what it's worth."

"Hmmm. Perhaps that's nothing, but I'd certainly like to know where he was last month, and even tonight, for that matter, before he's ruled out. We'll have to wait until I hear back from the War Department on him, however. As for Smith-Barton, I'll interview him again tomorrow afternoon."

"Again? You visited Albert?" Emma waited for the familiar feelings of failure at the thought of her broken engagement. Instead, gratefulness bloomed in her heart that she wasn't tied to the man. If that bounder had gone through with their marriage, she would never have had these past weeks with Derick.

Emma tried to picture the two men in the same room together. Albert was slight and pale and, in comparison to Derick at least, a little effeminate. Derick was tall, dark and wholly masculine—not in an overpowering way but in a subtle, inherently male way that stole her breath even to be near him. She realized she'd rather have had one afternoon in Derick's arms than a lifetime in any other man's, in spite of everything.

Didn't that answer all of her questions? She didn't know, but they were discussing Albert right now. "What on earth did you say to him?"

The dark half smile that lifted Derick's lips made Emma wish she'd been a fly on that wallpaper. Albert had likely been terribly intimidated. That thought brought Emma just a touch of guilty joy.

"I told him he was a bloody fool to let you go."

Emma caught her breath at the sudden heat in Derick's eyes. Whatever *was* between them was strong, unusual. When she allowed her hurt and anger and insecurities to get out of the way, she knew that—even in all of her inexperience.

Would *she* be a bloody fool to let Derick go? That was the real question, wasn't it? And one that she wouldn't be able to answer with him in the same room, enticing her senses, distracting her thoughts. She probably wouldn't even be able to think straight with him in the same house.

"Yes, well, it's late and we both should find our bed."

Derick's black eyebrows winged high.

"I mean beds." Emma felt her skin blotch red. "W-would you like me to meet you at the castle in the morning? It would make more sense for me to come to your mother's journals rather than have you bring them back here."

Derick's eyes had gone the same mossy green as they had earlier in the forest. "I'll escort you to the castle in the morning myself. I'll be staying at the manor tonight, Emma."

"Here?" A nervous thrill shot through her. "Why?"

"Someone tried to get into your house this very evening, and we now know for certain there is a killer on the loose. Maybe he will just watch and see, thinking that perhaps your finding Farnsworth will be no different than your finding the other couriers. Or maybe he's spooked now, knowing how close Farnsworth had come to him and thinks getting rid of you will ensure he's not caught. Either way, you can't really think I'm going to let you stay alone here, unprotected."

"But—"

"Perkins is having a room made up for me. The Blue Room, I think he said."

"But that's right across the hall from me!"

"The better to protect you, my dear." The slow smile that accompanied his jest was decidedly wolfish.

Yes, but who was going to protect her from herself?

"Don't you think you should sleep downstairs, closer to George?" she tried. "He'd be the one truly in danger."

Derick stepped close to her, the smile fading from his face. "Station an additional footman to guard your brother if you wish, Pygmy. But your safety is more important to me." He reached out and cupped her face with one hand, his thumb dragging slowly across her cheek.

"Don't call me that," she said automatically, but there was no heat to it. A slow smile spread across his face, and then he turned and was gone.

Oh my. How on earth was she going to sort out any of her jumbled thoughts and feelings knowing that Derick slept mere feet from her?

And more importantly, how was she going to keep herself from going to him in the night?

Chapter Twenty-one

Derick sat in an armchair in the Blue Room, next to the crackling fire that had been laid by one of Wallingford Manor's footmen. The unnaturally dyed blue leather had made him quite leery at first glance, but it was more comfortable than it looked. He was glad of it, as he doubted that sleep was in his near future.

He settled deeper into the cushion, slouching low as the leather creaked in protest, and raised a cut-glass snifter to the level of his eyes. Swirling its contents round and round, he watched the fire through the crystal, the flames distorted by the brandy inside his glass. The effect gave the amber liquid the appearance of being lit from within. Just like Emma's golden eyes.

He sat the brandy down on the table beside him, untouched. He might never be able to drink the stuff again, which was a damned shame. He *liked* brandy. But it would forever be a reminder of Emma, and of what he was choosing to leave behind.

And leave her behind he would. She was part of his past—maybe the only good part, but part just the same. And his past was what he intended to forget, along with all of the painful memories that went with it. It had worked for him before, and it would again.

So why did the idea of departing for the Americas all of a sudden leave him feeling empty and hollow?

He cut his eyes to the snifter on the table. A drink might fill the void, at least temporarily. He may be swearing off the stuff when he left Derbyshire, but it wouldn't hurt to enjoy a taste while he was still here, would it?

Of course not. He reached for the glass and took a swallow. *It wouldn't hurt to enjoy your last few days with Emma, either,* his conscience whispered darkly.

Derick choked as the liquor burned its way down his throat. Oh yes, it would hurt. Either her or him, or both, but it would most definitely hurt.

He set the snifter aside, the heavy glass clicking against the wooden tabletop, and rifled a hand through his hair. How the hell had Emma gotten under his skin so deeply so quickly? How many years had he made it through, how many women, without letting anyone inside? And now that he was *this* close to putting it all behind him, one tiny, stubborn slip of a woman had burrowed her way in and he feared she might never leave, even when he did.

It must be because she'd always been there. Not consciously, or even obviously, but rather like a single gold thread woven into the tapestry of his life. When he was young, he wouldn't have noticed it, instead drawn to the rich colors—the reds, the greens, the blues. But those vibrant shades had long been sullied, turned dark and dull, making the gold shine out even more. There all along, and all along the most valuable thread of all.

And now, as a man well aware of the preciousness of gold, he could no longer miss it—no longer miss her— and he greatly feared that now that he'd noticed her, she could never be unseen.

But he would do his damnedest.

A soft knock floated across the room, neither hesitant nor forceful. Emma. Every one of his senses shifted into sensual alert. It would be dangerous to allow her in now. He should pretend to be asleep . . .

But she didn't give him the choice. The knob turned and she entered like a whisper, reaching him almost as quickly. The clean scent of lavender filled his nose as she passed by him, coming to stand before the fire.

"You're awake," she murmured.

Derick's grip tightened on the arms of his chair. Emma stood before him in her night rail and wrapper, a plain, simple combination of pale green that was more alluring than even the most intricately revealing lingerie he'd ever uncovered. She'd clearly just bathed, as her skin was rosy from warm water and scrubbing, and her hair—her glorious chestnut hair—fell down her back and around her face in damp, drying curls.

"You shouldn't be here," he answered, aware that his voice had gone husky with the raging desire she always seemed to elicit in him.

"You're right. I shouldn't." She looked around her for a moment, then dragged a stool over and settled herself on it, just in front of him. So close that if she reached out she'd be able to place her hands upon his knees. She looked directly into his eyes, holding his gaze. "But I'm not going to leave unless you demand that I go."

He swallowed, somehow unable to say the words, even though he knew he should. And Emma saw it, he knew, saw his hesitation. Saw it and pounced on it.

"I thought not." She did reach forward then, caressing the tops of his thighs with both hands.

At his groan, she actually smiled, a slow, sensuous thing that threatened to undo him. "Emma . . ."

"I have a question I must ask you. And remember, you promised earlier you'd always tell me the truth as long as I was certain I wanted to know it." Her smile had faded, and despite her confident tone, her hands trembled upon his thighs. He felt the tiny quaking to his bones. She must very much fear the answer to whatever she was about to ask.

His heart sped. He was fairly certain that whatever she asked, he wouldn't want to answer as much or even more than she apparently wanted him to. But he nodded his head. He *had* promised. "All right."

Her trembling increased. Derick moved his own hands atop hers, pinning her palms against his thighs.

She took a breath.

"When you—" Emma swallowed, shaking her head. She started again. "When we made love, was it a means to an end? A tool of your profession, as you claimed it to be with all of the others?"

Ah, hell.

"Did you feel nothing for me?" she whispered.

Lie! his mind shrieked, like a damned scared old woman. *Lie to her! It would be kinder.*

But the vulnerability he saw in her eyes wouldn't let him. He couldn't do it. Couldn't let her think she'd meant less than she had.

Derick squeezed his eyes shut and a muscle ticked in his jaw. He felt it leaping in time with his pounding heart. "I've never experienced anything like what I felt with you in my arms, Emma. It was like . . ." He opened his eyes then, looked deeply into hers, and gave the most honest answer he knew. "It was like it was my very first time."

Speaking the words aloud broke something within him. A dam, a wall, a shell. And it hurt, a sharp, piercing pain through his heart.

"It was your first time making *love*," she whispered, nodding slowly as if he'd confirmed something she'd suspected. She turned her hands beneath his, now gripping him palm to palm. "It was mine, too. But . . ." Her tongue came out to wet her lips nervously. "But I don't want it to be my last."

He choked on a cross between a laugh and the unfamiliar tightness in his throat. "It won't be your last time. You're an incredible, desirable woman. There will be another man, a better ma—"

"No," she whispered fiercely. "There was ever only you. There will only ever *be* you, Derick." Emma dropped to her knees between his, kicking the stool away behind her and settling back on her heels like an entreating angel, swathed in green, preparing to pray for the soul of a lost sinner. "If you turn me away now, you will doom me to a life without love. I will awaken every day with your name on my lips. I will mourn every lonely night in my bed. I will always, always want you. And I think you will want me, too."

He suspected he would. Every moment. But that didn't mean they should be together. "Emma, you deserve more."

"But what if I don't want more?" she cried.

"Then I want more *for* you," he growled. God, he felt trapped. He couldn't bolt to his feet with her kneeling between his legs without kicking her, couldn't yank his hands from the tightness of her grip without hurting her. Sweat popped out on his brow, and his skin began to itch. "More than a bastard, more than a deceitful cad, more than a bloody impostor with no country of his own."

"Oh yes?" Emma rose off of her heels, as high as she could while still kneeling. Her face was very near his and her eyes blazed with indignation, or passion, or both. "Well, I want more for *you*, too. More than unwarranted shame, more than undeserved self-loathing, more than a bloody future with no *home* of your own." And then her voice and her gaze softened. "Not like the one I could give you."

He'd stopped breathing at her fierce avowal, whereas her breasts rose and fell rapidly as she took in great gulps of air.

She pulled her hands from his, and pressed them once again upon his thighs to help herself to rise.

Thank God. He burned to leap from the chair and put some distance between them—would as soon as she bloody moved away.

But she didn't. She simply stood firmly between his thighs once she'd gained her feet. She reached out and grasped either side of his face between her hands and leaned into him.

"Derick, no matter what has come before, no matter what you've done or who you've been . . . I don't care. You can start over. With me. Because no matter any of it, *I know you*. And I love you."

She brought her lips to his, a sweet, trembling kiss that was there and gone almost before it registered.

"Won't you love me, too?" she whispered against his mouth.

Derick's pulse drove hard and fast, desire—both physical and dangerously, unfamiliarly, emotional—pumped through his veins, pushing away his resistance beat by beat by beat.

She deserved better than him. And he deserved so much worse than her. But . . .

Could he have a fresh start with Emma? Could her love wash away his past? How could he forget the bad if she were always with him, a reminder of who he'd been and where he'd come from?

He reached out and cupped her face between his own hands, just as she still held him. He eased her back just enough that he could see her eyes, and his breath caught. They brimmed with an emotion he hadn't felt in years. One he'd almost forgotten. One he desperately needed.

Hope.

He widened his legs as his hands left her face and

pulled at her shoulders instead. He tugged Emma down upon his lap, cradling her across his thighs as he took her lips with his. She whimpered as his mouth crushed hers, but in relief rather than fear, he knew. Still, he gentled, his hands returning to her face in tender caresses.

God, he trembled like a boy as he touched her skin with reverent strokes. It was as if what he'd told her earlier was true, as if he'd never done this before. And he hadn't, he realized. Not even when he'd been with her, because then he hadn't *known* he loved her.

"Oh, Emma," he gasped between kisses, not wishing to part from her even long enough to draw breath. "I need you," he whispered, the truth falling from his lips before he could stop it. He closed his eyes so that he could breathe her in, experience her through his other senses. "God, how I need you."

"I know," she moaned. "I'm only glad you finally figured it out."

Derick's eyes flew open and he barked a startled laugh. Leave it to his darling Pygmy to say just what was on her mind. He pulled back and caressed her cheek. "Well," he chuckled, "we're not all as brilliant as you, love. It takes some of us longer than others."

Emma flushed a delicate rose. "I didn't mean it that w—"

"I know." And he kissed her again.

He spent long minutes simply playing about her lips. Their tongues intertwined, rubbed along each other, caressed, danced away, and caressed again. Never had he experienced such intimacy. He thought of nothing else but the pleasure to be had between just her mouth and his.

"Derick," she moaned. "Please . . ." She tugged at his wrist, as if begging him to move his hands from her face and touch her anywhere. Everywhere.

He blinked, trying to pull himself out of a daze. Lost as he'd been in her, he'd nearly forgotten there was anything in the world beyond her kiss. Had he ever felt this way? Such a desire to meld with another person, to melt into her so that he didn't know where he ended and she began?

No. It was amazing, this ability to lose himself, to forget. But now that she'd brought his attention to their burgeoning need, he felt it keenly. He slipped an arm beneath her knees and the other behind her back, gathering her to him as he rose from the chair.

"Where are we going?" Emma asked as she pressed tiny kisses against the corners of his mouth.

"I'm going to take you in a bed, properly this time."

Emma turned her head to the massive four-poster, draped in blue velvets of varying shades. "No, please. It's too dark. I want to see you when you touch me . . ." Her lashes fell, as did her voice. "When you're inside of me."

At her words, a fierce primal instinct clamored. Damn, how he wanted that, too. And then she raised her gaze to him. The intensity blazing from her eyes sent a hot shiver through him. "I want to see you when I touch you, too," she purred.

Her words stilled his feet, but sent his pulse racing faster than it ever had, even those times when he'd been nearly captured with information that would have gotten him tortured and killed.

"By the fire," she suggested huskily.

Derick started toward the bed again, and Emma moaned her protest. "I'm only snagging the coverlet, love," he promised as he reversed course, dragging the thick blanket along behind them. When they reached the hearth, he let her down gently, enjoying the slow glide of her body against his until she gained her feet. Silently she took one end of the coverlet while he took the other. They folded it over and spread it in front of the fire.

When it was settled, they stood facing each other, exchanging hungry looks but nothing more. Christ, he was at loose ends, unsure how to proceed when he had no agenda but pleasure. Hers *and* his . . . sex not as a device, but as a way to cherish another person and let that person cherish him.

Emma seemed to understand. She stepped forward and took his hand, tugging him to the center of the blanket. "Stand here," she murmured. He did, spreading his feet shoulder width apart. He found himself shifting nervously, like a virgin bride. Damnation.

Emma let go of his hand and rested her palm against his stomach. It leapt beneath her touch, and a hot thrill shot through his body. Then she circled him slowly, her palm dragging along his hip. She nudged him until he raised his arm, allowing her to pass under and behind, skimming across his buttocks. She did the same as she came around, caressing his other hip until she stood before him again. Heat as he'd never felt radiated above and below the sensual equator she'd traced.

And yet her touch had been more than sexual. It had been an exploration, a claiming. And that made him burn all the more.

Emma tugged his shirt from his trousers and placed both palms beneath the fabric, against the bare skin of his stomach. "Emma," he gasped. His entire body had been rock hard and rigid from the moment she'd first placed that trembling kiss upon his lips. He didn't know how he'd be able to stand much more, which was bloody laughable. She'd barely touched his body! Yet it was as if since he'd acknowledged his love for her, her ability to excite and entice him had magnified. "Whatever you're going to do, do it quickly."

A wholly seductive grin wreathed her face. "Bend down for me," she said, and pulled his shirt over his head when he complied.

When his mouth came free of the cotton, Emma captured it with hers and everything became a blur of sensation and emotion, touch and devotion. His mind could hardly keep track of where she touched, where he touched. Lips to neck, tongue to ear, hand to breast, mouth to nipple. Moans of pleasure and need, all charged with an undercurrent of tenderness, and the completely novel sense of giving himself to Emma.

Was this what it felt like to make love? Always he'd measured every movement—always in control. He'd focused solely on what he needed to do to drive a woman to tell him her darkest secrets while giving away nothing himself. Yet when Emma touched him, it was all he could do to think at all. And he was on the verge of confessing his very soul to her. He would give her anything right now.

When they'd been together before, she'd been able to push him beyond his conscious control at certain points, yes, but he hadn't allowed himself to wholly feel. But now that he'd accepted his love for her, he couldn't stop it, couldn't halt the sensations rioting through him at every touch of her hand, every stroke, every murmured word of love.

And then, somehow, his pants were gone. Her pale green bodice was well beneath her breasts and the flowing skirt high about her waist and he was poised above her, at the entrance of her body. They were still kissing— desperately, hungrily, intimately. And they held that kiss as he entered her, both emitting low moans that were captured by the other.

"Emma," he whispered when he was fully inside, encased by her heat, enveloped by her love. He withdrew slowly, savoring the slick slide as she gripped him, all the while understanding that the hold she had on him was so much more than physical.

"Emma," he said again as he drove back into her depths. "Emma. Emma. Emma." Her name became a litany upon his lips, murmured with every hard thrust, echoed by her cries of passion. It had never been like this. This urgency combined with a sense of rightness. That he was joining with the one person to whom he belonged.

Within him, the tumult built. Within her, too—he could feel her tightening around him. Mindless now, he pulled her hips harder to him as he continued to thrust, pulled her along with him toward glorious oblivion.

It burst upon them—first him, he thought, but his wild thrashing triggered her release right after. Then they flew together, clinging to each other as pleasure buffeted them, took them up in the whirling storm, and tossed them back out again. Pleasure so intense it bordered on painful, at least for him. It could only be because so much more than his body had been given, to Emma. Only Emma.

The first thing he registered as his conscious mind returned was her soft cheek resting against his, hot and damp with sweat. Then he heard their rasping breaths, his, hers, blending together in satiated harmony like the final movement of a symphony after a thrilling crescendo.

His arms trembled, his muscles spent and weak. He should move. He must be crushing her, and yet he couldn't fathom being apart from her, either. Ever. He shifted to his side, taking her with him so they might stay joined. Then he sealed their lips in another deep, languid kiss, wanting nothing more than to prolong this new intimacy between them forever.

Emma tasted of warm sunshine and fresh air and promise—impossible, he knew, but her kiss made him feel as if endless summer days stretched out before him once again. Carefree days, like the ones before his world had changed irrevocably.

She also tasted of salt and of . . . tears? Alarm chased away his sanguinity. Had he hurt her? She still kissed him as tenderly as he did her. She hadn't tensed in his arms, had made no sounds of distress. And yet he knew that not all pain was physical. Damn it all, he'd known one of them would get hurt if he gave in to his desire for her.

Derick framed Emma's face with his hands and eased back, prepared to demand why she cried, to do anything it took to soothe her. Her amber eyes had gone a deep gold and were dilated with spent passion . . . but they were also completely dry.

Derick licked his lips, the taste of tears still strong upon them, just as Emma gasped softly. She touched her hand to his face and caressed his cheek. "Oh, Derick," she whispered.

He frowned, bringing his own hand up to his other cheek, and was met with warm moisture. It was *he* who wept? Yes. Silently, unconsciously, moved by the beauty he'd found in her arms.

Despite the shock, a peace unlike any he'd ever known settled over Derick. One he would never have believed possible. Emma loved him. He pulled her tighter to him, melting as she tucked her face into the crook of his neck.

He never wanted to let her go.

"Emma," he whispered, "come with me." He brushed his hand over her hair, his fingers tangling in the damp curls. It might be a mistake. It might be unfair to her, but he no longer wanted to fight what had always been between them. What he knew now always would be. "Come with me to America . . . as my wife."

Wife? Elation burst in Emma's chest and her heart soared toward the stars . . . until it stalled . . . froze in midflight . . . hurtled back to the earth in an out-of-control spin. "A-America?"

She couldn't have heard him correctly.

Emma lifted her head, pulling back as far as Derick's embrace would allow. "Did you say America?"

His chin dropped in a determined nod. "It's where I

intend to make my home after my work for England is
complete."

"But—" Emma wiggled out of his arms. What was he
saying? She couldn't think properly tucked so close to
his hot skin, with his intoxicating scent fogging her
senses. She brought herself to a sitting position, glancing
down at her wanton state. She certainly couldn't think
half-naked, either. She tugged her bodice up, the soft
cotton scraping roughly against her still sensitive breasts.
Derick's eyes flared at the movement, as if he regretted
she'd removed them from his sight. Her hand shook as
she pushed the skirt of her night rail back down her legs
and scooched back from him. He actually sighed at that.

The bit of distance she'd put between them helped
her get control of her thoughts, but only a minor percentage. There was still the distraction of his magnifi-
cently muscled, utterly naked body lounging inches
from her. "But," she said again, "your work for England
will never be done. You may retire from spy work, but
you're a viscount, Derick. You have respons—"

"I'm no viscount," he said harshly, swinging his leg
around and rising to a seated position himself. All pretense of lounging vanished as he seemed to vibrate with
tension. "I am a French bastard, Emma. Not a British
aristocrat."

"What complete poppycock!" Why was he so hung
up on this erroneous conviction that it was blood that
made a man? She answered her own question—because
most people still were. Bloodlines were considered everything. People were fools.

But Derick wasn't, though he was likely entrenched
in his beliefs if he'd held them all these years. She wanted
to reach out to him, but she sensed that would be the
wrong way to handle this. If she tried to coddle him, he'd
probably just tell himself that she placated him rather
than admit his thinking was flawed. So she pointed an
aggressive finger at him instead, determined to use logic

to convince him he was wrong. "You're a British viscount in everyone's eyes but your own."

He scowled at her. "That's because they don't know—"

"So what if they did?" she challenged. "Under the law, any issue born within a legal union is legitimate. That alone makes you Scarsdale."

"Argh," he growled, gaining his feet. He stalked away from her, and despite the tension in the moment, Emma couldn't help but admire his lithe, potently masculine form. Couldn't help but remember him moving powerfully within her, and her core went all soft and warm even as the strain growing between them tightened the rest of her.

"That's not what matters here," he insisted.

"No?" She stood herself, following, unwilling to let him run from this fight. "Fine. So you're not descended from generations of Avelines. That doesn't matter, either. History is full of men who have had titles created for them to reward them for service to the king. Even men of common birth, which you are not," she pointed out, although she supposed he could be, at least partially. While his mother was the daughter of a French *compte*, she had no idea about the man who'd sired him. "Do you not think you, of all people, would qualify for such an honor after all you've done?"

"Emma . . ." he warned, his eyes gone dark and stormy.

"I'm right, and you know it. But you don't need to have a title created for you, because you were born to one."

"I was *born* into a lie," he shouted, turning to face her. "I've *lived* a lie." He slammed his fist into the center of his chest. "I *am* a lie."

Emma's breaths came rapid and tight, knowing they'd come to the heart of it. She reached out her hand, placing it tentatively over his fist, ready to attempt the most significant proof of her life—mathematical or otherwise.

She could do this. *First step, list your statements and the reasons the statements are true.*

"No, Derick," she said softly. "You may have been born into a lie, but you lived the life *given* to you to live. You may have French blood flowing through your veins, but you've proven by your actions, your service to England, that you are just as British as anyone else born here. *More* so. You've certainly given more to your country."

"Your country," he muttered, but without heat. She was getting through to him. She knew it.

"*Our* country."

His eyes drifted closed, midnight black lashes fanning over his cheeks in a way that made him look like a dark angel.

She almost had him. Just a couple more steps. Statements and reasons leading to the proper conclusion. "In your heart, Derick, I know you love England, or you wouldn't have spent the last fourteen years of your life doing everything you've had to do to protect her."

His lids flicked open and the stark sadness in them brought sharp tears to her eyes. "I do love England. And I've done what I can for her. Gladly." He lifted his fist, still enclosed in her palm, from his chest and slammed it back into himself. "But it has cost me, Emma. Bits of soul that I'll never get back."

Emma felt his pain as if it were her chest thumped by their joined hands. A sinking fear settled in her middle. This was where math failed her . . . when she tried to apply it to the messy world of real people. If only she were a fraction as proficient with them as she was with numbers. But numbers didn't come with feelings. With memories that could spoil everything.

Derick plucked her hand from his and then took both of hers in his warm grip.

"You said earlier that I could start over. That had always been my aim, but until today, I hadn't truly thought it possible. But you gave me hope, Emma. I believe that with you I just might be able to begin anew."

But it seemed it would be all right. Emma felt the smile building inside before it lifted her lips. "Oh, Derick, you can."

"But not here," he said quietly. "Not in Derbyshire. Not even in England." He squeezed her hands firmly, almost tugging her toward him. "Come with me."

Emma's smile froze on her face and her chest squeezed so, she couldn't catch her breath. Go with him? She'd always, *always* wanted to be his wife. As long as she could remember, even when she didn't dare to dream it anymore. And here was her chance, but . . . leave England? "I can't. My brother—"

"Can come with us."

Emma shook her head vehemently. "And leave *two* titles abandoned? It's bad enough you plan to desert your duties, but what of Wallingford lands, our tenants, our responsibilities to them?"

A muscle ticked in Derick's jaw. She felt low for implying he was shirking his duty after all he'd given to his country, but it was true! When you were of the noble class, duty never ended.

His voice was tight and low. "Hire a competent steward, as I have."

Emma scoffed, jerking her hands from his. She spun away from him to stare at the fire, grateful for any spot to focus aside from him. "The people here deserve better than that. They deserve landowners who are involved, who care about their prosperity. Besides, I have my work—"

"Which you could still do from America." Derick stood behind her now. His voice held a pleading quality that shook her resolve. His breath brushed against the side of her neck, sending shivers of longing that pricked through her despair. "The correspondence might take longer, but it could be done. My friend the Earl of Stratford could easily be persuaded to present your ideas to Parliament here. He's a crusader. This is just the sort of thing that would appeal to him."

He placed his hands on her shoulders, turning her slowly back to face him. "Or better yet, do your work *for* America. Think about it—she's a young country, not yet so set in her ways. Less civilized. Imagine if you used your findings about crimes and criminals there and helped *shape* the laws rather than spending your life fighting to change laws here that have been in place for centuries."

Emma damned him for tempting her, for using her tactics against her, for trying to appeal to her logic when, for once, this wasn't about logic. But it wasn't about logic for him, either, was it? Still, "No," she whispered, her voice cracking. "No," she said more firmly. "I know my place, and it's here."

His grip tightened on her shoulders. "Then I envy you, Emma." His green gaze bored into her. "I don't know my place. But I *do* know that it's *not* here. I can't live another day pretending to be something, *someone*, that I'm not. Can't you see that?"

"No," she cried. "What I see is a man who can't live another day pretending *not* to be something that you *are*! I don't care what the makeup of your blood is, Derick. You're an Englishman, through and through. You belong here, just as I do."

She knew the look of frustrated longing that twisted his features must be reflected in her own. She'd never felt such desperation, such an inability to affect her world. This was not some equation she could manipulate. She couldn't add or subtract, couldn't multiply or divide from either side of the equal sign and make things come out right. The truth of that pierced her.

When the light faded from his jewel-toned eyes, Emma knew that she'd failed. "No, Emma." He dropped his hands from her and turned away. "I don't."

Chapter Twenty-two

The late Viscountess Scarsdale's loopy, flowing hand-writing—so different from her own neat, efficient scrawl—blurred in front of Emma's eyes.

Ensconced on a chaise in the study at Aveline Castle, it seemed as if she had been reading for hours. She'd been summoned just after dawn to find Derick waiting for her in her downstairs parlor, anxious to drop her at the castle and take up the search for Harding.

She'd taken perverse pleasure in his haggard appearance, as it seemed he had spent the last awful hours of the night as she had—alone, sleepless and suffering. But then, of course, she'd felt guilty. She didn't truly wish upon Derick the soul-deep ache that gnawed at her, even if it was his fault that they both hurt so.

Emma sighed, tucking her legs more tightly beneath her, one of Lady Scarsdale's leather-bound journals forgotten upon her lap. Was it his fault any more than it was hers? Was his stubborn insistence to leave England any more to blame than her own to stay?

Yes, blast it all. It was. He had no ties to America, whereas her entire life was here in Derbyshire. He had lived all over the Continent these past fourteen years, whereas she'd never lived anywhere else. He was the adaptable one, whereas she . . .

She was afraid to leave. She controlled her life here in her little sphere. It was ordered just the way she liked it. Even her disorder, like her messy cloakroom and the careful chaos of her study, was that way because she chose it to be. Here, she knew exactly who she was. Here, everything made sense in an Emma sort of way that made her comfortable, content.

There was nothing wrong with that, was there? Should she toss everything she knew aside just because Derick was determined to run from who *he* was?

Emma forced her mind back to the book in her lap. The viscountess' writings were much like the woman herself had been—flighty and shallow with an interesting mix of wit and biting sarcasm. But there were also glimpses of a woman Emma hadn't known. A lonely woman. A sad woman. An angry woman.

Some journal entries were filled with Lady Scarsdale's observations of the small-town society around her. Those were the sardonically funny bits. The viscountess had had a flair for description. While Derick was correct that his mother had not named people in her journals, Emma had easily picked out various friends and neighbors throughout, including herself. And every one of their suspects. She'd jotted down names and dates next to each, to look for a pattern later against dates that were important to their investigation.

Other entries were filled with mourning and sorrow, rage and resentment. The sentiments on the page alternated between pining for a lost love and cursing fate and Scarsdale and everything else that stood between the woman and her lover.

Emma's chest grew tight. Is that how she would feel after a few years of being separated from Derick? Knowing her love was a country away, out of her reach? Not even in a neighboring country, close as France, but an entire *ocean* away. Would it turn her bitter and cold to be without him?

And would it make it better that their separation was not forced by a furious husband, but because both she and Derick were too afraid to be together? Or would that sad truth make it infinitely worse?

A drop of moisture splashed on the page, smearing the ink, joining older, long-dried tears that Lady Scarsdale must have cried years ago. Emma swiped at it with her thumb, which only served to blur part of a sentence.

She sniffed, disgusted with herself. This wasn't about her. She was reading these journals only to look for evidence that the viscountess had been a traitor and for insight into who might have been her accomplice.

She dug back into the journals, taking special note of dates when Lady Scarsdale had been with her brother. Perhaps Derick might have dates of when information was passed that corresponded.

All the while, Emma tried very hard to pretend the viscountess' steamy recollections of lovemaking were written about someone other than George. Still, it was easy to see that Derick's mother had felt no love for Emma's brother, although there was certainly affection. But then, how could Lady Scarsdale have ever loved George when she had apparently pined for the Frenchman who'd sired her son until her dying day?

Emma couldn't imagine taking another lover after Derick left for America.

Oh, why was she thinking of him again?

After a couple more hours, Emma closed the cover on the last journal and rose to her feet. She stretched her arms above her head, restoring blood to her tingling muscles. She hadn't been able to put Derick out of her mind, so the reading had taken much longer than it should have. Surely Derick would be back soon with news of how his searches had gone.

She gathered the volumes and stacked them neatly

on Derick's desk, then picked up the pages of her notes that would need to be cross-checked.

Even as she looked through them once more, something just didn't balance in her mind.

Through all her reading Emma never got the sense that Lady Scarsdale had been contemplating taking her own life. No explanations, no red flags that her melancholy was any more or less intense toward the end than it had always been.

If anything, these journal entries made Emma question Lady Scarsdale's suicide all the more. Derick's theory that his mother was afraid she was close to being discovered and chose to take her life rather than be captured would at least explain it, but it still didn't feel right to Emma.

So what if . . .

What if she hadn't?

Emma couldn't dispute Derick's theory that Lady Scarsdale had had the best access to George, through either herself or Harding. Nor could she deny that the viscountess would be the most likely person in the area to have the French connections necessary to perpetrate a long deception. She'd certainly had enough pull to learn what had become of her son during wartime. And Derick had said that the staff at Aveline Castle claimed his mother had become very anxious and jumpy during the last days of her life.

So what could all of that mean? Well, what if Lady Scarsdale hadn't been the traitor, but the traitor's accomplice . . . maybe even unwittingly? And what if she'd come to suspect something was wrong, and that was why she'd gotten anxious . . . maybe she'd even confronted the real traitor. What if her death wasn't what it seemed either?

After all, nothing else in this whole twisted tale was what it seemed.

Emma looked behind her, to the wall. The map Derick had taken such offense at her marking up the first night he'd come back had been re-hung. She snagged it and pulled it from its frame once again. From memory, she marked the four bodies she knew—two couriers, Farnsworth and Molly.

After she'd included Molly's murder in her calculations, Emma had discovered that four points of data still weren't enough to make her equation work. But perhaps *five* would be sufficient to point to the villain's residence. It wouldn't be the first time she couldn't get an equation to work without enough data points. And if her instincts were right . . .

She drew a mark where Lady Scarsdale's body had been found.

Her hand started to shake. *When this is over, Derick will leave again.*

Emma closed her eyes. *And he won't come back this time.*

Be that as it may, a killer needed to be caught and as magistrate, she ultimately had the responsibility to catch him. This was her home, after all.

It took much snooping to find a ruler to make her distance measurements, but once she had them for five bodies now, she plugged the information into the formula she'd tweaked.

She stared at the new coordinates that should point to where the killer lived.

Then she plotted them on the map.

Derick handed his reins to a stable boy at the Swan and Stag. "Just water," he told the groom. "I won't be long."

The youth nodded and led the horse away.

Derick's shadow followed him as he made his way toward the entrance of the inn and pub. The sun had long passed the midpoint in the sky and now arced farther west with every passing hour.

It had been a day of confirmations and frustrations. This morning's exhumations had proven Emma's guess correct, and the two missing couriers had now officially been found. In both boot compartments had been the men's identification, as well as both of their vials of last resort, still full.

But there had been no word about Harding's whereabouts. No one, it seemed, had seen or heard from the man. Interviews with the village's ostlers told Derick the footman hadn't taken a coach from town unless he had stowed away, and no one had reported any stolen horseflesh. Harding either traveled on foot, or more likely, was hiding out somewhere in the area. If that were the case, Derick knew very well it could take days or perhaps even weeks to run the man to ground.

Days or weeks of strained cooperation between him and Emma. Days or weeks of awkward, tormented silences like this morning's, each desperately wanting the other but needing something neither was willing to give. Days or weeks of torture.

And what if Harding didn't surface? How long would it be before Derick felt safe that the man was gone for good? Safe enough to leave Emma without his protection, that was. Their mutual suffering could go on for bloody ever.

Unless you decide to stay . . .

Derick stomped his boots on the ground, kicking away the clumping Derbyshire mud before entering the tap. If he stomped harder than necessary, no one seemed to notice.

Hell, he didn't blame Emma for not understanding why he had to leave. How could she when her security, her sense of self lay here, in England? In Derbyshire. He'd meant it when he'd said he envied her. These days spent with her had unlocked enough of his childhood memories that he could almost recall how it had been to feel the same. Enough to realize he'd be cruel to ask her to give that up for him.

So, he would make this last stop and then he'd go back to the castle and discuss the progress with Emma as if yesterday had never happened. He would listen to whatever she'd found, without giving in to the urge to drop to his knees and beg her, again, to come with him. He would tell her what he'd learned today and what he hadn't, all the while pretending that his heart wasn't bleeding inside his chest. And then he would escort her home and lie awake all night in the room across from hers, ignoring his body when it demanded that he march across the hallway and take her over and over again until she agreed to be his wife and leave the country with him.

Derick ducked his head to clear a low-hanging beam as he entered the taproom, his eyes scouring the room for the pub's owner.

"G'd afternoon, m'lord," the portly man greeted him from behind the bar, almost affably. That was a change from his last visit. Indeed, as Derick glanced around at the tap's patrons, he recognized many of the same faces as before, but he also noticed more nods and tentative smiles than distrustful stares.

It was because of Emma, he knew. Since she'd accepted him, the other townspeople had come around—just as he had planned when he'd made his decision to stay close to her. Unfortunately, he hadn't counted on her ability to steal into his soul, or he would have found another way to complete his mission.

Liar. He would do it all again, he realized. No matter how badly the memories would torment him later. At least with Emma, he'd remembered how to *feel*, and that was a gift.

"I'm sure you've heard that I'm looking for Thomas Harding." Derick slipped a coin onto the bar. "Have you seen or heard anything of him lately?"

The owner pulled the coin across the bar with one

hand and slid a pint to Derick at the same time with the other. "Nope, but I 'ave something else ye might be interested in 'earing, if ye can give me a minute."

"Of course."

"Marie!" the man yelled over his shoulder to the equally plump woman drying mugs at the end of the bar. "Go fetch the boy." Then the owner turned back to Derick and nodded to a table in the corner. "I'll meet ye over there as soon as I finish up 'ere."

Intrigued, Derick settled himself in a scuffed wooden chair, his back against the wall so he could survey the whole room. He couldn't imagine what the barkeep could have to tell him, but he certainly knew that information often came when and from places he'd least expected.

He took a long draw of the ale while he waited, enjoying the simple stout flavor that washed his tongue — different from the lighter brews he'd sampled in France, Belgium and Vienna. He wondered how the ale in America would taste, whether he would like it.

The thought struck him that he had never once before wondered whether or not he would *like* living in America. Rather, it had just been a place far from Europe where he could make a fresh start. A land of opportunity, where his name would mean nothing, where he could forg—

"Thanks for yer patience, m'lord." The owner of the Swan and Stag sidled up to the table and pulled out the other chair, his brow raised in question. Derick nodded and the man lowered his girth as the chair groaned. "As I was sayin', I 'aven't seen Harding in days, but just yesterday, I did see one of them other fellows I'd told you about."

Derick straightened in his chair as the hairs on the back of his neck followed suit. "Yesterday?" He'd assumed when the barkeep had first mentioned the stranger that he'd been referring to Farnsworth. Was there another player entirely? Or was the man just a vagabond or a tourist? "Where? When exactly? What was he doing?"

"Don't know what 'e'd been in town doing," the man said, "but I saw 'im cutting across the field behind me stable 'ere, 'eading away from the village. Near dark, I'd say."

"Which direction?"

"East—southeast, more like."

The same direction as Aveline Castle and Wallingford Manor. Damnation.

"And you're absolutely sure it wasn't Harding you saw?"

The owner pursed his lips. "O'course."

Who was this stranger? Was *he* the man that had snuck into Wallingford Manor while they'd been recovering Farnsworth? And how the hell was Derick going to find him, too?

"Seeing 'ow interested ye was in 'earing if I ever saw the man again, I set one of me grooms to follow 'im," the barkeep said with a sly smile. He raised a beefy hand and flicked his fingers. A young lad shuffled over to the table, head bent. "William 'ere can take you right to 'im."

Energy buzzed through Derick, as did a multitude of questions. "Excellent, but I'd rather pay a visit to this stranger alone." If this man were mixed up in any way with treason and murder, Derick wasn't about to put the groom at any more risk than the barkeep already had. He hoped the boy had been smart enough not to have been seen—not only for his own protection but so he hadn't scared the man off. "Can you describe exactly where you followed him to?"

The boy nodded. "Yes, sir. He went into one of them caves, north of the creek. Not the big one, but the one what sort of looks like a keyhole. Do you know it?"

"Yes." Derick drummed his fingers against the scarred tabletop in a slow rhythm, belying how quickly thoughts flew through his mind. Hadn't Emma's first attempt at her equation pointed about there? Yes, he remembered making a joke about a cave-dwelling hermit living there for the past decade. But that was ridiculous, wasn't it? Though hermits were not unusual, they were typically well known to the estate owners and townsfolk—some even making their livelihood in such "hermitages." Whoever this man was, he was no hermit.

But what if he was a killer, a traitor who'd used the cave as his home base when he was in the area? What if Emma had gotten that part right?

Derick leapt to his feet, dropping coins on the table—some for the owner, more for the boy. "With my thanks," he said over his shoulder as he rushed to get his horse.

He briefly thought about getting Emma as well. But no, she was safely tucked away at Aveline Castle with his mother's journals. He wouldn't risk her any more than he would that young groom. After he'd interrogated this stranger would be soon enough to let Emma in on whatever he discovered.

Half an hour later, Derick tied his mount off about a quarter mile from the cave. He'd go the rest of the way on foot. He checked his pistol and tucked it away, just in case he needed it, then headed deeper into the woods.

He smelled the smoke first, a light wisp on the breeze, like that from a cook fire. It was soon followed by the aroma of roasting meat. He slowed his step, moved more quietly. As he got closer to the small clearing where the keyhole cave was situated, it was evident from the tamped-down undergrowth that at least one person had been passing here fairly regularly. He could now see tendrils of smoke rising from a small unattended fire just outside the mouth of the cave. A rough spit had been erected over the fire with what looked to be a large rabbit skewered on it.

Derick crouched low, hidden by a large oak, and waited for the stranger to show himself. Could this be the man he was truly after? If so, it raised more questions than it answered, but that was nothing new. Things so often were more complicated than they seemed, particularly when it came to treason. His instincts told him he was close to uncovering the truth now, and the thrill of the hunt pumped through his veins as he waited for his quarry to show himself.

He didn't have to wait long. Less than a minute passed before a man emerged from the mouth of the cave. A tallish man, though not overly so, a lean build, dark hair—just as the owner of the Swan and Stag had described. A wave of gray smoke from the cook fire obscured Derick's view of his face, however, and by the time it cleared, the man had come around and now stood with his back to Derick. He crouched down to check his supper.

Derick took the opportunity to catch the stranger unaware. He pulled his pistol, hoping he wouldn't need it but intending to be prepared for any eventuality.

"Stop what you are doing and place your hands where I can see them."

The man tensed—Derick felt it as much as saw it— but did as he was ordered. When the man's hands came into view, Derick noticed the man was older than he'd expected, knuckles more pronounced, skin more lined. But still strong enough to kill Farnsworth, he'd wager.

"Now, stand slowly and turn around."

The stranger obeyed and Derick got his first look at the man's face.

His heart kicked so violently, he nearly dropped his gun. It listed sideways in his grip, almost forgotten. His first thought was that there was no way he could have been prepared for this. His second was that he was staring.

Staring into eyes so familiar that he might as well be looking into a mirror.

"Hello, my son."

Chapter Twenty-three

Derick's grip on his pistol tightened, and he righted the weapon, aiming straight at the Frenchman's heart. "It was you?"

Hardly the first thing he'd ever imagined saying upon finally meeting the man who'd sired him, but there it was. Of course, he'd never expected to meet the man under these circumstances.

Damnation. Could any person alive have ever been born of more duplicitous parents than he had been? Should he prick his finger right now, he wouldn't be surprised if the blood that welled from the wound was as black as the ebony hair he and his sire had in common.

He couldn't seem to stop staring at Charles Moreau. While he'd never met him, Derick knew his name well. During that last ugly confrontation he'd had with his mother, she'd gloated over how she'd insisted upon Charles as Derick's middle name to honor her lover and how Scarsdale had never suspected, as Charles was as common an English name as it was French.

"It was me, what?" Moreau asked carefully. His English was very cultured, very natural—but why shouldn't it be? The man had lived here as his mother's secret lover for more than a decade before Scarsdale had discovered them. Moreau still held his hands in the air and his eyes had not left the pistol Derick held on him. A perplexed frown formed between his eyebrows.

As the shock of seeing Moreau dimmed, Derick's thinking cleared. Moreau clearly played some part in this. However, if the Frenchman had been his mother's accomplice, why hadn't he just left England when she killed herself? It made little sense for him to still be around . . . He had no reputation in England to protect.

Something was off. He'd best guard his words carefully and let Moreau do the talking so he could get to the truth.

Derick affected a casual shrug with the shoulder not attached to the hand that held his pistol. "Squatting on my land. I'd heard reports and came to investigate."

"I see." Yet one black brow winged high in clear disbelief. Derick wondered if he looked so arrogant when he made the same gesture, as he knew he did often. "And reports of a vagrant necessitate a pistol?"

Derick narrowed his eyes. "Yes. Now what in the hell are you doing in England, much less here?"

Moreau's eyes narrowed in much the same way, then flicked to the pistol once more. He squared his shoulders. "Why? Are you planning on carrying out your English father's threat?"

"What?" Derick frowned, and then understanding dawned. His mother had told him that when Scarsdale had uncovered the truth, he'd had Moreau severely beaten. Before he was sent back to France, Moreau had been warned that he'd be killed if he ever set foot on English soil again. Derick slowly lowered the pistol. "Of course not."

The Frenchman gave one hard nod of his head, then slowly lowered his hands. *"Merci."*

"You haven't answered my question."

"You haven't answered mine, either. Why the pistol?

Who did you really think might be out here?" he asked, suspicion clear in his voice.

"I told you why I'm here."

Moreau snorted. "Fine. Keep your secrets. God knows you come by them honestly." Moreau turned his back on Derick, crouching to turn the rabbit on the spit, so he didn't see Derick flinch at that hard truth. "I thought maybe you were hunting the man that killed your mother, as I am."

Killed my— He couldn't have heard Moreau correctly. Derick came around the fire so he could see the Frenchman's face. "She killed herself."

Moreau stood and raised his eyes to Derick's. The stark grief in them made Derick wish to look away. Grief and a naked love that was hard to look upon, even all of these years later. Derick couldn't breathe. If he'd felt as if he were looking in a mirror before, it was magnified now . . . only he saw how he would look in the future. Every time he thought of Emma.

"Vivienne would never do such a thing."

Surely Moreau hadn't come all the way from France upon learning of his mother's death because he couldn't believe she'd committed suicide. If he had, that was terribly sad, and Derick didn't wish to be the one to have to convince him of the truth. But he would have to be. "Perhaps, not under normal circumstances," Derick said gently, awkwardly. "But there are things you don't know."

Moreau threw a hand out in an effusive gesture of agitation, or perhaps denial. "There are things you don't know, either."

Yes, there were. About his mother, about Moreau, about why Moreau was here today. And he wanted to know them all. "Then why don't you tell me?" he asked, not sure which answer he sought the most.

Moreau's shoulders relaxed and he nodded. "*Oui.* I will tell you why I am here. Then you can help me avenge my Vivienne." He removed the skewered rabbit from the fire. "Come, sit with me."

Derick followed Moreau to the mouth of the cave, where a crude campsite was set just inside. He refused the man's offer of roasted meat, but did sit on a log that had been pulled in to serve as a seat.

"Your mother, she wrote to me these many years we were kept apart. During wartime, the letters did not come so regularly, but they always came. I begged her, year after year, to come as well, to run away and join me in France. But Vivienne, she never would."

"Why not?" Derick always had had the impression that she would have gone to France in a heartbeat if she were able.

"At first, it was because Scarsdale threatened to stop her family's allowance if she tried to leave."

Derick nodded. That made sense.

"But then," Moreau went on, "even after her parents died and her sisters married, she still would not come."

Derick could sense Moreau's sadness, his confusion. Then the man lifted a shoulder and a bittersweet smile turned his lips.

"I'm sure I don't have to tell you that your mother was spoiled. She'd never lived in anything less than a fine castle, and that was the one thing I couldn't offer her. I'd given up everything to follow her to England when she was forced to marry Scarsdale, you see. We were so young. Stupid. But even if I hadn't left everything behind to be with Vivienne, my family's money and holdings were lost in the Terror. The only wealth I have now is what I have earned, and that was never enough for her. She had no wish to live in a small cottage, nor to do for herself."

Moreau rose from his seat, and began to pace. "It was hard for me to understand. I didn't care where I lived, as long as I could be with Vivienne. I would have come and lived in this *cave*"—he swung his arm in an agitated swipe—"risking my life if I were caught by Scarsdale, just to be with your mother." Moreau let out a long, pained sigh. "And I was very angry that she didn't feel the same."

Derick shook his head. This poor man, so besotted by a selfish woman who didn't deserve such devotion. Not like Emma, who was so very worthy of love.

"Life is too short not to be with the one you love," Moreau said. Derick's body went very still. Would he risk his life in a country he was warned never to enter again, just to be near Emma? *Hell, yes.* So why wouldn't he stay in England to be with her?

Moreau started talking again. "But Vivienne begged me to hold on. Scarsdale was so much older than she. I'm sure you know, her family had negotiated an extremely generous widow's portion for her. She promised that when Scarsdale died, we would use it to purchase a small château near the sea where we could live out the rest of our lives together. I loved her so much, I couldn't have denied her. So we waited. And waited. Twenty-three years, we waited."

What hell that must have been. He couldn't imagine *one* year without Emma. Hell, not one *week*.

"And finally, I received her letter that Scarsdale was dead. Ah, that letter." The Frenchman's eyes closed slowly, as if in remembered bliss. "So full of joy and excitement and promise. Vivienne bade me to come to England and join her here, be with her until the estate was settled and her portion under her own control, and then we would leave England together, just as we had arrived together so many years ago."

What a fool he was being. He wasn't going to be like his parents. He wasn't going to let anything stand in the way of his and Emma's love. If she wouldn't come to America, then he would have to stay here. He could do nothing else.

"But then, only two days after I received that letter, another came, telling me to stay where I am. Vivienne said that she was in trouble and that I was to expect her imminently."

Derick's attention jerked fully back to Moreau. "She was planning to come to you?" That explained her hastily packed valuables. So what happened between her dashing off a letter to Moreau and her jumping off a cliff? Had Farnsworth caught up to her? Had she realized there was no escape from justice?

"Yes, but she never arrived. So after several days' wait, I came here. . . only to find her dead. I will never believe that when we were so close to finally being together Vivienne would take her life. *Non.*"

Moreau's story was worrying, on many levels. Derick chose to focus only on the part that pertained to his mission. His instincts told him to believe Moreau's tale, so he decided to be honest with the man in return. He stood to face him.

"Mother *was* in trouble, which is *why* she killed herself, rather than be arrested." Derick briefly outlined his own version of events—noticing how Moreau flinched when Derick mentioned her long-running affair with George Wallingford—and ending with her taking her own life to avoid being captured as a traitor.

Moreau's ruddy complexion reddened with rising emotion during the telling. "How could you believe such a thing of your mother?"

"Well, in addition to mountains of circumstantial evidence, my mother was a liar and a deceiver, who felt nothing for anyone but herself," he said. Although in light of what he'd just learned, "And perhaps you," he allowed.

"That is not true! She loved *you.* You were her son!"

"She hated me!" Derick shot back, old hurts and fresh anger boiling up.

"No, Derick. You must remember how your mother doted on you."

Flashes of memory, of her perfumed arms cuddling him close, her lilting voice singing lullabies in French, of kisses and hugs, assaulted him, twisting him with an old longing. He'd loved Maman so much, and had known, with a little boy's certainty, that she loved him, too. Which is why her sudden coldness had wounded him so grievously. "She loved me until you were gone. Then she hated me."

Moreau's eyes filled with sadness. "She never hated you. When Scarsdale sent me away, your mother clung to you—not only as her child but as the only part of me she had left. When Scarsdale became aware of what you meant to her, in that way, he took you from her, too. He told her you were *his* heir—the only one he was going to get, at any rate—and that you would be raised by an Englishman, not some French whore. That's when he sent her here."

Derick stared at Moreau, stunned.

"I know, from Vivienne's letters, that she did not treat you well when you came to visit her. You must understand, Derick . . . You were a source of both joy and misery to her, a reminder of everything she couldn't have. Me. You. Love. She believed Scarsdale only sent you to torture her. She never meant to hurt you . . . She just wasn't capable of anything else at the time."

Derick closed his eyes, shutting out Moreau's entreating, sympathetic gaze. Could it be that Vivienne Aveline was not as heartless as she'd seemed?

"And you're wrong about her. When you left for France, Vivienne did her best to keep track of you. She poured out her worry for you in her letters to me. In time, she came to suspect what role you played in the war. We both did. She would never have betrayed England, never have done anything to put you in danger."

If not her, then who?

"Vivienne's letter said she'd seen something she shouldn't have. Now you say there is a traitor here. Maybe she saw something that got her killed."

Derick's eyes flew open. "Wait—she said she *saw* something she shouldn't have?"

"Yes."

"Did she say what?"

"*Non*. The letter was very short, rushed, her hand-writing hurried and scribbled, agitated."

Damnation. This could change everything. "Do you have it?"

"*Non*. I left it safe in France, with all of her other letters to me. But I tell you, it said only that I should stay in France, that she'd seen something she shouldn't have, that she didn't feel safe here any longer, and that she was coming to me immediately."

Derick scrambled to reevaluate everything he'd thought he knew. But first he needed everything Moreau knew. "So when you got here, you learned that Mother was dead. Then what did you do?"

"I could not believe it, so I decided I must stay until I learned what truly befell my Vivienne, and avenged her. I didn't have much money, not enough to stay at an inn for long, so I decided to conserve my coin for food and find a place in the woods to stay. I found this place and then started investigating."

"*You* were the man asking questions in town about her," Derick realized.

"Yes, as discreetly as I could. But I learned nothing that I didn't already know . . . except that the Wallingford man had been Vivienne's lover for many years before his accident." A look of jealous distaste crossed Moreau's features, followed by resignation. "She never shared that with me. Alas, I cannot fault her. It's not as if I've been a monk all this time. And your mother was a woman of strong passions. But I know her heart belonged to me, as mine does to her."

Derick had no wish to think about his mother and her passions. "Then what did you do?"

"I tried to retrace Vivienne's steps, to discover what she may have seen. I learned from one of your maids that the day news arrived of Scarsdale's death, Vivienne went to Wallingford Manor, presumably to share the wonderful news with her . . . *friend*. It is unknown whether she ever made it that far because when she came back, she was very upset, but wouldn't tell the maid anything. Two days later, Vivienne was dead."

What the hell had happened between the castle and the manor?

"When you arrived, I thought about reaching out to you for help, but I could not bring myself to do it. Yet I cannot bring myself to leave, either, not knowing what happened to your mother." The Frenchman let out a growl of frustration. "So I find myself watching Wallingford Manor more often than not, since that was the last place she was known to have gone. I can think of nothing else to do."

"You've been watching Wallingford Manor?"

"As much as I am able without rousing suspicion."

"Were you there last night?"

Moreau nodded.

"Was it you who snuck into the house?"

But Moreau gave a quick shake of his head. "*Non*. It was another man."

"You saw him?"

"*Oui*. He caught my attention because of how he crept through the shadows, sticking very close to the house, as if he didn't wish to be seen. It seemed very suspicious. When he reached the house, he stopped, very sudden like, and then dashed in through an open set of French doors."

"What did he look like?"

Moreau tipped his head back and forth. "It was dark, so I couldn't see much. He was of average height and build."

Harding was average, but that didn't help much. "Did you see which direction he went when he left? Was it toward town or into the woods—"

"He didn't leave. Moments after he snuck in, the parlor lit up and Wallingford's sister appeared to pull the doors closed."

That made no sense. Moreau must have his timing off.

"Not long after, I saw *you* sneaking up to the house, also, but like I said—I never saw anyone leave."

Impossible. Derick, Perkins and the rest of the staff had thoroughly searched the house. No one had been there. "When you say moments later, how long do you truly mean?"

Moreau pushed his lips out, thinking. "Less than a minute, I'd say."

Then Emma should have seen him, but the only person inside the parlor with her when she lit the lamps was . . . No. It couldn't be. "You're certain, absolutely certain, you saw no one leaving the manor between the time you saw the man enter and when you saw me?"

Moreau narrowed his gaze on Derick, very alertly. "You know who killed my Vivienne . . ."

It wasn't a question, but Derick shook his head nonetheless. "No." It was impossible. Yet . . . what better way to hide in plain sight than to pretend a debilitating infirmity. It was diabolical, but not impossible.

Christ. How could he have missed such a thing?

Because he'd been so wrapped up in Emma, that's how.

Emma. Thank God she was safely tucked away at the castle. If her brother had been the traitor all along . . . it would devastate her.

There had to be another explanation.

"Do you think you could recognize the man you saw?" he asked Moreau.

The Frenchman's nose scrunched. "I might be able to."

Derick scrutinized the man's expression. He couldn't tell whether Moreau was telling the truth or just over-promising so as not to be left behind now that he suspected that Derick knew something about "his Vivienne's" death. "Fine. Come with me, if you wish."

Moreau gave a hasty nod and scrambled to put out

the cook fire. The two men journeyed to Aveline Castle at a pace that discouraged conversation.

"Emma?" Derick called out as he entered his study, with Moreau fast on his heels.

But only her faint lavender scent lingered in the room. Derick looked around. A frame leaned empty against the wall—she'd pulled out the Burnett map once again. Why? He strode over to the desk, where it lay spread across the top.

What he saw chilled his blood.

Emma had marked where his mother had been found, as if she, like Moreau, suspected she'd been murdered. A piece of paper filled with Emma's mathematical scribblings told him she'd worked her equation again, and this time Wallingford Manor was circled several times. A note, in Emma's efficient handwriting, rested atop his mother's journals.

> *Derick,*
> *The killer lives in my house. It* must *be Harding. I've returned home to protect George. Meet me there.*
> *Emma*

Derick's heart started pounding hard in his chest. What if it was Emma who needed protection *from* George? What if she shared her theory with her brother, and he panicked, thinking they were too close for comfort, even if they'd had it all wrong? If he'd been willing to kill to protect his secret, what would he be willing to do to maintain it—even to his own sister?

"Come," he barked to Moreau, not bothering to see if the Frenchman followed.

He had to get to Emma before it was too late.

Chapter Twenty-four

"Why have you posted two footmen at my door?"
Emma glanced up from the tea service, where she'd been absentmindedly pouring cups for herself and George as they sat near the fire in the downstairs parlor. She didn't even want tea, really. It was just the quintessential English way of occupying herself while she waited, she supposed. Waited for Derick to bring news of his search for Harding. Waited for Harding to make a move against George, if he would.

The footman-cum-traitor might not ever come back, she knew. He may already be far gone from here, deciding it was best to get out of Derbyshire while he could. Still, she touched the burled wood handle of one of her father's old pistols, which she'd carefully loaded and then tucked discreetly onto the tea tray within easy reach, just in case she needed it to defend her brother.

She pasted a reassuring smile on her face for George's benefit. What should she say? "Just as a precaution," she demurred, hoping he would be pacified with that. It depended on his mood.

George frowned as he pulled his lap blanket more snugly around him. "Is this because of last night? Because you found me asleep alone in the dark?" His frown deepened. "Did you reprimand Perkins? I told you to leave well enough alone. I don't need to be watched every second of the day."

"No, no, George," she rushed to assure him, setting his tea on the table where he could reach it easily. "It's nothing to do with last night."

"Emma . . ." George's tone said he knew she was lying.

"Well," she hedged, interlacing her fingers as she wrung her hands together, "that's not entirely true." She sighed, debating how much to tell him. She'd promised to keep Derick's secret, but surely George needed to be aware of the danger. Maybe she could relay only part of the story? "It does have to do with last night, only not in the way you think."

George quirked a woolly brow.

"You see, last night Thomas Harding ran off. We believe he may have killed the maid from Aveline Castle, and were holding him until we could prove it. He is dangerous. Until he is captured again, I'd rather be safe than sorry."

"I see." George nodded slowly as he reached for his tea, gripping it with his stronger left hand, rather than right-handed as he would have before the stroke. "Terrible business, that. I still can't quite believe it of Thomas. But . . ." He took a sip before setting the cup carefully back down. "I don't understand . . . even if he killed the maid, why would you think he poses any danger to us?"

Emma pressed her lips together tightly. How many percentage points down the good sister scale would she fall if she wished for one of George's spells to save her from this conversation?

Shame on you, Emma!

She didn't *really* mean that. On the other hand, if she continued the conversation to its logical conclusion and George got upset, it could throw him into one of his spells.

So, how many points might she move *up* the scale if she deceived him just a little bit? Hmmm . . . was there a balance point in there somewhere?

You're sounding like Derick again.

Yes, she was. "I'm afraid Harding may have done worse than that, George. He may have been responsible for the death of that man we found in the woods yesterday, too."

"Thomas? You don't say. Why would he do such a thing?"

Emma shrugged, tried to demur. "Why would anyone do such a thing?"

George actually rolled his eyes at her. "Do you have any proof?"

"I think the fact that he ran off after word came that the remains were found is very telling."

"Emma," George said in a chiding tone. "You've never been one to leap to conclusions. You must have *some* reason to think Harding is responsible for whatever befell that poor man."

She shook her head. "Nothing definite . . . just theories." That was, at least, true. "But I don't need proof to be vigilant. Until Harding is caught, I plan to be extra-cautious with yo—*our*—safety."

Her brother crossed his arms and cocked his head, eyeing her in a way that made her feel like he saw straight through her. Which he probably did.

Oh, why did George have to be so much his old self today? He might not have the mathematical mind she and her father had shared, but George had always been clever in his own way—at least before his stroke.

"You've also never been one to keep secrets from me before, Em. And yet I feel certain you're not telling me everything. Is it because you're afraid to upset me?"

Emma squirmed guiltily.

"I understand. I know you coddle me more and more as my faculties deteriorate, but I'm feeling quite up to snuff of late. Or at least I would be if I didn't suspect that something was worrying my baby sister. Why don't you talk it through with me, like we used to?"

Emma pursed her lips, shut tight.

"Or is it that you now have someone else to share your confidences with?" George asked. "I know that Aveline spent the night here last night. In the Blue Room, I'm told." George raised his eyebrows and looked down his nose at her. "I'll wager *he* is privy to your suspicions." A hurt note had crept into George's voice, and it pulled at her heart.

"George . . ." He was right. She did coddle him, tried not to allow any unpleasantness near him. But he was going to learn the truth eventually. Wouldn't it be better if he heard it from her, on a day when he was in his right mind? She didn't have to tell him about Derick, just about Harding.

Emma took a deep breath and let it out again before she began. "The reason I think Harding is dangerous enough to merit safety precautions is . . . complicated. First, the man we found in the forest yesterday wasn't just some poor unfortunate. He was an agent of the War Department."

George's eyes flew wide. She'd clearly startled him. "What? How did you . . ." He coughed. "The War Department, you say? How could you know such a thing?"

"We, um, discovered some identification secreted on the body." She didn't have to say that Derick knew right where to look because he, himself, was an agent of the War Department, now did she?

"Secreted? Where?"

She waved a dismissive hand. "Hidden in the heel of his boot."

"Ah . . ." George said softly. "Whatever made you think to look there?"

"That's not important. What matters is that it struck a chord in my memory. I went through my files and found two similar deaths in which the bodies had been stripped, not only of belongings but of anything that might obviously identify them. Derick is overseeing the exhumations to be sure, but I suspect they will carry the same hidden identification as the man we found yesterday, proving them as having worked for the War Department as well."

"My God," George whispered, his face drained of color. Was he already beginning to suspect what must have happened?

"Yes. We have three dead agents of the Crown, killed here in upper Derbyshire."

"You can draw only one conclusion from that . . ." George murmured. Emma noticed his knuckles had also gone white where his hands were fisted in his lap. Poor George. He would feel awful when he realized how he'd been used by Harding and possibly by Lady Scarsdale, though Emma wasn't quite convinced of the viscountess' involvement.

"That we've been living with a traitor in our midst, yes."

"And you're convinced it is Harding?" George asked, with an urgency that seemed misplaced. "You're sure?"

"It has to be. You see, I decided to plot the crimes on a map, like I would my research, to see what they might tell me about the criminal, and everything pointed to the killer having lived here—"

"*Emma.*"

She jumped as Derick's hard voice cracked across the room. She turned to find him standing in the doorway, his stance as stiff as his tone. His gaze was fixed on George, even though he'd addressed her. Emma scowled at Derick even as guilt pricked her. She hadn't done anything wrong—she hadn't betrayed *his* secret. She just hadn't felt George deserved to be left totally in the dark when it was *he* who was in the most danger.

She turned her gaze back to her brother, and was

alarmed at how his eyes had narrowed, how ruddy his face had suddenly gone. "George?" She rushed to him, laying a hand against his forehead. His skin was dry and hot against her palm, and his chest pumped as his breathing grew shallow and rapid. Perhaps telling him had been a mistake, after all. One of his attacks seemed to be coming on fast.

"*That's* Wallingford?" A voice Emma had never heard before jerked her attention back to the doorway. An older man with hair the color of Derick's stepped into the room, peering around Derick at her brother. Peering with green eyes exactly like—

"But how can that be?" the stranger asked, his brow furrowing much as Derick's did. "I was told he was confined to a chair."

"Hush," Derick ordered.

Emma stared at the man blankly, her mind fighting to process what she was seeing versus what she was hearing. *What* had he said about George? "He is," she answered automatically. George's rolling chair was quite obvious.

"*Non,*" he spat. The stranger was French. With those eyes, he could be none other than Derick's sire. But what in the world was he doing *here*? "*That's* the man I saw outside last night," the man went on, "creeping into this house!"

"What?" Emma's gaze flew to Derick, who didn't seem surprised by the stranger's accusation. No, he was staring at George much like the spider who'd caught the fly.

"*That's* the man you think killed my Vivienne?" The Frenchman started forward, only to be halted when Derick threw an arm in front of him.

"Are you mad?" Emma cried, placing herself protectively in front of George. She wasn't sure what was going on here, but the stranger glared at her brother as if he meant to throttle him.

Nothing made any sense.

"Emma," Derick barked, and she jumped. "Come here," he urged, more gently. "Come to me."

"Why?" she whispered.

But the word was drowned out by a shuffling behind her. Emma started to turn, but George's arm blocked her as he reached for the tea tray and just as suddenly, his other arm snaked around from behind, trapping her arm against her waist.

"Because your lover doesn't want me to be able to use you as a shield," George said as his grip tightened painfully. "Stay back!" he growled at Derick, and something hard jammed into her left side, just below her ribs. Emma glanced down to see her father's pistol in her brother's hand. She stared at it dumbly, as if it wasn't she who was being held at gunpoint, even though the sharp pain digging into her ribs told her it most certainly was.

And then she felt George move. No—*stand*—behind her. "George?" Emma's world stopped spinning, everything seeming to slow, her usually quick mind suddenly struggling to process what was happening. Both the arm around her hips and the one holding the gun moved up her body, until George had pinned her back against him with an arm across her chest and the gun pressed tight against her temple. And then he pulled, tugging her with him toward the French doors.

"You can walk." She couldn't keep from spouting the obvious, like the stupid fool she was.

"For years now," George confirmed.

"Years?" Emma hated the imbecilic high-pitched squeak her voice had taken on. Thoughts, memories, ruffled through her mind. But much like it seemed with Derick, when her heart was involved, her memory wasn't acute. As if, when she trusted, her mind didn't feel it had to hold on to everything. "Was it all just a ruse, George?" Even as she asked the question, she knew the answer. She could feel the trembling in his right arm, sense the weakness in that side as he shuffled her along.

"No, Em. The stroke was real enough. But as I started to recover my senses, I realized it would be the perfect front to hide behind. To cast off suspicion, should anyone come looking for me."

"Like the agent we found yesterday?"

"Yes. Now, do be quiet, Emma."

Oh, God. How could she have been so naive? Emma cut her eyes to the French doors. George had succeeded in pulling her just under halfway there. Her chest tightened with her growing alarm. What did he intend to do? He couldn't possibly have a plan—everything had happened so fast. Which would make him more desperate, and more volatile.

"There's nowhere for you go, Wallingford."

Derick. His voice cut through her panic. He sounded so calm, so relaxed. Emma turned her gaze to him. She'd been afraid to look at him, fearing that if she did she might lose the fragile control she had on her emotions. Yet now that she had, she latched onto him like a lifeline. Though he appeared relaxed, she could see he was anything but. He took his eyes off of George for just a moment, long enough to make eye contact with her, to give her an almost imperceptible nod of encouragement. His steadiness gave her strength.

Then George snarled, "Like hell," and Emma's insides curled in on themselves. George may have been able to hide that he'd recovered his strength, but she would never believe he'd faked all of his rages. The doctors had told her they were common when a brain had been damaged by stroke. She knew just how fast this situation could devolve.

"I can see you love my sister."

"What?" she blurted, startled. "George!" she scoffed over her shoulder, though her gaze never left Derick. "Don't be ridiculous . . ."

And then she saw it. Derick's eyes flashed. Though stark fear warred with impotent fury for control of his beautifully perfect features, his eyes glittered with . . . *love.* The kind of love that promised he'd sacrifice anything to save her.

"Oh," she whispered, stunned. *Derick loved her?*

"Oh, indeed," George answered softly. "*If* you want her to live, Aveline, you'll do exactly as I say," he continued, almost conversationally now—another worrying signal that his stability was waning. All the while, he inched them ever closer to the door. "I'm taking her with me. When I'm safely away, I'll let her go. But if I even suspect you've made to follow us, I swear I'll kill her. You and I both know she won't have been my first." George pressed the gun tighter against her temple and Emma couldn't contain a whimper.

"Whatever you say," Derick agreed, but his soothing tone sent an even sharper alarm coursing through Emma. She might not know Derick as well as she'd foolishly assured herself she had, but she did understand him well enough to know that he was lying. He wasn't going to let George walk away with her. "Just don't hurt her."

Who she didn't know anymore was George, if she ever had. Whether he'd always had murderous potential or whether it had been triggered by the damage to his brain, she couldn't know. Nor could she trust that George would keep his word. And if Derick tried to rescue her and was hurt—or, God forbid, killed—she'd never forgive herself. George was *her* brother. *She* should have seen what he was capable of. Derick shouldn't have to put himself at risk because she had been blind.

They were less than two feet from the door now. Twenty-two and a half inches, if she had to guess. Emma saw Derick tense, as if he were preparing to strike.

She closed her eyes. She calculated the approximate angle at which George held the gun to her head. She factored in his height compared to hers, and the fact that his strong hand held the gun, whereas his weaker side held her. She envisioned the precise arc of her elbow, where it would strike him, how she would have to move to roll into his weak leg. He might fire, she knew, but she considered how the gun might shift, where her head would be when she rolled, possible angles of the bullet in relation to her. She swiftly tabulated the probabilities of being fatally hit.

She opened her eyes, and a tremble wracked her. Was she seriously considering wagering her life on probabilities?

Derick's words came back to her. *But there were times, in the field, when things weren't so clear. When I had to go with only what knowledge I had and with my gut. With instinct and probabilities.*

Her instincts told her she couldn't let George get her out the door. Nor could she risk Derick, who looked ready to pounce. This had to end here.

Every muscle in Derick's body hummed with energy, and adrenaline sang through him as Wallingford dragged Emma inexorably away from him. If he leapt at Wallingford, would the man turn the gun on him to protect himself from attack, or would he simply react and shoot Emma? As close as the gun was pressed to her head, she'd never survive the wound. Christ. He'd never felt so bloody impotent in his life. He'd cornered many a traitor, but he'd never seen the level of desperation and madness in someone's eyes as he saw in Wallingford's.

Yet that wasn't what terrified him the most. His heart had lodged itself in his throat the moment he saw Emma close her eyes, the second he noticed her thumb working furiously on her fingers. She was plotting something, calculating the risk, and that scared the hell out of him.

She moved so quickly, he couldn't have helped her if he'd tried. All he could do was watch in horrified stillness as it unfolded before him. Emma's elbow swung in a blur, and then she seemed to throw herself into Wallingford's right thigh. A roaring boom echoed in the room, and the acrid smell of sulfured gunpowder scented the air.

"Emma!" The cry ripped from Derick's dry throat as she collapsed. She'd fallen like dead weight, trapping Wallingford's leg beneath her, and *she wasn't moving*.

As he ran toward Emma, some part of him registered that Wallingford was scrambling free, that he'd made it through the door, that he was escaping. But for the first time in his career, Derick let a traitor go without a thought of giving chase. Emma was all that mattered.

He dropped to his knees beside her, scooping her under the shoulders and pulling her into his lap. Her head lolled to the side and gorge rose in Derick's throat, fighting with the naked fear that strangled him. *Christ, so much blood.* It covered the side of her face, pooled and matted in her hair, turning the chestnut even darker. The skin not smeared with blood was pale as death.

"Oh God, Emma," he groaned. This was his fault. He'd made so many mistakes since he'd arrived here, missed so many things wrapped up in his emotions, his memories. Wrapped up in Emma. Had his bloody carelessness cost the woman he loved her life? How would he go on without her?

Emma's chest rose in a shallow breath. Not much, but he saw it, felt it, and relief crashed over him. The sharp ache that preceded tears twinged inside his throat and chest, and he let them fall hot against his cheeks.

A streak of color flew past him. Derick heard a guttural growl of rage, followed by the sick crunch of one body tackling another somewhere behind him. *Moreau.* The Frenchman refused to let Wallingford escape justice, it seemed. Wallingford's shrieks stopped abruptly, and Derick had a brief thought that Moreau could be choking the life out of the man. But he didn't care. All he cared about was Emma.

He wiped blood from her face with his bare hand, trying to find the wound, but as he swiped at the slippery warmth, more took its place, its coppery smell blending with the metallic taste in his mouth. His hand moved higher into her scalp until he felt torn flesh. He probed gently with his fingers, relying on feel since he couldn't see the wound through hair and blood.

The wound didn't feel deep, but rather shallow and long, as if the bullet had grazed her rather than punctured. Oh, thank God. He knew that didn't mean she was out of the woods, but her chances were a hell of a lot better than if she had a bullet lodged in her brain. Derick eased her gently to the floor and then tugged at his cravat, pressing the linen tightly to Emma's head to stanch the flow. She didn't even moan, telling him she was deeply unconscious.

Around him, servants poured into the room, drawn by the gunshot. Behind him, he heard men struggling to drag Moreau off of their master. Perkins dropped to his knees on the other side of Emma's prone body, and raised a shaky gaze to Derick.

"My lord? What—what happened?"

Derick could hear Moreau howling, having been pulled off of his prey. Wallingford's choking gasps told him the man still lived. He was sorry for it. Things would have been easier for all of them if Wallingford was dead, especially Emma.

As much as he wished to shut out the world around him and stay with Emma, assure himself that she was all right, that she would live, he couldn't. If he didn't deal with this situation, the staff might mistakenly injure Moreau. Wallingford might escape. He caressed Emma's still face, then ordered Perkins to keep the pressure on her wound. Derick rose and turned, barking orders at the men who battled the struggling Moreau.

"Let that man loose," he shouted, stepping into the fray to yank Moreau free. When he was assured that the Frenchman was relatively unscathed, Derick turned to Wallingford.

Emma's brother had been pulled to a seated position. Wallingford Manor's housekeeper hovered over him, clucking as she examined the angry purple bruises that bloomed on his neck.

Derick slowly, deliberately walked over to Wallingford, his rage growing with every step. He had to yank the leash of his control tighter than he ever had in his life. Everything in him demanded that he knock the solicitous servant out of the way and finish the job Moreau had started. He had to curl his fingers into tight fists to resist the temptation.

He motioned for two of the burlier-looking men. "Detain Lord Wallingford in his rooms," he commanded. "And post sentries at the doors and windows."

Several heads turned to Derick, their expressions reflecting various states of confusion and shock. Many glanced over at the still unconscious Emma, then at Moreau and to Wallingford, before settling back on him. He offered no explanations, however, and they didn't refuse his command.

Derick moved to return to Emma when a hand snaked around his boot, pulling at his ankle.

"Emma?" Wallingford croaked.

Derick turned his gaze to the man, a scathing reply on his tongue, but he held it in. Wallingford's face was tight with remorse, and his eyes implored for news of his sister. Derick gritted his teeth.

"She lives."

Relief loosened Wallingford's features, which fueled Derick's anger.

"Barely," he spat. He kicked the man's hand from his boot. "For your sake, you'd best hope she makes a full recovery, or spending the rest of your life in Newgate will seem like heaven compared to what I'll do to you."

Chapter Twenty-five

Derick nodded at the footmen who guarded Wallingford's bedroom. He couldn't imagine what the staff must be thinking. Only the four people who were in the parlor knew exactly what had happened, and it would be best for Emma if it stayed that way. Moreau had promised his silence. Derick had only to take care of Wallingford to ensure that the truth stayed buried, and that was best done while Emma was still unconscious. He prayed she would understand.

Derick silently let himself in.

Emma's brother paced slowly before the fire in the dimly lit room, the flames casting him in flickering shadows cut by orange light. Wallingford walked stiffly, dragging his right side noticeably, as if the events of the day had taken their toll on his strength, and his shoulders and head hung low, as if all that had happened weighed heavily on more than just his body.

Derick didn't want to be away from Emma when she woke. He had best get this over with quickly. He came farther into the room, not bothering to conceal his footsteps. Wallingford stopped and turned toward the sound.

"Aveline." The man sounded tired, much older than

his forty-five years, and his voice was tinged with anxiety. "How . . . how is my sister?"

Now that the madness had left Wallingford's eyes, he looked innocent. Fragile, even. After years of reading people, Derick knew the man's concern was genuine. He took some pity on him.

"She's breathing steadily and her heartbeat is strong," he replied. Yet his voice roughened with anger as he continued. "She hasn't woken yet, but the doctor says that's not uncommon. The force of the bullet bruised her severely. Taking into account the shock she's had today and the blood loss . . . it's no wonder she is slow to wake."

Wallingford dropped his head. "But she'll recover?"

"She should. The doctor says much depends on whether she's bruised internally as well as externally. I should know in a day or two."

Derick very deliberately didn't say "we." Wallingford wouldn't be around to find out if Derick had his way.

The man swallowed audibly. Perhaps he'd understood. Derick hoped to hell he had.

"How did you figure it out?" Wallingford asked. "If you only discovered the body in the woods was a War Department agent yesterday, how in the hell did you trace that to *me*, and so damned fast? Emma didn't know, but you did. I saw it in your eyes."

Derick considered letting the man die without ever knowing the answer, but decided against it. "Because I came here suspecting you." He gave Wallingford a brief but concise accounting of exactly who he was and everything that had happened, every bit of evidence the Crown had on him. He wanted him to understand that there was no way out for him.

"It was brilliant, sending you," Wallingford murmured. "When you were spending so much time with my sister, I just thought you were developing a *tendre* for her, or perhaps rekindling an old one. God knows she's loved you forever." A rueful smile, if you could call it that, lifted one side of his mouth. "I never suspected you were really here for me."

"I do love your sister," Derick stated. He wasn't sure why. Maybe because despite what had happened this afternoon, he could see that George Wallingford cared for Emma in his own way. "I intend to marry her."

The shorter man stared into Derick's eyes for a long moment, then nodded. "I'm glad she'll be taken care of." Wallingford tunneled his fingers through his thinning brown hair. "What happens now?" he asked soberly.

Now was the part where Derick would normally interrogate a traitor before his or her execution, extracting every bit of information he could. But Emma was lying upstairs and he wanted nothing more than to be done with this awful business and start a new life with her when she awoke. So he intended to ask Wallingford only three questions.

"Thomas Harding," Derick said. "Do I need to continue to hunt him as a murderer?"

Wallingford turned his face away. "No. I killed the maid. She—she happened across me while I was out of my chair. She was sneaking away from a lovers' tryst with Harding in the hours before dawn. That's when I would strengthen my legs . . . when no one was around to see me. She just happened to be in the wrong place at the wrong time."

Derick clenched his fists. Bloody senseless. Wallingford deserved to die for that alone. But he needed two more questions answered. "My mother. What happened to her?"

Wallingford wouldn't even look at him. "She saw me strangle the agent who came after me. I'd received word, you see, from my contact in France, to be on my guard. So when the stranger came snooping around, I took no chances . . . I took him by surprise, instead. It was . . . unfortunate that Vivienne happened to be coming to see me that day. She fled, and at first I let her go. I mean,

I loved her in my own way, and I thought she loved me. I don't even think she knew at the time that I'd seen her, so I waited to see what she would do. But then, paranoia set in and I went to talk with her. We . . . argued, and in the end . . . I didn't trust her to keep my secret."

A quiet fury roiled just beneath Derick's skin. His mother must have been terrified in the last days, moments, of her life. Whatever her faults, she hadn't deserved such an end. None of Wallingford's victims had. Wallingford probably deserved a worse end than he was going to get. But first Derick needed to know one last thing.

"Look at me, Wallingford," he ordered. When the man complied, Derick said, "Your sister. Do you love *her*?"

Wallingford's face crumpled. "I do."

Derick believed him.

So he walked over to the bed and leaned against it. He lifted his heel, pulled it across the opposite knee and flicked the catch on his boot. "I love her, too. And for some misguided reason, she loves you." Derick put his fingers inside the small compartment, pulling out the vial of last resort he'd carried for just over thirteen years now. Its contents would still be potent, he knew. And he didn't need it anymore.

"I'm sure you've gathered that part of my duty to the Crown is to terminate the traitors I run to ground."

Wallingford closed his eyes, even as he nodded.

"But I don't want that standing between me and my wife," Derick said. "So I would let her decide. You know she'd choose for you to live." Derick closed the compartment in his boot and put his foot back onto the floor. "You'd be turned over to the Crown, sent up for trial. Your family's reputation—Emma's reputation—would be dragged through the mud. It would be awful for her." Derick rolled the vial slowly between his palms. "She'll have me to help her through, but you know she'll suffer for it."

Wallingford covered his face with both shaking hands.

"Or you can take this," Derick said, holding the tiny clear vial between his thumb and forefinger. "It's fast-acting, and better than you deserve."

A quiet sob escaped from Wallingford. Derick walked to him, setting the vial on the table closest to him.

"It's your choice, Wallingford," he said, and the glass vial clicked against the wood table. "I'll be there for Emma either way. But if you love your sister, you know what you have to do."

Derick turned and walked away. Another first in his career—he let a traitor live.

As he snicked the door open to leave this part of his life behind and walk into a new life with Emma, he heard Wallingford's quiet whisper. "Take care of her, Aveline."

He stopped in the doorway, but didn't bother to look back at the man. "I mean to."

Consciousness didn't sneak up on Emma. Awareness didn't gently pull her from the depths of sleep. Rather, they slammed into her, pounding her awake so forcefully that her head throbbed even as she blinked to clear her vision.

But the pain in her head didn't stop. Fig! It was as if she'd been run over by a carriage, or struck with a mallet, or . . . or *shot.*

Memories screamed in. "Derick!" she gasped, reaching blindly for him.

"Shhh . . . shhh. I'm here."

His voice rumbled from her left and she turned her head toward him. His warm hand stole over hers and she gripped him tight. For a moment, she saw three of him, a trio of dark angels backlit by a dim glow that gave the impression of tarnished halos. But a few more blinks merged them into one. One glorious, handsome, per-

fectly flawed man, sitting—she glanced around, noting
the familiar furnishings—at her bedside in her darkened
room. How had she gotten here?

Derick's green gaze devoured her in the low light, his
face lined with worry. Emma tried to speak, but her
tongue felt dry as limestone dust and as if it had quadrupled in size. She raised her hand to soothe the vicious
burning in her head and winced as she encountered
scratchy linen that covered a horribly tender spot. She
ached terribly, but she lived. Her calculated risk must
have worked.

Emma sucked in a breath. "George!" she croaked.
"Where is my brother?" How could she have forgotten
him? Her thoughts swam through her mind slower than
a slug through molasses.

Derick's grip tightened on her hand. "He's . . . seques-
tered in his room."

"But he's all right?"

"He was when I saw him last," Derick said.

Alarm gripped her, knowing when Derick gave nu-
anced answers, they could mean many things. She tried
to sit up, but the sudden movement sent her head spinning one direction and her stomach circling her insides
in the other. She moaned piteously.

"When, *exactly*, did you see him?" she insisted,
though how she got the words through the roiling tumult in her body, she wasn't sure.

"Hush, love." Derick pressed his hand against her
chest, trying to ease her back into the pillows. "The doctor said you would be weak for some time after you
woke. You must rest."

But Emma struggled against him. "When?"

Derick stilled, and expelled a long breath. "Not an
hour ago. I went to check on him, and asked him a few
questions."

Emma took shallow breaths as she fought to quell

her nausea, which must have been caused when she tried to move too quickly. But it worsened as she listened to Derick explain that George had confessed to killing not only Farnsworth but Derick's mother and poor Molly Simms, too. Tears leaked unchecked from her eyes as she considered all of the pain her brother had caused.

And yet he was her brother, in spite of everything. "I must see him."

Derick nodded, as if he'd expected that. He slipped his hands beneath her shoulders and gently helped her to sit.

"Thank you," she whispered.

They didn't speak as he helped her down the hall and down the stairs to her brother's chamber. It took all of Emma's strength, even leaning heavily on Derick, to make it that far—there was none left for conversation.

At any rate, they didn't need to speak. Emma could sense Derick's growing tension and his building worry for her as they approached George's door. It intensified her own until she trembled with it.

What would she say to her brother? That she understood? She didn't, couldn't. That she forgave him? She did, even though she was fairly certain she didn't yet know the extent of what he'd done. She couldn't fathom where they went from here, what awful things were in store for George, and for her, when he was brought to justice. How life would change irrevocably. But she couldn't think about that now. All she really wanted to say to him, she realized, was that she loved him.

Perkins and John Coachman stood guard on either side of George's door. Her longtime servants blanched when they saw her. Emma automatically brushed at the linen bandage circling her head. She must look a fright. The thought brought an unlikely smile. It quickly faded, however, when she wondered if everyone already knew what George had done.

Emma looked up at Derick. His face was solemn, closed . . . but his eyes told her he was here to be whatever she needed. She interlaced her fingers with his, grateful, not caring if the servants saw. Derick was her support, her strength, and she needed him right now. She delivered three raps to the door.

Her heart sped with every moment that passed with no answering call from George. "Perhaps he's asleep?"

Derick didn't reply, only squeezed her hand tightly and opened the door.

A dying fire lit the room, just barely. Emma scanned the space for George. There he was, lying abed as she'd thought. And yet . . . the room was swathed in an eerie stillness that raised gooseflesh on her skin. Emma hurried over to George's bedside with Derick's assistance, but she knew long before she reached him that her brother was gone.

His face, which had been etched with strain most of their lives—the strain of never living up to their father's expectations, the strain of his stroke, and the strain that must have come from hiding his traitorous activities for so long, had smoothed in death. George looked . . . peaceful, in a way she couldn't remember him looking since their mother had been alive. He probably didn't deserve such peace after all he'd done, but Emma still fiercely wished it for him in whatever life he went to next.

Emotion stung her nose, curled her lungs, squeezed her heart. She turned to Derick with tear-filled eyes. He didn't look surprised, and that squeezed her heart exponentially more. "Did you do this?"

Derick turned to her, taking her other hand in his. "No, Emma. I left your brother alive and well. I swear it."

She couldn't speak, only nodded as she felt her face crumple. She couldn't have blamed Derick if he had taken her brother's life, any more than she prayed Derick didn't blame her that her brother took his mother's. But she was glad he hadn't.

Emma pulled away from him and approached the bed. George's hands rested on his stomach, each curled around something. She reached out and touched his cooling skin, easily prying his fingers open—rigor mortis hadn't set in yet, of course. The smooth kiss of glass met her skin as she plucked a small empty vial from his left hand. "Poison," she whispered.

In his right he held a letter, addressed to her. She opened it with trembling fingers, and bit her lip at George's familiar handwriting.

> *My dearest Em,*
> *I can't ask for your forgiveness, though you'll likely give it anyway. I've always known that it's your heart that truly sets you apart from all others—not your mind.*
> *I can ask that you don't mourn me. I don't deserve it.*
> *I know my choice tonight will cause you pain, and that's the only thing I truly regret. But I hope one day you'll come to see that what I do now, at least, I do out of love. You were my heart, darling sister—the only one I had left.*
> *George*

Emma brought the letter to her forehead, which she'd dropped to meet it, as sobs wracked her.

She felt Derick's arms settle around her shoulders. "Come, Emma," he murmured.

She covered her face with her hands, but allowed him to lead her away from the bed, through an interior doorway into a small sitting room. Once inside, Derick opened his arms to her. He said nothing, only folded her into his embrace, cocooned her in bergamot and bay, in him, and held her while she wept.

She wept for poor Molly Simms and her parents. She wept for Lady Scarsdale and for Moreau. And she wept for herself, for the loss of her brother—regardless of what he'd done, he had been her only family.

When she felt strong enough to pull back, she held the letter out before her with a hand that shook. "But . . . but he doesn't say *why* . . ." She took a shuddering breath, trying to regain her composure. "How can I ever quantify it when I don't understand *why*?"

Derick caressed her face, wiping tears away with his thumbs. "We may never know why, Emma."

"But I don't understand," she cried. "How could George and I be so very different? It doesn't fit either side of the argument! Our blood was the same *and* we grew up with the same advantages. Yes, maybe his stroke exacerbated some evil part of his personality, but he was committing treason before then. How can that be?"

Derick slowly shook his head as he continued to stroke her skin. "I don't know."

The enormity of all that had happened today settled on Emma's chest with a crushing weight. She struggled to breathe. "Everything is gone, Derick. George. My position as de facto magistrate. Even the work I've dedicated years of my life to makes no *sense* to me anymore." She dropped her chin, resting her head heavily in his palms as she closed her eyes. "Has it all been for naught? Have I just been tilting at pinwheels all of this time?"

Derick's barking laugh startled her so, she snapped her head back up and opened her eyes to stare at him. "Pinwheels?" A deep chuckle rumbled from his chest and echoed through the room. "I think you mean 'windmills,' love."

Emma huffed, the laugh starting low and haltingly in her stomach. But it quickly bubbled forth until she was gasping with it. "Windmills. Of course," she said on a hiccup, which made them laugh all the harder.

It felt good to release some of her angst, to dispel a little of the tension that had strangled her. It felt even better when Derick hugged her to him as their laughter subsided.

"All I know," Derick said, "is that people are complex, messy . . . not all of them will fit neatly into your equations, regardless of which argument ultimately proves to be true." Derick gently tipped her face back to look at him. "But your project? Your passion for it will never be for naught. I believe you *can* make things better, Emma. You can give people opportunities to make good choices—and I believe you should, because *some* of them will."

Emma pondered his words. Could the answers really be somewhere in the middle? And even if they were, did that make what she was trying to accomplish any less important? Or less effective?

"But some of them won't, Emma. And you can't choose for them."

Any good humor that still lingered in Emma's heart fled. No, she couldn't. Just look at her brother. George had had every opportunity and he'd chosen to become a traitor. She dropped her head back to Derick's chest, defeated. He would have to tell his superiors, of course. There would be an inquest . . . She couldn't even imagine how horrible the next few weeks would be. Maybe Derick would stay in England until it was all finished, to see his duty through. Maybe she wouldn't have to be alone through it all.

She *needed* him. Needed his friendship at least.

She held no illusions that Derick would still want her for his wife, even if she would go to America with him. He might feel some love for her, but look at how he painted himself with his parents' sins just because he carried their blood. How much more would he hate that she shared blood with a traitor? He would abhor even the thought of having a family with her.

"What happens now?" she murmured against his chest.

"Now," he said, gently prying the vial she still held from her and dropping it into his pocket, "we inform the staff that your brother has succumbed to another, more massive stroke."

Emma stepped back so she could see Derick's face clearly. "What?"

"We bury him in the morning, quietly."

"But your superiors . . ."

"It will be enough for them that I assure them the traitor has been neutralized. Only you, me and Moreau know what really happened, Emma. There's no reason for you to suffer any more than you have."

Emma considered for a moment, relief washing through her. Until . . . "Molly Simms' parents deserve to know the truth of what happened to their daughter."

Derick nodded. "All right. But there's no need to name your brother as the traitor. We'll simply tell them what happened and that the traitor has been caught and executed. Knowing the way gossip spreads in a small town, people will blame Moreau, since he was a stranger here. But he'll be long gone by then."

She widened her eyes. "What about Harding?"

"I'll continue to hunt for the man. If he wants to stay in Derbyshire, the story we'll tell the Simms family should clear his name. If not, we'll offer him a job on one of our other estates, let him start fresh."

"We'll?" Emma blinked, hope daring to push out the darkness clouding her heart. "Our? Does . . . does that mean you still want me to come with you to America?"

But Derick shook his head slowly. "No, Emma."

She hadn't thought she had any more room for pain inside her tonight, but she'd been wrong. It pushed out even the breath from her lungs.

"I want us to make our home in England."

Emma sucked air in through her nose. "I—what about my tainted blood?"

Derick gently tucked a finger under her chin. "You don't believe that nonsense," he reminded her.

"But *you* do," she reminded him right back.

"I'm not so sure anymore," he said. "You've given me much to consider in the past weeks, Emma." And then he told her what he'd learned about his parents today. He finished with a shrug. "Perhaps my blood is not as black as I thought."

She opened her mouth, but he moved his fingers to her lips to shush her.

"I meant what I said a moment ago. I'm beginning to believe our lives come down to the choices we make." He dropped his hand back to his side. "I can accept that I chose to become everything that I did. I also think I can make my peace with it, given time," he finished.

"I'm glad," she said as a single tear leaked from her eye. If anyone deserved peace, it was Derick.

Emma took a deep breath, then another. Could it be that all would be well? That after everything they had experienced and been—in their pasts, in their presents— she and Derick could choose happiness together? And by choosing it, make it so?

Lightness ballooned inside her, lifting her spirits higher and higher . . . until a dampening thought popped it. "But what of your feeling that England is not your home? I wouldn't wish you to be unhappy." Even if she had to leave behind everything she knew.

"My home is where my heart is, Emma." Derick took her hand and brought it to his chest, then placed his hand over her heart. "And my heart is here with you. If you want to stay in Derbyshire, we will. If you would rather come to Shropshire, we'll live there."

"Truly?" she whispered.

"Truly," he answered. And yet, despite his assurance, she sensed he would not be happy in either place. She didn't even know if she would be happy in Derbyshire anymore, not after all that had happened.

Upper Derbyshire would always hold a special place in her heart—it was her birthplace, the home of her youth. It was where she'd first met Derick and fallen in love with him. It was where he'd come back and fallen in love with her. Yet maybe they needed to start fresh, too. Make new memories. With him, she realized she wasn't afraid to try. But perhaps they wouldn't have to go so far as the Americas.

"Can we move to London?" she asked. "I hear there's a terrible crime problem that could use some serious analysis."

Derick's quick grin flashed, telling her he liked the idea. "London? I don't know if Bow Street and the House of Lords are ready for the lady magistrate and the French viscount . . ."

"So we'll practice a little deception," Emma said, hugging him tightly to her. "We'll pretend to be plain old Lord and Lady Scarsdale. By the time they figure out we're not exactly what we seem . . ." She shrugged.

Derick's booming laugh filled her with joy. "I love you, Pygmy."

She poked him playfully in the chest. "How many times do I have to tell you? Don't call me Pyg—"

But he cut her off with a kiss, and the last thing Emma could remember thinking was that if he kissed her like that, he could call her whatever he wanted.

Epilogue

Derick slipped unnoticed into Emma's study, melting into the shadows along the far wall. It wasn't even a challenge, as she didn't pay him a bit of mind. No, she was standing at her blackboards, lost in her equations.

Her cheeks were dusted with green, blue and white, with a dot of pinkish-red on her nose for good measure. A smile of satisfaction crept over his face. He wouldn't have her any other way.

He slid quietly behind Emma and waited until she lowered her hand and stepped back to study her work. He held his breath for a few long seconds and then snaked his arms around her from behind.

"Oh!" she shrieked, instinctively clasping her hands over his across her middle. "Curse your damnably silent spy footsteps," she muttered, but there was laughter in her voice.

He turned her in his arms, affectionately wiping chalk dust from her nose with his thumb. "There was no need for stealth, my love," he chuckled. "The clacking of chalk on board was so loud an elephant could have snuck up on you."

He eyed the board she'd been working on. Her strokes seemed different than usual . . . harsh and heavy-handed. Almost angry. "Is something bothering you, Emma? I know you're disappointed that Parliament refused to institute a nationalized system of crime reporting, but Stratford won't give up. He'll be back at them again next season, you can be assured."

Emma blew out a breath, fluttering a lock of chestnut hair that had come loose from the knot at the back of her neck. "Yes, of course. I know he will, and I *am* disappointed, but . . ."

Her shoulders slumped and she brought a hand up to rub at her eyes.

Alarm clenched Derick's gut. He took a closer look at her face, noted the dark circles shadowing her eyes. "Emma, what is it?"

Her brows dipped and her lower lip began to tremble. "I don't know," she cried plaintively. "Maybe I'm fighting some melancholy." Her amber eyes filled with tears and a sharp ache squeezed in his throat as his unease mounted. Emma rarely cried. "I just don't feel myself. And I'm so *tired* all of the time . . ."

Derick tipped her face up, staring at her for a long moment with concern. Then he let his gaze travel over the rest of her body. Was it a trick of the light, or did he detect a subtle rounding . . . Of course! He closed his eyes, his body relaxing as fear left him only to be replaced by an elation that filled his entire chest. He couldn't contain the grin that split his face.

Emma frowned. "This makes you happy?" she grumbled.

"Yes."

His darling wife actually scowled at him then. "I don't understand."

"I know." He glanced up at her blackboards. "Here, let me put it in a language you will understand."

He felt Emma's eyes on his back as he picked up a piece of her chalk. A few strokes later, he stepped back to Emma's side. "There."

Emma narrowed her eyes on his equation.

$$1 + 1 = 3$$

"One plus one equals *three*?" she scoffed. "That makes no sense at all," she said, planting her arms akimbo on her hips.

"It does if one is *you*," he said slowly. "And the other one is *me* . . ."

He waited patiently as his brilliant, literal wife worked it out.

"Oh!" she exclaimed, her eyes widening as she comprehended his meaning. One of her hands instinctively cradled her stomach. "Oh, do you think?"

"I do," he said, reaching for her. He hugged her tightly to him and simply breathed her in.

"A baby," she murmured against his chest.

"Indeed." Derick tried to imagine what it would be like, having a child of his own. Would he get to relive his youth, only this time through the eyes of his own son or daughter? "Perhaps we could spend summers in Derbyshire," he said, surprising himself.

"Do you mean it?" Emma said, turning up her face to look at him.

Neither he nor Emma had been back there for more than a day or two since they'd married. Maybe it was time.

"Well, we had such fun running those woods together. I just thought . . . it would be a shame not to share that with our children. The creeks—"

"My cave," Emma interjected, a smile lighting her face.

"*My* cave," he retorted. Then he huffed as another thought occurred. "You know, if it's a boy, the viscountcy will finally have some English blood in it again, if not that of a true Aveline."

A troubled frown tangled Emma's brow. "You don't still think that's what matters, do you?" she asked softly, hugging him closer to her.

Derick dropped a kiss on his wife's forehead. She still tasted of warm sunshine and fresh air and promise to him—even though it was autumn now and the London air hadn't been fresh in years. It was time to go back. To put the past to rest and look only to the future. "Of course not, darling," he assured her, as overwhelming gratitude filled his heart. "You've taught me that nothing matters but love."

Author's Note

I hope you enjoyed reading *Sweet Deception*! The original idea for this story centered on a missing maid that led to the discovery of other missing women. It did feature the crude geographical profiling that Emma does in the book, but it had her hunting a serial killer instead of a traitor. However, as characters are sometimes wont to do, Derick showed up on the page and insisted that this was *his* story as much as it was Emma's, and that *he* was a traitor hunter, thank you very much. He hadn't spent fourteen years behind enemy lines just to show up at his family home and get drawn into someone else's murder investigation. He wanted to be there for his own reasons. He was all fine and good with letting Emma work out most of the crime, but he fully intended on bringing his expertise to bear, as well. Therefore, they would be hunting a traitor—end of story.

Pesky characters.

Still, I was able to put most of the research I had already done to use. I just had to come up with a different set of bodies for them to find—rather than missing women, they were now looking for missing couriers and War Department agents, etc.

Emma was only a little ahead of her time in combining her moral statistics project with crime statistics to try to affect policy. According to an essay by Michael Friendly in the journal *Statistical Science*, the systematic study of social numbers by mathematicians (such as population data, mortality, ability to raise an army, etc.) had begun in the 1660s, and by the mid-1700s, those numbers were already being used to affect state policy in other areas. But it wasn't until the period following Napoleon's defeat in 1815 that crime became a pressing enough concern for policy makers to take notice, amidst the perfect storm of an exploding population, widespread inflation and unemployment that followed the wars. Because of the new class of desperate, dangerous petty criminals, people started seriously looking at how that growing problem could be addressed.

Nowhere was the crisis more prevalent than in Paris (think of the times depicted in Victor Hugo's fabulous novel *Les Misérables*, set from 1815 to the Paris Uprising in 1832). Consequently, the Ministry of Justice in France was the first to institute a centralized national system of crime reporting (something Emma wished England would do in *Sweet Deception*). A young mathematician named André-Michel Guerry was able to harness that wealth of numbers, and by doing so, became the father of modern social science, criminology and profiling through his moral statistics mapping project. Geographic profilers and criminologists will tell you that his work, combined with similar work of a Belgian named Adolphe Quetelet, became the springboard for much of the criminal profiling that helps us capture criminals today. By analyzing the raw data, Guerry was able to show, for the first time, numerical proof that overturned widespread beliefs about the nature and causes of crimes. He also proved that human actions are governed by social laws, in the same way the laws of physics govern the universe, opening the door to further study in the social sciences.

As for Emma trying to discover a killer's residence from the position of the crimes he'd committed, the methods she used were crude, but they were certainly methods she could have devised at the time and ones that also could have worked. In fact, simple as they are, police forces still use the methods depicted in *Sweet Deception*, though their accuracy leaves something to be desired. Nowadays, of course, we have much more sophisticated equations—the most famous being the Rossmo formula, which you may have seen employed to catch killers in a couple of episodes of the television series, *NUMB3RS*. This incredibly complex equation, run by computers, takes in account everything we know about how killers operate, derived from nearly two centuries of crime analysis.

Were Emma working in law enforcement today, I fancy she'd be something of a criminal profiler, one of those brilliant researchers who analyzes the connection between people and the crimes they commit, searching not only for a way to catch criminals but also for a way to predict who might commit future crimes, and a way to stop them before they do.

Don't miss the next novel
in the Veiled Seduction series,

SWEET MADNESS

Coming from Signet Eclipse in June 2013.

Prologue

Leeds, June 1817

Yellow suited her. Gabriel Devereaux's gaze followed the young woman's lithe form as she floated around the dance floor in her partner's arms. Her flowing skirts of lemon, shot with some sort of white embroidered flowers he couldn't name, barely brushed the ground as she twirled in the moves of the waltz.

He'd never liked blondes who wore yellow. They faded into their ensemble, like a monochrome painting that failed to draw the eye. Not so Lady Penelope. No, she seemed to glow, brightening everything and everyone around her like a ray of early-summer sunshine. Having known her but a few days, Gabriel had a feeling Lady Penelope was the type who refused to fade into anything.

He was glad of it, for her sake. Michael had a tendency to overshadow most ordinary people.

"Lusting after our cousin's new bride, are you?"

Gabriel's jaw clenched with indignation at the insult as his gaze snapped to the man who'd sidled up to him. He bit his tongue against a stinging retort, however. Even the most scathingly witty rejoinder would have been lost on Edward, even were the man sober enough to comprehend it.

"Don't be ridiculous," Gabriel drawled lazily. Of course he wasn't lusting after Lady Penelope, even if his skin tingled with inconvenient awareness as the happy couple twirled near. He fought the strange need to follow them with his eyes and instead turned toward his younger brother.

Edward's bulbous nose shone bright with the redness of drink. Gabriel frowned. When had his brother become such a sot? The night was much too young to be so far gone. But even foxed as Edward was, his eyes glinted with a knowing look.

Hell. Edward might have become a drunkard in the years Gabriel had been away, but his brother also knew him better than perhaps anyone. Edward must have seen something in his expression to speak as he had, and Gabriel feared he knew what it was.

Jealousy.

His gaze strayed back to the dancers as he lost the battle not to look. This time, however, he forced himself to focus on his cousin, Michael, third Baron Manton, whose teeth were bared in a beatific smile. And why wouldn't he be in raptures? Michael, it seemed, had found love.

And *that* was what Gabriel envied. Not the lady in specific, but the *idea* of her. Could finding the right wife bring back *his* smile?

Not that I deserve it.

Gabriel forced his gaze away.

"Well, it's too late now," Edward sniffed, taking a healthy swig of what must have been some rather potent punch. "For both of us."

Gabriel glanced sharply at Edward, drawn by the hollow anger in the man's voice. Surely he wasn't saying . . . But Edward wasn't looking anywhere near the dance floor, or the newlyweds. Instead he stared toward the west corner of the ballroom.

Gabriel followed his line of sight, wincing as he recognized his brother's wife, Amelia, flirting shamelessly with a well-known rake.

Edward tossed back the remains of his punch with a low growl, then wiped his mouth against the inside of his cuff. "Excuse me, brother," he said curtly before stalking off.

Hell and hell again. Gabriel made to follow. He was head of the family now, much as he didn't relish the role. It was his duty to head off any potential scene that might spoil his cousin's wedding ball.

Gabriel slowed as Edward made an abrupt turn, in the opposite direction from his wife, and pushed out a set of French doors into the night instead.

He watched his brother's departure with frustrated sadness. How things had changed, for all of them.

"Lord Bromwich?"

Gabriel jerked as a gloved hand slid over his forearm and gripped him lightly. He fisted his own hands before he even realized what he was doing.

"Oh—I—" A nervous laugh bubbled from Lady Penelope's lips, making her seem younger than her twenty years. Her pale green eyes widened at whatever she saw upon his face and her hand fell away from his arm.

Wariness crept into her expression, darkening her eyes much as a quick-moving storm cloud shaded spring grass into a deeper hue.

And that made him feel much older than his own seven and twenty.

He forced a smile, even as he forced muscles tensed to strike into relaxation. "Lady Penelope, forgive me. I—" What could he say? *I'm sorry that I nearly just planted you a facer?* Ever since the wars, he didn't do well with the unexpected. "I was deep in thought and . . . didn't hear your approach."

"Of course," she murmured, and to Gabriel's surprise, she placed her hand on his arm once again. "And I startled you," she continued, nodding thoughtfully. "How insensitive of me. Forgive *me*, my lord. I shall endeavor not to take you by surprise again."

Gabriel felt his brow knitting over the bridge of his nose. He didn't know Lady Penelope well. Was she mocking him? Or was she simply being polite? Because she couldn't possibly understand how the long years spent fighting on the battlefields of Europe had changed him, could she? He'd never spoken of it.

"Now, however," she said brightly, her bow-shaped lips spreading in a smile that seemed to burst through any cloud that still lingered over them, "I do believe you are meant to stand up with me for this dance."

Gabriel blinked rapidly at her sudden change in countenance. He couldn't help but draw in a sharp, deep breath, quite dazzled by it. How could a simple smile dispel the remaining tension in his limbs? But it had, and more than that, it filled his chest with something . . . warm. Something pleasant. Something he was afraid to name.

He was saved from trying as Lady Penelope tugged at him. "The dancers are already lined up." Her blond head, with ringlets adorned by yellow violas, tipped toward the top of the room as she looked up at him expectantly.

Of course. As head of his family, he was to partner his cousin's bride as she led the next dance. *That* was why she'd approached him. Gabriel shook off the strange sense of connection he'd felt with her, and hastened his step to follow.

Unease curdled in his stomach as they reached the head of the line. Gabriel generally avoided dancing. In fact, he made it a point to steer clear of ballrooms altogether. Since his return, it all just seemed too . . . close. Too many people jostling about for space. Too much noise. As far from and yet more like a battlefield than he felt comfortable with.

Not to mention it had been years since he'd last danced. He knew nothing of the current steps.

But he hadn't been able to refuse his place at a family wedding. A fine sheen of sweat chilled the back of his neck. All he had to do was make it through this one dance, and then he could retire for the evening.

As they took their place perpendicular to the split line of dancers, Lady Penelope slipped her hand in his and raised their joined arms.

Time to gird your loins, old man.

The strains of violins filled the air first, joined almost immediately by the notes of a pianoforte in a lively tune he didn't recognize. All he could tell was that it was in three-quarters time.

Gabriel did his best not to grimace, waiting to see what dance his partner would choose. He hoped it was something simple that he could easily emulate without making an arse of himself.

A flute piped up in merry accompaniment, signaling the start of the dancing.

Lady Penelope squeezed his hand. "Never fear, my lord," she whispered. "'Twill be over in a trice."

Before Gabriel could reply, she flashed her smile at him once more, and bent her torso away from him. Then she turned in a vaguely familiar step. When she grasped both of his hands and pulled him into the move, his body went easily, willingly, as if his muscles remembered the dance from long ago.

Only a few steps in and he realized that was because they did. Lady Penelope had chosen a simple country dance, popular in years past, and one blessedly that he knew. Relief washed over him, his cold sweat breaking into a warm one as she pulled him into the energetic skips and turns that left him unable to think of anything but the dance.

Like a battalion of soldiers following their commander, the next set of dancers fell in behind them as they made their way down the line in the progressive dance, one pair after another, until all were stepping lively.

All in all, the dance took nearly half an hour to complete. Gabriel would have wagered he smiled more in that thirty-minute span than he had in the previous month. Blood coursed through his veins, exhilarating in a way he'd forgotten he could feel.

Perhaps he should take up dancing as a pastime. If it made him feel like this, it could well be the cure to all of his ills.

But was it the dancing? Or the dancing partner?

He glanced over at Lady Penelope as they stood across from each other, their part of the dance now finished. She grinned and clapped in time with the music, watching the other dancers finish their sets. But Gabriel couldn't take his eyes from her.

Her face was flushed from exertion, her green eyes bright with merriment. Tiny ringlets of her blond hair had dampened with perspiration and now clung to her temples and nape. She was the quintessential picture of an English rose—all slight and pale and graceful, with delicate ankles and wrists, a patrician nose and dewy skin. Everything a young Englishwoman should be.

Everything he'd fought to preserve.

Why shouldn't I seek my happiness? he thought. There was more than one Lady Penelope in the world. Perhaps it was time he ventured out from his self-imposed exile and found a wife of his own. A lady a bit older than Michael's bride, of course. And perhaps one not quite so . . . sunny. All that brightness might be a shock to his system all at once, accustomed to living in darkness as he was. But the point remained.

A spot of applause broke out as the last of the dancers came to a breathless stop. Gabriel broke his gaze away from his cousin's wife and joined in.

Michael bounded over from his place in the line as the clapping died down. "Gad, Pen. Haven't danced that one in an age."

Damn, but Michael seemed like such a young pup. It

was hard to remember he was only two years Gabriel's junior. Gabe had often envied the seemingly inexhaustible energy Michael exuded. His cousin never tired. With his typical exuberance, he threw an arm around his bride and brushed a kiss on her temple. "Were you feeling nostalgic, dearling?"

Lady Penelope returned her husband's squeeze with a fond smile. "Indeed, I was," she answered lightly, but her eyes met Gabriel's.

And in that moment, Gabriel knew she'd chosen the dance specifically with him in mind. She'd sensed his distress, had correctly interpreted it for what it was and so had picked a dance he was likely to know. He marveled at her intuitiveness. And at her consideration.

Just as he realized that she hadn't been mocking him before. Somehow, she'd understood. How, he couldn't fathom. Perhaps someone else she knew suffered as he did? Her cousin had recently married the Earl of Stratford, a man who'd been grievously injured in the same battle Gabriel had been. Maybe Stratford experienced the same gnawing restlessness, the overvigilance, the insomnia . . . the nightmares. Reliving battles won and lost, night after night after night . . .

"Well, no more of that, my love," Michael declared. "From this moment on, we only look forward." He swiped a glass of champagne from the tray of a passing footman. The servant stopped, and thirsty dancers swarmed him for the rest of the libations as the poor man's eyes widened comically.

Michael snagged a flute for his bride and another for Gabriel before raising his own in an impromptu toast. "To our future!" He touched his glass to Penelope's, the crystal kiss ringing with a high-pitched *ting*.

"To your future," Gabriel agreed. His gaze strayed once again to Lady Penelope. "I wish you very happy."

Michael gave him a hearty slap on the shoulder that tipped champagne over the rim of Gabe's glass, splashing his hand and wrist with the frigidly sticky stuff. His cousin followed that up with a half-squeeze that constituted affection amongst the males of the species, sloshing yet more liquor onto Gabriel's shoes.

Lady Penelope simply murmured, "Thank you, Lord Bromwich."

"Gabriel," he insisted, for reasons he couldn't define. At the dip of her brow, he tried anyway. "We're family now," he explained gruffly, kicking droplets of champagne from his feet.

"Then, thank you, Gabriel."

"Yes, thank you, Gabriel," Michael parroted before plucking the still full champagne flute from Lady Penelope's fingers. "Now come, wife," he said with an exaggerated waggle of his blond brows, as if he relished the word. Then his voice dropped to a low tone, infused with an intimacy that made Gabriel turn his head. "Let us away."

"Let's do," Lady Penelope answered eagerly, and the happy couple hurried off together.

As he watched them depart, Gabriel was finally able to name that elusive feeling that had filled his chest when Lady Penelope had first smiled at him.

Hope.

Hope for *his* future.

Gabriel swallowed what little champagne remained in his glass, raising it in his own toast. "May it be as blissful as theirs."

Chapter One

The West Midlands, February 1820
Two and one half years later, shortly after the
death of Mad King George III

Lady Penelope Bridgeman, Baroness Manton, alighted from the carriage, her sturdy black kid boots crunching gravel beneath them as she stepped onto the drive of Vickering Place.

At first glance, the seventeenth-century mansion looked like any other palatial spread. No fewer than a dozen chimney blocks jutted from the slate roof, each spouting puffs of smoke that spoke of toasty fires within, keeping the residents of the brown brick home warm in defiance of the chilly February winter.

Ivy strangled the west wing of the structure, as well as the walls leading up to the entrance of the main house. The vines were brownish green and barren now, but Penelope imagined they would be beautiful to behold come springtime. As would the large ornamental fountain that fronted the house when it was once again filled with water, as well as the acres upon acres of parkland that surrounded it when they were greened up and in bloom.

However, Penelope fervently hoped she would have no occasion to visit Vickering Place in the spring. Indeed, she wished she wasn't here now.

The carved oak door was opened for her before she even gained the top step of the stoop.

"Lady Manton." A thin man, clad in a serviceable black suit, greeted her by her name, though they had never met. She supposed she shouldn't have been surprised. Visitors were likely regulated here, and expected well in advance.

"Mr. Allen, I presume?" she inquired, pulling her dark wool greatcoat tighter around her as a frigid wind nipped across her nape. She stamped her feet in an effort to warm them, her eyes shifting involuntarily over the man's shoulder to the roaring fire she could see blazing from a hearth within.

"I am he," Allen confirmed, stepping back into the doorway so that Penelope might enter. "Please do come in."

She slid sideways past him, grateful for the blast of warmth as she crossed the threshold into a well-lit foyer. Her eyes were immediately drawn to the painted ceiling that arced high above, depicting fluffy clouds in a blue summer sky that faded into the throes of a brilliant sunset around the edges.

She hadn't expected such a cheerful scene.

A woman's desolate wail sliced through the hall, raising the hair on Penelope's arms, even covered as they were with layers of wool and bombazine. The high-pitched cry was cut off abruptly, leaving only an eerie echo ricocheting off of the marble walls of the foyer.

Penelope shivered. *That* was more in line with her expectation of Vickering Place.

Mr. Allen, she noted, seemed unruffled by the noise, almost as if he hadn't even noticed. One grew used to it, she supposed. Allen extended an arm to usher her into what appeared to be his office, and as Penelope took a seat in a plush armchair across from his stark, imposing desk, she strove for a similar sangfroid even as her stomach churned with nerves.

"I'm afraid your journey may have been in vain, my lady," Mr. Allen began, lowering himself stiffly into his own seat. "It seems his lordship has descended into a fit of mania this morning. When he gets like this, he can be very dangerous. I cannot, in good conscience, allow you near him. For your safety's sake."

Penelope winged a brow high at the subtle condescension in the director's tone. She pursed her lips.

Allen, apparently misinterpreting the reason for her irritation, said defensively, "I *did* send a messenger to the White Horse, but he must have just missed you. I am sorry you had to come all this way."

Penelope waved a dismissive hand. "Your man delivered the message in plenty of time. However—" However, what? She'd been a fool not to anticipate this sort of resistance. She'd gotten spoiled, working with her cousin Liliana, the Countess of Stratford, over the past year and a half treating ex-soldiers and their families. No one ever questioned Liliana because she was female, not anymore.

How Penelope wished her cousin was here with her now, but she was far into her second confinement and hadn't been able to travel. Pen chewed her lip, trying to imagine how Liliana would have handled Mr. Allen. She took a deep breath through her nose and stiffened her spine. Well, she didn't know exactly what Liliana would have done, but Penelope knew how her own mother would have handled the man if this were a domestic situation. And since it involved her family, she supposed it was.

She adopted her best "lady of the house" tone, all clipped and commanding. "*However*, it is my understanding that Vickering Place is a *private* sanatorium. Your guests are here voluntarily, at the behest of their families, are they not?" She raised both brows now, staring Allen down. "At their very *expensive* behest."

At his stiff nod, Penelope could almost taste her victory. She reached into her greatcoat, efficiently pulling out a packet of letters from her husband's family, detailing their wishes. Her hand trembled a bit as she leaned forward and handed them across the desk. "Then I expect to see my—his lordship immediately. In whatever condition he may be in."

It was Allen's turn to purse his lips, which thinned to the point of almost disappearing as he skimmed the letters. Disapproval lined his features but all he said was, "Very well."

Penelope gave the director a curt nod and rose to her feet. She exited the office on her own, not waiting to see if he followed. He did, of course. Couldn't risk the little lady wandering about the sanatorium on her own, could he?

"This way, my lady." Allen rattled a heavy set of keys, plucking the head of one between his fingers as the others settled with a jangling clank on the ring.

And that was when the illusion that Vickering Place was still a country mansion fell completely away. Certainly the flocked wall paper of gold damask, the plaster molding and expensive artwork that lined the hallway spoke of its aristocratic history, but Penelope knew that Vickering Place had been sold by its owner and converted to a private sanatorium for lunatics. A place where the wealthy sent their sons and daughters, or their mothers and fathers, for treatment, or simply to hide them away from society.

As Michael's family had done to poor Gabriel.

Another howl rent the air, this time a man's, Penelope thought, though not Gabriel's. The cry was accompanied by a harsh, rhythmic clanking, as if the poor soul banged something against the metal bars she knew had been installed in the doorways.

An ache pierced her chest. She couldn't imagine Michael's cousin in a place such as this. Though she hadn't known Gabriel well, she'd sensed he was cut from similar cloth as Geoffrey, Liliana's husband, and many other brave ex-soldiers she'd known. Gabriel had a commanding air, an independent and self-reliant streak that must have chafed against confinement. It had to be driving him mad to be locked up so.

No, madness is what brought him here.

Penelope shivered. She'd have never believed such a thing about Gabriel two and a half years ago, but he *was* blood related to Michael, and if Penelope knew anything, she knew now that Michael had been mad.

The affliction had driven her husband to take his own life barely six months after they'd been married.

Penelope's steps faltered. Oh Lord. What made her think she could be of any help to Gabriel Devereaux? She'd been worthless to Michael when he'd needed her. Worthless.

Mr. Allen halted, as if noticing his footfalls were now the only ones ringing on the marble floors. He turned to look over his shoulder. "Have you changed your mind, then, Lady Manton?"

Yes.

Penelope's chest tightened, her breaths coming with great difficulty as the horror of another frosty winter morning invaded her mind.

He's not breathing! Michael!

Penelope shook her head, as much to dislodge the memories as to reply to the director. "No. No, of course not." Yet her voice was much more assured than her feet. Pen had to force them to get moving again.

Allen fixed her with a doubtful look before turning back to lead the way once more.

She was not that naive young society wife anymore, Pen reminded herself. For the past two years, with Liliana's encouragement, she'd thrown herself into studying the inner workings and maladies of the mind. At first, it had been a way to distract her from her grief, but then she'd realized she had a gift.

People of all classes had often told her she was easy to talk to, so when Liliana had suggested she spend time talking to the ex-soldiers served by the private clinic that Stratford had built, it had been easy to say yes. And that one yes had turned into a calling, one that had met with some success.

Which was why Edward Devereaux had visited her in London and begged her to visit Gabriel. Well, that, and that the Devereauxs knew she would keep their shame private. She'd married into their family, after all, and they counted on that loyalty for her silence.

Mr. Allen stopped before a massive wooden door, its brass knob polished to a high shine. The director pulled the door open easily, revealing the heavy iron bars that barricaded the entrance to the suite of rooms that had become the Marquess of Bromwich's home.

He slid the key into the lock, twisting it with an efficient click. The bars swung open noiselessly, too new yet to creak with rust.

Penelope schooled her features, trying to prepare herself for anything. She smoothed a nervous hand over her widow's weeds, her mood now as somber and dark as the colors she always wore.

What kind of Gabriel would she encounter beyond that threshold? If his affliction was similar to Michael's, he could be flying high, gregarious and grandiose, awake for days with no end in sight. Or he could be a man in the depths of despair, wallowing in a dark place where no one could reach him, least of all her.

Was she ready to be faced with the stuff of her nightmares?

Penelope swallowed, hard. Yes. Because Gabriel was still alive, still able to be saved. Whatever she must do, she would do it, if only as penance for what she *hadn't* been able to do for Michael.

Penelope stepped into the room, at least as far as she could before shock stilled her feet.

"Oh . . . my . . . God," she whispered. She could have never prepared herself for this. "Oh, Gabriel. What's become of you?"

Also available from

Heather Snow

First book in the Veiled Seduction series

Sweet Enemy

With a gaggle of husband-hunters vying for his attention, Geoffrey Wentworth, Earl of Stratford, finds Miss Liliana Claremont a notable exception. She has no desire to marry the son of the man she believes killed her father. Determined to find evidence of the crime, Liliana rouses the Earl's suspicions, as well as her own undeniable attraction to him.

**Available wherever books are sold or at
penguin.com**

facebook.com/LoveAlwaysBooks

S0373

LOVE
ROMANCE NOVELS?

For news on all your favorite romance authors,
sneak peeks into the newest releases, book
giveaways, and much more—

"Like" Love Always on Facebook!

 LoveAlwaysBooks

49€